Christmas 2013

Dear Friends,

Merry Christmas! I'm excited that two of my favorite holiday stories are being published together. *Call Me Mrs. Miracle* was written after the success of the Hallmark adaptation of *Mrs. Miracle*, which ranked as their highest rated movie of 2009. *Call Me Mrs. Miracle*, also starring the talented Doris Roberts, again scored as the network's most viewed movie of the year.

The bonus story in this collection, *The Christmas Basket*, is another of my favorites. It won a RITA® Award, which is Romance Writers of America's highest award for excellence in writing. That's especially gratifying, because it was chosen by my peers. So you can see that both books signify high points in my writing career.

The holidays are a special time with our children and grandchildren, a time of gathering together, building memories, of laughter and fun. My wish is that these two books will be part of your holiday enjoyment.

Merry Christmas!

Debbie Macomber

P.S. You can reach me in a number of ways—through my webpage at www.debbiemacomber.com or on Facebook. Or if you wish, you can reach me at P.O. Box 1458, Port Orchard, WA 98366.

Praise for Debbie Macomber's Christmas stories

"*Call Me Mrs. Miracle* is an entertaining holiday story that will surely touch the heart…. Best of all, readers will rediscover the magic of Christmas."
—*Bookreporter.com*

There's Something About Christmas is "a tale of romance in the lives of ordinary people, with a message that life is like a fruitcake: full of unexpected delights."
—*Publishers Weekly*

"*There's Something About Christmas* is a wonderfully funny, and at times heart-wrenching story of finding the right person to love at the most delightful time of year."
—*Times Record News* (Wichita Falls, Texas)

"Macomber once again demonstrates her impressive skills with characterization and her flair for humor."
—*RT Book Reviews* on *When Christmas Comes*

When Christmas Comes "is a sweetly satisfying, gently humorous story that celebrates the joy and love of the holiday season."
—*Booklist*

"A fast, frothy fantasy for those looking to add some romance to their holidays."
—*Publishers Weekly* on *The Snow Bride*

"Macomber's latest charming contemporary Christmas romance is a sweetly satisfying, gently humorous story that celebrates the joy and love of the holiday season."
—*Booklist* on *Christmas Letters*

"*New York Times* bestselling author Debbie Macomber has written a delightful holiday story filled with romance, conflict and lots of humor."
—*BookReporter.com* on *The Christmas Basket*

"It's just not Christmas without a Debbie Macomber story."
—*Armchair Interviews*

DEBBIE MACOMBER

Call Me Mrs. Miracle

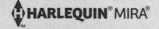

ISBN-13: 978-0-7783-1458-5

CALL ME MRS. MIRACLE

Copyright © 2013 by Harlequin Books S.A.

The publisher acknowledges the copyright holder of the individual works as follows:

CALL ME MRS. MIRACLE
Copyright © 2010 by Debbie Macomber

THE CHRISTMAS BASKET
Copyright © 2002 by Debbie Macomber

Recycling programs for this product may not exist in your area.

Printed in U.S.A.

HARLEQUIN®
www.Harlequin.com

Also by Debbie Macomber

Blossom Street Books

The Shop on Blossom Street
A Good Yarn
Susannah's Garden
Back on Blossom Street
Twenty Wishes
Summer on Blossom Street
Hannah's List
The Knitting Diaries
  "The Twenty-First Wish"
A Turn in the Road

Cedar Cove Books

16 Lighthouse Road
204 Rosewood Lane
311 Pelican Court
44 Cranberry Point
50 Harbor Street
6 Rainier Drive
74 Seaside Avenue
8 Sandpiper Way
92 Pacific Boulevard
1022 Evergreen Place
Christmas in Cedar Cove
  (*5-B Poppy Lane* and
  A Cedar Cove Christmas)
1105 Yakima Street
1225 Christmas Tree Lane

Dakota Series

Dakota Born
Dakota Home
Always Dakota

The Manning Family

The Manning Sisters
The Manning Brides
The Manning Grooms

Christmas Books

A Gift to Last
On a Snowy Night
Home for the Holidays
Glad Tidings
Christmas Wishes
Small Town Christmas
When Christmas Comes
  (now retitled *Trading
  Christmas*)
*There's Something About
  Christmas*
Christmas Letters
Where Angels Go
The Perfect Christmas
Angels at Christmas
  (*Those Christmas Angels*
  and *Where Angels Go*)
Call Me Mrs. Miracle

Heart of Texas Series

VOLUME 1
(*Lonesome Cowboy* and
  Texas Two-Step)
VOLUME 2
(*Caroline's Child* and
  Dr. Texas)
VOLUME 3
(*Nell's Cowboy* and
  Lone Star Baby)
Promise, Texas
Return to Promise

Look for Debbie Macomber's
This Matter of Marriage
available soon from Harlequin MIRA

CONTENTS

CALL ME MRS. MIRACLE

To
Dan and Sally Wigutow
and
Caroline Moore
in appreciation for bringing
Mrs. Miracle
to life

One

Need a new life? God takes trade-ins.
                                        —Mrs. Miracle

Jake Finley waited impatiently to be ushered into his father's executive office—the office that would one day be his. The thought of eventually stepping into J. R. Finley's shoes excited him. Even though he'd slowly been working his way through the ranks, he'd be the first to admit he still had a lot to learn. However, he was willing to do whatever it took to prove himself.

Finley's was the last of the family-owned department stores in New York City. His great-grandfather had begun the small mercantile on East 34th Street more than seventy years earlier. In the decades since, succeeding Finleys had opened branches in the other boroughs and then in nearby towns. Eventually the chain had spread up and down the East Coast.

"Your father will see you now," Mrs. Coffey said. Dora Coffey had served as J.R.'s executive assistant for at least twenty-five years and knew as much about the company as Jake did—maybe more. He hoped that when the time came she'd stay on, although she had to be close to retirement age.

"Thank you." He walked into the large office with its panoramic view of the Manhattan skyline. He'd lived in the city all his life, but this view never failed to stir him, never failed to lift his heart. No place on earth was more enchanting than New York in December. He could see a light snow drifting down, and the city appeared even more magical through that delicate veil.

Jacob R. Finley, however, wasn't looking at the view. His gaze remained focused on the computer screen. And his frown told Jake everything he needed to know.

He cleared his throat, intending to catch J.R.'s attention, although he suspected that his father was well aware of his presence. "You asked to see me?" he said. Now that he was here, he had a fairly good idea what had initiated this summons. Jake had hoped it wouldn't happen quite so soon, but he should've guessed Mike Scott would go running to his father at the first opportunity. Unfortunately, Jake hadn't had enough time to prove that he was right—and Mike was wrong.

"How many of those SuperRobot toys did you order?" J.R. demanded, getting straight to the point. His father had never been one to lead gently into a subject. "Intellytron," he added scornfully.

"Also known as Telly," Jake said in a mild voice.

"How many?"

"Five hundred." As if J.R. didn't know.

"What?"

Jake struggled not to flinch at his father's angry tone, which was something he rarely heard. They had a good relationship, but until now, Jake hadn't defied one of his father's experienced buyers.

"For how many stores?"

"Just here."

J.R.'s brow relaxed, but only slightly. "Do you real-ize those things retail for two hundred and fifty dol-lars apiece?"

J.R. knew the answer to that as well as Jake did. "Yes."

His father stood and walked over to the window, pac-ing back and forth with long, vigorous strides. Although in his early sixties, J.R. was in excellent shape. Tall and lean, like Jake himself, he had dark hair streaked with gray and his features were well-defined. No one could doubt that they were father and son. J.R. whirled around, hands linked behind him. "Did you clear the order with…anyone?"

Jake was as straightforward as his father. "No."

"Any particular reason you went over Scott's head?"

Jake had a very good reason. "We discussed it. He didn't agree, but I felt this was the right thing to do." Mike Scott had wanted to bring a maximum of fifty robots into the Manhattan location. Jake had tried to persuade him, but Mike wasn't interested in listening to speculation or taking what he saw as a risk—one that had the potential of leaving them with a huge overstock. He relied on cold, hard figures and years of purchasing experience. When their discussion was over, Mike still refused to go against what he considered his own bet-ter judgment. Jake continued to argue, presenting in-ternet research and what his gut was telling him about this toy. When he'd finished, Mike Scott had coun-tered with a list of reasons why fifty units per store would be adequate. *More* than adequate, in his opin-ion. While Jake couldn't disagree with the other man's logic, he had a strong hunch that the much larger order was worth the risk.

"You *felt* it was right?" his father repeated in a scathing voice. "Mike Scott told me we'd be fortunate to sell fifty in each store, yet you, with your vast experience of two months in the toy department, decided the Manhattan store needed ten times that number."

Jake didn't have anything to add.

"I don't suppose you happened to notice that there's been a downturn in the economy? Parents don't *have* two hundred and fifty bucks for a toy. Not when a lot of families are pinching pennies."

"You made me manager of the toy department." Jake wasn't stupid or reckless. "I'm convinced we'll sell those robots before Christmas." As manager, it was his responsibility—and his right—to order as he deemed fit. And if that meant overriding a buyer's decision—well, he could live with that.

"You think you can sell *all* five hundred of those robots?" Skepticism weighted each word. "In two weeks?"

"Yes." Jake had to work hard to maintain his air of confidence. Still he held firm.

His father took a moment to consider Jake's answer, walking a full circle around his desk as he did. "As of this morning, how many units have you sold?"

That was an uncomfortable question and Jake glanced down at the floor. "Three."

"Three." J.R. shook his head and stalked to the far side of the room, then back again as if debating how to address the situation. "So what you're saying is that our storeroom has four hundred and ninety-seven expensive SuperRobots clogging it up?"

"They're going to sell, Dad."

"It hasn't happened yet, though, has it?"

"No, but I believe the robot's going to be the hottest toy of the season. I've done the research—this is the toy kids are talking about."

"Maybe, but let me remind you, *kids* aren't our customers. Their parents are. Which is why no one else in the industry shares your opinion."

"I know it's a risk, Dad, but it's a calculated one. Have faith."

His father snorted harshly at the word *faith*. "My faith died along with your mother and sister," he snapped.

Involuntarily Jake's eyes sought out the photograph of his mother and sister. Both had been killed in a freak car accident on Christmas Eve twenty-one years ago. Neither Jake nor his father had celebrated Christmas since that tragic night. Ironically, the holiday season was what kept Finley's in the black financially. Without the three-month Christmas shopping craze, the department-store chain would be out of business.

Because of the accident, Jake and his father ignored anything to do with Christmas in their personal lives. Every December twenty-fourth, soon after the store closed, the two of them got on a plane and flew to Saint John in the Virgin Islands. From the time Jake was twelve, there hadn't been a Christmas tree or presents or anything else that would remind him of the holiday. Except, of course, at the store…

"Trust me in this, Dad," Jake pleaded. "Telly the SuperRobot will be the biggest seller of the season, and pretty soon Finley's will be the only store in Manhattan where people can find them."

His father reached for a pen and rolled it between his fingers as he mulled over Jake's words. "I put you in charge of the toy department because I thought it would be a valuable experience for you. One day you'll sit in this chair. The fate of the company will rest in your hands."

His father wasn't telling him anything Jake didn't already know.

"If the toy department doesn't show a profit because you went over Mike Scott's head, then you'll have a lot to answer for." He locked eyes with Jake. "Do I make myself clear?"

Jake nodded. If the toy department reported a loss as a result of his judgment, his father would question Jake's readiness to take over the company.

"Got it," Jake assured his father.

"Good. I want a report on the sale of that robot every week until Christmas."

"You'll have it," Jake promised. He turned to leave.

"I hope you're right about this toy, son," J.R. said as Jake opened the office door. "You've taken a big risk. I hope it pays off."

He wasn't the only one. Still, Jake believed. He'd counted on having proof that the robots were selling by the time his father learned what he'd done. Black Friday, the day after Thanksgiving, which was generally the biggest shopping day of the year, had been a major disappointment. He'd fantasized watching the robots fly off the shelves.

It hadn't happened.

Although they'd been prominently displayed, just one of the expensive toys had sold. He supposed his father had a point; in a faltering economy, people were evaluating their Christmas budgets, so toys, especially expensive ones, had taken a hit. Children might want the robots but it was their parents who did the buying.

Jake's head throbbed as he made his way to the toy department. In his rush to get to the store that morning, he'd skipped his usual stop at a nearby Starbucks. He needed his caffeine fix.

"Welcome to Finley's. May I be of assistance?" an older woman asked him. The store badge pinned prominently on her neat gray cardigan told him her name was Mrs. Emily Miracle. Her smile was cheerful and engaging. She must be the new sales assistant Human Resources had been promising him—but she simply wouldn't do. Good grief, what were they thinking up in HR? Sales in the toy department could be brisk, demanding hours of standing, not to mention dealing with cranky kids and short-tempered parents. He needed someone young. Energetic.

"What can I show you?" the woman asked.

Jake blinked, taken aback by her question. "I beg your pardon?"

"Are you shopping for one of your children?"

"Well, no. I—"

She didn't allow him to finish and steered him toward the center aisle. "We have an excellent selection of toys for any age group. If you're looking for suggestions, I'd be more than happy to help."

She seemed completely oblivious to the fact that he was the department manager—and therefore her boss. "Excuse me, Mrs...." He glanced at her name tag a second time. "Mrs. Miracle."

"Actually, it's Merkle."

"The badge says Miracle."

"Right," she said, looking a bit chagrined. "HR made

a mistake, but I don't mind. You can call me Mrs. Miracle."

Speaking of miracles... If ever Jake needed one, it was now. Those robots *had* to sell. His entire future with the company could depend on this toy.

"I'd be more than happy to assist you," Mrs. Miracle said again, breaking into his thoughts.

"I'm Jake Finley."

"Pleased to meet you. Do you have a son or a daughter?" she asked.

"This is *Finley's* Department Store," he said pointedly.

Apparently this new employee had yet to make the connection, which left Jake wondering exactly where HR found their seasonal help. There had to be someone more capable than this woman.

"Finley," Mrs. Miracle repeated slowly. "Jacob Robert is your father, then?"

"Yes," he said, frowning. Only family and close friends knew his father's middle name.

Her eyes brightened, and a smile slid into place. "Ahh," she said knowingly.

"You're acquainted with my father?" That could explain why she'd been hired. Maybe she had some connection to his family he knew nothing about.

"No, no, not directly, but I *have* heard a great deal about him."

So had half the population on the East Coast. "I'm the manager here in the toy department," he told her. He clipped on his badge as he spoke, realizing he'd stuck it in his pocket. The badge said simply "Manager," without including his name, since his policy was to be as anonymous as possible, to be known by his role, not his relationship to the owner.

"The manager. Yes," she said, nodding happily. "This works out beautifully."

"What does?" Her comments struck him as odd.

"Oh, nothing," she returned with the same smile.

She certainly looked pleased with herself, although Jake couldn't imagine why. He doubted she'd last a week. He'd see about getting her transferred to a more suitable department for someone her age. Oh, he'd be subtle about it. He had no desire to risk a discrimination suit.

Jake examined the robot display, hoping that while he'd been gone another one might have sold. But if that was the case, he didn't see any evidence of it.

"Have you had your morning coffee?" Mrs. Miracle asked.

"No," he muttered. His head throbbed, reminding him of his craving for caffeine.

"It seems quiet here at the moment. Why don't you take your break?" she suggested. "The other sales associate and I can handle anything that comes along."

Jake hesitated.

"Go on," she urged. "Everyone needs their morning coffee."

"You go," he said. He was, after all, the department manager, so he should be the last to leave.

"Oh, heavens, no. I just finished a cup." Looking around, she gestured toward the empty aisles. "It's slow right now but it's sure to pick up later, don't you think?"

She was right. In another half hour or so, he might not get a chance. His gaze rested on the robots and he pointed in their direction. "Do what you can to interest shoppers in those."

"Telly the SuperRobot?" she said. Not waiting for his reply, she added, "You won't have any worries there. They're going to be the hottest item this Christmas."

Jake felt a surge of excitement. "You heard that?"

"No…" she answered thoughtfully.

"Then you must've seen a news report." Jake had been waiting for exactly this kind of confirmation. He'd played a hunch, taken a chance, and in his heart of hearts felt it had been a good decision. But he had four hundred and ninety-seven of these robots on his hands. If his projections didn't pan out, it would take a long time—like maybe forever—to live it down.

"Coffee," Mrs. Miracle said, without explaining why she was so sure of the robot's success.

Jake checked his watch, then nodded. "I'll be back soon."

"Take whatever time you need."

Jake thanked her and hurriedly left, stopping by HR on his way out. The head of the department, Gloria Palmer, glanced up when Jake entered the office. "I've got a new woman on the floor this morning. Emily Miracle," he said.

Gloria frowned. "Miracle?" She tapped some keys on her computer and looked back at Jake. "I don't show anyone with that name working in your department."

Jake remembered that Emily Miracle had said there'd been an error on her name tag. He rubbed his hand across his forehead, momentarily closing his eyes as he tried to remember the name she'd mentioned. "It starts with an *M*—McKinsey, Merk, something like that."

Gloria's phone rang and she reached for it, holding it

between her shoulder and ear as her fingers flew across the keyboard. She tried to divide her attention between Jake and the person on the line. Catching Jake's eye, she motioned toward the computer screen, shrugged and shook her head.

Jake raised his hand and mouthed, "I'll catch you later."

Gloria nodded and returned her attention to the caller. Clearly she had more pressing issues to attend to just then. Jake would seek her out later that afternoon and suggest Mrs. Miracle be switched to another department. A less demanding one.

As he rushed out the door onto Thirty-fourth and headed into the still-falling snow, he decided it would be only fair to give the older woman a chance. If she managed to sell one of the robots while he collected his morning cup of java, he'd consider keeping her. And if she managed to sell *two,* she'd be living up to her name!

Two

If God is your copilot, trade places.
                                        —*Mrs. Miracle*

Friday morning, and Holly Larson was right on schedule—even a few minutes ahead. This was a vast improvement over the past two months, ever since her eight-year-old nephew, Gabe, had come to live with her. It'd taken effort on both their parts to make this arrangement work. Mickey, Holly's brother, had been called up by the National Guard and sent to Afghanistan for the next fifteen months. He was a widower, and with her parents doing volunteer medical work in Haiti, the only option for Gabe was to move in with Holly, who lived in a small Brooklyn apartment. Fortunately, she'd been able to turn her minuscule home office into a bedroom for Gabe.

They were doing okay, but it hadn't been easy. Never having spent much time with children Gabe's age, the biggest adjustment had been Holly's—in her opinion, anyway.

Gabe might not agree, however. He didn't think sun-dried tomatoes with fresh mozzarella cheese was a special dinner. He turned up his nose and refused even one bite. So she was learning. Boxed macaroni and cheese suited him just fine, although she couldn't tolerate the stuff. At least it was cheap. Adding food for a growing boy to her already strained budget had been a challenge. Mickey, who was the manager of a large grocery store in his civilian life, sent what he could but he had his own financial difficulties; she knew he was still paying off his wife's medical bills and funeral expenses. And he had a mortgage to maintain on his Trenton, New Jersey, home. Poor Gabe. The little boy had lost his mother when he was an infant. Now his father was gone, too. Holly considered herself a poor replacement for either parent, let alone both, although she was giving it her best shot.

Since she had a few minutes to spare before she was due at the office, she hurried into Starbucks to reward herself with her favorite latte. It'd been two weeks since she'd had one. A hot, freshly brewed latte was an extravagance these days, so she only bought them occasionally.

Getting Gabe to school and then hurrying to the office was as difficult as collecting him from the after-school facility at the end of the day. Lindy Lee, her boss, hadn't taken kindly to Holly's rushing out the instant the clock struck five. But the child-care center at Gabe's school charged by the minute when she was late. *By the minute.*

Stepping out of the cold into the warmth of the coffee shop, Holly breathed in the pungent scent of fresh coffee. A cheery evergreen swag was draped across the display case. She dared not look because she had a weakness for cranberry scones. She missed her morning ritual of a latte and a scone almost as much as she did her independence. But giving it up was a small sacrifice if it meant she could help her brother and Gabe. Not only that, she'd come to adore her young nephew and, despite everything, knew she'd miss him when her brother returned.

The line moved quickly, and she placed her order for a skinny latte with vanilla flavoring. The man behind her ordered a large coffee. He smiled at her and Holly smiled back. She'd seen him in this Starbucks before, although they'd never spoken.

"Merry Christmas," she said.

"Same to you."

The girl at the cash register told Holly her total and she opened her purse to pay. That was when she remembered—she'd given the last of her cash to Gabe for lunch money. It seemed ridiculous to use a credit card for such a small amount, but she didn't have any choice. She took out her card and handed it to the barista. The young woman slid it through the machine, then leaned forward and whispered, "It's been declined."

Hot embarrassment reddened her face. She'd maxed out her card the month before but thought her payment would've been credited by now. Scrambling, she searched for coins in the bottom of her purse. It didn't take her long to realize she didn't have nearly enough change to cover the latte. "I have a debit card in here someplace," she muttered, grabbing her card case again.

"Excuse me." The good-looking man behind her pulled his wallet from his hip pocket.

"I'm…I'm sorry," she whispered, unable to meet his eyes. This was embarrassing, humiliating, downright mortifying.

"Allow me to pay for your latte," he said.

Holly sent him a shocked look. "You don't need to do that."

The woman standing behind him frowned impatiently at Holly. "If I'm going to get to work on time, he does."

"Oh, sorry."

Not waiting for her to agree, the stranger stepped forward and paid for both her latte and his coffee.

"Thank you," she said in a low, strangled voice.

"I'll consider it my good deed for the day."

"I'll pay for your coffee the next time I see you."

He grinned. "You've got a deal." He moved down to the end of the counter, where she went to wait for her latte. "I'm Jake Finley."

"Holly Larson." She extended her hand.

"Holly," he repeated.

"People assume I was born around Christmas but I wasn't. Actually, I was born in June and named after my mother's favorite aunt," she said. She didn't know why she'd blurted out such ridiculous information. Perhaps because she still felt embarrassed and was trying to disguise her chagrin with conversation. "I do love Christmas, though, don't you?"

"Not particularly." Frowning, he glanced at his watch. "I've got to get back to work."

"Oh, sure. Thank you again." He'd been thoughtful and generous.

"See you soon," Jake said as he turned toward the door.

"I owe you," she said. "I won't forget."

He smiled at her. "I hope I'll run into you again."

"That would be great." She meant it, and next time she'd make sure she had enough cash to treat him. She felt a glow of pleasure as Jake left Starbucks.

Holly stopped to calculate—it'd been more than three months since her last date. That was pitiful! Three months. Nuns had a more active social life than she did.

Her last relationship had been with Bill Carter. For a while it had seemed promising. As a divorced father, Bill was protective and caring toward his young son. Holly had only met Billy once. Unfortunately, the trip to the Central Park Zoo hadn't gone well. Billy had been whiny and overtired, and Bill had seemed to want *her* to deal with the boy. She'd tried but Billy didn't know her and she didn't know him, and the entire outing had been strained and uncomfortable. Holly had tried—unsuccessfully—to make the trip as much fun as possible. Shortly thereafter, Bill called to tell her their relationship wasn't "working" for him. He'd made a point of letting her know he was interested in finding someone more "suitable" for his son because he didn't feel she'd make a good mother. His words had stung.

Holly hadn't argued. Really, how could she? Her one experience with Billy had been a disaster. Then, just a month after Bill's heartless comment, Gabe had entered her life. These days she was more inclined to agree with Bill's assessment of her parenting skills. She didn't seem to have what it took to raise a child, which deeply concerned her.

Things were getting easier with Gabe, but progress had been slow, and it didn't help that her nephew seemed to sense her unease. She had a lot to learn about being an effective and nurturing parent.

Dating Bill had been enjoyable enough, but there'd never been much chemistry between them, so not seeing him wasn't a huge loss. She categorized it as more of a disappointment. A letdown. His parting words, however, had left her with doubts and regrets.

Carrying her latte, Holly walked the three blocks to the office. She actually arrived a minute early. Working as an assistant to a fashion designer sounded glamorous but it wasn't. She didn't get to take home designer purses for a fraction of their retail price— except for the knockoff versions she could buy on the street—or acquire fashion-model hand-me-downs.

She was paid a pittance and had become the go-to person for practically everyone on staff, and that added up to at least forty people. Her boss, Lindy Lee, was often unreasonable. Unfortunately, most of the time it was Holly's job to make sure that whatever Lindy wanted actually happened. Lindy wasn't much older than Holly, but she was well connected in the fashion world and had quickly risen to the top. Because her work as a designer of upscale women's sportswear was in high demand, Lindy Lee frequently worked under impossible deadlines. One thing was certain; she had no tolerance for the fact that Holly now had to stick to her official nine-to-five schedule, which meant her job as Lindy Lee's assistant might be in jeopardy. She'd explained the situation with Gabe, but her boss didn't care about Holly's problems at home.

Rushing to her desk, Holly set the latte down, shrugged off her coat and readied herself for the day. She was responsible for decorating the office for Christmas, and so far, there just hadn't been time. On Saturday she'd bring Gabe into the office and the two of them would get it done. That meant her own apartment would have to wait, but…oh, well.

Despite her boss's complaints about one thing or another, Holly's smile stayed in place all morning. A kind deed by a virtual stranger buffered her from four hours of commands, criticism and complaints.

Jack…no, Jake. He'd said his name was Jake, and he was cute, too. Maybe *handsome* was a more accurate description. Classically handsome, like those 1940s movie stars in the old films she loved. Tall, nicely trimmed dark hair, broad shoulders, expressive eyes and…probably married. She'd been too shocked by his generosity to see whether he had a wedding band. Yeah, he was probably taken. Par for the course, she thought a little glumly. Holly was thirty, but being single at that age wasn't uncommon among her friends. Her parents seemed more worried about it than she was.

Most of her girlfriends didn't even *think* about settling down until after they turned thirty. Holly knew she wanted a husband and eventually a family. What she hadn't expected was becoming a sole parent to Gabe. This time with her nephew was like a dress rehearsal for being a mother, her friends told her. Unfortunately, there weren't any lines to memorize and the script changed almost every day.

At lunch she heated her Cup-a-Soup in the microwave and logged on to the internet to check for messages from Mickey. Her brother kept in touch with Gabe every day and sent her a quick note whenever he could. Sure enough, there was an email waiting for her.

From: "Lieutenant Mickey Larson" <larsonmichael@goarmy.com>
To: "Holly Larson"<hollylarson@msm.com>
Sent: December 10
Subject: Gabe's email

Hi, sis,
Gabe's last note to me was hilarious. What's this about you making him put down the toilet seat? He thinks girls should do it themselves. This is what happens when men live together. The seat's perpetually up.

Has he told you what he wants for Christmas yet? He generally mentions a toy before now, but he's been suspiciously quiet about it this year. Let me know when he drops his hints.

I wish I could be with you both, but that's out of the question. Next year for sure.

I know it's been rough on you having to fit Gabe into your apartment and your life, but I have no idea what I would've done without you.

By the way, I heard from Mom and Dad. The dental clinic Dad set up is going well. Who'd have guessed our parents would be doing volunteer work after retirement? They send their love…but now that I think about it, you got the same email as me, didn't you? They both sound happy but really busy. Mom was concerned about you taking Gabe, but she seems reassured now.

Well, I better get some shut-eye. Not to worry— I reminded Gabe that when he's staying at a house with a woman living in it, the correct thing to do is put down the toilet seat.

Check in with you later.

Thank you again for everything.
Love,
Mickey

Holly read the message twice, then sent him a note. She'd always been close to her brother and admired him for picking up the pieces of his life after Sally died of a rare blood disease. Gabe hadn't even been a year old. Holly had a lot more respect for the demands of parenthood—and especially single parenthood—now that Gabe lived with her.

At five o'clock, she was out the door. Lindy Lee threw her an evil look, which Holly pretended not to see. She caught the subway and had to stand, holding tight to one of the poles, for the whole rush-hour ride into Brooklyn.

As she was lurched and jolted on the train, her mind wandered back to Mickey's email. Gabe hadn't said anything about Christmas to her, either. And yet he had to know that the holidays were almost upon them; all the decorations in the neighborhood and the ads on TV made it hard to miss. For the first time in his life, Gabe wouldn't be spending Christmas with his father and grandparents. This year, there'd be just the two of them. Maybe he'd rather not celebrate until his father came home, she thought. That didn't seem right, though. Holly was determined to make this the best Christmas possible.

Not once had Gabe told her what he wanted. She wondered whether she should ask him, maybe encourage him to write Santa a letter—did he still believe in Santa?—or try to guess what he might like. Her other question was what she could buy on a limited income.

A toy? She knew next to nothing about toys, especially the kind that would intrigue an eight-year-old boy. She felt besieged by even more insecurities.

She stepped off the subway, climbed the stairs to the street and hurried to Gabe's school, which housed the after-hours activity program set up for working parents. At least it wasn't snowing anymore. Which was a good thing, since she'd forgotten to make Gabe wear his boots that morning.

What happened the first day she'd gone to collect Gabe still made her cringe. She'd been thirty-two minutes late. The financial penalty was steep and cut into her carefully planned budget, but that didn't bother her nearly as much as the look on Gabe's face.

He must have assumed she'd abandoned him. His haunted expression brought her to the edge of tears every time she thought about it. That was the same night she'd prepared her favorite dinner for him—another disaster. Now she knew better and kept an unending supply of hot dogs—God help them both—plus boxes of macaroni and cheese. He'd deign to eat carrot sticks and bananas, but those were his only concessions, no matter how much she talked about balanced nutrition. He found it hilarious to claim that the relish he slathered on his hot dogs was a "vegetable."

She waited by the row of hooks, each marked with a child's name. Gabe ran over the instant he saw her, his face bright with excitement. "I made a new friend!"

"That's great." Thankfully Gabe appeared to have adjusted well to his new school and teacher.

"Billy!" he called. "Come and meet my aunt Holly."

Holly's smile froze. This wasn't just any Billy. It was

Bill Carter, Junior, son of the man who'd broken up with her three months earlier.

"Hello, Billy," she said, wondering if he'd recognize her.

The boy gazed up at her quizzically. Apparently he didn't. Or maybe he did remember her but wasn't sure when they'd met. Either way, Holly was relieved.

"Can I go over to Billy's house?" Gabe asked. The two boys linked arms like long-lost brothers.

"Ah, when?" she hedged. Seeing Bill again would be difficult. Holly wasn't eager to talk to the man who'd dumped her—especially considering why. It would be uncomfortable for both of them.

"I want him to come tonight," Billy said. "My dad's making sloppy joes. And we've got marshmallow ice cream for dessert."

"Well…" Her meals could hardly compete with that—not if you were an eight-year-old boy. Personally, Holly couldn't think of a less appetizing combination.

Before she could come up with a response, Gabe tugged at her sleeve. "Billy doesn't have a mom, either," he told her.

"I have a mom," Billy countered, "only she doesn't live with us anymore."

"My mother's in heaven with the angels," Gabe said. "I live with my dad, too, 'cept he's in Afghanistan now."

"So that's why you're staying with your aunt Holly." Billy nodded.

"Yeah." Gabe reached for his jacket and backpack.

"I'm sorry, Billy," she finally managed to say, "but Gabe and I already have plans for tonight."

Gabe whirled around. "We do?"

"We're going shopping," she said, thinking on her feet.

Gabe scowled and crossed his arms. "I hate shopping."

"You won't this time," she promised and helped him put on his winter jacket, along with his hat and mitts.

"Yes, I will," Gabe insisted, his head lowered.

"You and Billy can have a playdate later," she said, forcing herself to speak cheerfully.

"When?" Billy asked, unwilling to let the matter drop.

"How about next week?" She'd call or email Bill so it wouldn't come as a big shock when she showed up on his doorstep.

"Okay," Billy agreed.

"That suit you?" Holly asked Gabe. She wanted to leave *now,* just in case Bill was picking up his son today. She recalled that their housekeeper usually did this—but why take chances? Bill was the very last person she wanted to see.

Gabe shrugged, unhappy with the compromise. He let her take his hand as they left the school, but as soon as they were outdoors, he promptly snatched it away.

"Where are we going shopping?" he asked, still pouting as they headed in the opposite direction of her apartment building. The streetlights glowed and she saw Christmas decorations in apartment windows—wreaths, small potted trees and strings of colored lights. So far Holly hadn't done anything. Perhaps this weekend she'd find time to put up their tree—after she'd finished decorating the office, of course.

"I thought we'd go see Santa this evening," Holly announced.

"Santa?" He raised his head and eyed her speculatively.

"Would you like that?"

Gabe seemed to need a moment to consider the question. "I guess."

Holly assumed he was past the age of believing in Santa but wasn't quite ready to admit it, for fear of losing out on extra gifts. Still, she didn't feel she could ask him. "I want you to hold my hand while we're on the subway, okay?"

"Okay," he said in a grumpy voice.

They'd go to Finley's, she decided. She knew for sure that the store had a Santa. Besides, she wanted to look at the windows with their festive scenes and moving parts. Even in his current mood, Gabe would enjoy them, Holly thought. And so would she.

Three

Exercise daily—walk with the Lord.
                              —*Mrs. Miracle*

It was the second Friday in December and the streets were crowded with shoppers and tourists. As they left the subway, Holly kept a close watch on Gabe, terrified of becoming separated. She heaved a sigh of relief when they reached Finley's Department Store. The big display windows in the front of the fourteen-story structure were cleverly decorated. One showed a Santa's workshop scene, including animated elves wielding hammers and saws. Another was a mirrored pond that had teddy bears skating around and around. Still another, the window closest to the doors, featured a huge Christmas tree, circled by a toy train running on its own miniature track. The boxcars were filled with gaily wrapped gifts.

With the crowds pressing against them, Gabe and Holly moved from window to window, stopping at the final one. "Isn't that a great train set?" she asked.

Gabe nodded.

"Would you like one of those for Christmas?" she murmured. "You could ask Santa."

Gabe glanced up at her. "There's something else I want more."

"Okay, you can tell Santa that," she said.

They headed into the store, and had difficulty getting through the revolving doors, crushed in with other shoppers. "Can we go home and have dinner when we're done seeing Santa?" Gabe asked.

"Of course. What would you like?"

If he said hot dogs or macaroni and cheese Holly promised herself she wouldn't scream.

"Mashed potatoes with gravy and meat loaf with lots of ketchup."

That would take a certain amount of effort but was definitely something she could do. "You got it."

Gabe cast her one of his rare smiles, and Holly placed her hand on his shoulder. This was progress.

The ground floor of Finley's was crammed. The men's department was to the right and the cosmetics and perfume counters directly ahead. Holly inched her way forward, Gabe close by her side.

"We need to get to the escalator," she told him, steering the boy in that direction. She hoped that once they got up to the third floor, the crowds would have thinned out, at least a little.

"Okay." He voluntarily slipped his hand in hers.

More progress. Visiting Santa had clearly been a stroke of genius on her part.

Her guess about the crowds was accurate. When they reached the third floor Holly felt she could breathe again. If it wasn't for Gabe, she wouldn't come within ten miles of Thirty-fourth on a Friday night in December.

"Santa's over there," Gabe said, pointing.

The kid obviously had Santa Claus radar. Several spry elves in green tights and pointy hats surrounded the jolly old man in the red suit. This guy was good, too. His full white beard was real. He must've just gotten off break because he wore a huge smile.

The visit to Santa was free but for an extra twenty dollars, she could buy a picture. They'd stopped at an ATM on their way to the subway and she'd gotten cash. Although she couldn't help feeling a twinge at spending the money, a photo of Gabe with Santa would be the perfect Christmas gift for Mickey.

The line moved quickly. Gabe seemed excited and happy, chattering away about this and that, and his mood infected Holly. She hadn't felt much like Christmas until now. Classic carols rang through the store and soon Holly was humming along.

When it was Gabe's turn, he hopped onto Santa's knee as if the two of them were old friends.

"Hello there, young man," Santa said, adding a "Ho, ho, ho."

"Hello." Gabe looked him square in the eyes.

"And what would you like Santa to bring you?" the jolly old fellow inquired.

Her nephew didn't hesitate. "All I want for Christmas is Telly the SuperRobot."

What in heaven's name was that? A robot? Even without checking, Holly knew this wasn't going to be a cheap toy. A train set—a small one—she could manage, but an electronic toy was probably out of her price range.

"Very well, young man, Santa will see what he can do. Anything else you're interested in?"

"A train set," Gabe said, his eyes serious. "But I *really* want Intellytron."

"Intellytron," Holly muttered to herself.

Santa gestured at the camera. "Now smile big for me, and your mom can collect the photograph in five minutes."

"Okay." Gabe gave Santa a huge smile, then slid off his knee so the next child in line could have a turn. It took Holly a moment to realize that Gabe hadn't corrected Santa about who she was.

Holly went around to the counter behind Santa's chair to wait for the photograph, accompanied by Gabe.

"I don't know where Santa will find one of those robots," she said, trying to get as much information as she could.

"All the stores have them," Gabe assured her. "Billy wants an Intellytron, too."

So she could blame Billy for this sudden desire. But since this was the only toy Gabe wanted, she'd do her best to make sure that Intellytron the SuperRobot would be wrapped and under the tree Christmas morning.

"Maybe I should see what this robot friend of yours looks like," she suggested. A huge sign pointing to the toy department was strategically placed near Santa's residence. This, Holly felt certain, was no coincidence.

"Toys are this way," Gabe said, leading her by the hand.

Holly dutifully followed. "What if they don't have the robot?" she asked.

"They will," he said with sublime confidence.

"But what if they don't?"

Gabe frowned and then tilted his chin at a thought-ful angle. "Can Santa bring my dad home?"

Holly's heart sank. "Not this year, sweetheart."

"Then all I really want is my robot."

She'd been afraid of that.

They entered the toy department and were met by a grandmotherly woman with a name badge that identi-fied her as Mrs. Emily Miracle.

"Why, hello there," the woman greeted Gabe with a smile.

Gabe immediately smiled back at her. "Hello."

"I see you've been to visit Santa." She nodded at the photo Holly was holding.

"Yup," Gabe said happily. "He was nice."

"Did you tell Santa what you want for Christmas?"

"Intellytron the SuperRobot," he replied.

"Telly is a wonderful toy. Let me show you one."

"Please," Holly said, hoping against hope that the robot was reasonably priced. If fate was truly with her, it would also be on sale.

Mrs. Miracle took them to a display on the other side of the department, directly across from the elevator. The robots would be the first toys seen by those step-ping off. She wondered why they weren't by the esca-lator, but then it dawned on her. Mothers with young children usually came up via elevator. The manager of this department was no dummy.

"Look!" Gabe said, his eyes huge. "It's Telly! He's here. I told you he would be. Isn't he the best *ever?*"

"Would you like to see how he works?" the grand-motherly saleswoman asked.

"Yes, please."

Holly was impressed by Gabe's politeness, which

she'd never seen to quite this degree. Well, it was December, and this was the one toy he wanted more than any other. The saleswoman took down the display model and started to demonstrate it when a male voice caught Holly's attention.

"Hello again."

She turned to face Jake, the man she'd met in Starbucks that morning. For a moment she couldn't speak. Eventually she croaked out a subdued hello.

He looked curiously at Gabe. "Your son?"

"My nephew," she said, recovering her voice. "Gabe's living with me for the next year while his father's in Afghanistan."

"Nephew," he repeated, and his eyes sparked with renewed interest.

"I brought Gabe here to visit Santa and he said that what he wants for Christmas is Intellytron the Super-Robot."

"An excellent choice. Would you like me to wrap one for you now?"

"Ah…" Holly paused. "I need to know how much they are first." Just looking at the toy told her she wasn't getting off cheap.

"Two hundred and fifty dollars."

Holly's hand flew to her heart. "*How* much?"

"Two hundred and fifty dollars."

"Oh." She swallowed. "Will there be a sale on these later? A big sale?"

Jake shook his head. "I doubt it."

"Oh," she said again.

Jake seemed disappointed, too.

Holly bit her lip. This was the only gift Gabe had requested. He'd indicated mild interest in a train set, but that was more at her instigation. Watching his eyes light up as the robot maneuvered itself down the aisle filled her with a sense of delight. He loved this toy and it would mean so much to him. "I get my Christmas bonus at the end of next week. Will you still have the robot then?" Never mind that Lindy Lee might be less than generous this year....

"We should have plenty," Jake told her.

"Thank goodness," Holly said gratefully.

"We've sold a number today, but I brought in a large supply so you shouldn't have anything to worry about."

"Wonderful." She could hardly wait for Gabe to unwrap this special gift Christmas morning. Tonight, the spirit of Christmas had finally begun to take root in her own heart. Seeing the joy of the season in Gabe's eyes helped her accept that this year would be different but could still be good. Although she and Gabe were separated from their family, she intended to make it a Christmas the two of them would always remember.

"I want to thank you again for buying my latte this morning," she said to Jake. She was about to suggest she pay him back, because she had the cash now, but hesitated, hoping for the opportunity to return the favor and spend more time with him.

"Like I said, it was my good deed for the day."

"Do you often purchase a complete stranger a cup of coffee?"

"You're the first."

She laughed. "Then I'm doubly honored."

"Aunt Holly, did you see? Did you see Telly move?" Gabe asked, dashing to her side. "He can talk, too!"

She'd been so involved in chatting with Jake that she'd missed most of the demonstration. Other children had come over to the aisle, drawn by the robot's activities; in fact, a small crowd had formed to watch. Several boys Gabe's age were tugging at their parents' arms.

"We'll have to see what Santa brings," Holly told him.

"He'll bring me Telly, won't he?"

Holly shrugged, pretending nonchalance. "We'll have to wait and see."

"How many days until Christmas?" Gabe asked eagerly.

"Today's the tenth, so…fifteen days."

"That long?" He dragged out the words as if he could barely hang on all those weeks.

"The time will fly by, Gabe. I promise."

"Excuse me," Jake said as he turned to answer a customer's question. Her query was about the price of the robot, and the woman had nearly the same reaction as Holly. Two hundred and fifty dollars! A lot of money for a toy. Still, in Gabe's case it would be worth it.

Mrs. Miracle brought out the display robot to demonstrate again, and Gabe and a second youngster watched with rapt attention. The older woman was a marvel, a natural with children.

"So, you're the manager here," Holly said once Jake was free.

He nodded. "How'd you guess?" he asked with a grin.

"Your badge, among other things." She smiled back at him. "I was just thinking how smart you were to place Santa next to the toy section."

"That wasn't my idea," Jake said. "Santa's been in that location for years."

"What about the Intellytron display across from the elevator?"

"Now that *was* my idea."

"I thought as much."

Jake seemed pleased that she'd noticed. "I'm hoping it really takes off."

"Well, if Gabe's interest is any indication, I'm sure it will."

He seemed to appreciate her vote of confidence.

"Look!" Gabe said, grabbing Holly's hand. He pointed to a couple who were removing a boxed unit of Intellytron from the display. "My robot will still be here by Christmas, won't he?"

"Absolutely," she assured him.

Jake winked at her as Mrs. Miracle led the young couple toward the cash register.

"Hiring Mrs. Miracle was a smart move, too," she said.

"Oh, I can't really take credit for that," Jake responded.

"Well, you're lucky, then. She's exactly right for the toy department. It's like having someone's grandmother here. She's helping parents fulfill all their children's Christmas wishes."

Jake glanced at the older woman, then slowly nodded. "I guess so," he said, sounding a bit uncertain.

"Haven't you seen the way kids immediately take to her?" Holly asked.

"Not only can't I take credit for her being here, it's actually a mistake."

"A mistake," Holly echoed. "You're joking! She's *perfect*. It wouldn't surprise me if you sold out the whole toy department with her working here."

"Really?" He said this as if Holly had given him something to think about.

"I love her name, too. Mrs. Miracle—it has such a nice Christmas sound."

"That's a mistake, as well. Her name's not really Miracle. HR spelled it wrong on her badge, and I asked that it be corrected."

"Oh, let her keep the badge," Holly urged. "Mrs. Miracle. It couldn't be more appropriate."

Jake nodded again. "Perhaps you're right."

Mrs. Miracle finished the sale and joined them. "Very nice meeting you, Gabe and Holly," she said warmly.

Holly didn't remember giving the older woman her name. Gabe must have mentioned it.

"You, too, Emily," she said.

"Oh, please," she said with a charming smile. "Just call me Mrs. Miracle."

"Okay," Gabe piped up. "We will."

Four

Lead me not into temptation.
I can find the way myself.

—J. R. Finley

"I thought we'd bake cookies today," Holly said on Saturday morning as Gabe sat at the kitchen counter eating his breakfast cereal. When he didn't think she was looking, he picked up the bowl and slurped what was left of his milk.

"Cookies?" Gabe said, frowning. "Can't we just buy them?"

"We could," Holly answered, "but I figured it would be fun to bake them ourselves."

Gabe didn't seem convinced. "Dad and I always got ours at the store. We never had to *work* to get them."

"But it's fun," Holly insisted, unwilling to give up quite so easily. "You can roll out the dough. I even have special cookie cutters. After the cookies are baked and they've cooled down, we can frost and decorate them." She'd hoped this Christmas tradition would appeal to Gabe.

He slid down from his chair and carried his bowl to the dishwasher. "Can I go on the computer?"

"Sure." Holly made an effort to hide her disappointment. She'd really hoped the two of them would bond while they were baking Christmas cookies. Later, she intended to go into the office and put up decorations—with Gabe's help. She wanted that to be fun for him, too.

Gabe moved to the alcove between the kitchen and small living room with its sofa and television. Holly was astonished at how adept the eight-year-old was on the computer. While he logged on, she brought out the eggs and flour and the rest of the ingredients for sugar cookies and set them on the kitchen counter.

Gabe obviously didn't realize she could see the computer screen from her position. She was pleased that he was writing his father a note.

From: "Gabe Larson"<gabelarson@msm.com>
To: "Lieutenant Mickey Larson" <larsonmichael@ goarmy.com>
Sent: December 11
Subject: Cookies

Hi, Dad,
Guess what? Aunt Holly wants me to bake cookies. Doesn't she know I'm a BOY? Boys don't bake cookies. It's bad enough that I have to put the toilet seat down for her. I hope you get home soon because I'm afraid she's going to turn me into a girl!
Gabe

Holly tried to conceal her smile. "Would you like to go into the city this afternoon?" she asked as she added the butter she'd cubed to the sugar in the mixing bowl.

Gabe turned around to look at her. "You aren't going to make me go shopping, are you?"

"No. I'll take you to my office. Wouldn't you like that?"

"Yes," he said halfheartedly.

"I have to put up a few decorations. You can help me."

"Okay." Again he showed a decided lack of enthusiasm.

"The Rockefeller Center Christmas tree is up," she told him next.

Now that caught his interest. "Can we go ice-skating?"

"Ah…" Holly had never gone skating. "Maybe another time, okay?"

Gabe shrugged. "Okay. I bet Billy and his dad will take me."

The kid had no idea how much that comment irritated her. However, Holly knew she had to be an adult about it. She hadn't phoned Bill to discuss the fact that his son and her nephew were friends. She would, though, in order to arrange a playdate for the two boys.

"I thought we'd leave after lunch," she said, resuming their original conversation.

"Okay." Gabe returned to the computer and was soon involved in a game featuring beasts in some alien kingdom. Whatever it was held his attention for the next ten minutes.

Using the electric mixer, Holly blended the sugar, butter and eggs and was about to add the dry ingredients when Gabe climbed up on the stool beside her.

"I've never seen anyone make cookies before," he said.

"You can watch if you want." She made an effort

to sound matter-of-fact, not revealing how pleased she was at his interest.

"When we go into the city, would it be all right if we went to Finley's?" he asked.

Holly looked up. "I suppose so. Any particular reason?"

He stared at her as if it should be obvious. "I want to see Telly. He can do all kinds of tricks and stuff, and maybe Mrs. Miracle will be there."

"Oh."

"Mrs. Miracle said I could stop by anytime I want and she'd let me work the controls. She said they don't normally let kids play with the toys but she'd make an exception." He drew in a deep breath. "What's an 'exception'?"

"It means she'll allow you to do it even though other people can't."

"That's what I thought." He leaned forward and braced his elbows on the counter, nodding solemnly at this evidence of his elevated status—at least in Mrs. Miracle's view.

As soon as the dough was mixed, Holly covered it with plastic wrap and put it inside the refrigerator to chill. When she'd finished, she cleaned off the kitchen counter. "You want to lick the beaters?" she asked.

Gabe straightened and looked skeptically at the mixer. "You can do that?"

"Sure. That's one of the best parts of baking cookies."

"Okay."

She handed him one beater and took the second herself.

Gabe's eyes widened after his first lick. "Hey, this tastes *good*."

"Told you," she said with a smug smile.

"Why can't we just eat the dough? Why ruin cookies by baking 'em?"

"Well, they're not cookies unless you bake them."

"Oh."

Her response seemed to satisfy him.

"I'm going to roll the dough out in a few minutes. Would you help me decide which cookie cutters to use?"

"I guess." Gabe didn't display a lot of enthusiasm at the request.

Holly stood on tiptoe to take down the plastic bag she kept on the upper kitchen shelf. "Your grandma Larson gave these to me last year. When your dad and I were your age, we used to make sugar cookies."

Gabe sat up straighter. "You mean my dad baked cookies?"

"Every Christmas. After we decorated them, we chose special people to give them to."

Gabe was always interested in learning facts about Mickey. Every night he asked Holly to tell him a story about his father as a boy. She'd run out of stories, but it didn't matter; Gabe liked hearing them again and again.

"You gave the cookies to special people? Like who?"

"Well…" Holly had to think about that. "Once I brought a plate of cookies to my Sunday school teacher and one year—" she paused and smiled "—I was twelve and had a crush on a boy in my class, so I brought the cookies to school for him."

"Who'd my dad give the cookies to?"

"I don't remember. You'll have to ask him."

"I will." Gabe propped his chin on one hand. "Can I take a plate of cookies to Mrs. Miracle?"

Holly was about to tell him that would be a wonderful idea, then hesitated. "The problem is, if I baked the cookies and decorated them, they'd be from me and not from you."

Gabe frowned. "I could help with cutting them out and stuff. You won't tell anyone, will you?"

"Not if you don't want me to."

"I don't want any of my friends to think I'm a sissy."

She crossed her heart. "I promise not to say a word."

"Okay, then, I'll do it." Gabe dug into the bag of cookie cutters and made his selections, removing the Christmas tree, the star and several others. Then, as if a thought had suddenly struck him, he pointed at her apron. "I don't have to put on one of those, do I?"

"You don't like my apron?"

"They're okay for girls, but not boys."

"You don't have to wear one if you'd rather not."

He shook his head adamantly.

"But you might get flour on your clothes, and your friends would guess you were baking." This was a clever argument, if she did say so herself.

Gabe nibbled on his lower lip, apparently undecided. "Then I'll change clothes. I'm not wearing any girlie apron."

"That's fine," Holly said, grinning.

The rest of the morning was spent baking and decorating cookies. Once he got started, Gabe appeared to enjoy himself. He frosted the Christmas tree with green icing and sprinkled red sugar over it.

Then, with a sideways glance at Holly, he promptly ate the cookie. She let him assume she hadn't noticed.

"Who are you giving your cookies to?" Gabe asked.

Actually, Holly hadn't thought about it. "I'm not sure." A heartbeat later, the decision was made. "Jake."

"The man in the toy department at Finley's?"

Holly nodded. "He did something kind for me on Friday. He bought my coffee."

Gabe cocked his head. "Is he your boyfriend?"

"Oh, no. But he's very nice and I want to repay him." She got two plastic plates and, together, they arranged the cookies. Holly bundled each plate in green-tinted cellophane wrap and added silver bows for a festive look.

"You ready to head into town?" she asked.

Gabe raced into his bedroom for his coat, hat and mittens. "I'm ready."

"Me, too." The truth was, Holly felt excited about seeing Jake again. Of course, there was always the possibility that he wouldn't be working today—but she had to admit she hoped he was. Her reaction surprised her; since Bill had broken off their relationship she'd been reluctant to even consider dating someone new.

Meeting Jake had been an unexpected bonus. He'd been so— She stopped abruptly. Here she was, doing it again. Jake had paid for her coffee. He was obviously a generous man... or he might've been in a rush to get back to the store. Either way, he'd been kind to her. But that didn't mean he was *attracted* to her. In reality it meant nada. Zilch. Zip. Gazing down at the plate of cookies, Holly felt she might be pushing this too far.

"Aunt Holly?"

She looked at her nephew, who was staring quizzically at her. "Is something wrong?" he asked.

"Oh, sorry... No, nothing's wrong. I was just thinking maybe I should give these cookies to someone else."

"How come?"

"I...I don't know."

"Give them to Jake," Gabe said without a second's
doubt. "Didn't you say he bought your coffee?"

"He did." Gabe was right. The cookies were simply
a way of thanking him. That was all. She was returning a kindness. With her quandary settled, they walked
over to the subway station.

When they arrived at Finley's, the streets and the
store were even more crowded than they'd been the
night before. Again Holly kept a close eye on her
nephew. She'd made a contingency plan—if they did
happen to get separated, they were to meet in the toy
department by the robots.

They rode up on the escalator, after braving the cosmetics aisles, with staff handing out perfume samples.
Gabe held his nose, but Holly was delighted to accept
several tiny vials of perfume. When they finally reached
the toy department, it was far busier than it had been
the previous evening. Both Gabe and Holly studied the
display of robots. There did seem to be fewer of the
large boxes, but Jake had assured her there'd be plenty
left by the time she received her Christmas bonus. She
sincerely hoped that was true.

The moment Gabe saw Mrs. Miracle, he rushed to
her side. "We made you sugar cookies," he said, giving her the plate.

"Oh, my, these are lovely." The grandmotherly woman
smiled. "They look good enough to eat."

"You *are* supposed to eat them," Gabe said with a giggle.

"And I will." She bent down and hugged the boy. "Thank you so much."

Gabe whispered, "Don't tell anyone, but I helped Aunt Holly make them."

Holly was standing close enough to hear him and exchanged a smile with Mrs. Miracle.

"You should be proud of that," Mrs. Miracle said as she led him toward the Intellytron display, holding the plate of cookies aloft. "Lots of men cook. You should have your aunt Holly turn on the Food Network so you see for yourself."

"Men bake cookies?"

"Oh, my, yes," she told him. "Now that you're here, why don't we go and show these other children how to work this special robot. You can be my assistant."

"Can I?" Wide-eyed, Gabe looked at Holly for permission.

She nodded, and Mrs. Miracle and Gabe went to the other side of the toy department. Holly noticed that Jake was busy with customers, so she wandered down a randomly chosen aisle, examining the Barbie dolls and all their accoutrements. She felt a bit foolish carrying a plate of decorated cookies.

As soon as he was free, Jake made a beeline toward her. "Hi," he said. "I didn't expect to see you again so soon."

"Hi." Looking away, she tried to explain the reason for her visit. "Gabe wanted to check out his robot again. After that, we're going to my office and then Rockefeller Center to see the Christmas tree…but we decided to come here first." The words tumbled out so quickly she wondered if he'd understood a thing she'd said.

He glanced at the cookies.

"These are for you," she said, shoving the plate in his direction. "Sugar cookies. In appreciation for my latte."

"Homemade sugar cookies," he murmured as if he'd never seen anything like them before.

He continued to stare at the plate for an awkward moment. Holly was afraid she'd committed a social faux pas.

"My mother used to bake sugar cookies every Christmas," Jake finally said. His eyes narrowed, and the memory seemed to bring him pain.

Holly had the absurd notion that she should apologize.

"I remember the star and the bell." He spoke in a low voice, as though transported through the years. "Oh, and look, that one's a reindeer, and of course the Christmas tree with the little cinnamon candies as ornaments."

"Gabe actually decorated that one," she said.

He looked up and his smile banished all doubt. "Thank you, Holly."

"You're welcome, Jake."

"Excuse me." A woman spoke from behind Holly. "Is there someone here who could show me the electronic games?"

Jake seemed reluctant to leave her, and Holly was loath to see him go. "I'll be happy to help you," he said. He set the cookies behind the counter and escorted the woman to another section of the department.

Holly moved to the area where Gabe and Mrs. Miracle were demonstrating Intellytron. A small crowd had gathered, and Gabe's face shone with happiness as he put the robot through its paces. In all the weeks her nephew had lived with her, she'd never seen him so excited, so fully engaged. She knew Gabe wanted this toy for Christmas; what Holly hadn't understood until this very second was just how much it meant to him.

Regardless of the cost, Holly intended to get her nephew that robot.

Holiday Sugar Cookies

(from Debbie Macomber's Cedar Cove Cookbook)

This foolproof sugar cookie recipe makes a sturdy, sweet treat that's a perfect gift or a great addition to a holiday cookie platter.

2 cups (4 sticks) unsalted butter, at room temperature
2 cups brown sugar
2 large eggs
2 teaspoons vanilla extract or grated lemon peel
6 cups all-purpose flour, plus extra for rolling
2 teaspoons baking powder
1 teaspoon salt

1. In a large bowl with electric mixer on medium speed, cream butter and sugar until light and fluffy. Add eggs and vanilla; beat until combined.

2. In a separate bowl, combine flour, baking powder and salt. Reduce mixer speed to low; beat in flour mixture just until combined. Shape dough into two disks; wrap and refrigerate at least 2 hours or up to overnight.

3. Preheat oven to 350°F. Line baking sheets with parchment paper. Remove 1 dough disk from the refrigerator. Cut disk in half; cover remaining half. On a lightly floured surface with floured rolling pin, roll dough 1/4-inch thick. Using cookie cut-

ters, cut dough into as many cookies as possible; reserve trimmings for rerolling.

4. Place cookies on prepared sheets about 1 inch apart. Bake 10 to 12 minutes (depending on the size of cookies) until pale gold. Transfer to wire rack to cool. Repeat with remaining dough and rerolled scraps.

TIP: Decorate baked cookies with prepared frosting or sprinkle unbaked cookies with colored sugars before putting them in the oven.

Makes about 48 cookies.

Five

People are like tea bags—you have to drop them in hot water before you know how strong they are.

—*Mrs. Miracle*

"Sugar cookies," Jake said to himself. A rush of memories warmed him. Memories of his mother and sister at Christmas. Spicy scents in the air—cinnamon and ginger and cloves. Those sensory memories had been so deeply buried, he'd all but forgotten them.

"We sold three of the SuperRobots this afternoon," Mrs. Miracle said, breaking into his thoughts.

Just three? Jake felt a sense of dread. He'd need to sell a lot more than three a day to unload the five hundred robots he'd ordered. He checked the computer, which instantly gave him the total number sold since Black Friday. When he saw the screen, his heart sank down to his shoes. This wasn't good. Not good at all. Jake had made a bold decision, hoping to prove himself to his father, and he was about to fall flat on his face.

"I'll be leaving for the night," Mrs. Miracle announced. "Karen—" the other sales associate "—is already gone."

He glanced at his watch. Five after nine. "By all means. You've put in a full day."

"So have you."

As the owner's son, Jake was expected to stay late. He wouldn't ask anything of his staff that he wasn't willing to do himself. That had been drilled into him by his father, who lived by the same rules.

"It's a lovely night for a walk in the park, don't you think?" the older woman said wistfully.

Jake lived directly across from Central Park. He often jogged through the grounds during the summer months, but winter was a different story.

Mrs. Miracle patted him on the back. "I appreciate that you let me stay here in the toy department," she said.

Jake turned to look at her. He hadn't said anything to the older woman about getting her transferred. He couldn't imagine HR had, either. He wondered how she'd found out about his sudden decision to keep her with him. Actually, it'd been Holly's comment about having a grandmotherly figure around that had influenced him. That, and Emily's obvious rapport with children.

"Good night, Mrs. Miracle," he said.

"Good night, Mr. Finley. Oh, and I don't think you need to worry about that robot," she said. "It's going to do very well. Mark my words."

Now it appeared the woman was a mind reader, too.

"I hope you're right," he murmured.

"I am," she said, reaching for her purse. "And remember, this is a lovely evening for a stroll through the park. It's an excellent way to clear your head of worries."

Again, she'd caught him unawares. Jake had no idea he could be so easily read. Good thing he didn't play high-stakes poker. That thought amused him as he finished up for the day and left the store.

He was grateful not to run into his father because J.R. would certainly question him about those robots. No doubt his father already knew the dismal truth; the click of a computer key would show him everything.

When Jake reached his apartment, he was hungry and restless. He unwrapped the plate of cookies and quickly ate two. If this wasn't his mother's recipe, then it was a very similar one. They tasted the same as the cookies he recalled from his childhood.

Standing by the picture window that overlooked the park, he remembered the Christmas his mother and sister had been killed. The shock and pain of it seemed as fresh now as it'd been all those years ago. No wonder his father still refused to celebrate the holiday. Jake couldn't, either.

When he looked out, he noticed how brightly lit the park was. Horse-drawn carriages clattered past, and although he couldn't hear the clopping of the horses' hooves, it sounded in his mind as clearly as if he'd been out on the street. He suddenly saw himself with his parents and his sister, all huddled under a blanket in a carriage. The horse had been named Silver, he remembered, and the snow had drifted softly down. That was almost twenty-one years ago, the winter they'd died, and he hadn't taken a carriage ride since.

Mrs. Miracle had suggested he go for a walk that evening. An odd idea, he thought, especially after a long day spent dealing with harried shoppers. The last thing he'd normally want to do was spend even more time on his feet. And yet he felt irresistibly attracted to the park. The cheerful lights, the elegant carriages, the man on the corner selling roasted chestnuts, drew him like a kid to a Christmas tree.

None of this made any sense. He was exhausted, doubting himself and his judgment, entangled in memories he'd rather ignore. Perhaps a swift walk would chase away the demons that hounded him.

Putting on his coat, he wrapped the cashmere scarf around his neck. George, the building doorman, opened the front door and, hunching his shoulders against the wind, Jake hurried across the street.

"Aunt Holly, can we buy hot chestnuts?"

The young boy's voice immediately caught Jake's attention. He turned abruptly and came face-to-face with Holly Larson. The fourth time in less than twenty-four hours.

"Jake!"

"Holly."

They stared at each other, both apparently too shocked to speak.

She found her voice first. "What are you doing here?"

He pointed to the apartment building on the other side of the street. "I live over there. What are you doing here this late?"

"How late *is* it?"

He checked his watch. "Twenty to ten."

"Ten!" she cried. "You've got to be kidding. I had no idea it was so late. Hurry up, Gabe, it's time we got to the subway."

"Can we buy some chestnuts first?" he asked, gazing longingly at the vendor's cart.

"Not now. Come on, we have to go."

"I've never had roasted chestnuts before," the boy complained.

"Neither have I," Jake said, although that wasn't strictly true, and stepped up to the vendor. "Three, please."

"Jake, you shouldn't."

"Oh, come on, it'll be fun." He paid for the chestnuts, then handed bags to Holly and Gabe.

"I'm not sure how we got this far north," Holly said, walking close to his side as the three of them strolled down the street, eating chestnuts. "Gabe wanted to see the carriages in the park."

"Lindy told me about them." Gabe spoke with his mouth full. "Lindy Lee."

"Lindy Lee's my boss," Holly explained. "The designer."

Jake knew who she was, impressed that Holly worked for such a respected industry name.

"We went into Holly's office to decorate for Christmas, and Lindy was there and she let me put up stuff around her desk. That's when she told me about the horses in the park," Gabe said.

"Did you go for a ride?" Jake asked.

Gabe shook his head sadly. "Aunt Holly said it costs a lot of money."

"It is expensive," Jake agreed. "But sometimes you can make a deal with the driver. Do you want me to try?"

"Yeah!" Gabe said excitedly. "I've never been in a carriage before—not even once."

"Jake, no," Holly whispered, and laid a restraining hand on his arm. "I should get him home and in bed."

"Aunt Holly, *please!*" The eight-year-old's plaintive cry rang out. "It's Saturday."

"You're turning down a carriage ride?" Jake asked. He saw the dreamy look that came over Holly as a carriage rolled past—a white carriage drawn by a midnight-black horse. "Have you ever been on one?"

"No…"

"Then that settles it. The three of us are going." Several carriages had lined up along the street. Jake walked over to the first one and asked his price, which he willingly paid. All that talk about negotiating had been just that—talk. This was the perfect end to a magical day. Magical because of a plate of silly sugar cookies. Magical because of Holly and Gabe. Magical because of Christmas, reluctant though he was to admit it.

He helped Holly up into the carriage. When she was seated, he lifted Gabe so the boy could climb aboard, too. Finally he hoisted himself onto the bench across from Holly and Gabe. They shared a thick fuzzy blanket.

"This is great," Gabe exclaimed. "I can hardly wait to tell my dad."

Holly smiled delightedly. "I'm surprised he's still awake," she said. "We've been on the go for hours."

"There's nothing like seeing Christmas through the eyes of a child, is there?"

"Nothing."

"Reminds me of when I was a kid…"

The carriage moved into Central Park and, even at this hour, the place was alive with activity.

"Oh, look, Gabe," Holly said, pointing at the carousel. She wrapped her arm around the boy, who snuggled closer. "We'll go on the carousel this spring."

He nodded sleepily. The ride lasted about thirty minutes, and by the time they returned to the park entrance, Gabe's eyes had drifted shut.

"I was afraid this would happen," Holly whispered.

"We'll go to my apartment, and I'll contact a car service to get you home."

Holly shook her head. "I…appreciate that, but we'll take the subway."

"Nonsense," Jake said.

"Jake, I can't afford a car service."

"It's on me."

"No." She shook her head again. "I can't let you do that."

"You can and you will. If I hadn't insisted on the carriage ride, you'd have been home by now."

She looked as if she wanted to argue more but changed her mind. "Then I'll graciously accept and say thank-you. It's been a magical evening."

Magical. The same word he'd used himself. He leaped down, helped her and Gabe out, then carried Gabe across the street. The doorman held the door for them.

"Evening, Mr. Finley."

"Evening, George."

Holly followed him onto the elevator. When they reached the tenth floor and the doors glided open, he led the way down the hall to his apartment. He had to shift the boy in his arms to get his key in the lock.

Once inside Holly looked around her, eyes wide. By New York standards, his apartment was huge. His father had lived in it for fifteen years before moving to a different place. This apartment had suited Jake, so he'd taken it over.

"I see you're like me. I haven't had time to decorate for Christmas, either," she finally said. "I was so late getting the office done that I had to come in on a Saturday to do it."

"I don't decorate for the holidays," he said without explaining the reasons. He knew he probably sounded a little brusque; he hadn't meant to.

"I suppose you get enough of that working for the store."

He nodded, again avoiding an explanation. He laid a sleeping Gabe on the sofa.

"I'll see how long we'll have to wait for a car," he said. The number was on speed dial; he used it often, since he didn't own a car himself. In midtown Manhattan car ownership could be more of a liability than a benefit. He watched Holly walk over to the picture window and gaze outside. Apparently she found the scene as mesmerizing as he had earlier. Although he made every effort to ignore Christmas, it stared back at him from the street, the city, the park. New York was always intensely alive but never more so than in December.

The call connected with the dispatcher. "How may I help you?"

Jake identified himself and gave his account number and address, and was assured a car would be there in fifteen minutes.

"I'll ride with you," Jake told her when he'd hung up the phone.

His offer appeared to surprise her. "You don't need to do that."

"True, but I'd like to," he said with a smile.

She smiled shyly back. "I'd like it, too." Walking away from the window, she sighed. "I don't understand why, but I feel like I've known you for ages."

"I feel the same way."

"Was it only yesterday morning that you paid for my latte?"

"You were a damsel in distress."

"And you were my knight in shining armor," she said warmly. "You're still in character this evening."

He sensed that she wanted to change the subject because she turned away from him, resting her gaze on something across the room. "You know, you have the ideal spot for a Christmas tree in that corner," she said.

"I haven't celebrated Christmas in more than twenty years," Jake blurted out, shocking himself even more than Holly.

"I beg your pardon?"

Jake went back into the kitchen and found that his throat had gone dry and his hands sweaty. He never talked about his mother and sister. Not with anyone. Including his father.

"You don't believe in Christmas?" she asked, trailing after him. "What about Hanukkah?"

"Neither." He'd dug himself into a hole and the only way out was to explain. "My mother and sister were killed on Christmas Eve twenty-one years ago. A freak car accident that happened in the middle of a snowstorm, when two taxis collided."

"Oh, Jake. I'm so sorry."

"Dad and I agreed to forget about Christmas from that point forward."

Holly moved to his side. She didn't say a word and he was grateful. When people learned of the tragedy—almost always from someone other than him—they rarely knew what to say or how to react. It was an uncomfortable situation and still painful; he usually mumbled some remark about how long ago the accident had been and then tried to put it out of his mind. But he *couldn't,* any more than his father could.

Holly slid her arms around him and simply laid her head against his chest. For a moment, Jake stood unmoving as she held him. Then he placed his own arms around her. It felt as though she was an anchor, securing him in an unsteady sea. He needed her. *Wanted* her. Before he fully realized what he was doing, he lifted her head and lowered his mouth to hers.

The kiss was filled with urgency and need. She slipped her arms around his neck, and her touch had a powerful effect on him.

He tangled his fingers in her dark shoulder-length hair and brought his mouth to hers a second time. Soon they were so involved in each other that it took him far longer than it should to hear the ringing of his phone.

He broke away in order to answer; as he suspected, the car was downstairs, waiting. When he told Holly, she immediately put on her coat. Gabe continued to sleep as Jake scooped him up, holding the boy carefully in both arms.

George opened the lobby door for them. Holly slid into the vehicle first, and then as Jake started to hand her the boy, he noticed a movement on the other side of the street.

"Jake?" Holly called from the car. "Please, there's no need for you to come. You've been so kind already."

"I want to see you safely home," he said as he stared

across the street. For just an instant—it must have been his imagination—he was sure he'd seen Emily Merkle, better known as Mrs. Miracle.

Six

Forbidden fruit creates many jams.
—*Mrs. Miracle*

The phone rang just as Holly and Gabe walked into the apartment after church the next morning. For one wild second Holly thought it might be Jake.

Or rather, *hoped* it was Jake.

Although she'd been dead on her feet by the time they got to Brooklyn, she couldn't sleep. She'd lain awake for hours, thinking about the kisses they'd shared, replaying every minute of their time together. All of this was so unexpected and yet so welcome. Jake was—

"Hello," she said, sounding breathless with anticipation.

"What's this I hear about you turning my son into a girl?"

"Mickey!" Her brother's voice was as clear as if he were in the next room. He tried to phone on a regular basis, but it wasn't easy. The most reliable form of communication had proved to be email.

"So you're baking cookies with my son, are you?" he teased.

"We had a blast." Gabe was leaping up and down, eager to speak to his father. "Here, I'll let Gabe tell you about it himself." She passed the phone to her nephew, who immediately grabbed it.

"Dad! Dad, guess what? I went to Aunt Holly's office to help her decorate and then she took me to see the big tree at Rockefeller Center and we watched the skaters and had hot chocolate and then we walked to Central Park and had hot dogs for dinner, and, oh, we went to see Mrs. Miracle. I helped Aunt Holly roll out cookies and…" He paused for breath.

Evidently Mickey took the opportunity to ask a few questions, because Gabe nodded a couple of times.

"Mrs. Miracle is the lady in the toy department at Finley's," he said.

He was silent for a few seconds.

"She's really nice," Gabe continued. "She reminds me of Grandma Larson. I gave her a plate of cookies, and Aunt Holly gave cookies to Jake." Silence again, followed by "He's Aunt Holly's new boyfriend and he's really, really nice."

"Maybe I should talk to your father now," Holly inserted, wishing Gabe hadn't been so quick to mention Jake's name.

Gabe clutched the receiver in both hands and turned his back, unwilling to relinquish the phone.

"Jake took us on a carriage ride in Central Park and then…" Gabe stopped talking for a few seconds. "I don't know what happened after that 'cause I fell asleep."

Mickey was asking something else, and although Holly strained to hear what it was, she couldn't.

Whatever his question, Gabe responded by glancing at Holly, grinning widely and saying, "Oh, yeah."

"Are you two talking about me?" she demanded, half laughing and half annoyed.

She was ignored. Apparently Gabe felt there was a lot to tell his father, because he cupped his hand around the mouthpiece and whispered loudly, "I think they *kissed*."

"Gabe!" she protested. If she wanted her brother to know this, she'd tell him herself.

"Okay," Gabe said, nodding. He held out the phone to her. "Dad wants to talk to you."

Holly took it from him and glared down at her nephew.

"So I hear you've found a new love interest," Mickey said in the same tone he'd used to tease her when they were teenagers.

"Oh, stop. Jake and I hardly know each other."

"How'd you meet?"

"At Starbucks. Mickey, please, it's nothing. I only met him on Friday." It felt longer than two days, but this was far too soon to even suggest they were in a relationship.

"Gabe doesn't seem to feel that's a problem."

"Okay, so I took Jake a plate of cookies like Gabe said—it was just a thank-you for buying me a coffee—and…and we happened to run into him last evening in Central Park. It's no big deal. He's a nice person and, well…like I said, we've just met."

"But it looks promising," her brother added.

Holly hated to acknowledge how true that was. Joy and anticipation had surged through her from the moment she and Jake kissed. Still, she was afraid to admit this to her brother—and, for that matter, afraid to admit it to herself. "It's too soon to say that yet."

"Ah, so you're still hung up on Bill?"

Was she? Holly didn't think so. If Bill had ended the relationship by telling her the chemistry just wasn't there, she could've accepted that. Instead, he'd left her with serious doubts regarding her parenting abilities.

"Is that it?" Mickey pressed.

"No," she said. "Not at all. Bill and I weren't really meant to be together. I think we both realized that early on, only neither of us was ready to be honest about it."

"Mmm." Mickey made a sound of agreement. "Things are going better with Gabe, aren't they?"

"Much better."

"Good."

"He's adjusting and so am I." This past week seemed to have been a turning point. They were more at ease with each other. Gabe had made new friends and was getting used to life without his father—and with her. She knew she insisted on rules Mickey didn't bother with—like making their beds every morning, drinking milk with breakfast and, of course, putting the toilet seat down. But Gabe hardly complained at all anymore.

"What was it he told Santa he wanted for Christmas?" Mickey asked.

"So he emailed you about the visit with Santa, did he?"

"Yup, he sent the email right after he got home. He seemed quite excited."

"It's Intellytron the SuperRobot."

At her reference to the toy, Gabe's eyes lit up and he nodded vigorously.

"We found them in Finley's Department Store. Mrs.

Miracle, the woman Gabe mentioned, works there...
and Jake does, too."

"Didn't Gabe tell me Jake's name is Finley?" Mickey
asked. "He said he heard Mrs. Miracle call him that—
Mr. Finley. Is he related to the guy who owns the store?"

"Y-e-s." How dense could she be? Holly felt like slapping her forehead. She'd known his name was Finley
from the beginning and it hadn't meant a thing to her.
But now... now she realized Jake was probably related
to the Finley family—was possibly even the owner's
son. No wonder he could afford to live where he did.
He hadn't given the price of the carriage ride or the car
service a second thought, either.

She had the sudden, awful feeling that she was swimming in treacherous waters and there wasn't a life pre-
server in sight.

"Holly?"

"I...I think he must be." She'd been so caught up in
her juvenile fantasies, based on the coincidence of their
meetings, that she hadn't paid attention to anything else.

"You sound like this is shocking news."

"I hadn't put two and two together," she confessed.

"And now you're scared."

"I guess I am."

"Don't be. He puts his pants on one leg at a time
like everyone else, if you'll pardon the cliché. He's just
a guy."

"Right."

"You don't seem too sure of that."

Holly wasn't. A chill had overtaken her and she
hugged herself with one arm. "I need to think about
this."

"While you're thinking, tell me more about this robot that's got my son so excited."

"It's expensive."

"How...expensive?"

Holly heard the hesitation in her brother's voice. He had his own financial problems. "Don't worry—I've got it. This is on me."

"You're sure about that?"

"Positive." The Christmas bonus checks were due the following Friday. If all went well, hers should cover the price of the toy with enough left over for a really special Christmas dinner.

Christmas.

When she woke that morning, still warm under the covers, Holly's first thought had been of Jake. She'd had the craziest idea that...well, it was out of the question now.

What Jake had confided about his mother and sister had nearly broken her heart. The tragedy had not only robbed him of his mother and sibling, it had destroyed his pleasure in Christmas. Holly had hoped to change that, but the mere notion seemed ridiculous now. She'd actually planned to invite Jake to spend Christmas Day with her and Gabe. She knew now that he'd never accept. He was a Finley, after all, a man whose background was vastly different from her own.

Half-asleep, she'd pictured the three of them sitting around her table, a lovely golden-brown turkey with sage stuffing resting in the center. She'd imagined Christmas music playing and the tree lights blinking merrily, enhancing the celebratory mood. She couldn't believe she'd even considered such a thing, knowing what she did now.

"I have a Christmas surprise coming your way," Mickey said. "I'm just hoping it arrives in time for the holidays."

"It doesn't matter," she assured her brother, dragging her thoughts away from Jake. She focused on her brother and nephew—which was exactly what she intended to do from this point forward. She needed to forget this romantic fantasy she'd invented within a day of meeting Jake Finley.

"I can guarantee Gabe will like it and so will you," Mickey was saying.

Holly couldn't begin to guess what Mickey might have purchased in Afghanistan for Christmas, but then her brother had always been full of surprises. He'd probably ordered something over the internet, she decided.

"Mom and Dad mailed us a package, as well," she told him. "The box got here this week."

"From Haiti? What would they be sending?"

"I don't have a clue," she said. Once the tree was up she'd arrange the gifts underneath it.

"You're going to wait until Christmas morning, aren't you?" he asked. "Don't open anything before that."

"Of course we'll wait." Even as kids, they'd managed not to peek at their gifts.

Mickey laughed, then grew serious. "This won't be an ordinary Christmas, will it?"

Holly hadn't dwelled on not being with her parents. Her father, a retired dentist, and her mother, a retired nurse, had offered their services in a health clinic for twelve months after the devastating earthquake. They'd been happy about the idea of giving back, and Holly had been happy for them. This Christmas was supposed to be Mickey, Gabe and her for the holidays—and then Mickey's National Guard unit had been called up and he'd left to serve his country.

"It could be worse," she said, and her thoughts involuntarily went to Jake and his father, who refused to celebrate Christmas at all.

"Next year everything will be different," Mickey told her.

"Yes, it will," she agreed.

Her brother spoke to Gabe for a few more minutes and then said goodbye. Gabe was pensive after the conversation with his father and so was Holly, but for different reasons.

"How about toasted cheese sandwiches and tomato soup for lunch?" she suggested, hoping to lighten the mood. "That was your dad's and my favorite Sunday lunch when we were growing up."

Gabe looked at her suspiciously. "What kind of cheese?"

Holly shrugged. "Regular cheese?" By that she meant the plastic-wrapped slices, Gabe's idea of cheese.

"You won't use any of that buffalo stuff, will you?"

She grinned. "Buffalo mozzarella. Nope, this is plain old sliced regular cheese in a package."

"Okay, as long as the soup comes from a can. That's the way Dad made it and that's how I like it."

"You got it," she said, and moved into the kitchen.

Gabe sat on a stool and watched her work, leaning his elbows on the kitchen counter. Holly wasn't fooled by his intent expression. He wasn't interested in spending time with her; he was keeping a close eye on their lunch in case she tried to slip in a foreign ingredient. After a moment he released a deep sigh.

"What's that about?" she asked.

"I miss my dad."

"I know you do, sweetheart. I miss him, too."

"And Grandma and Grandpa."

"And they miss us."

Gabe nodded. "It's not so bad living with you. I thought it was at first, but you're okay."

"Thanks." She hid a smile and set a piece of buttered bread on the heated griddle, then carefully placed a slice of processed cheese on top before adding the second piece of bread. She planned to have a plain cheese sandwich herself—one with *real* cheese.

Obviously satisfied that she was preparing his lunch according to his specifications, Gabe clambered off the stool. "Can we go to the movies this afternoon?"

"Maybe." She had to be careful with her entertainment budget, especially since there were additional expenses coming up this month. "It might be better if we got a video."

"Can I invite a friend over?"

She hesitated a moment, afraid he might want to ask his new friend, Billy.

"Sure," she said. "How about Jonathan Krantz?" Jonathan was another eight-year-old who lived in the building, and Caroline, his mother, sometimes babysat for her.

That was acceptable to Gabe.

After lunch they walked down to the neighborhood video store, found a movie they could both agree on and then asked Jonathan to join them.

Holly did her best to pay attention to the movie; however, her mind had a will of its own. No matter how hard she tried, all she could think about was Jake. He didn't phone and that was just as well. She wasn't sure what she would've said if he had.

Then again, he hadn't asked for her phone number. Still, he could get it easily enough if he wanted....

Late Sunday night, after Gabe was asleep, Holly went on the computer and did a bit of research. Sure enough, Jake was related to the owner. Not only that, he was the son and heir.

Monday morning, Holly dropped Gabe off at school and took the subway into Manhattan. As she walked past Starbucks, she felt a twinge of longing—for more than just the coffee they served. This was where she'd met Jake. Jake Finley.

As she walked briskly past Starbucks, the door flew open and Jake Finley dashed out, calling her name.

Holly pretended not to hear.

"Holly!" he shouted, running after her. "Wait up!"

Seven

*Coincidence is when God chooses
to remain anonymous.*

—*Mrs. Miracle*

"Wait up!" Jake called. Holly acted as if she hadn't heard him. Jake knew better. She was clearly upset about something, although he couldn't figure out what. His mind raced with possibilities, but he couldn't come up with a single one that made sense.

Finally she turned around.

Jake relaxed. Just seeing her again brought him a feeling of happiness he couldn't define. He barely knew Holly Larson, yet he hadn't been able to forget her. She was constantly in his thoughts, constantly with him, and perhaps the most puzzling of all was the *rightness* he felt in her presence. He couldn't think of any other way to describe it.

Jake had resisted the urge to contact her on Sunday, afraid of coming on too strong. They'd seen quite a bit of each other in the past few days, seemingly thrown together by fate. Coincidence? He supposed so, and yet... It was as though a providential hand was behind all this. Admittedly that sounded fanciful, even melodramatic. Nevertheless, four chance meetings in quick succession was hard to explain.

With someone else, a different kind of woman, Jake might have suspected these meetings had been contrived, and certainly this morning's was pure manipulation on his part. He'd hoped to run into her casually. But he hadn't expected to see Holly walk directly past the coffee shop. He couldn't allow this opportunity to pass.

She looked up at him expectantly; she didn't say anything.

"Good morning," he said, unsure of her mood.

"Hi." She just missed making eye contact.

He felt her reluctance and frowned, unable to fathom what he might have done to upset her. "What's wrong?" he asked.

"Nothing."

"Then why won't you look at me?"

The question forced her to raise her eyes and meet his. She held his gaze for only a fraction of a second before glancing away.

The traffic light changed and, side by side, they crossed the street.

"I'd like to take you to dinner," he said. He'd decided that if he invited her out on a real date they could straighten out the problem, whatever it was.

"When?"

At least she hadn't turned him down flat. That was encouraging. "Whenever you say." He'd rearrange his schedule if necessary. "Tonight? Tomorrow? I'm free every evening. Or I can be." He wanted it understood that he wasn't involved with anyone else. In fact, he hadn't been in a serious relationship in years.

His primary goal for the past decade had been to learn the retail business from the ground up, and as a result his social life had suffered. He worked long hours and that had taken a toll on his relationships. After his last breakup, which was in... Jake had to stop and think. June, he remembered. Had it really been that long? At any rate, Judith had told him it was over before they'd really begun.

At the time he'd felt bad, but agreed it was probably for the best. Funny how easily he could let go of a woman with hardly a pause after just four weeks. Judith had been attractive, successful, intelligent, but there'd been no real connection between them. The thought of letting Holly walk out of his life was a completely different scenario, one that filled him with dread.

All he could think about on Sunday was when he'd see her again. His pride had influenced his decision not to call her; he didn't want her to know how important she'd become to him in such a short time. Despite that, he'd gone to Starbucks first thing this morning.

"Tonight?" she repeated, referring to his dinner invitation. "You mean this evening?"

"Sure," he said with a shrug. "I'm available Tuesday night if that's better for you."

She hesitated, as if considering his offer. "Thanks, but I don't have anyone to look after Gabe."

"I could bring us dinner." He wasn't willing to give up that quickly.

Her eyes narrowed. "Why are you trying so hard?"

"Why are you inventing excuses not to see me?"

He didn't understand her reluctance. Saturday, when

he'd dropped her off at her Brooklyn apartment and kissed her good-night, she'd practically melted in his arms. Now she couldn't get away from him fast enough.

Holly stared down at the sidewalk. People hurried past them and around them. They stood like boulders in the middle of a fast-moving stream, neither of them moving, neither talking.

"I...I didn't know who you were," she eventually admitted. "Not until later."

"I told you my name's Jake Finley." He didn't pretend not to understand what she meant. This wasn't the first time his family name had intimidated someone. He just hadn't expected that sort of reaction from Holly. He'd assumed she knew, and that was part of her charm because it hadn't mattered to her.

"I know you did," she countered swiftly. "And I feel stupid for not connecting the dots."

He stiffened. "And my name bothers you?"

"Not really," she said, and her gaze locked with his before she slowly lowered her lashes. "I guess it does, but not for the reasons you're assuming."

"What exactly am I assuming?" he asked.

"That I'd use you."

"For what?" he demanded.

"Well, for one thing, that robot toy. We both know how badly Gabe wants it for Christmas and it's expensive and you might think I..."

"*What* would I think?" he asked forcefully when she didn't complete her sentence.

"That I'd want you to get me the toy."

"Would you ask me to do that?" If she did, he'd gladly purchase it—retail price—on her behalf.

"No. Never." Her eyes flared with the intensity of her response. She started to leave and Jake followed.

"Then it's a moot point." He began to walk, carefully matching his longer stride to her shorter one. "Under no circumstances will I purchase that toy for you. Agreed?"

"Agreed," she said.

"Anything else?"

Holly looked at him and then away. "I don't come from a powerful family or know famous people or—"

"Do you think I care?"

"No, but if you did, you'd be plain out of luck."

He smiled. "That's fine with me."

"Okay," she said, stopping abruptly. "Can you explain why you want to see me?"

Jake wished he had a logical response. He felt drawn to her in ways he hadn't with other women. "I can't say for sure, but deep down I feel that if we were to walk away from each other right now, I'd regret it."

"You do?" she asked softly, and pressed her hand to her heart. "Jake, I feel the same way. What's happening to us?"

He didn't have an answer. "I don't know." But he definitely felt it, and that feeling intensified with each meeting.

They started walking again. "So, can I see you tonight?" he asked. That was important, necessary.

Her face fell. "I wasn't making it up, about not having anyone to take care of Gabe. If you were serious about bringing us dinner…"

"I was."

Her face brightened. "Then that would work out perfectly."

"Do you like take-out Chinese?" he asked, thinking Gabe would enjoy it, as well.

"Love it."

"Me, too, but you'll have to use chopsticks."

"Okay, I'll give it a try."

"Great." Jake breathed easier. Everything was falling into place, just the way he'd hoped it would. He glanced at his watch and grimaced. He was late for work. He hoped Karen or Mrs. Miracle had covered for him.

Retreating now, taking two steps backward, he called out to Holly, "Six-thirty? At your place?"

She nodded eagerly. "Yes. And thank you, Jake, thank you so much."

He raised his hand. "See you tonight."

"Tonight," she echoed, and they both turned and hurried off to their respective jobs.

Jake's step was noticeably lighter as he rushed toward the department store. By the time he arrived, ten minutes later than usual, he was breathless. He'd just clocked in and headed for the elevator when his father stopped him, wearing a frown that told him J.R. wasn't happy.

"Are you keeping bankers' hours these days?"

"No," Jake told him. "I had an appointment." A slight stretch of the truth.

"I was looking for you."

"Any particular reason?" Jake asked. He'd bet his lunch break this sudden interest in the toy department had to do with those robots.

His father surprised him, however, with a completely different question. "I heard from HR that you requested a transfer for one of the seasonal staff...."

"Mrs. Miracle."

"Who? No, that wasn't the name."

"No, it's Merkle or Michaels or something like that. The name badge mistakenly says Miracle, and she insisted that's what we call her."

His father seemed confused, which was fine with Jake. He felt he was being rather clever to keep J.R.'s attention away from the robots.

J.R. ignored the comment. "You asked for this Mrs. Miracle or whoever she is to be transferred and then you changed your mind. Do I understand correctly?"

"Yes. After I made the initial request, I realized she was a good fit for the department—a grandmotherly figure who relates well to kids *and* parents. She adds exactly the right touch."

"I see," his father murmured. "Okay, whatever you decide is fine."

That was generous, seeing that *he* was the department head, Jake mused with more affection than sarcasm.

"While I have you, tell me, how are sales of that expensive robot going?"

Jake wasn't fooled. His father already knew the answer to that. "Sales are picking up. We sold a total of twenty-five over the weekend."

"Twenty-five," his father said slowly. "There're still a lot of robots left in the storeroom, though, aren't there?"

"Yes," Jake admitted.

"That's what I thought."

He made some additional remark Jake couldn't quite grasp, but it didn't sound like something he wanted to hear, anyway, so he didn't ask J.R. to repeat it.

As he entered the toy department, clipping on his

"Manager" badge, Jake was glad to see Mrs. Miracle on duty.

"Good morning, Mr. Finley," she said, looking pleased with herself.

"Good morning. I apologize for being late—"

"No problem. I sold two Intellytrons this morning."

"Already?" This was encouraging news and improved his workday almost before it had started. "That's wonderful!"

"They seem to be catching on."

The phone rang just then, and Jake stepped behind the counter to answer. The woman at the other end of the line was looking for Intellytron and sighed with audible relief when Jake assured her he had plenty in stock. She asked that he hold one for her.

"I'll be happy to," Jake said. He found Mrs. Miracle watching him, smiling, when he ended the conversation. "I think you might be right," he said. "That was a woman calling about Intellytron. She sounded excited when I told her we've got them."

Mrs. Miracle rubbed her palms together. "I knew it." The morning lull was about to end; in another half hour, the store would explode with customers. Since toys were on the third floor, it took time for shoppers to drift up the escalators and elevators, so they still had a few minutes of relative peace. Jake decided to take advantage of it by questioning his rather unusual employee.

"I thought I saw you on Saturday night," he commented in a nonchalant voice, watching her closely.

"Me?" she asked.

Jake noted that she looked a bit sheepish. "Did you happen to take a walk around Central Park around ten or ten-thirty?"

"My heavens, no! After spending all day on my feet, the last thing I'd do is wander aimlessly around Central Park. At that time of night, no less." Her expression turned serious. "What makes you ask?"

"I could've sworn that was you I saw across from the park."

She laughed as though the question was ludicrous. "You're joking, aren't you?"

"No." Jake grew even more suspicious. Her nervous reaction seemed to imply that she wasn't being completely truthful. "Don't you remember? You suggested I take a stroll through the park."

"I said that?"

"You did," he insisted. He wasn't about to be dismissed quite this easily. "You said it would help clear my head."

"After a long day at work? My goodness, what was I thinking?"

Jake figured the question was rhetorical, so he didn't respond. "I met Holly Larson and her nephew there," he told her.

"My, that was a nice coincidence, wasn't it?"

"Very nice," he agreed.

"Are you seeing her again?" the older woman asked.

"Yes, as a matter of fact, I am." He didn't share any details. The less she knew about his personal life, the better. Mrs. Miracle might appear to be an innocent senior citizen, but he had his doubts. Not that he suspected anything underhanded or nefarious. She seemed… Jake couldn't come up with the right word. He liked Mrs. Miracle and she was an excellent employee, a natural saleswoman. And yet… He didn't really know much about her.

And what he did know didn't seem to add up.

Eight

Aspire to inspire before you expire.
　　　　　　　　　　　　　　　—*Mrs. Miracle*

Holly felt as if she was walking on air the rest of the way into the office. It didn't matter how rotten her day turned out to be; no one was going to ruin it after her conversation with Jake.

She'd spent a miserable Sunday and had worked herself into a state after she'd discovered Jake's position with the department store. Son and heir. Now, having talked to him, she realized her concerns were irrelevant. Okay, so his family was rich and influential; that didn't define him or say anything about the person he really was.

The question that, inevitably, kept going around and around in her mind was why someone like Jake Finley would be interested in *her*. The reality was that he could have his pick of women. To further complicate the situation, she was taking care of Gabe. Lots of men would see her nephew as an encumbrance. Apparently not Jake.

Holly was happy they'd gotten this settled. She felt reassured about his interest—and about the fact that he'd promised not to purchase the robot for her. Mickey had offered, too, but she knew he was financially strapped. Besides, getting Gabe this toy for Christmas—as *her* gift to him—was important to Holly.

She couldn't entirely explain why. Maybe because of Bill's implication that she wasn't good with kids. She had something to prove—if not to Bill or Mickey or even Jake, she had to prove it to herself. Nothing was going to keep her from making this the best possible Christmas for Gabe.

Holly entered her cubicle outside Lindy Lee's office and hung up her coat. She'd been surprised to find her boss in the office on Saturday afternoon and had tried to keep Gabe occupied so he wouldn't pester her. Unfortunately, Holly's efforts hadn't worked. She'd caught Gabe with Lindy Lee twice. One look made her suspect Lindy didn't really appreciate the intrusion. As soon as they'd finished putting up the decorations, Holly had dragged Gabe out with her. But this morning, as she looked around the office, she was pleased with her work. The bright red bulbs that hung outside her cubicle created an air of festivity. She couldn't help it—she started singing "Jingle Bells."

"Where is that file?" Lindy Lee shouted. She was obviously in her usual Monday-morning bad mood. Her employer was sorting through her in-basket, cursing impatiently under her breath.

Of course, Lindy Lee didn't mention *which* file she needed. But deciphering vague demands was all part and parcel of Holly's job. And fortunately she had a pretty good idea which one her boss required.

Walking into Lindy Lee's office, Holly reached across the top of the desk, picked up a file and handed it to her.

Lindy Lee growled something back, opened the file and then smiled. "Thank you."

"You're welcome," Holly said cheerfully.

The designer eyed her suspiciously. "What are *you* so happy about?" she asked.

"Nothing…I met up with a friend this morning, that's all."

"I take it this *friend* is a man."

Holly nodded. "A very special man."

"Honey, don't believe it." She laughed as though to say Holly had a lot to learn about the opposite sex. "Men will break your heart before breakfast and flush it down the toilet just for fun."

Holly didn't bother to explain about Jake. Lindy Lee's experience with men might be far more extensive than her own, but it was obviously different. Jake would never do anything to hurt her; she was sure of it. Besides, Lindy Lee socialized in different circles—Jake's circles, she realized with a start. Still, Holly couldn't make herself believe Jake was the kind of man who'd mislead her. Even though they'd known each other so briefly, every instinct she had told her she could trust him, and she did.

No irrational demand or bad temper was going to spoil her day, Holly decided. Because that evening she was seeing Jake.

Holly guessed wrong. Her day was ruined.

Early that afternoon she slipped back into her cubicle after delivering Lindy Lee's latest sketches to the tech department, where they'd be translated into patterns, which would then be sewn up as samples. Lindy was talking to the bookkeeper and apparently neither one noticed that she'd returned.

Holly hadn't intended to listen in on the conversation, but it would've been impossible not to with Lindy Lee's office door wide open. In Holly's opinion, if Lindy wanted to keep the conversation private, then it was up to her to close the door.

"Christmas bonuses are due this Friday," Marsha, the bookkeeper, reminded their boss.

"Due." Lindy Lee pounced on the word. "Since when is a bonus *due?* It's my understanding that a bonus is exactly that—a bonus—an extra that's distributed at my discretion."

"Well, yes, but you've given us one every year since you went out on your own."

"That's because I could afford to."

"You've had a decent year," Marsha said calmly.

Holly wanted to stand and cheer. Marsha was right; profits were steady despite the economy. The staff had worked hard, although their employer took them for granted. Lindy Lee didn't appear to notice or value the team who backed her both personally and professionally. More times than she cared to count, Holly had dropped off and picked up Lindy's dry cleaning or run errands for her. She often went above and beyond anything listed in her job description.

Not once had she complained. The way Holly figured it, her main task was to give Lindy Lee the freedom to be creative and do what she did best and that was design clothes.

"A *decent* year, perhaps," Lindy Lee repeated. "But not a stellar one."

"True," Marsha agreed. "But you're holding your own in a terrible economy."

"All right, I'll reconsider." Lindy Lee walked over to the window, her back to Holly. Not wanting to be caught listening, Holly quietly stood. There was plenty to do away from her desk—like filing. Clutching a sheaf of documents, she held her breath as she waited for Lindy's decision.

"Everyone gets the same bonus as last year," Lindy Lee said with a beleaguered sigh.

Holly released her breath.

"Everyone except Holly Larson."

Her heart seemed to stop.

"Why not Holly?" Marsha asked.

"She doesn't deserve it," Lindy Lee said flippantly. "She's out of the office at the stroke of five and she's been late for work a number of mornings, as well."

The bookkeeper was quick to defend Holly. "Yes, but she's looking after her nephew while her brother's in Afghanistan. This hasn't been easy for her, you know."

Lindy Lee whirled around and Holly moved from her line of vision in the nick of time. She flattened herself against the wall and continued to listen.

"Yes, yes, I met the boy this weekend. She brought him on Saturday when she came in to decorate."

"On her own time," Marsha said pointedly.

"True, but if she managed her time better, Holly could've done it earlier. As it is, the decorations are up much later than in previous years. If I was giving out bleeding-heart awards this Christmas, I'd make sure Holly got one. No, I won't change my mind," she snapped as Marsha began to protest. "A bonus is a bonus, and as far as I'm concerned Holly doesn't deserve one. It's about merit, you know, and going the extra mile, and she hasn't done that."

Holly gasped.

"But—"

"I've made my decision."

Marsha didn't argue further.

Holly didn't blame her. The bookkeeper had tried. Holly felt tears well up but blinked them away. She was a good employee; she worked hard. While Lindy Lee was correct—these days she *did* leave the office on time—there'd been many a night earlier in the year when she'd stayed late without being asked. She'd often gone that extra mile for her employer. Yet all Lindy seemed to remember was the past three months.

She felt sick to her stomach. So there'd be no bonus for her. Although the amount of money wasn't substantial—maybe five hundred dollars—it would've made all the difference. But somehow, she promised herself, she'd find a way to buy Gabe his special Christmas toy.

Even though she was distracted by her financial worries, Holly managed to enjoy dinner with Jake and Gabe that evening. Jake brought chopsticks along with their take-out Chinese—an order large enough to feed a family of eight. Several of the dishes were new to Holly. He'd chosen moo shu pork and shrimp in lobster sauce, plus barbecue pork, egg rolls, fried rice and almond fried chicken.

Gabe loved every minute of their time with Jake. As he so eloquently said, "It's nice being around a guy."

"I don't know," Jake commented as he slipped his arm around Holly's waist. "Women aren't so bad."

Gabe considered his comment carefully. "Aunt Holly's okay, I guess."

"You *guess*," she sputtered. Using her chopsticks she removed the last bit of almond fried chicken from her nephew's plate.

"Hey, that was mine," Gabe cried.

"That's what you get for criticizing women," Holly told him, and then, to prove her point, she reached for his fried dumpling, too. In retaliation, Gabe reached across for her egg roll, dropping it on the table.

Jake immediately retrieved it and stuck one end in his mouth. "Five-second rule," he said just before he bit down.

When they'd finished, they cleared the table and settled down in front of the television.

As Jake flipped through the channels, Gabe asked, "When are we gonna put up the Christmas tree?"

"This week," Holly told him. She'd need to budget carefully now that she wasn't going to get her bonus. The tree—she'd hoped to buy a real one—was an added expense she'd planned to cover with the extra money. This year she'd have to resort to the small artificial tree she'd stuck in the back of her coat closet.

The news that she wouldn't be receiving the bonus was devastating. Holly's first instinct had been to strike back. If everyone else was getting a bonus, it didn't seem fair that she wasn't. Still, Lindy Lee had a point. Holly hadn't been as dedicated to her job since Gabe came into her life. She had other responsibilities now.

That afternoon she'd toyed with the idea of looking for a new job. She could walk out—that would show Lindy Lee. Reason quickly asserted itself. She couldn't leave her job and survive financially. It could take her months to find a new one. And although this was an entry-level position, the chance to advance in the fashion world was an inducement she simply couldn't reject that easily. She'd made friends at the office, too. Friends like Marsha, who'd willingly defended her to their employer.

Besides, if she left her job, there'd be dozens who'd leap at the opportunity to take her place. No, Holly would swallow her disappointment and ride this out until Mickey returned. Next Christmas would be different.

"Can Jake help decorate the Christmas tree?" Gabe asked.

Jake was sitting next to her and Holly felt him tense. His face was pale, his expression shocked.

"Jake." Holly said his name softly and laid her hand on his forearm. "Are you okay?"

"Sure. Sorry, no decorating trees for me this year," he said in an offhand way.

"Why not?" Gabe pressed. "It's really fun. Aunt Holly said she'd make popcorn and we'd have cider. She has some ornaments from when she and my dad were kids. She won't let me see them until we put up the tree. It'll be lots of fun." His young face pleaded with Jake to reconsider.

Holly gently placed her hand on her nephew's shoulder. "Jake said another time," she reminded him. Jake hadn't participated in any of the usual Christmas traditions or activities in more than twenty years, ever since he'd lost his mother and sister.

"But there won't be another time," her nephew sulked. "I'll be with my dad next year."

"Jake's busy," Holly said, offering yet another excuse.

"Sorry to let you down, buddy," Jake told Gabe. "We'll do something else, all right?"

Gabe shrugged, his head hanging. "Okay."

"How about if I take you ice-skating at Rockefeller Center? Would you like that?"

"Wow!" In his excitement, Gabe propelled himself off the sofa and landed with a thud on the living room carpet. "I wanted to go skating last Saturday but Aunt Holly doesn't know how."

"She's a girl," Jake said in a stage whisper. Then he looked at her and grinned boyishly. "Frankly, I'm glad of it."

"As you should be," she returned under her breath.

"When can we go?" Gabe wasn't letting this opportunity slip through his fingers. He wanted to nail down the date as soon as possible. "I took skating lessons last winter," he said proudly.

Jake hesitated. "I'll need to get back to you once I see how everything goes at the store. It's the Christmas season, you know, so we might have to wait until the first week of the new year. How about Sunday the second?"

"That *long?*"

"Yes, but then I'll have more time to show you some classic moves. Deal?"

Gabe considered this compromise and finally nodded. "Deal." They clenched their fists and bumped them together to seal the bargain.

The three of them sat side by side and watched a rerun of *Everybody Loves Raymond* for the next half hour. Jake was beside her, his arm around her shoulders. Gabe sat to her left with his feet tucked beneath him.

When the program ended, Gabe turned to Jake. "Do you want me to leave the room so you can kiss my aunt Holly?"

"Gabe!" Holly's cheeks were warm with embarrassment.

"What makes you suggest that?" Jake asked the boy.

Gabe stood in the center of the room. "My dad emailed and said if you came to the apartment, I should dis-discreetly leave for a few minutes, only I don't know what that word means. I think it means you want to kiss Aunt Holly without me watching. Right?"

Jake nodded solemnly. "Something like that."

"I thought so. Okay, I'm going to go and get ready for bed." He enunciated each word as if reading a line of dialogue from an unfamiliar play.

Jake winked at Holly. "Pucker up, sweetheart," he said, doing a recognizable imitation of Humphrey Bogart.

Holly rolled her eyes and clasped her hands prayerfully. "Ah, sweet romance."

As soon as the bedroom door closed, Jake pulled her into his arms. The kiss was everything she'd remembered and more. They kissed repeatedly until Gabe came back and stood in front of them. He cleared his throat.

"Should I go away again?" he asked.

"No, that's fine," Holly said. She had trouble speaking.

"Your timing is perfect," Jake assured the boy.

Jake left shortly after that, and once she'd let him out of the apartment, Holly leaned against the door, still a little breathless. Being with Jake was very nice, indeed,

but she had something else on her mind at the moment—
Intellytron the SuperRobot and how she was going to
afford one before Christmas.

Nine

It's hard to stumble when you're down on your knees.
—Shirley, Goodness and Mercy,
friends of Mrs. Miracle

Holly gave the situation regarding Gabe and the robot careful thought during the sleepless night that followed their dinner. She'd asked Jake about it when Gabe was out of earshot.

"There are still plenty left," he'd told her.

"But they're selling, aren't they?"

"Yes, sales are picking up."

That was good for him but unsettling for her. If she couldn't afford to pay for the robot until closer to Christmas, then she'd need to make a small deposit and put one on layaway now. She didn't know if Finley's offered that option; not many stores did anymore. She'd have to check with Jake. She dared not take a chance that Intellytron would sell out before she had the cash.

While she was dead set against letting Jake purchase the robot for her, she hoped he'd be willing to put one aside, even if layaway wasn't a current practice at higher-end department stores. If she made their lunches, cut back on groceries and bought only what was absolutely necessary, she should be able to pay cash for the robot just before Christmas.

Tuesday morning she packed a hard-boiled egg and an apple for lunch. For Gabe she prepared a peanut butter and jelly sandwich, adding an apple for him, too, plus the last of the sugar cookies. Gabe hadn't been happy to take a packed lunch. He much preferred to buy his meal with his friends. But it was so much cheaper for him to bring it—and, at this point, necessary, although of course she couldn't tell him why. The leftover Chinese food figured into her money-saving calculations, too. It would make a great dinner.

On her lunch hour, after she'd eaten her apple and boiled egg, Holly hurried to Finley's to talk to Jake. She'd been uneasy from the moment she'd learned she wasn't getting a Christmas bonus. She wouldn't relax until she knew the SuperRobot would still be available the following week.

Unfortunately, Jake wasn't in the toy department.

"He's not here?" Holly asked Mrs. Miracle, unable to hide her disappointment.

"He's with his father just now," the older woman told her, and then frowned. "I do hope the meeting goes smoothly. It can be difficult to read the senior Mr. Finley sometimes. But I have faith that all will end well." Her eyes twinkled as she spoke.

Holly hoped she'd explain, and Mrs. Miracle obliged.

"In case you didn't hear, Jake went over the department buyer's head when he ordered those extra robots," she confided, "and that's caused some difficulty with his father. J. R. Finley has a real stubborn streak."

Mrs. Miracle seemed very well informed about the relationship between Jake and his father. "The robots are selling, though. Isn't that right?" she asked, again torn between pleasure at Jake's success and worry about laying her hands on one of the toys. The display appeared to be much smaller than last week.

"Thankfully, yes," Mrs. Miracle told her. "Jake took quite a risk, you know?"

Holly shook her head.

"Jake tried to talk Mike Scott into ordering more of the robots, but Mike refused to listen, so Jake did what he felt was best." Her expression sobered. "His father was not pleased, to put it mildly."

"But you said they're selling."

"Oh, yes. We sold another twenty-five over the weekend and double that on Monday." She nodded sagely. "I can only assume J.R. is feeling somewhat reassured."

"That's great." Holly meant it, but a shiver of dread went through her.

"Several of our competitors have already sold out," Mrs. Miracle said with a gleeful smile.

"That's terrific news." And it was—for Finley's. Parents searching for the toy would now flock to one of the few department stores in town with enough inventory to meet demand.

"How's Gabe?" Mrs. Miracle asked, changing the subject.

"He's doing fine." Holly chewed her lip, her thoughts still on the robot. "Seeing how well the robot's selling, would it be possible for me to set one aside on a layaway plan?"

The older woman's smile faded. "Oh, dear, the store

doesn't have a layaway option. They haven't in years. Is that going to be a problem for you?"

Holly wasn't surprised that layaway was no longer offered, but she figured it was worth asking. Holly clutched her purse. "I...I don't know." Her mind spinning, she looked hopefully at the older woman. "Do you think you could hold one of the robots for me?" She hated to make that kind of request, but with her credit card temporarily out of commission and no layaway plan, she didn't have any other choice. The payment she'd made on her card would've been processed by now, but she didn't dare risk a purchase as big as this.

"Oh, dear, I'm really not sure."

"Could you ask Jake for me?" Holly inquired. She'd do it herself if he was there.

"Of course. I just don't think I could go against store policy, being seasonal staff and all."

"I wouldn't want you to do that, Mrs. Miracle."

"However, I'm positive Jake would be happy to help if he can." She leaned closer and lowered her voice. "He's rather sweet on you."

Sweet? That was a nice, old-fashioned word. "He's been wonderful to me and Gabe."

"So I understand. Didn't he bring you dinner last night?"

Holly wondered how Mrs. Miracle knew about that, unless Jake had mentioned it. No reason not to, she supposed. "Yes, and it was a lovely evening," she said. The only disappointment had come when Gabe asked him to help decorate the tree and Jake refused. The mere suggestion had distressed him. She hadn't realized that the trauma of those family deaths was as intense and painful as if the accident had just happened. If it was this traumatic for Jake, Holly could only imagine what it was like for his father.

"Did you know Jake and his father leave New York every Christmas Eve?" Mrs. Miracle whispered.

It was as if the older woman had been reading her mind. "I beg your pardon?"

"Jake and his father leave New York every Christmas Eve," she repeated.

Holly hadn't known this and wasn't sure what to say.

"Isn't that a shame?"

Holly shrugged. "Everyone deals with grief differently," she murmured. Her brother handled the loss of his wife with composure and resolve. That was his personality. Practical. Responsible. As he'd said himself, he couldn't fall apart; he had a boy to raise.

Sally had been sick for a long while, giving Mickey time to prepare for the inevitable—at least to the extent anyone can. He'd loved Sally and missed her terribly, especially in the beginning. Yet he'd gone on with his life, determined to be a good father.

Perhaps the difference was that for the Finleys, the deaths had come suddenly, without warning. The family had awakened the morning of Christmas Eve, excited about the holiday. There'd been no indication that by the end of the day tragedy would befall them. The shock, the grief, the complete unexpectedness of the accident, had remained an unhealed wound all these years.

"He needs you," Mrs. Miracle said.

"Me?" Holly responded with a short laugh. "We barely know each other."

"Really?"

"We met last week, remember?"

"Last week," she echoed, with that same twinkle in her eye. "But you like him, don't you?"

"Yes, I guess I do," Holly admitted.

"You should invite him for a home-cooked dinner."

Funny, Holly had been thinking exactly that. She'd wait, not wanting to appear too eager—although heaven knew that was how she felt. And of course there was the problem of her finances....

"I'd like to have Jake over," she began. "He—"

"Did I hear someone mention my name?" Jake said from behind her.

"Jake!" She turned to face him as his assistant moved away to help a young couple who'd approached the department. From the corner of her eye, Holly saw that the husband and wife Mrs. Miracle had greeted were pointing at the SuperRobot. Mrs. Miracle picked up a box and walked over to the cash register to ring up the sale.

"Holly?" Jake asked.

"I need to put Intellytron on layaway but Mrs. Miracle told me you don't do that," she said in a rush.

"Sorry, no. I thought you were going to use your Christmas bonus to purchase the robot this week."

"I'm not getting one," she blurted out. She was close to tears, which embarrassed her.

"Listen, I'll buy the robot for Gabe and—"

"No," she broke in. "We already talked about that, remember? I won't let you."

"Why not?"

"Because...I just won't. Let's leave it at that."

He frowned but reluctantly agreed. "Okay, if that's the way you want it."

"That's the way it has to be."

"At least let me hold one for you," Jake said before she could compose herself enough to ask.

"You can do that?"

Jake nodded. "Sure. I'll set one aside right away and put your name on it. I'll tell everyone on staff that it isn't to be sold. How does that sound?"

She closed her eyes as relief washed over her. "Thank you. That would be perfect."

"Are you all right now?" He placed his hand on her shoulder in a comforting gesture.

"I'm fine. I apologize if I seem unreasonable."

"I understand."

"You do?" Holly wasn't convinced she could explain it herself. She just knew she had to do this. For Gabe, for Mickey…and for herself. The robot had become more than a toy. It was a symbol of her commitment to her nephew and her desire to give him the Christmas he deserved.

She saw that the department was busy and she was keeping Jake from his customers. "I have to get back to the office," she said.

He grinned. "Next time maybe you could stay longer."

Holly smiled back. "Next time I will."

"I'll call you. You're in the phone directory?"

She nodded, hoping she'd hear from him soon. "See you, Jake."

"See you, Holly."

As she walked toward the elevator, Mrs. Miracle joined her. "Mr. Finley suggested I take my lunch hour now," she said as they stepped into the empty car together. "What I feel like having is fried chicken."

"Fried chicken," Holly echoed. "My mother, who

was born and raised in the South, has a special family recipe but she hasn't made it in years. I can't even remember the last time we ate fried chicken." In this age of heart-healthy diets, her mother had focused on lean, low-carb meals.

"A special recipe?" Mrs. Miracle murmured. "I'll bet it was good."

"The best." Now that she thought about it, Holly figured she might have a copy in her kitchen. "Mom put together a book of family recipes for me when I left home. I wonder if she included that one." Fried chicken was the ultimate comfort food and would make a wonderful dinner when she invited Jake over—sometime in the new year.

"She probably did. That sounds just like her."

"You know my mother?" Holly asked, surprised.

"No...no, but having met you, I know she must be a very considerate woman, someone who cares about family and traditions."

What a lovely compliment. The kind words helped take the sting out of her employer's refusal to give Holly a Christmas bonus. Lindy Lee was a modern-day Scrooge as far as Holly was concerned.

That evening, as dinner heated in the microwave, Holly searched through her kitchen drawers for the notebook where her mother had written various recipes passed down through her family.

"What would you think of homemade fried chicken for Christmas?" Holly asked Gabe. It wasn't the traditional dinner but roast turkey with all the fixings was out of her budget now. If Gabe considered her fried chicken a success, she'd serve it again when Jake came over.

"I've had take-out chicken. Is that the same?"

"The same?" she repeated incredulously. "Not even close!"

"Then I've never had it." He shrugged. "If it's not frozen or out of a can Dad doesn't know how to make it," Gabe said. "Except for macaroni and cheese in the box." He sat down at the computer and logged on to the internet, preparing to send an email to his father, as he did every night. He hadn't typed more than a few words when he turned and looked at Holly. "What's for dinner tonight?"

"Leftover Chinese. You okay with that?"

"Sure." Gabe returned to the computer screen.

Ten minutes later, he asked, "Can you invite Jake for Christmas dinner?"

"He won't be able to come."

"Why not?"

"He's going away for Christmas."

Gabe was off the internet and playing one of his games, jerking the game stick left and right as he battled aliens. "Why?"

"You'll have to ask him."

"I will." Apparently he'd won the battle because he let go of the stick and faced her. "You're going to see him again, right? You want to, don't you?"

Even an eight-year-old boy could easily see through her.

"I hope so."

"Me, too," Gabe said, then added, "Billy wants me to come over after school on Friday. I can go, can't I?" He regarded her hopefully.

The boys had obviously remained friends. "I'll clear it with his dad first." Holly had been meaning to talk to Bill before this. She'd make a point of doing it soon, although she wasn't looking forward to contacting him.

The good news was that she'd found the recipe in her mother's book.

Fried Chicken

(from *Debbie Macomber's Cedar Cove Cookbook*)

The key to crisp fried chicken is cooking at a high temperature. Stick a candy or deep-frying thermometer in the chicken as you fry to make sure the oil temperature remains between 250° and 300°F.

1 whole chicken (about 31/2 pounds), cut into 10
   pieces
1 quart buttermilk
2 tablespoons Tabasco or other hot sauce
2 cups all-purpose flour
Salt and pepper, to taste
2 large eggs
1 teaspoon baking powder
1/2 teaspoon baking soda
Vegetable oil or shortening

1. Rinse chicken. In a large bowl or resealable plastic bag, combine buttermilk and Tabasco. Add chicken pieces, turn to coat. Refrigerate, covered, for at least 8 hours and up to 16, turning the pieces occasionally. Remove chicken from buttermilk; shake off excess. Arrange in a single layer on large wire rack set over rimmed baking sheet. Refrigerate, uncovered, for 2 hours.

2. Measure flour into large shallow dish; whisk in some salt and pepper. In a medium bowl, beat

eggs, baking powder and baking soda. Working in batches of 3, drop chicken pieces in flour and shake dish to coat. Shake excess flour from each piece. Using tongs, dip chicken pieces into egg mixture, turning to coat well and allowing excess to drip off. Return chicken pieces to flour; coat again, shake off excess and set on wire rack.

3. Preheat oven to 200°F. Set oven rack to middle position. Set another wire rack over a rimmed baking sheet, and place in oven. Line a large plate with paper towels. Pour oil about 1/2 inch up the side of a large, heavy skillet. Place skillet over high heat; let pan warm until oil shimmers.

4. Place half of chicken, skin-side down, in hot oil. Reduce heat to medium and fry 8 minutes, until deep golden brown. Turn chicken pieces; cook an additional eight minutes, turning to fry evenly on all sides. Using tongs, transfer chicken to paper towel–lined plate. After draining, transfer chicken to wire rack in oven. Fry remaining chicken, transferring pieces to paper towel–lined plate to drain, then to wire rack in oven to keep warm.

Serves 4 to 6.

Ten

May you live all the days of your life.
                                                —*Mrs. Miracle*

Emily Merkle smiled to herself. This latest assignment was going well. She enjoyed the ones that took place during the Christmas season most of all. She hadn't expected the romance between Jake and Holly to develop quite this quickly, so that was a bonus. Those two were very good together—and good for each other.

She attached her name badge to her sweater and hung her purse in the employee locker, then headed up to the toy department. She'd grown fond of Jake Finley. He was a kindhearted young man, a bit reserved, to be sure, but willing to take a risk he believed in. The robots were one example of that, his pursuit of Holly another.

Walking toward the elevator, she saw J. R. Finley, who'd just come into the hallway. He stopped, and his eyes automatically went to her badge.

"Mrs. Miracle," he said thoughtfully. He seemed to be mulling over where he'd heard it before.

"Mr. Finley," she said in the same thoughtful tone.

"To the best of my recollection, we don't have an employee here at Finley's named Miracle."

Emily was about to identify herself, but before she could, J.R. continued.

"I pride myself on knowing the name of every employee at the Thirty-fourth Street Finley's. Including seasonal staff." He narrowed his eyes. "Just a minute. I remember my son mentioning you earlier."

"The name is Merkle," Emily told him. "Emily Merkle."

Finley shook his head. "Can't say I'm familiar with that name, either."

"If you check with HR, I'm sure—"

"You're working with my son in the toy department, aren't you?" he said abruptly.

Emily frowned. "Are you always this rude, or are you making an exception in my case?"

He blinked twice.

He was used to everyone kowtowing to him. Well, *she* wouldn't do it.

"I beg your pardon?"

Emily met his look boldly. "I was saying something, young man."

J.R.'s head reared back and he released a howl of laughter. "*Young* man? My dear woman, it's been a long time since anyone referred to me as young."

Compared to her, he was practically in diapers. "That's beside the point."

He seemed confused.

"As I was saying," Emily continued politely, "if you care to check with HR, you'll find that I was hired last week as seasonal help."

"Only last week?" J.R. smiled at her. "That explains it, then."

"It does, indeed." She started down the hallway and was surprised when J.R. kept pace with her.

"You *are* working with my son, correct?"

"Yes. The toy department is extremely busy this time of year, as you well know." She glanced pointedly at her watch, wanting him to realize she should be on the floor that very moment.

"My son made a huge error in judgment by ordering five hundred of those expensive robots."

She was puzzled by his willingness to discuss business—and family—matters with a short-term employee. But she couldn't let his comment go unchallenged. "You think so, do you?" she asked mildly.

He gave her a startled look, as if no one had dared question his opinion before. "I know so," he insisted.

Emily was curious as to why he felt Jake was wrong and he was right. "Please tell me why you're so convinced your son's about to fail."

"Good grief, woman—"

"Call me Mrs. Miracle."

"Fine, Mrs. Miracle. Do you realize exactly how many of these…Intellytromps he needs to sell by Christmas? That's less than two weeks from now. It'll never happen."

"They're Intelly*trons*."

"Tromps, trons, whatever. They won't sell. Mark my words. It would take a miracle." He grinned broadly, obviously thinking himself very clever.

"You called?" she said, and laughed.

J.R. apparently didn't like the fact that she'd responded to his joke with one of her own. Instead of laughing, he scowled.

"Never mind," she said with a sigh. "I just wish you had more faith in your son."

He quickly took offense. "My son is my concern."

"He *is* your concern," she agreed. "And your future. So it's time you trusted his judgment."

She'd really ruffled his feathers now. He grew red in the face and puffed up like an angry rooster, his chest expanding. "Now listen here. I won't have an employee talking to me as if I'm some messenger boy."

Emily stood her ground. "Someone needs to tell you the truth and it might as well be me."

"Is that so?"

He sounded like a third-grader exchanging insults on the playground.

"You need to give your son a bit of leeway to make his own mistakes instead of second-guessing all his decisions."

He opened and closed his mouth as if he couldn't speak fast enough to say what was on his mind. He thrust out one hand. "Your badge."

So he intended to fire her. "You don't want to do that," she told him calmly.

"I will not have an insubordinate employee working in my store!"

"I'm temporary help," she reminded him. "I'll be gone soon enough."

"I expect you gone *today.*"

"Sorry, I'm afraid that would be impossible. You'll need to reconsider."

Once again he couldn't seem to speak. "Are...are

you refusing to leave the premises?" he finally managed to sputter.

"Jacob Robert, settle down. You've always had a problem with your temper, haven't you? Now, take a deep breath and listen to me. You do not want to fire me this close to Christmas."

"Are you threatening me?" he growled. "And how do you know my middle name?"

"Not in the least," she said, answering his first question and ignoring his second.

"I'm calling Security and having you escorted from the building. Your check will be mailed to you."

"Security?" The image of two beefy security guards lifting her by the arms and marching her outside was so comical it made Emily laugh.

That seemed to infuriate him even more. "Do you find this humorous?"

"Frankly, yes." She wouldn't lie; the man was insufferable. Oh, heavens, she did have her work cut out for her. "Now, if you'll excuse me, your son needs my help."

His jaw sagged as she scurried past him and walked quickly to the elevator.

As she suspected, the toy department was in chaos. Poor Jake was run ragged—thanks, in part, to his father, who'd taken too much pleasure in making her late for her shift. That man was about to meet his match. Emily Merkle was not going to let one overstuffed, pigheaded man stand in the way of her mission.

She'd been on the floor for thirty minutes or so when J.R. unexpectedly showed up. When he saw how busy the department was, he did a double take.

"Don't stand there gawking," Emily said as she marched past him, leading a customer to the cash register. Brenda and Karen, also on duty, were bustling around, answering questions, ringing up sales, demonstrating toys.

He stared at her blankly.

"Help," she told him. "We could use an extra pair of hands, in case you hadn't noticed."

"Ah..." He froze, as if he didn't know where to start.

"That couple over there," Emily said, pointing in the direction of the board games. "They have a three-year-old and a six-year-old and they're looking for suggestions. Give them a few."

"Ah..."

"Don't just stand there with your mouth hanging open," she ordered. "Get to work!"

To his credit, J.R. rolled up his sleeves and dug in. J. R. Finley might know the name of every employee in his store—with minor exceptions, of course—but he was in way over his head when it came to recommending board games. To *her* credit, Emily kept her mouth shut.

At four o'clock there was a slight lull. "Dad," Jake greeted his father. "What brings you down here?"

J.R. squinted at Emily but didn't answer.

"Whatever it was, I'm grateful." He turned to Emily. "How many Intellytrons did we sell this afternoon?"

"Sixteen."

"Fabulous!" Jake couldn't conceal his excitement.

His father, however, looked as though he needed to sit down, put up his feet and have a cup of hot tea. In Emily's view, it would do the man good to work the floor once in a while. He might actually learn something that way.

"I came to talk to you about this woman." J.R. stabbed a menacing finger at Emily.

"Ah, you mean Mrs. Miracle," Jake said fondly. "She's a wonder, isn't she?"

"She's a nuisance," J.R. snapped. "I want her fired."

Jake laughed, which was clearly the opposite reaction of what his father expected.

"This is not a joke."

"Yes, it is," Jake insisted. "Didn't you see what a madhouse this place was? It's like that every day now. I can't afford to lose Mrs. Miracle."

Emily sauntered over to J.R.'s side and whispered saucily, "Told you so."

He shook his finger. "I don't care if I have to work this department on my own," he yelled, "I will not tolerate insubordination."

"Excuse me, Dad, I've got another customer."

"I do, too," Emily said. "But you can keep standing there for a while. You make a nice fixture."

A kid of about five stepped in front of J.R. and stared up at him. "Is that a trick, mister?"

J.R. lowered his arms. "What, son?"

The boy was completely enthralled. "The way you get your cheeks to puff out like that."

Difficult though it was, Emily managed not to laugh. The boy was quite observant. J.R. had the puffing of cheeks down to an art form.

Jake finished with his customer and hurried back to his father. "Dad, I am *not* firing Mrs. Miracle."

"No, you're not. I am," J.R. said. "It will give me great pleasure to make sure she never works in this store again."

"What did she do that was so terrible?" Jake demanded.

"She insulted me and meddled in my personal affairs," his father burst out.

"How?" Jake asked, calm and collected. He was the perfect contrast to his father, who waved both arms wildly and spoke loudly enough to attract attention from every corner of the third floor.

When J.R. didn't answer, Jake shrugged and said, "Sorry, Dad, I need her."

Emily smiled ever so sweetly.

"She's out of here," J.R. roared, making a chopping motion with his arm. She thought he resembled an umpire signaling a strikeout.

Jake shook his head. "She's our best sales associate by a mile, so if she goes, we might as well close down the entire department. You wouldn't want that, would you, Dad?"

J.R. hesitated.

"And if we close the department, you won't have a chance to prove how wrong I was by ordering five hundred Intellytrons," he said, as if that should be sufficient inducement to keep her on staff.

Emily suspected J.R. wanted Jake to fall flat on his face over this robot. He'd pay a high price for being right—and, as a matter of fact, he was dead wrong. She'd seen for herself how popular the toy was. She'd hoped it would be and had done her best to sell it. However, after the past twenty-four hours, she didn't need to try very hard; the toy sold itself. Apparently, its sudden popularity had begun like so many trends, on the West Coast. Now, the moment someone heard that Finley's still had robots in stock, they dashed over. Then they couldn't whip out their credit cards fast enough.

"I'd better stay," Emily murmured to Jake. "As much

as I'd like to walk away right now, I wouldn't give your father the satisfaction."

J.R. stomped his foot.

"Are you having a temper tantrum?" she asked sweetly.

Jake only laughed. "Dad, I think it might be best if you went back to your office now. Or you could go home."

"This is *my* store and I'll stay anywhere I darn well please."

Jake leaned closer to his father and whispered, "You're scaring off my customers."

"Oh, sorry."

"We want customers, don't we, Dad? Isn't that the whole idea?"

"Don't get smart with me," J.R. muttered.

"Yes, Dad." Jake winked at Emily, who winked back.

J.R. must have caught sight of what they were doing. "What's that about?"

"What?" Emily asked, again the picture of politeness.

"What?" Jake echoed.

Seeing that he'd forfeited even the pretense of control, J.R. sighed. "Forget it."

"I can stay on, then?" Emily asked the store owner.

"Why ask me? I seem to have lost complete control of this company to a man I no longer recognize—my son." With that he marched toward the elevator that would deliver him to his private office on the fourteenth floor.

Eleven

*People are funny. They want the front of the bus,
the middle of the road and the back of the church.*
— Mrs. Miracle

Holly knew she couldn't postpone calling Bill Carter,
since the boys wanted to get together two days from
now. It would be petty to allow her awkward relationship with Bill to stand in the way of her nephew being
friends with his son.

The problem was how to approach him. She waited
until Gabe was in bed on Wednesday night. Then she
drew in a deep breath and looked up Bill's home number, which she'd made a point of erasing from her
mind—and her phone. She hated feeling nervous about
this. It was a courtesy call and nothing more.

Bill picked up on the fourth ring, when she was about
to hang up, almost relieved he hadn't answered. Then
all of a sudden, she heard, "Hello."

"Bill, it's Holly."

"Do you realize what time it is?"

"Uh, yes… It's nine-thirty. Am I calling too late?"

He didn't respond immediately. "I know why you're calling and I—"

"You do?" So all this angst had been for nothing. She should've noticed earlier how silly she was being, how badly she'd overreacted.

"It's about Tiffany, isn't it?"

"No…who's Tiffany?"

"You mean you *don't* know?"

Obviously she didn't. "Sorry, I think we're talking at cross-purposes here. I don't know any Tiffany—well, other than the one I met through work. I'm calling about Billy."

"My son?"

He sounded both relieved and worried, which confused Holly. "Listen, can we start over?" she asked.

"It's too late for that."

Just how obtuse *was* the man? "I don't mean our relationship, Bill. I was referring to our conversation."

"Just tell me why you called," he said, with more than a hint of impatience.

"I'm trying to, but you keep interrupting me. This isn't an easy phone call for me and your attitude's not helping." If Bill was a decent human being, he should understand this was difficult and appreciate the courage it had taken her to contact him. The fact that he didn't angered her. "No wonder the two of us aren't dating anymore," she muttered.

"Okay, fine. But what's that got to do with my son?"

She sighed loudly. "Since you haven't worked it out for yourself, I'll tell you. Billy and Gabe have become friends."

"Yeah? So what?"

"Well, I—" Before she could answer his rudely phrased question, he broke in.

"Wait a minute," he said suspiciously. "How do you know my son's friends with this kid?"

The way he said it practically implied that Holly had been stalking his son. "That's the most ridiculous question I've ever heard! I know because Gabe's my nephew."

"So?"

"So Billy wants Gabe to come home with him after school on Friday."

"Fine. And this concerns you how?"

"I thought I should tell you we're related."

"That still doesn't explain why you're calling. Shouldn't Gabe's parents clear this with me? Not you."

Holly gritted her teeth at his offensive tone. What she'd ever seen in this man was completely lost on her now. At the moment, she was grateful he'd broken it off.

"I have custody of Gabe," she said calmly. She didn't feel like describing how that had come about; it was none of his business—and besides, she wanted to keep the conversation as short as possible.

"*You* have custody?"

The question grated on her nerves. "Yes, *me,* and it's working out very nicely, I might add."

"Ah…" Bill apparently hadn't figured out yet how to react.

Holly had no intention of allowing him to make any more derogatory comments about her mothering skills. She launched right into her question, not giving him a chance to say much of anything. "Is it still okay if Gabe comes to your house after school?"

"Uh, sure."

"Do you have the same housekeeper looking after Billy as before?"

The suspicious voice was back. "Why do you ask?"

"Because I don't want Gabe visiting Billy if there isn't any adult supervision." The after-school program only went until five-thirty, and Bill was often home much later than that, which meant the part-time housekeeper picked the boy up and then stayed at the apartment to supervise him.

"Oh, yeah, Mrs. Henry still looks after Billy from five-thirty to seven, except for the nights I have social engagements. Then she stays until I get home."

He seemed to delight in letting her know—in what he probably thought was a subtle fashion—that he'd started dating again. Well, she had social engagements, too, even if they mostly involved going out with friends, but was mature enough not to mention it. Let him think what he liked.

Holly waited a moment, hoping he'd realize how juvenile his reaction had been. "Talking civilly isn't so hard, is it?" she asked.

"No," he agreed.

"Great. Now that's settled, what time would you like me to pick Gabe up?"

"You'll pick him up?"

"Would you rather bring him back to my apartment?" That certainly made it easier for her. Maybe he didn't want Holly showing up at his house, but if so, she didn't care enough to be offended.

"I can do that," he said.

"Fine."

"Fine," he echoed.

"What time should I expect you?"

"Seven-thirty, I guess."

"I'll be here."

She was about to disconnect when Bill's soft chuckle caught her off guard. "So Gabe's your nephew, huh?"

"I already told you that."

"You did. His last name's Larson?"

"Yes, Gabe Larson." She didn't see the humor in this. "I apologize for calling so late, but I thought it would be best if you and I talked when Gabe was in bed."

"Did you think I'd refuse to let the two boys be friends?"

"I wasn't sure. Our last conversation wasn't very pleasant and, well, it seemed better to ask."

"I'm glad you did."

She was glad to hear that because he sure hadn't acted like it.

Holly met Jake for lunch on Thursday. He'd called her at the office that morning and suggested a nearby restaurant; thankfully he'd insisted on buying. She might've sounded a bit too eager to accept, because she was sick of making do with leftovers. By cutting back, packing lunches and not spending a penny more than necessary Holly had managed to save seventy-five dollars toward the robot. According to her calculations, she'd have the funds to make the purchase but it would be close. Every cent counted.

Jake had arrived at the restaurant before her and secured a booth. "Hi," he said with a smile when she slid in across from him.

"Hi. This is nice. Thanks so much." She reached for the menu and quickly scanned the day's specials. She was so hungry, Jake would be fortunate if she could limit her selection to one entrée. As it was, she ordered a cup of wild-mushroom soup, half a turkey sandwich with salad and a slice of apple pie à la mode for dessert.

Jake didn't seem to mind.

"That was delicious," she said as she sat back half an hour later and pressed her hands over her stomach. "I probably ate twice as much as any other woman you've ever gone out with."

"It's a relief to be with someone who isn't constantly worried about her weight."

"I do watch my calories but I've been doing without breakfast, and lunches have been pretty skimpy and—"

"No breakfast?"

"That's not entirely accurate. I have breakfast, sort of. Just not much."

"And the reason is?"

Holly wished she'd kept her mouth shut. She pretended not to hear his question and glanced at her watch instead. "Oh, it's almost one. I should get back to work."

"Holly." Jake wasn't easily distracted. "Answer the question."

Her shoulders sagged. "I really do need to go."

"You're going without breakfast to save money for the robot, aren't you?"

"Sorry, I have to run." She slid out of the booth and grabbed her coat and purse. "Oh, before I forget. Gabe wanted me to invite you to come and watch us decorate our Christmas tree tomorrow night, if you can. He'll be at a friend's place and won't get home until seven-thirty."

He hesitated, and Holly knew why. "I won't be able to leave the store until at least nine," he said.

"I let Gabe stay up until ten on Friday and Saturday nights."

He hesitated again. Holly hadn't forgotten his reaction when Gabe had first mentioned decorating for Christmas. She knew that, like his father, he ignored the holiday—apart from being surrounded by all that bright and shiny yuletide evidence at the store. Perhaps it was selfish of her, but she wanted to show him the joy of Christmas, prove that not all his Christmas memories were bad. She was convinced there must be happy remembrances, too, and she hoped to revive those so he could let go of the past. Holly held her breath as she waited for his response.

Jake stared into the distance for what seemed like a long time before he said, "Okay, I'll come."

Her breath whooshed out in relief and she gave him her brightest, happiest smile. "Thank you, Jake." She finished putting on her coat, hoping he understood how much she appreciated his decision.

"Can we do this again?" he asked. "It's been crazy in the toy department. Mrs. Miracle insisted I take my lunch break early—and she said I should invite you. I need to get back to work, but I wanted to see you."

"I wanted to see you, too."

They left the restaurant together and went their separate ways. Holly's spirits were high. She'd cleared the air with Bill as much as possible, and Gabe had been excited to learn he'd be able to go to his friend's house on Friday.

When she returned to work, she found her boss on the phone, talking in her usual emphatic manner. Despite the fact that Holly wouldn't be receiving a Christmas bonus, she'd tried not to let that influence her job performance.

As soon as Lindy Lee saw her, she waved one arm to get her attention.

Holly stepped into her employer's office. "You're back late from lunch," Lindy said as she slammed down the phone.

"I have an hour lunch," Holly reminded her. She rarely took that long and often ate at her desk. Taking the full time allotted her was the exception rather than the rule.

"It's one-fifteen," Lindy Lee said pointedly, tapping her index finger against her wristwatch.

"And I left the office at twelve-thirty. Technically I still have fifteen minutes." Holly could see that she might have said more than necessary and decided it would be best to stop while she was ahead. "Is there something you need me to do?" she asked.

Frowning, Lindy handed her a thick file folder. "I need you to get these sketches over to Design."

"Right away." She took the folder and hurried out of the office, catching the elevator to the sixth floor. As she entered the design department she caught sight of one of the models regularly hired by the company. Tiffani White was tall, slim and elegant and she possessed about as perfect a body as one could hope to have. She was a favorite of Lindy Lee's and no wonder. The model showed Lindy's creations to their peak potential.

Tiffani saw Holly and blinked, as if she had trouble placing her, which was odd. They'd spent a fair amount of time together, since Holly had been backstage at several runway events with her.

"Lindy Lee asked me to deliver these sketches," she

said to the head of the technical department. She turned to Tiffani.

"Hi, Tiff," she said casually.

"Hi." The model smiled—a smile that didn't quite reach her eyes.

Holly smiled back, but there was something strange going on. Tiffani had always been friendly. They'd even had coffee together now and then. Once, nearly a year ago when she'd been dating Bill, they'd run into Tiffani and—

Just a minute!

Thoughts and memories collided inside Holly's head. The conversation with Bill the night before played back in her mind. He'd made an unusual comment when they'd first spoken, mentioning the name Tiffany—or rather, Tiffani, with an *i*. The pieces were falling into place....

"Tiffani," Holly said. "I talked to Bill the other night."

"You did?"

"Yes, and your name came up."

The model brought one beautifully manicured hand to her mouth. "It did? Then you know?"

"Well, not everything."

"I wanted him to tell you before now, but Bill said it wasn't really any of your business. I told him that sometimes we see each other at work and it would make things better for me if you knew."

"So the two of you are...dating?"

"Actually we're...talking about marriage."

Marriage. Bill was planning to *marry* Tiffani? This didn't make sense. The model was about the least motherly woman Holly had ever met; she'd even told Holly she didn't like children. And she'd demonstrated it, too.

They'd had a shoot earlier in the year with a couple of child models and Tiffani had been difficult and cranky all day. She'd made it clear that she didn't enjoy being around kids.

Holly wondered if Bill had any idea of the other woman's feelings. Probably not, she thought uncharitably. All he saw was Tiffani's perfect body and how good she looked on his arm.

In some ways, she had to concede, Bill and Tiffani were a good match. Bill had his own graphic design business and often hosted clients. Tiffani would do well entertaining, but Holly suspected she didn't have a lot to offer as a stepmother to Billy.

Yet that'd been the excuse Bill had used when he'd broken off *their* relationship.

That was exactly what it'd been. An excuse, and a convenient one. He'd wanted Holly out of his life and he didn't care how badly he hurt her to make that happen. Granted, the relationship would've ended anyway, but in the process of hastening its demise, he'd damaged her confidence—in herself and in her maternal instincts.

Bill Carter was a jerk, no question about it. Tiffani was welcome to him.

Twelve

*Be ye fishers of men. You catch 'em
and God'll clean 'em.*

—Mrs. Miracle

"Can I go see Telly the robot after school?" Gabe asked as Holly walked him to school Monday morning.

"Not today," she said, stepping up her speed so she'd make it to work on time. The last thing she needed was to show up late. As it was, Gabe would get out of school at eleven-thirty this morning for winter break, and there was no after-school care today. Thankfully her neighbor, Caroline Krantz, had children of her own, including a son, Jonathan, who was Gabe's age, and Gabe enjoyed going there. Today, however, he obviously had a different agenda.

"But it's been so *long* since I saw him and I want—"

"I know. I'm sorry, Gabe. But Christmas will be here soon," she said, cutting him off.

"Do you think Santa's going to bring me my robot?"

"We won't find out until Christmas, will we?" she said, ushering him along. At the school, she bent down and kissed his cheek. "Remember, you're going to Mrs. Krantz's house with Jonathan after school."

"Yeah," he said, kicking at the sidewalk with the toe of his boot.

"Call me at the office when you get there, okay?"

"Okay."

Holly watched him walk into the building and then half ran to the subway station.

She was jostled by the crowd and once again had to stand, clutching the pole as she rode into the city. Her weekend had been everything she'd hoped for. Jake had stopped by on Friday night, arriving later than expected. She'd assembled the small artificial tree, which she'd bought years before; she would've preferred a real one but didn't want to spend the money this year. Then she'd draped it with lights, and she and Gabe had carefully arranged the ornaments. They were almost done by the time Jake came over, and Gabe insisted that he place the angel on top of the tree. Holly wasn't sure how he'd react to that request. At first he'd hesitated until she explained it was an honor and that it meant a lot to Gabe. Then he reluctantly set the angel on the tree.

Maybe it wasn't up to her to change—or try to change—his feelings about Christmas, but she hoped to coax him by creating new memories and by reminding him of happy ones from his own childhood.

On Friday, after school and his playdate with Billy, Gabe had been exhausted by ten o'clock. Holly tucked him in, and then she and Jake had cuddled and kissed in front of the television. She couldn't remember what TV program they'd started to watch because they were soon more focused on each other than on the TV.

Thinking about Friday night with Jake made her tingle with excitement and anticipation. Bill could have his Tiffani. Holly would rather be with Jake. Their relationship held such promise....

Unfortunately, Jake was so busy at the store on Saturday that a couple of quick phone calls had to suffice. On Sunday evening he came to the apartment, bringing a take-out pizza and a bottle of lovely, smooth merlot— the best wine she'd had in ages. Jake had been full of tales about the store, and especially how well Intellytron was now selling. Rumor had it that Finley's was the only place in Manhattan that had the robot available, and customers had flooded the store, many of them going straight from Santa's throne to the toy department. No one else had guessed that Intellytron would be one of the hottest retail trends of the season.

While Holly was thrilled for Jake, she was still concerned that there wouldn't be any left once she could afford to make the purchase. Jake had again assured her she didn't need to worry; he'd put one aside for Gabe. It was safely hidden away in the back of the storeroom, with a note that said it wasn't to be sold.

Holly dashed into the office just in time. She saw Lindy Lee glance at her watch but Holly knew she had three minutes to spare. While Lindy Lee might not appreciate her new work habits, she was well within the bounds of what was required. Before Gabe's advent into her life, she'd often arrived early and stayed late. That wasn't possible now, and she was paying the price for her earlier generosity, which Lindy Lee had quickly taken for granted. Still, she enjoyed her job and believed she was a credit to her employer, even if Lindy didn't agree.

"Good morning," she said to her boss, sounding

more cheerful than she felt. Holly was determined not to allow Lindy Lee's attitude to affect her day.

At noon, Holly began to check her watch every few minutes. She kept her cell phone on her desk, ready to receive Gabe's call. He should be phoning any time now; school was out, and he'd be going home with Jonathan. At twelve-thirty Holly started to worry. Gabe should be at the Krantzes'. Why hadn't he called? She felt too anxious to eat the crackers and cheese she'd brought, too anxious to do anything productive. She'd give him until one-fifteen and then she'd call.

At one-thirteen, her cell phone chirped, and she recognized the Krantzes' number. Holly heaved a grateful sigh. "Hello," she said.

"Holly?" It was Caroline.

"Oh, hi. Did everything go as scheduled? Did Gabe and Jonathan walk home from school together?"

"Well, that's the reason I'm phoning. Gabe didn't come home with Jonathan."

A chill raced down her spine. "What do you mean?"

"He told Jonathan there was something he needed to do first, so Jonathan came home by himself. I…I feel really bad about this."

"Where is he?" Holly asked, struggling not to panic.

"That's just it. I don't know."

There was a huge knot in Holly's chest, and she found it difficult to breathe. How could she tell her brother that Gabe had gone missing?

Panicked thoughts surged through her mind. He'd been abducted, kidnapped, held for ransom. Or even worse, simply taken, never to be seen or heard from again.

"I'll call you if I hear anything," Caroline told her.

"I'd go look myself but I can't leave the children. If he's not here in an hour, we'll reassess, call the police. In the meantime, I'll phone some of the other kids' parents."

"Yes… Thank you." Holly disconnected the line, her cell phone clenched in her fist.

"Holly?" Lindy Lee asked, staring at her. "What's wrong?"

Holly didn't realize she'd bolted to her feet. She felt herself swaying and wondered if she was going to faint. "My—my nephew's missing."

"Missing," Lindy Lee repeated. "What do you mean, missing?"

"He didn't show up at the sitter's house after school."

Lindy Lee looked at her watch. "It's a bit early for him to be out of school, isn't it?"

"No, not today," she said, panic making her sound curt. She was torn by indecision. Her first inclination was to contact the police immediately, not to wait an other hour as Caroline had suggested. They should start a neighborhood search. Ask questions.

She wondered crazily if she should get his picture to the authorities so they could place it on milk cartons all across America.

Her cell phone chirped again and she nearly dropped it in her rush to answer.

"Yes?" she blurted out.

"Holly, it's Jake."

"I don't have time to talk now. Gabe's missing and we've got to contact the police and get a search organized and—"

"Gabe's with me," Jake interrupted.

She sank into her chair, weak with relief. "He's with you?"

"Yes. He came into the city."

"On his own?" This was unbelievable!

"Yup."

"You mean to say he walked from school to the subway station, took the train and then walked to Finley's by *himself?*" It seemed almost impossible to comprehend. She held her head in one hand and leaned back in her chair, eyes closed. She remembered what he'd said that morning, about wanting to see the robot, but she'd had no idea he'd actually try to do it.

"Would you like to talk to him?" Jake was asking.

"Please."

"Aunt Holly?" Gabe's voice was small and meek.

"So," she said, releasing a long sigh. Although the urge to lambaste him was nearly overwhelming, she resisted. "You didn't walk home with Jonathan the way you were supposed to?"

"No."

"Can you tell me why?"

"Because…"

"Because *what?*"

"I wanted to see Intellytron again and you said we couldn't and I thought, well, I know you have to work and everything, but I could come by myself, so I did. I remembered to take the green line and then I walked from the subway station." Despite the fact that he was obviously in trouble, there was a hint of pride in his voice.

Gabe had traveled into the city on his own just to see his favorite toy. The possibility hadn't even occurred to her. Holly suppressed the urge to break into sobs.

"I'm coming to get you right this minute," she declared. "Stay with Jake and Mrs. Miracle, and I'll be there as soon as I can. Now put Jake back on the phone."

His voice, strong and clear, came through a moment later. "Holly, it's Jake."

"I'm on my way."

"He'll be fine until you get here," he said.

"Thank you, thank you so much." This time, the urge to weep nearly overcame her.

"Everything's fine. Relax."

"I'm trying." She closed her cell, then looked up to see her boss standing in front of her desk.

"I take it you've located the little scoundrel?"

Holly nodded. "He came into the city on his own. Would it be okay if I brought him to the office for the rest of the day?" Taking him back to Brooklyn would be time-consuming and Lindy Lee would no doubt dock her pay. Holly needed every penny of her next paycheck. "I promise he won't make a sound."

Lindy Lee considered the request, then slowly nodded. "I enjoyed meeting Gabe that Saturday.... I wouldn't mind seeing him again."

Lindy Lee wanted to see Gabe again? *This* was an interesting development, as well as an unexpected one. Her employer wasn't the motherly type—to put it mildly. Lindy Lee was all about Lindy Lee.

Grabbing her coat and purse, Holly rushed over to Finley's, calling Caroline Krantz en route. The store was crowded, and by the time she reached the third floor Holly felt as though she'd run a marathon. She saw Mrs. Miracle first, and the woman's eyes brightened the instant she noticed Holly.

"You don't have a thing to worry about, my dear. Gabe is perfectly safe with Jake."

"Aunt Holly!" Gabe raced to her side and Jake followed.

"You're in a lot of trouble, young man," she said sternly, hands on her hips.

Gabe hung his head. "I'm sorry," he whispered, his voice so low she could hardly hear it.

Customers thronged the toy department, several of them carrying the boxes that held the SuperRobot. A line had already formed at the customer service desk, and she noted that a couple of extra sales associates were out on the floor today. Everyone was busy.

"You'll have to come back to the office with me," Holly told Gabe. "I'm warning you it won't be nearly as much fun as it would've been with Jonathan and his mother."

"I know," he muttered. "Am I grounded?"

"We'll discuss that once we're home."

"Okay, but nothing happened...."

"You mean nothing other than the fact that you nearly gave me a heart attack."

Jake murmured a quick goodbye and started to leave to help a customer but Mrs. Miracle stopped him. "I'll take care of them," she said. "Besides, I believe there was something you wanted to ask Holly?"

"There was?" He looked surprised, wrinkling his brow as if he couldn't recall any such question.

"The Christmas party," Mrs. Miracle said under her breath. "You mentioned asking Holly to go with you."

Jake's mouth sagged open. "I'd thought about it, but I didn't realize I'd said it out loud." Now, instead of looking surprised, he seemed confused. "My father and I usually just make a token appearance."

"This year is different," the older woman insisted.

"You need to be there for your staff. After all, the toy department's the busiest of the whole store at Christmastime. And," she continued sagely, "I predict record sales this year. Your staff needs to know you appreciate them."

"But—"

"I can't go," Holly said, resolving the issue. "There's no one to watch Gabe."

"Oh, but there is, my dear," Mrs. Miracle told her.

Holly frowned. Finding someone to stay with Gabe had always been a problem. She didn't want to impose on Caroline any more than she already did, especially since her neighbor wouldn't take any payment. With Jake they'd managed to work around it, which was easy enough, since Jake had mostly come to her apartment.

"I'll be more than happy to stay with Gabe while the two of you attend the party," Mrs. Miracle said.

It was generous of her to offer, but Holly couldn't accept. She shook her head. "You should be at the party yourself, Mrs. Miracle."

"Oh, heavens, no. After a full day on my feet I'll look forward to sitting in that comfy blue chair of yours. The one your parents gave you."

Before she could question how Mrs. Miracle knew about her chair, Jake asked, "Would you like to go to the party with me?" His eyes met hers, and she found herself nodding.

"Yes," she whispered. "When is it?"

"Wednesday night, after the store closes."

"Wednesday," she repeated.

"I'll pick you up at nine-thirty. I know that's late but—"

"I'll be ready."

"I'll come over a bit earlier," Mrs. Miracle added. "The two of you will have a *lovely* evening." She spoke with the utmost confidence, as if no other outcome was possible.

Holly and Gabe left a few minutes later, and Jake walked them to the elevator. "I'll see you Wednesday," he said as he pressed the button.

"Listen, Jake, you don't need to do this. I mean, it's fairly obvious you didn't intend to ask me and—"

"I'd really like it if you'd come to the party with me," he said, and she couldn't doubt his sincerity.

"Then I will," she murmured. "I'll look forward to it."

In the elevator, Holly remembered Mrs. Miracle's comment. The woman had never been to her apartment and yet somehow she knew about the chair her parents had given her. Furthermore, she seemed to know her address, too.

Oh, well. Gabe had probably told her. He obviously felt comfortable with the older woman and for that Holly could only be grateful.

Thirteen

Cars are not the only thing recalled by their maker.
—Mrs. Miracle

On Wednesday at nine-fifteen, Emily stood at Holly's door, her large purse draped over one arm and her knitting bag in the other hand. Holly answered, smiling in welcome. She absolutely sparkled. In her fancy black dress and high heels, her hair gathered up and held in place with a jeweled comb, she looked stunning.

"Mrs. Miracle, I can't thank you enough." Holly stepped aside so Emily could enter the apartment. "Tonight wouldn't be possible if not for you."

"The pleasure's all mine," she said. She put down her bags, then unwrapped the knitted scarf from around her neck and removed her heavy wool coat. Holly hung them in the hallway closet as Emily arranged her bags by the chair, prepared to settle down for the evening. The toy department had kept her busy all day and she was eager to get off her feet.

Holly followed her into the small living room. "I feel bad that you won't be attending the party."

"Oh, no, my dear." Emily dismissed her concern. "I'm not a party girl anymore." She chuckled at her own humor. "Besides, I intend to have a good visit here with my young friend Gabe."

"He's been pretty subdued since the episode on Monday. He's promised to be on his best behavior."

"Don't you worry. We'll have a grand time together." And they would.

"Hi, Mrs. Miracle."

She was surprised to see Jake standing on the other side of the room. He'd arrived early, she thought approvingly, and he looked quite debonair in his dark suit and red tie. She'd seen an improvement in his attitude toward Christmas, mostly due to Holly and Gabe. And she had it on excellent authority that it would improve even more before the actual holiday.

"Gabe's on the computer," Holly said, pointing at the alcove between the living room and kitchen. "He's had his dinner and he can stay up until ten tonight."

Gabe twisted around and waved.

Emily waved back. "I'll make sure he's in bed by ten."

Jake held Holly's coat and the young woman slipped her arms into the sleeves. "I appreciate your volunteering to watch Gabe," he said with a smile for Emily.

"As I told Holly, I'm delighted to do it." She walked over to where Gabe sat at the small desk and put her hand on his shoulder. "Now, you two go. Have fun."

Holly kissed the top of Gabe's head. "Be good."

"I will," the boy said without taking his eyes from the screen.

Holly and Jake left, and Emily had to grin as she

glanced over Gabe's shoulder at the message he was emailing his father.

From: "Gabe Larson"<gabelarson@msm.com>
To: "Lieutenant Mickey Larson" <larsonmichael@goarmy.com>
Sent: December 22
Subject: Me and Aunt Holly

Hi, Dad,
I made Aunt Holly cry. Instead of going to Jonathan's house like I was supposed to, I went to see the robot. I was afraid the store would run out before Santa got my Intellytron. Aunt Holly came and picked me up and when we were outside she started to cry. When I asked her why she was crying she said it was because she was happy I was safe.

Are you mad at me? I wish Aunt Holly had gotten mad instead of crying. I felt awful inside and got a tummy ache. She took me back to her office and made me sit quiet all afternoon. But that was okay because I knew I didn't do the right thing. Her boss is real pretty. I don't think she's around kids much because she talked to me like I was in kindergarten or something. I think she's nice, though.

You said you had a gift coming for me for Christmas. It isn't here yet. I know I was bad, so you don't have to send it if you don't want. I'm sorry I made Aunt Holly cry.
Love,
Gabe

Emily sank down in the big comfortable chair, rested her feet on the matching ottoman and took out her knitting. She turned on the television and had just finished the first row when Gabe joined her. He didn't say anything for a long time, but Emily could see his mind working.

After a while he said, "My dad's going to be mad at me."

"It was brave of you to tell him you did something you weren't supposed to," she murmured.

Gabe looked away. "I told him he doesn't need to send me anything for Christmas. He said there was a special gift on the way but it hasn't come. He probably won't send it now."

"Don't be so sure." She pulled on the skein of yarn as she continued knitting.

"What if Santa finds out what I did?" His face crumpled in a frown. "Do you think maybe he won't bring me the robot 'cause I went to Finley's by myself and I didn't tell anyone where I was going?"

"Well, now, that remains to be seen, doesn't it?"

Gabe climbed onto the sofa and rested his head against the arm. "I didn't think Aunt Holly would be so worried when I didn't go to Jonathan's house after school. She got all weird."

"Weird?"

"Yeah. When we were still at her office, all of a sudden she put her arms around my neck and hugged me really hard. Isn't that weird?"

Emily shrugged but didn't answer. "Are you ready for Christmas?" she asked instead.

Gabe nodded. "I made Aunt Holly an origami purse. A Japanese lady came to my school and showed us how to fold them. She said they were purses, but it looks more like a wallet to me, all flat and skinny." He sighed dejectedly. "I wrapped it up but you can't really see where the wrapping stops and the gift starts."

"I bet Holly will really like the purse because you made it yourself," Emily said with an encouraging smile.

"I made my dad a gift, too. But Aunt Holly and I mailed off his Christmas present a long time ago. They take days and days to get to Afghanistan so we had to go shopping before Thanksgiving and wrap up stuff for my dad. Oh, we mailed him the picture of me and Santa, too. And I made him a key ring. And I sent him nuts. My dad likes cashews. I've never seen a cashew in the shell, have you?"

"Why, yes, as a matter of fact I have," she said conversationally.

Gabe sat up. "What do they look like?"

"Well, a cashew is a rather unusual nut. My goodness, God was so creative with that one. Did you know the cashew is both a fruit *and* a nut?"

"It is?"

"The fruit part looks like a small apple and it has a big stem."

The boy's eyes were wide with curiosity.

"The stem part is the nut, the cashew," she explained.

"Wow."

"And they're delicious," she said. "Good for you, too," she couldn't resist adding.

"What are you doing for Christmas?" Gabe asked.

"I've been invited to a party, a big one with lots of celebrating. I'll be with my friends Shirley, Goodness—"

"Goodness? That's a funny name."

"Yes, you're right. Anyway, the party preparations have already begun. It won't be long now."

"Oh." Gabe looked disappointed.

"Why the sad face?"

"I was going to ask you to come here for Christmas."

Emily was touched by his invitation. "I know you'll have a wonderful Christmas with Holly," she said.

"I invited Aunt Holly's boss, too."

She had to make an effort to hide her smile. This was all working out very nicely. Very nicely, indeed.

"Lindy didn't say she'd come for sure but she might." He paused. "She said to call her Lindy, not Ms. Lee like Aunt Holly said I should."

"Well, I hope she comes."

"Me, too. I think she's lonely."

"So do I," Emily agreed. The boy was very perceptive for his age, she thought.

"I asked her what she wants for Christmas and she said she didn't know. Can you *believe* that?"

In Emily's experience, many people walked through life completely unaware of what they wanted—or needed. "I brought along a book," she said, changing the subject. "Would you like to read it to me?" She'd put the children's book with its worn cover on the arm of her chair.

Gabe considered this. "I'm not in school now. Can you read it to me?"

"The way your dad used to when you were little?" she asked.

Gabe nodded eagerly. "I used to sit on his lap and he'd read me stories until I fell asleep." His face grew sad. "I miss my dad a lot."

"I know you do." Emily set aside her knitting. "Would you like to sit in my lap?"

"I'm too big for that," he insisted.

Emily could see that despite his words he was mulling it over. "You're not too big," she assured him.

Indecision showed on his face. Gabe wanted to snuggle with her, yet he hesitated because he was eight now and eight was too old for such things.

"What book did you bring?" he asked.

"It's a special one your grandma Larson once read to your dad and your aunt Holly."

"Really? How'd you know that?"

"Oh, I just do. It's the Christmas story."

"I like when the angels came to announce the birth of Baby Jesus to the shepherds."

She closed her eyes for a moment. "It was the most glorious night," she said. "The sky was bright and clear and—"

"And the angels sang," Gabe finished enthusiastically. "Angels have beautiful voices, don't they?"

"Yes, they do," Emily confirmed. "They make music we know nothing about here on earth…I'm sure," she added quickly. "Glorious, heavenly music."

"They do?" He cocked his head to one side.

"You'll hear it yourself one day, many years from now."

"What about you? When will you hear it?"

"Soon," she told him. He climbed into her lap and she held him close. He really was a sweet boy and would become a fine young man like his father. He'd be a wonderful brother to his half brother and half sister, as well—but she was getting ahead of herself.

"Tell me more about the angels," Gabe implored. "Is my mom an angel now?"

"No, sweetheart. Humans don't become angels. They're completely separate beings, although both were created by God."

"How come you know so much about angels?"

"I read my Bible," she said, and he seemed to accept her explanation.

"I never knew my mom," he said somberly. "Dad has pictures of her at the house. I look at her face and she smiles at me but I don't remember her."

"But you do understand that she loved you very much, right?"

"Dad said she did, and before she died she made him promise that he'd tell me every night how much she loved me."

"I know," she whispered.

"Do you think there are lots of angels in heaven?" Gabe asked.

"Oh, yes, and there are different kinds of angels, too."

"What kinds are there?"

"Well, they have a variety of different tasks. For instance, Gabriel came to Mary as a messenger. Other angels are warriors."

"When I get to heaven, I want to meet the warrior angels."

"And you shall."

"Do you think I was named after the angel Gabriel?" he asked.

Emily pressed her cheek against the top of his head, inhaling the clean, little-boy scent of his hair. "Now, that's something you'll need to ask your father when you see him."

"Okay, I will."

"Gabriel had one of the most important tasks ever assigned," Emily said. "He's the angel God sent to tell Mary about Baby Jesus."

He yawned. "Can people see angels?"

Emily's mouth quivered with a smile she couldn't quite suppress. "Oh, yes, but most people don't recognize them."

Gabe lifted his head. "How come?"

"Not all angels show their wings," she said.

"They don't?"

"No, some angels look like ordinary people."

"How come?"

"Well, sometimes God sends angels to earth. But if people saw their wings, they'd get all excited and they'd miss the lesson God wanted to teach them. That's why angels are often disguised."

"Are they always disguised?"

"No, some are invisible. Other times they look like ordinary people."

"Do angels only come to teach people a lesson?"

"No, they come to help, too."

Gabe yawned again. "How do angels help?"

"Oh, in too many ways to count."

He thought about that for a while, his eyelids beginning to droop.

"Are you ready for me to read you the story?" Emily asked.

"Sure." He rested his head against her shoulder as

she opened the book. She read for a few minutes before she noticed that Gabe had fallen asleep. And she hadn't even gotten to the good part.

Fourteen

When you flee temptation,
don't leave a forwarding address.
                 —Shirley, Goodness and Mercy,
                         friends of Mrs. Miracle

The Christmas party was well under way by the time Holly and Jake arrived. When they entered the gala event, the entire room seemed to go still. Holly kept her arm in Jake's, self-conscious about being the center of attention.

"Why's everyone looking at us?" she whispered.

Jake patted her hand reassuringly. "My father and I usually show up toward the end of the party, say a few words and then leave. No one expected me this early."

He'd mentioned that before. Still, she hadn't realized his arrival would cause such a stir. Jake immediately began to walk through the room, shaking hands and introducing Holly. At first she tried to keep track of the names, but soon gave up. She was deeply impressed by Jake's familiarity with the staff.

"How do you remember all their names?" she asked when she had a chance.

"I've worked with them in each department," he explained. "My father felt I needed to know the retail business from the mail room up."

"You started in the mail room?"

"I did, but don't for a minute consider the mail room unimportant. I made that mistake and quickly learned how vital it is."

"Your father is a wise man."

"He is," Jake said. "And a generous one, too. But he'd describe himself as *fair*. He's always recognized the value of hiring good people and keeping them happy. I believe it's why we've managed to hold on to the company despite several attempts to buy us out."

It went without saying that Jake intended to follow his father's tradition of treating employees with respect and compensating them generously.

Ninety minutes later Holly's head buzzed with names and faces. They sipped champagne and got supper from the buffet; the food was delicious. Numerous people commented happily on seeing Jake at the party.

His father appeared at about midnight and immediately sought out his son and Holly.

"So this is the young lady you've talked about," J. R. Finley said, slapping Jake jovially on the back.

"Dad, meet Holly Larson."

J.R. shook her hand. "I'm pleased to meet you, young lady. You've made a big impression on my son."

Holly glanced at Jake and smiled. "He's made a big impression on me."

J. R. Finley turned to his son. "When did you get here?"

"Before ten," Jake said.

His father frowned, then moved toward the microphone. As was apparently his practice, he gave a short talk, handed out dozens of awards and bonuses and promptly left.

The party wound down after J.R.'s speech. People started to leave, but almost every employee, singly and in groups, approached Jake to thank him for attending the party. Holly couldn't tell how their gratitude affected Jake, but it had a strong impact on her.

"They love you," she said when they went to collect their coats.

"They're family," Jake said simply.

She noticed that he didn't say Finley's employees were *like* family but that they *were* family. The difference was subtle but significant. J.R. had lost his wife and daughter and had turned to his friends and employees to fill the huge hole left by the loss of his loved ones. Jake had, too.

As they stepped outside, Holly was thrilled by the falling snow. "Jake, look!" She held out her hand to catch the soft flakes that floated down from the night sky. "It's just so beautiful!"

Jake wrapped his scarf more securely around his neck. "I can't believe you're so excited about a little snow."

"I love it…. It's so Christmassy."

He grinned and clasped her hand. "Do you want to go for a short walk?"

"I'd love to." It was cold, but even without boots or gloves or a hat, Holly felt warm, and more than that, *happy.*

"Where would you like to go?" Jake asked.

"Wherever you'd like to take me." Late though it was, she didn't want the night to end. Lindy Lee had never thrown a Christmas party for her staff. Maybe she'd talk to Lindy about planning one for next December; she could discuss the benefits—employee satisfaction and loyalty, which would lead to higher productivity. Those were the terms Lindy would respond to. Not appreciation or enjoyment or fun. Having worked with Lindy as long as she had, Holly suspected her employer wasn't a happy person. And she wasn't someone who cared about the pleasure of others.

"I thought this would be a miserable Christmas," Holly confessed, leaning close to Jake as they moved down the busy sidewalk. They weren't the only couple reveling in the falling snow.

"Why?" Jake asked. "Because of your brother?"

"Well, yes. It's also the first Christmas without my parents, and then Mickey got called up for Afghanistan so there's just Gabe and me."

"What changed?"

"A number of things, actually," she said. "Meeting you, of course."

"Thank you." He bent down and touched his lips to hers in the briefest of kisses.

"My attitude," she said. "I was worried that Gabe would resent living with me. For months we didn't really bond."

"You have now, though, haven't you?"

"Oh, yes. I didn't realize how much I loved him until he went missing the other day. I...I don't normally panic, but I did then."

Holly was still surprised by how accommodating her employer had been during and after that crisis. First

Lindy Lee had allowed Gabe to come to the office and then she'd actually chatted with him. Holly didn't know what the two of them had talked about, but her employer had seemed almost pleasant afterward.

"Remember the other night when you and Gabe decorated your Christmas tree?" Jake asked.

"Of course."

"Gabe asked me about mine."

"Right." It'd been an awkward moment. Gabe had been full of questions. He couldn't understand why some people chose not to make Christmas part of their lives. No tree. No presents. No family dinner. The closest Jake and his father got to celebrating the holidays was their yearly sojourn to the Virgin Islands.

Holly knew this was his father's way of ignoring the holiday. Jake and J.R. left on Christmas Eve and didn't return until after New Year's.

She was sure they'd depart sooner if they could. The only reason they stayed in New York as long as they did was because of the business. The holiday season made their year financially. Without the last-quarter sales, many retailers would struggle to survive. Finley's Department Store was no different.

"You told Gabe you didn't put up a tree," Holly reminded him.

"I might've misled him."

"You have a tree?" After everything he'd said, that shocked her.

"You'll see." His stride was purposeful as they continued walking. She soon figured out where they were headed.

"I can't wait," she said with a laugh.

When they reached Rockefeller Center, they stood

gazing up at the huge Christmas tree, bright with thousands of lights and gleaming decorations. Jake gestured toward it. "*That's* my Christmas tree," he said.

"Gabe's going to be jealous that I got to see it again—with you."

Music swirled all around them as Jake slipped his arm about her waist. "When I was young, I found it hard to give up the kind of Christmas I'd known when my mother and sister were alive. Dad refused to have anything to do with the holidays but I still wanted the tree and the gifts."

Holly hadn't fully grasped how difficult those years must've been for him.

"Dad said if I wanted a Christmas tree, I could pick one in the store and make it my own. Better yet, I could claim the one in Rockefeller Center and that's what I did."

Instinctively she knew Jake had never shared this information with anyone else.

"Well, you've got the biggest, most beautiful Christmas tree in the city," she said, leaning her head against his shoulder.

"I do," he murmured.

"Jake," she said carefully. "Would you consider having Christmas dinner with Gabe and me?"

He didn't answer, and she wondered if she'd crossed some invisible line by issuing the invitation. Nevertheless she had to ask.

"I know that would mean not joining your father when he leaves for the Caribbean, but you could fly out the next day, couldn't you?" Holly felt she needed to press the issue. If he was ever going to agree, it would be tonight, after he'd witnessed how much it meant to Finley's employees that he'd attended their party.

"I could fly out later," he said. "But then I'd be leaving my father alone on the saddest day of his life."

"I'd like to invite him, too."

Jake's smile was somber and poignant. "He'll never come, Holly. He hates anything to do with Christmas outside of the business, anyway."

"Maybe so, but I'd still like to ask him." She wasn't sure why she couldn't simply drop this. It took audacity to invite two wealthy men to her small apartment, when their alternative was an elaborate meal in an exotic location.

She was embarrassed now. "I apologize, Jake. I don't know what made me think you'd want to give up the sunshine and warmth of a Caribbean island for dinner with me and Gabe."

"Don't say that! I want to be with you both."

"But you don't feel you can leave your father."

"That's true, but maybe it's time I started creating traditions of my own. I'd be honored to spend Christmas Day with the two of you," he said formally.

Holly felt tears spring to her eyes. "Thank you," she whispered.

She turned to face him. He smiled as she slid her hands up his chest and around his neck. Standing on the tips of her toes with a light snow falling down on them, she pressed her mouth to his.

Jake held her tight. Holly sensed that they'd crossed a barrier in their relationship and established a real commitment to each other.

"When I come, I'll bring the robot for Gabe and hide it under the tree so it'll be a real surprise."

"I'll give you the money on Friday—Christmas Eve."
Christmas Eve.

"Okay." She knew he'd rather not take it, but there was no question—she had every intention of paying.

Jake called his car service, and a limousine met them at Rockefeller Center fifteen minutes later. When he dropped her off at the apartment Mrs. Miracle was sound asleep, still in the blue chair. Jake helped her out to the car, then had the driver take her home. Holly was touched by his thoughtfulness.

Even after Jake had left, Holly had trouble falling asleep. Her mind whirled as she relived scenes and moments of what had been one of the most memorable evenings of her life. When the alarm woke her early Thursday morning, she couldn't get up and just dozed off again. She finally roused herself, horrified to discover that she was almost half an hour behind schedule.

She managed to drag herself out of bed, gulp down a cup of coffee and get Gabe up and dressed and over to the Krantzes'.

Filled with dread, Holly rushed to work. As she yanked off her coat, she heard her name being called. Breathless, she flew into Lindy Lee's office; as usual, Lindy looked pointedly at her watch.

Holly tried to apologize. "I'm sorry I'm late. I'll make up the twenty-five minutes, I promise."

Lindy Lee raised one eyebrow. "Make sure you do."

Holly stood waiting for the lecture that inevitably followed. To her astonishment, this time it didn't. "Thank you for understanding."

"See to it that this doesn't happen again," her employer said, dismissing Holly with a wave of her hand.

"It won't…I just couldn't seem to get moving this

morning." Thinking she'd probably said too much already, she started to leave, then remembered her resolve to discuss a Christmas party with Lindy Lee.

Aware that Holly was lingering, Lindy Lee raised her head and frowned. "Was there something else?"

"Well, yes. Do you mind if I speak freely?"

"That depends on what you have to say." Lindy Lee held her pen poised over a sheet of paper.

"I was at the employees' party for Finley's Department Store last evening," she said, choosing her words carefully. "It was a wonderful event. The employees work together as a team and…and they feel such loyalty to the company. You could just tell. They feel valued, and I doubt there's anything they wouldn't do to help the company succeed."

"And your point is?" Lindy Lee said impatiently.

"My point is we all need to work as a team here, too, and it seemed to me that maybe we should have a Christmas party."

Lindy Lee leaned back in her chair and crossed her arms. "In a faltering economy, with flat sales and an uncertain future, you want me to throw a *Christmas party?*"

"It's…it's just an idea for next year," Holly said, and regretted making the suggestion. Still, she couldn't seem to stop. "The future is always uncertain, isn't it? And there'll always be ups and downs in the economy. But the one constant is the fact that as long as you're in business you'll have a staff, right? And you need them to be committed and—"

"I get it," Lindy Lee said dryly.

Holly waited.

And waited.

"Let me think about it," Lindy Lee finally mumbled.

She'd actually agreed to think about it. Now, this was progress—more progress than Holly had dared to expect.

Fifteen

The best vitamin for a Christian is B1.
—*Mrs. Miracle*

Jake Finley was in love. Logically, he knew, it was too soon to be so sure of his feelings, and yet he couldn't deny his heart. Love wasn't about logic. He'd been attracted to Holly from the moment he met her, but this was more than attraction. He felt…connected to Holly, absorbed in her. He thought about her constantly. Over the years he'd been in other relationships, but no woman had made him feel the way Holly did.

When he arrived at work Thursday morning, he went directly to his father's office. Dora Coffey seemed surprised to see him.

"Is my father in yet?" Jake asked her.

"Yes, he's been here for a couple of hours. You know your father—this store is his life."

"Does he have time to see me?" Jake asked next. "No meetings or conference calls?"

"He's free for a few minutes." She left her desk and announced Jake, who trailed behind her.

When Jake entered the office, his father stood. "Good morning, son. What can I do for you?" He gestured for Jake to take a seat, which he did, and settled back in his own chair.

Jake leaned forward, unsure where to start. He should've worked out what he was going to say before coming up here.

"I suppose you want to gloat." J.R. chuckled. "You were right about that robot. Hardly anyone else forecast this trend. I turned on the TV this morning and there was a story on Telly the SuperRobot. Hottest toy of the season, they said. Who would've guessed it? Not me, that's for sure."

"Not Mike Scott, either," Jake added, although he didn't fault the buyer.

"True enough. And yet Mike was the first to admit he didn't see this coming."

So Scott had mentioned it to J.R. but not to him. Still, it must've taken real humility to acknowledge that he'd been wrong.

"I'm proud of you, son," J.R. continued. "You went with your gut and you were right to do it."

Jake wondered what would've happened if Finley's had been stuck with four hundred leftover robots. Fortunately, however, he wouldn't have to find out.

"I checked inventory this morning, and we have less than twenty of the robots in stock."

Jake didn't need to point out the benefits of being the only store in the tristate area with *any* robots in stock. Having a supply—even a rapidly dwindling supply—of the season's most popular toy brought more shoppers into the store and created customer loyalty.

"They're selling fast. The entire quantity will be gone before Christmas."

"Good. Good," his father said. He grinned as he tilted back in his high leather chair. "Oh, I enjoyed meeting your lady friend last night."

"Holly enjoyed meeting you."

"She's special, isn't she?"

Jake was astonished that his father had immediately discerned his feelings for Holly. "Yes, but... What makes you say that?" He had to ask why it had been so obvious to his father.

J.R. didn't respond for a moment. Finally he said, "I recognized it from the way you looked at her. The way you looked at each other."

Jake nodded but didn't speak.

"I remember when I met your mother." There was a faraway expression in his eyes. "I think I fell in love with Helene as soon as I saw her. She was the daughter of one of my competitors and so beautiful I had trouble getting out a complete sentence. It's a wonder she ever agreed to that first date." He smiled at the memory.

So rarely did his father discuss his mother and sister that Jake kept quiet, afraid that any questions would distract J.R. He craved details, but knew he had to be cautious.

"I loved your mother more than life itself. I still do."

"I know," Jake said softly.

"She wasn't just beautiful," he murmured, and the same faraway look stole over him. "She had a heart unlike anyone I've ever known. Everyone came to her when they needed something, whether it was a kind word, a job, some advice. She never turned anyone away." His face, so often tense, relaxed as he sighed.

"I felt that my world ended the day your mother and Kaitlyn died. Since then you've been my only reason for going on."

"Well, I hope your grandchildren will be another good reason," Jake teased, hoping to lighten the moment.

J.R. gave a hearty laugh. "They certainly will. So…I was right about you and Holly."

"It's too early to say for sure," Jake hedged. Confident though he was about his own feelings, he didn't want to speak for Holly. Not yet…

"But you *know*."

"It looks…promising."

Slapping the top of his desk, J.R. laughed again. "I thought so. I'm happy for you, Jake."

"Thanks, Dad." But he doubted J.R. would be as happy when he found out what that meant, at least as far as Christmas was concerned.

"Oh, before I forget," J.R. said with exquisite timing. "Dora's ordered the plane tickets for Christmas Eve. We leave JFK at seven and land in Saint John around—"

"Dad, I'll need to change my ticket," Jake said, interrupting his father.

That brought J.R. up short. "Change your ticket? Why?"

"I'll join you on the twenty-sixth," Jake explained. "Holly invited me to spend Christmas Day with her and her nephew."

J.R.'s frown was back as he mulled over that statement. "You're going to do it?"

"Yes. I told her I would."

J.R. stood and walked to the window, turning his back to Jake. "I don't know what to say."

"Holly invited you, too."

"You told her it was out of the question, didn't you?"

More or less. "You'd be welcome if you chose to come."

Slowly J.R. turned around. "Well," he said with a sigh, "I suppose it was unrealistic of me not to realize times are changing." He paused. "I look forward to our vacation every year."

Jake had never thought of their trip to the Caribbean as a getaway. His father always brought work with him and they spent their week discussing trends, reading reports and forecasting budgets. It was business, not relaxation.

"You call it a *vacation?*" Jake asked, amused.

"Well, yes. What would you call it?" J.R. frowned in confusion.

Jake hesitated, then decided to tell the truth, even if his father wasn't ready to hear it. "I call it an escape from reality—but not from work. A vacation is supposed to be fun, a break, a chance to do nothing or else do something completely out of the ordinary. Not sit in a hotel room and do exactly the same thing you'd be doing here."

J.R.'s frown deepened.

"Admit it, Dad," Jake said. "You don't go to the islands to lounge on the beach or snorkel or take sightseeing trips. Far from it. You escape New York because you can't bear to be here over Christmas."

J.R. shook his head.

Jake wasn't willing to let it go. "From the time Mom and Kaitlyn died, you've done everything possible to pretend there's no Christmas.

"As a businessman you need the holidays to survive

financially but if it wasn't for that, you'd ban anything to do with Christmas from your life—and mine."

J.R. glared at Jake. "I believe you've said enough."

"You need to accept that Christmas had nothing to do with the accident. It happened, and it changed both our lives forever, but it was a fluke, a twist of fate. I wish with everything in me that Mom and Kaitlyn had stayed home that afternoon, but the fact is, they didn't. They went out, and because their cab collided with another one, they were killed."

"Enough!" J.R. shouted.

Jake stood. "I didn't mean to upset you, Dad."

"If that's the case, then you've failed. I *am* upset."

Jake regretted that; nevertheless, he felt this had to be said. "I'm tired of running away on Christmas Eve. You can do it if you want, but I'm through."

"Fine. Spend the day with Holly if you prefer. It's not going to bother me."

"I wish you'd reconsider and join us."

J.R. tightened his lips. "No, thanks. You might think I'm hiding my head in the sand, but the truth is, I enjoy the islands."

Jake might have believed him if J.R. had walked along the beach even once or taken any pleasure in their surroundings. Instead, he worked from early morning to late evening, burying himself in his work in a desperate effort to ignore the time of year—the anniversary of his loss.

"Yes, Dad," Jake said rather than allow their discussion to escalate into a full-scale argument.

"You'll come the next day, then?"

Jake nodded. He'd make his own flight arrangements. They always stayed at the same four-star hotel,
the same suite of rooms.

"Good."

Jake left the office and hurried down to the toy department. He was surprised to see Mrs. Miracle on
the floor. According to the schedule she wasn't even
supposed to be in. That was his decision; since she'd
volunteered to watch Gabe, he'd given her the day off.

"I didn't expect to see you this morning," he said.

"Oh, I thought I'd come in and do a bit of shopping
myself."

"I didn't realize you had grandchildren," he said.
In fact, he knew next to nothing about Mrs. Miracle's
personal life, including her address. He'd offered to
have the driver take her home and she'd agreed, but
only on the condition that he be dropped off first. For
some reason, he had the impression that she lived close
to the store....

"So how'd the meeting with your father go?" she
asked, disregarding his remark about grandchildren.

"How did you know that's where I was?" Jake asked,
peering at her suspiciously.

"I didn't, but you looked so concerned, I guessed it
had to do with J.R."

"It went fine," he said, unwilling to reveal the details
of his conversation with an employee, even if she'd become a special friend. He didn't plan to mention it to
Holly, either. All he'd say was that he'd extended the
dinner invitation to his father and J.R. had thanked her
but sent his regrets.

"I'm worried about J.R.," Mrs. Miracle said, again surprising him.

"Why? He's in good health."

"Physically, yes, he's doing well for a man of his age."

"Then why are you worried?" Jake pressed.

Instead of answering, the older woman patted his back. "I'm leaving in a few minutes. Would you like me to wrap Gabe's robot before I go?"

"Ah, sure," he said.

"You *are* taking it with you when you go to Holly's for Christmas, aren't you?"

"Yes."

"Then I'll wrap it for you. I'll get some ribbon and nice paper from the gift-wrapping kiosk."

"Thank you," Jake said, still wondering what she'd meant about J.R.

The older woman disappeared, leaving Jake standing in the toy department scratching his head. He valued Mrs. Miracle as an employee and as a new friend, and yet every now and then she'd say something that totally confused him. How did she know so much about him and his father? Perhaps she'd met his parents years ago. Or...

Well, he couldn't waste time trying to figure it out now.

Jake was walking to the customer service counter when his cell phone rang. Holly. He answered immediately.

"Can you talk?" she asked. "I know it's probably insane at the store, but I had to tell you something."

"What is it? Everything okay?"

"It's my boss, Lindy Lee. Oh, Jake, I think I'm going to cry."

"What's wrong?" he asked, alarmed.

"Nothing. This is *good.* Lindy just called me into her office. I spoke with her this morning about a Christmas party. I saw what a great time your employees had. I thought it would help morale, so I mentioned it to Lindy Lee."

"She's going to have a party?"

"No, even better than that. I can have a real Christmas dinner now with a turkey and stuffing and all the extras like I originally planned. I…I'd decided to make fried chicken because I couldn't really afford anything else, and now I can prepare a traditional meal."

"You got your bonus?"

"Yes! And it's bigger than last year's, so I can pay for the robot now."

"That's fabulous news!"

"It is, Jake, it really is." She took a deep breath. "If you don't mind, I'd like to call your father and invite him personally."

Jake's smile faded. "I should tell you I already talked to Dad about joining us on Christmas Day."

"I hope he will."

"Don't count on it." Jake felt bad about discouraging her. "I think he'd like to, but he can't let go of his grief. He feels he'd dishonor the memory of my mother and sister if he celebrated Christmas. For him, their deaths and Christmas are all tied together."

"Oh, Jake, that's so sad."

"Yes…" He didn't say what he knew was obvious— that, until now, the same thing had been true of him.

"I'm looking forward to spending the day with you,"

Jake said, and he meant every word. "Can you meet me for lunch this afternoon?" he asked, not sure he could wait until Christmas to see her again.

When she agreed, he smiled, a smile so wide that several customers looked at him curiously…and smiled back.

Sixteen

*Happiest are the people who give the most
happiness to others.*
                                    —Mrs. Miracle

That same morning Lindy Lee called Holly into her
office again. Saving the document she was working on,
Holly grabbed a pad and pen and rushed inside. Ges-
turing toward the chair, Lindy invited her to sit. This
was unusual in itself; Lindy Lee never went out of her
way to make Holly comfortable. In fact, it was generally the opposite.

"I've given your suggestion some thought," she said
crisply.

"You mean about the Christmas party for next year?"

Lindy Lee's eyes narrowed. "Of course I mean the
Christmas party. I want you to organize one for tomorrow."

"*Tomorrow?* But—"

"No excuses. *You're* the one who asked for this."

"I'll need a budget," Holly said desperately. It was
a little late to be organizing a party. Every caterer in

New York would've been booked months ago. Finding a restaurant with an opening the day before Christmas would be hopeless. What was she thinking when she'd suggested the idea to Lindy Lee? Hadn't she emphasized that she was talking about the *following* year? Not this one? Holly hardly knew where to start.

Lindy Lee glared at her. "I'm aware that you'll require a budget. Please wait until I'm finished. You can ask your questions then."

"Okay, sorry." Holly wasn't sure how she was supposed to manage this on such short notice.

Lindy explained that she'd close the office at two, that she wanted festive decorations and Christmas music, and that attendance was mandatory. "You can bring your nephew if you like," she added, after setting a more than generous budget.

"In other words, the family of staff is included?"

"Good grief, no."

"But Gabe's family."

"He's adorable. He even—" Lindy Lee stopped abruptly.

Holly was in complete agreement about Gabe's cuteness, but it wouldn't go over well if Gabe was invited and no one else's children were. "The others might get upset," Holly said, broaching the subject cautiously. "I mean, if I bring Gabe and no other children are allowed, it might look bad."

Lindy Lee sat back and crossed her arms, frowning. "If we invite family, then the place will be overrun with the little darlings," she muttered sarcastically. She sighed. "*Should* we include them?"

Holly shook her head. "There are too many practical considerations. People with kids would have to go home and pick them up and… Well, I think it's too much trouble, so let's not."

"Okay," Lindy said with evident relief.

"I'll get right on this."

"You might invite Gabe to the office again," Lindy Lee shocked her by saying. "Maybe in the new year."

Holly wondered if she'd misunderstood. "You want me to bring Gabe into the office?"

"A half day perhaps," her boss said, amending her original thought.

"Okay." So Gabe had succeeded in charming Lindy Lee, something Holly had once considered impossible.

Lindy Lee turned back to her computer, effectively dismissing Holly. Head whirling with the difficulty of her assignment, Holly returned to her own desk. She immediately got a list of nearby restaurants and began making calls, all of which netted quick rejections. In fact, the people she spoke with nearly laughed her off the phone. By noon she was growing desperate and worried.

"How's it going?" Lindy Lee asked as she stepped out of her office to meet someone for lunch. "Don't answer. I can tell by the look on your face."

"If only we'd scheduled the party a bit sooner…"

"You shouldn't have waited until the last minute to spring it on me," she said, laying the blame squarely on Holly.

That seemed unfair and a little harsh, even for Lindy Lee.

"We could have our event here in the building," Lindy Lee suggested, apparently relenting. "The sixth floor has a big open space. Check with them and see if that's available."

"I'll do it right away."

"Good," Lindy said, and turned to leave.

"I'll make this party happen," Holly promised through gritted teeth.

"I'll hold you to that," Lindy Lee tossed over her shoulder on her way out the door.

As soon as she'd left, Holly called the sixth floor. As luck would have it, the only time available was the afternoon of Christmas Eve—exactly what she needed. That solved one problem, but there was still an equally large hurdle to jump. Finding a caterer.

Despite the urgency of this task, Holly kept her lunch date with Jake. These last days before Christmas made getting away for more than a few minutes difficult for him. Yet he managed with the help of his staff who, according to Jake, were determined to smooth the course of romance. Mrs. Miracle, God bless her, had spearheaded the effort.

Holly picked up a pastrami on rye at the deli and two coffees, and walked to Finley's; that was all they really had time for. Now that she'd been assured of her Christmas bonus, Holly had resumed the luxury of buying lunch. When she arrived at the store, white bag in hand, Jake was busy with a customer.

Mrs. Miracle saw her and came over to greet Holly. "My dear, what's wrong?"

Once again Holly was surprised at how readable she must be. "I'm on an impossible mission," she said.

"And what's that?" the older woman asked.

Holly explained. As soon as she'd finished, Mrs. Miracle smiled. "I believe I can help you."

"You can?" she asked excitedly.

"Yes, a friend of mine just opened a small restaurant

in the Village. She's still getting herself established, but she'd certainly be capable of handling this party. What are you planning to serve? Sandwiches? Appetizers? Cookies? That sort of thing?"

"The party will be in the early afternoon, so small sandwiches and cookies would be perfect. It doesn't have to be elaborate." At this point she'd accept almost anything.

"I'll get you my friend's number."

"Yes, please, and, Mrs. Miracle, thank you so much."

"No problem, my dear. None whatsoever." The older woman beamed her a smile. "By the way, I've set up a table in the back of the storeroom for you and Jake to have your lunch."

"How thoughtful."

"You go on back and Jake'll be along any minute. Meanwhile, I'll get you that phone number."

"Thanks," she said again. "Could you tell me your friend's name?"

"It's Wendy," she said. "Now don't you worry about a thing, you hear?"

Feeling deeply relieved, Holly went to the storeroom. Sure enough, Mrs. Miracle had set up a card table, complete with a white tablecloth and a small poinsettia in the middle. Holly put down the sandwich, plus a couple of pickles and the two cups of coffee.

Jake came in a few minutes later, looking harassed. He kissed her, then took his place. "It's crazy out there," he said, slumping in his chair.

"I can tell." She noticed that the rest of the staff was diligently avoiding the storeroom, no doubt under orders from Mrs. Miracle.

He reached for his half of the massive sandwich. "I sold the last of the robots this morning."

"That's wonderful!"

"It is and it isn't," he said between bites. "I wish I'd ordered another hundred. We could've sold those, as well. Now we have to turn people away. I hate disappointing anyone."

"Is there any other store in town with inventory?"

"Nope, and believe me, I've checked. Another shipment is due in a week after Christmas but by then it'll be too late."

Holly hated to bring up the subject of Gabe's Intellytron, but she needed Jake's reassurance that the one he'd set aside hadn't been sold in the robot-buying frenzy. "You still have Gabe's, don't you?"

Still chewing on his sandwich, Jake nodded. "Mrs. Miracle wrapped it herself. It's sitting right over there." He pointed to a counter across from her. The large, brightly decorated package rested in one corner.

"I'm so grateful you did this for me," she told him. Meeting Jake had been one of the greatest blessings of the year—in so many ways.

"Thank Mrs. Miracle, too," he said. "She wasn't even supposed to be in today, but she ended up staying to help us out."

The few minutes they'd grabbed flew by much too quickly. Jake stood, kissed her again, and they left the storeroom together. As they stepped onto the floor, Mrs. Miracle handed her a slip of paper. "The name of the restaurant is Heavenly Delights and here's the number."

"Heavenly Delights," Holly repeated. "I'll give your friend a call as soon as I'm back at my desk."

"You do that."

Holly tucked the paper in her coat pocket and nearly danced all the way to the office. With a little help from Mrs. Miracle, she'd be able to pull off a miracle of her own—she'd organize this Christmas party, regardless of the difficulties and challenges.

Once at her desk, Holly reached for the phone and called the number Mrs. Miracle had written down for her.

"Hello." A woman answered on the third ring.

"Hello," Holly returned brightly. "Is this Wendy?"

"Yes. And you are?"

"I'm Holly Larson, and I'm phoning on behalf of Lindy Lee."

"Lindy Lee, the designer?" Wendy sounded impressed.

"Yes," Holly answered. "I know I'm probably calling at the worst time, but I felt I should contact you as soon as possible." She assumed the restaurant would be busy with the lunch crowd.

"No, no, this is fine."

"I was given your phone number by Emily Miracle."

"Who?"

"Oh, sorry. Her badge says Miracle, but that's a mistake. Rather than cause a fuss, she asked that we call her Mrs. Miracle, although that's not actually her name. I apologize, but I can't remember what it is. I'm so accustomed to calling her Mrs. Miracle." Holly hoped she wasn't rambling.

"Go on," Wendy urged without commenting on all the confusion about names.

"Long story short, she suggested I call you about catering Lindy Lee's Christmas party for her employees."

"She did?"

"Yes… She highly recommended you and the restaurant."

"What restaurant?"

"Heavenly Delights," Holly said. Wendy must own more than one. "The location in the Village."

"Heavenly Delights," Wendy gasped, then started to laugh. "Heavenly Delights?"

"Yes." Holly's spirits took a sharp dive; nevertheless, she forged ahead. "I'm wondering if you could work us into your schedule."

"Oh, dear."

Holly's spirits sank even further. "You can't do it?"

"I didn't say that."

Her emotions went from hopeful to disheartened and back again. "Then you could?"

"I…I don't know what to say." The woman seemed completely overwhelmed.

Yes, I can do it would certainly make Holly's day, but the words weren't immediately forthcoming.

"Unfortunately, the party's scheduled for tomorrow afternoon—Christmas Eve." Holly suspected that, by then, practically everyone in the restaurant business would be closing down and heading home to their families. As an incentive, she mentioned the amount she could offer. The catering would take up most of the budget, with a little left over for decorations.

"That sounds fair," Wendy said.

"Would you be able to accommodate us?" she asked hopefully. "We're talking about forty people, give or take."

"I…"

Holly closed her eyes, fearing the worst.

"I think I could. However, there's something you should know."

"What's that?"

"First, I can't imagine who this Mrs. Miracle is."

"As I said, that isn't her real name. But I can find out for you, if you like."

"No, it doesn't matter. What I wanted to tell you is that I don't have a restaurant."

"No restaurant?" Holly's mouth went dry.

"The thing is, I've been talking with my daughter about opening one. She's attending culinary school. I've been praying about it, too. However, a lot of problems stand in the way—one of which is money."

"Oh."

"When I applied for a loan, the bank officer asked me what we intended to call the restaurant. Lucie and I have gone over dozens of names and nothing felt right. Our specialty would be desserts.... I like the name Heavenly Delights. If you don't mind, I'll borrow it."

"I... That's the name Mrs. Miracle gave me."

"Well, if *she* doesn't mind, we'll definitely use it." She paused. "Maybe I know her, but right now I can't figure out who she is."

"Um, so if you don't have a restaurant yet, you can't cater the event?"

"I can't," Wendy agreed. "But perhaps Lucie and her friends from culinary school could."

"Really?" Holly asked excitedly.

"Give me your number and I'll call her to see if we can make this happen."

"Great!"

Holly fidgeted until Wendy called back five minutes later. "We'll do it," Wendy told her. "Lucie talked to several of her colleagues and they're all interested. I can promise you'll *love* their menu. Lucie's already working on it."

"Fabulous. Thank you! Oh, thank you so much." Her relief was so great that she felt like weeping.

She disconnected just as Lindy returned from lunch.

"The party's all set," Holly said happily.

"Really?" She'd impressed Lindy Lee, which was no small feat.

"Christmas Eve from two to four."

Her employer nodded. "Good job, Holly."

Holly closed her eyes and basked in the glow of Lindy Lee's approval.

Seventeen

We don't change God's message.
His message changes us.
                    —Mrs. Miracle

Jake glanced at his watch and felt a surge of relief. Five-thirty on Christmas Eve; in half an hour, the store would close its doors for the season.

Finley's would open again on the twenty-sixth for the year-end frenzy. He felt good that toy sales for this quarter were twenty percent higher than the previous year. He attributed the boost in revenue to Intellytron the SuperRobot. Jake felt vindicated that his hunch had been proven right. He'd be proud to take these latest figures to his father. While the robot alone didn't explain the increase, the fact that it was available at Finley's had brought new customers into the store.

Holly was occupied with her boss and the Christmas party, which she'd arranged for Lindy Lee at the last moment. The poor girl had worked herself into a nervous state to pull off the event, and Jake was confident that the afternoon had gone well. He knew Holly had obsessed over each and every detail.

No doubt exhausted, she'd go home to her Brooklyn apartment as soon as she was finished with the cleanup. Jake would come by later that evening to spend time with her and Gabe. The three of them would enjoy a quiet dinner and then attend Christmas Eve services at her church.

It felt strangely luxurious not to be rushing away from the city with his father, although Jake was saddened that he hadn't been able to convince J.R. to join them on Christmas Day.

His cell chirped, and even before he looked, Jake knew it was Holly.

"Hi," he said. "How'd the party go?"

"Great! Wonderful. Even Lindy Lee was pleased. The caterers did a fabulous job, above and beyond my expectations. Wendy told me that Heavenly Delights plans to specialize in desserts and they should. Everything was spectacular."

"I'm glad."

"Don't forget to bring over Gabe's gift tonight," she said in a tired voice. As he'd expected, Holly was worn out.

"Sure thing."

"We'll hide it in my bedroom until he goes to sleep, and then we can put it under the tree. That way it'll be the first thing he sees Christmas morning."

"Sounds like a plan."

"I'll distract him when you arrive so you can shove it in my closet."

"Okay."

She hesitated. "Are you sure you can't talk your father into coming for Christmas dinner?"

"I don't think so, Holly. He isn't ready to give up his...vacation." He nearly choked on the word.

"Ask him again, would you?" she said softly.

"I will," he agreed with some reluctance, knowing it wouldn't have any effect.

"And thank Mrs. Miracle for me. She saved the day with this recommendation."

"Of course. Although I believe she's already left."

"She'll be back, won't she?"

"As seasonal help, she'll stay on until the end of January when we finish inventory." The older woman had been a real success in the department. She'd reassured parents and entertained their kids. If she was interested, Jake would like to offer her full-time employment.

He ended his conversation with Holly and went into the storeroom to pick up Gabe's robot.

He stopped short. The package that had lain on the counter, the package so beautifully wrapped by Mrs. Miracle, was missing.

Gone.

"Karen," Jake said, walking directly past a customer to confront one of the other sales associates. If this was a practical joke, he was not amused. "Where's the robot that was on the counter in the storeroom?" he demanded, ignoring the last-minute shopper she was assisting.

Karen blinked as though he was speaking in a foreign language. "I beg your pardon?"

"The wrapped gift in the storage room?" he repeated.

"I...I don't have a clue."

"You know what I'm talking about, don't you?"

Her face became flushed. "I'm not sure."

"It was wrapped and ready for delivery and now it's missing." Jake couldn't believe anyone would steal the robot. He knew his employees, and there wasn't a single one who was capable of such a deed. He'd stake his career on it.

"Did you ask John?"

"No." Jake quickly sought out the youngest sales associate. John had just finished with a customer and looked expectantly at Jake.

"The robot's missing," he said without preamble.

John stared back at him. "The one in the storeroom?"

"Are there any others in this department?" he snapped. If there were, he'd grab one and be done with it. However, no one knew better than Jake that there wasn't an Intellytron to be had.

"I saw it," Gail said, joining them.

Relief washed over Jake. Someone had moved it without telling him; that was obviously what had happened. The prospect of facing Holly and telling her he didn't have the robot didn't bear thinking about.

That morning, the moment she'd received her Christmas bonus, Holly had rushed over to Finley's to pay for the toy. Her face had been alight with happiness as she described how excited Gabe would be when he found his gift under the Christmas tree. That robot meant so much to the boy. If Jake didn't bring it as promised, Holly might not forgive him. He hoped that wouldn't happen, but the thought sent a chill through him nonetheless.

Frances, another sales associate, came over, too. "Mrs. Miracle had it," she said.

"When?"

"This morning," Frances explained. "She didn't mention it to you?"

"No." Jake shook his head. "What did she do with it?"

Frances stared down at the floor. "She sold it."

"*Sold* it?" Jake exploded. This had to be some kind of joke—didn't it? "How could she do that? It was already paid for by someone else." That robot belonged to Gabe Larson. She knew that as well as anyone.

"Why would she sell it?" he burst out again, completely bewildered.

"I…I don't know. You'll have to ask her," Frances said. "I'm so sorry, Mr. Finley. I'm sure there's a logical explanation."

There'd better be. Not that it would help now.

Sick at heart, Jake left the department and went up to his father's office. Dora had already gone home; the whole administrative floor was deserted. He didn't know what he'd tell Holly. He should've taken the robot to his apartment and kept it there. Then he could've been guaranteed that nothing like this would happen. Still, berating himself now wouldn't serve any useful purpose.

Preparing for his flight, J. R. Finley was busy stuffing paperwork in his computer case when Jake entered the office. J.R. looked up at him. "What's the matter with you? Did you decide to come with me, after all?"

"No. Have you decided to stay in New York?" Jake countered.

"You're kidding, right?"

Jake slumped into a chair and ran his fingers through his hair. "Gabe's robot is missing," he said quietly. "Emily Miracle, or whatever her name is, sold it."

"Mrs. Miracle?" J.R.'s face tightened and he waved his index finger at Jake. "I told you that woman was up to no good, butting into other people's business. She's a troublemaker. Didn't I tell you that?"

"Dad, stop it. She's a sweet grandmotherly woman."

"She's ruined a little boy's Christmas and you call that *sweet?*" He made a scoffing sound and resumed his task of collecting papers and shoving them into his case.

"Do you have any connections—someone who can locate a spare Intellytron at the last minute?" This was Jake's only hope.

Frowning, his father checked his watch. "I'll make some phone calls, but I can't promise anything."

Jake was grateful for whatever his father could do. "What about your flight?"

J.R. looked at his watch again and shrugged. "I'll catch a later one."

Jake started to remind his father that changing flights at this point might be difficult, but stopped himself. If J.R. was going to offer his assistance, Jake would be a fool to refuse.

"I'll shut down the department and meet you back here in twenty minutes," Jake said.

His father had picked up his phone and was punching out numbers. One thing Jake could be assured of— if there was a single Intellytron left in the tristate area, J.R. would locate it and have it delivered to Gabe.

He hurried back to the toy department and saw that the last-minute customers were being ushered out, bags in hand, and the day's sales tallied. The store was officially closed. His staff was waiting to exchange Christmas greetings with Jake so they could go home to their families.

"Is there anything we can do before we leave?" John asked, speaking for the others.

"No, thanks. You guys have been great. Merry Christmas, everyone!"

As soon as they'd left, he got Mrs. Miracle's contact information and called the phone number she'd given HR. To his shock, a recorded voice message informed him that the number was no longer in service. That wasn't the only shock, either—she'd handed in her notice that afternoon.

He groaned. Mrs. Miracle was unreachable and had absconded with precious information regarding the robot—like why she'd sold it and to whom.

Jake returned to his father's office to find him pacing the floor with the receiver pressed to his ear. J.R. glanced in Jake's direction, then quickly looked away. That tight-lipped expression told Jake everything he needed to know—his father hadn't been successful.

He waited until J.R. hung up the phone.

"No luck," Jake said, not bothering to phrase it in the form of a question.

J.R. shook his head. "Everyone I talked to said as far as they knew we're the only store in five states to have the robot."

"*Had.* We sold out."

"Apparently there isn't another one to be found anywhere till after Christmas."

Jake had expected that. A sick feeling attacked the pit of his stomach as he sank into a chair and sighed loudly. "I appreciate your help, Dad. Thanks for trying."

"I'm sorry I couldn't do more." J.R. nodded and placed a consoling hand on Jake's shoulder. "I know how you feel."

Jake doubted that but he wasn't in the mood to argue.

"Holly's special," J.R. said. "I've known that since the first time you mentioned her."

"She is." Jake was in full agreement there.

"If it'd been your mother who needed that thing, I would've moved heaven and earth to make sure she got it."

He reconsidered. Maybe his father *did* know what he was feeling. He'd done his utmost to keep Holly and Gabe from being disappointed. Unfortunately, nothing he or J.R. did now would make any difference. It was simply too late.

"Every Intellytron in New York State and beyond is wrapped and under some youngster's tree," J.R. said.

Jake rubbed his face. "I'll come up with something to tell Holly and Gabe," he said, thinking out loud.

"Is there anything else the boy might like?" his father asked.

The only toy Gabe had referred to, at least in Jake's hearing, was the robot. He'd even risked Holly's wrath and traveled into the city on his own just to see it again and watch it in action.

"What about a train set?" his father suggested. "Every little boy wants a train set."

Jake had. He'd longed for one the Christmas his mother and sister had died. But there'd been no presents the next morning or any Christmas morning since the accident.

"He might," Jake said. "But—"

"Well, we have one of those."

Jake wondered what his father was talking about. As head of the toy department Jake was well aware of the inventory left in stock and there were no train sets.

This season had been record-breaking in more ways than one; not only the robot but a number of other toys had sold out. The trains, a popular new doll, a couple of computer games... "Exactly where is there a train set?" he asked. "Unless you mean the one in the window..."

"Not the display train. A brand-new one. Except that it's twenty-one years old." J.R. swallowed visibly. "I have it," he said. "It's still wrapped in the original paper. Your mother bought it for you just before..." He didn't need to finish the sentence.

"Mom bought me the train set I wanted?" Jake asked, his voice hoarse with emotion.

J.R. grinned. "You were spoiled, young man. Your mother loved you deeply. And your little sister adored you."

A sense of loss hit him hard and for a moment that was all Jake could think about. "You kept the train set all these years?" he finally asked.

J.R. nodded solemnly. "I always meant to give it to you but I could never part with it. In a way, holding on to it was like...having your mother still with me. I could pretend it was Christmas Eve twenty-one years ago and she hadn't died. Don't worry, I didn't *actually* believe that, but I could indulge the fantasy of what Christmas should've been. That train set made the memory so real...."

"And you're willing to give it up for Gabe?"

"No" was his father's blunt reply. "I'm willing to give it up for *you*."

Jake smiled and whispered, "Thanks, Dad."

"You're welcome. Now we've got a bit of digging to do. I don't remember where I put that train set but I know it's somewhere in the condo. Or maybe the storage locker. Or…"

"Do we have time? Did you change your flight?"

"Flight?" J.R. repeated, then seemed to remember he was scheduled to fly out that evening. Shaking his head, he muttered, "It's fine. I'll catch one tomorrow if I have to."

Jake didn't want to pressure his father, but he'd promised Holly he'd invite J.R. to dinner at her apartment. Although he'd already tried once, he'd ask again. If he was going to disappoint her on one front, then the least he could do was surprise her on another.

"Since you're apparently staying over…" he began.

"Yes?"

"Have Christmas dinner with Holly and Gabe and me tomorrow afternoon. Will you do that, Dad?"

His father took a long moment to consider the invitation. Then, as if the words were difficult to say, he slowly whispered, "I believe I will. Something tells me your mother would want me to."

Eighteen

God isn't politically correct. He's just correct.
—Mrs. Miracle

Holly set the phone down and forced herself to keep the smile on her face. Gabe's robot was missing. Because Gabe was in earshot, she couldn't ask Jake the questions that clamored in her mind. He'd said something about Mrs. Miracle, but Holly had been too disheartened to remember what followed.

Adding to her distress, Jake had said there was something he needed to do with his father, which meant he'd have to renege on dinner that night. In addition to the bad news about the missing robot, Jake had passed on some good news, too. Evidently his father had changed his plans and would be joining them on Christmas Day, after all, which delighted Holly and greatly encouraged her. She recognized that this was no small concession on J.R.'s part.

"Isn't Jake coming for dinner?" Gabe asked, looking up from his handheld video game. He lay on the sofa as he expertly manipulated the keys.

"I... No. Unfortunately, Jake has something else he has to do," Holly explained, doing her best to maintain an even voice. "Something really important," she emphasized.

Gabe frowned and sat up. "What's more important than Christmas Eve?"

Again Holly made an effort to pretend nothing was wrong. "We'll have to ask when we see him tomorrow," she said airily.

Her nephew slouched back onto the sofa. His downcast look prompted Holly to sit beside him. She felt as depressed as Gabe did, but was trying hard not to show it. In the larger scheme of life, these disappointments were minor. Nevertheless, she'd hoped to give Gabe a very special gift this year. And she'd hoped—so had Gabe—to spend Christmas Eve with Jake.

"Did Jake promise to come tomorrow?"

"He'll be here."

"But he said he'd come for dinner tonight, too—and he didn't."

"We'll have a wonderful time this evening, just the two of us." She slipped her arm around his small frame and squeezed gently.

Gabe didn't seem too sure of that. "Can I email my dad?"

"Of course." Holly would come up with ways to keep them both occupied until it was time to walk to church for the Christmas Eve service. They could watch a Christmas movie; Gabe might enjoy *The Bishop's Wife,* Holly's favorite, or *A Christmas Carol* with Alastair Sim as the ultimate Scrooge. Still cheering herself up, she headed into her kitchen to start frying the chicken, which had been marinating in buttermilk since six that morning. They'd have turkey tomorrow, but tonight she'd make the meal she associated with her mother... with comfort.

Gabe leaped up from the sofa and hurried into the kitchen. "Can we invite Mrs. Miracle for dinner?" he asked excitedly.

"Oh, Gabe, I wish we'd thought of that sooner."

"I like Mrs. Miracle."

"I like her, too." The older woman had never mentioned whether she had family in the area, which made Holly wonder if she was spending this evening by herself.

Gabe returned to writing his email. "Dad's surprise didn't come, did it?" he said in a pensive voice.

Holly suddenly realized it hadn't. This complicated everything. Not only wouldn't she be able to give her nephew the only toy he'd requested for Christmas, but the gift his father had mailed hadn't arrived, either.

"He might be mad at me for going into the city by myself," Gabe murmured.

"Oh, sweetie, I'm positive that's not it."

Before she could finish her reassurances, the doorbell chimed. Hoping, despite everything, that it was Jake, Holly answered the door, still wearing her apron. To her astonishment, Emily Miracle was standing in the hall.

"I hope you don't mind me dropping in unexpectedly like this."

"Mrs. Miracle! Mrs. Miracle!" Gabe rushed to the door. "We were just talking about you." He grabbed her free hand and tugged her into the apartment. "Can you stay for dinner? Aunt Holly's making fried chicken and there's corn and mashed potatoes and cake, too.

You can stay, can't you? Jake said he was coming and now he can't."

"Oh, dear," Emily said, laughing softly. "I suppose I could. I came by to bring you my Christmas salad. It's a family favorite and I wanted to share it with you."

"That's so nice of you, Emily," Holly said, adding a place setting to the table. Her mood instantly lightened.

"Jake *said* he'd come," Gabe pouted.

"He's doing something important," Holly reminded her nephew.

"I'm sure he is," Emily said, giving Holly a covered ceramic bowl and removing her coat. "It isn't like Jake to cancel at the last moment without a good reason. He's a very responsible young man—in his personal life and in business, too. He'll do his father proud." She held out her hands for the bowl.

"You mean *does* his father proud," Holly corrected, passing it back. She had every confidence that Jake would one day step up to the helm at Finley's, but that was sometime in the future. Jake seemed to think it might take as long as five years, and he said that suited him fine.

"Yes, that's what I mean. I've enjoyed working with him this Christmas season." Emily made her way into the kitchen and put her salad in the refrigerator.

"Can you come to church with us?" Gabe asked, following her. "It's Christmas Eve, and there's a special program and singing, too."

"I'd like that very much, but unfortunately I already have other plans."

"We're grateful you could have dinner with us," Holly said. She waited until Gabe had left the room before she asked Emily about the robot.

"Do you have any idea what happened to the you-know-what Jake put aside?" She spoke guardedly because the apartment was small and she wanted to ensure that Gabe didn't hear anything that would upset him.

Mrs. Miracle was about to answer when he dashed into the kitchen again.

Grasping the situation, she immediately distracted him. "Do you want to help me fill the water glasses?" she asked.

"Okay," Gabe agreed.

Emily poured water into the pitcher, which she handed to Gabe. Holding it carefully, he walked over to the dining area, which was actually part of the living room. The older woman turned to Holly. "I think there was a misunderstanding between Jake and me," she said in a low voice. "I'll clear everything up as soon as I can."

"Please do," Holly whispered. She tried to recall her conversation with Jake. He seemed to imply that Emily had sold the robot to someone else. That didn't seem possible. She'd never do anything to hurt a little boy; Holly was convinced of it.

The fried chicken couldn't have been better; in fact, it was as good as when her mother had prepared this dish. Holly had wanted tonight's meal to be memorable for Gabe, and because Mrs. Miracle was with them, it was.

During dinner, Emily entertained them with story after story of various jobs she'd taken through the years. She'd certainly had her share of interesting experiences, working as a waitress, a nanny, a nurse and now a salesperson.

All too soon, it was time to get ready for church. Holly reluctantly stood up from the table.

"Everything was lovely," Mrs. Miracle told her with a smile of appreciation. "I've never had chicken that was more delicious." She carried her empty dessert plate to the kitchen sink. "And that coconut cake…"

"I liked the sauce best," Gabe chimed in, putting his plate in the sink, too.

"I loved the salad," Holly said, and was sincere. "I hope you'll give me the recipe."

"Of course. I'll be happy to write it out for you now if you'll get me some paper and a pen."

Holly tore a page from a notebook and grabbed Gabe's Santa pen; minutes later, Mrs. Miracle handed her the recipe with a flourish. "Here you go." Then she frowned at her watch. "Oh, my. I hate to run, but I'm afraid I must."

"No, no, don't worry," Holly assured her. "We have to leave for church, anyway. I'm just glad you could be with us this evening. It meant a lot to Gabe and me."

The older woman bent down and kissed the boy's cheek. "This is going to be a very special Christmas for you, young man. Just you wait. It's one you'll remember your whole life. Someday you'll tell your grandchildren about the best Christmas of your life."

"Do you really think so?" Gabe asked, eyes alight with happiness.

She reached for her coat and put it on before she hugged Holly goodbye. "It's going to be a special Christmas for you, as well, my dear."

Holly smiled politely. Maybe Mrs. Miracle was right, but it definitely hadn't started out that way.

Gabe woke at six o'clock Christmas morning. He knocked on Holly's bedroom door and shouted, "It's

Christmas!" Apparently he suspected she might have forgotten.

Holly opened one eye. Still half-asleep, she sat up and stretched her arms above her head.

"Can we open our presents?" Gabe asked, leaping onto her bed.

"What about breakfast?" she said.

"I'm not hungry. You aren't, either, are you?" The question had a hopeful lilt, as though any thought of food would be equally irrelevant to her.

"I could eat," she said.

Gabe's face fell.

"I could eat…later," she amended.

His jubilant smile reappeared.

"Shall we see what Santa brought you?" she asked, tossing aside her covers. She threw on her housecoat and accompanied him into the living room, where the gifts beneath the small tree awaited their inspection.

Gabe fell to his knees and began rooting through the packages she'd set out the night before, after he'd gone to sleep. He must've known from the size of the wrapped boxes that the robot wasn't among them. He sat back on his heels. "Santa didn't get me Intellytron, did he?"

"I don't know, sweetie. I hear Santa sometimes makes late deliveries."

"He does?" Hope shone in his face. "When?"

"That I can't say." Rather than discuss the subject further, Holly hurried into the kitchen.

While she put on a pot of coffee, Gabe arranged the gifts in two small piles. Most of them had been mailed by Holly's parents, and Gabe's didn't take long to unwrap. He was wonderful, sweetly expressing gratitude and happiness with his few gifts. A number of times Holly had to wipe tears from her eyes.

"I hope you're not too disappointed," she said when she could speak. "I know how badly you wanted the robot—and I'm sure Santa has one for you but it might be a little late."

Gabe looked up from the new video game she'd purchased on her way home from work. "I bet I'll still get Intellytron. Mrs. Miracle said this was going to be my best Christmas ever, remember? And it wouldn't be without my robot." He jumped up and slid his arms around Holly's neck and gave her a tight hug.

She opened her gifts after that—a book from her parents, plus a calendar and a peasant-style blouse. And the origami purse from Gabe, which brought fresh tears to her eyes.

They had a leisurely breakfast of French toast and then, while Gabe played with his new video game, Holly got the turkey in the oven. The doorbell rang around eleven o'clock.

Jake and his father came in, carrying a large wrapped box between them. Holly's heartbeat accelerated. It must be Intellytron, although the box actually seemed too big.

"Merry Christmas," Jake said, and held her close. "Don't get excited—this isn't what you think it is," he whispered in her ear just before he kissed her.

"Merry Christmas, young man," J.R. said, and shook Gabe's hand.

"What's that?" Gabe asked, eyeing the box Jake had set on the carpet.

"Why don't you open it and see?" J.R. suggested.

Jake stood at Holly's side with his arm around her waist. "I'm sorry I had to cancel last night," he said in a low voice.

"It's fine, don't worry."

"Mrs. Miracle came over," Gabe said as he sat on the floor beside the box.

"Emily Miracle?" Jake frowned. "Did she happen to deliver something?" he asked, his eyes narrowing.

"She brought a Christmas salad for dinner," Gabe told him, tearing away the ribbon. He looked up. "We didn't eat it all. Do you want to taste it?" He wrinkled his nose. "For green stuff, it was pretty good."

"I wouldn't want to ruin my dinner," J.R. said, smiling down at him. "Go ahead, young man, and let 'er rip."

Gabe didn't need any encouragement. He tore away the wrapping paper. "It's a train set," he said. "That was the second thing on my Christmas list, after Intellytron. Can we set it up now?"

"I don't see why not," Jake told him and got down on his knees with Gabe. "I wanted one when I was around your age, too."

"Did you get one?" Gabe asked.

Jake looked at his father, who sat on the sofa, and nodded. "I certainly did, and it was the best train set money could buy."

Gabe took the engine out of the box. "Wow, this is heavy."

"Let's lay out the track first, shall we?"

Holly sat on the sofa next to Jake's father. "I'm so glad you could have dinner with us."

"I am, too." A pained look came over him and he

gave a slight shake of his head. "I was sure I'd never want to celebrate Christmas again, but I've decided it's time I released the past and started to prepare for the future."

"The future?" she repeated uncertainly.

"Grandchildren," J.R. said with a sheepish grin. "I have the distinct feeling that my son has met the woman he's going to love as much as I loved his mother."

Embarrassed, Holly looked away. With all her heart she hoped she was that woman.

"Jake would be furious with me if he knew I'd said anything. It's too soon—I realize that. He probably isn't aware of how strongly he feels, but I know. I've seen my son with other women. He's in love with you, the same way I was in love with Helene."

Holly was about to make some excuse about dinner and return to the kitchen when the doorbell chimed again. Everyone looked at her as if she knew who it would be.

"I...I wonder who that is," she murmured, walking to the door.

"It could be Mrs. Miracle," Gabe said hopefully.

Only it wasn't.

Holly opened the apartment door to find her brother standing there in his army fatigues, wearing a smile of pure happiness. In his arms he held a large wrapped box.

"Mickey!" she screamed. He put down the box and hugged her fiercely.

"Dad!" Gabe flew off the floor as though jet-propelled and launched himself into his father's arms.

Eyes closed, Mickey held the boy for a long, long time.

Merry Christmas, Holly thought, tears slipping down her face. Just as Emily Miracle had predicted, this was destined to be the best Christmas of Gabe's life.

Baby Arugula Salad with Goat Cheese, Pecans and Pomegranate Seeds

(from Debbie Macomber's Cedar Cove Cookbook)

This salad is a lively blend of sharp arugula, tangy goat cheese, mellow pecans and tart pomegranates. If you can't find arugula, substitute any delicate salad green.

1 small shallot, minced
3 tablespoons balsamic vinegar
1 teaspoon Dijon mustard
Salt and pepper, to taste
1/2 cup extra-virgin olive oil
10 to 12 cups baby arugula (about 10 ounces)
1 cup pomegranate seeds (from one pomegranate)
1/2 cup toasted pecans, chopped
1 cup crumbled goat cheese

1. In a measuring cup, whisk shallot, vinegar, mustard, salt and pepper until combined. Slowly pour oil in a stream until blended.

2. In a large serving bowl, combine arugula, pomegranate seeds and pecans. Add dressing; toss to coat. Top salad with cheese; toss once.

TIP: Extra-virgin olive oil, which comes from the first cold pressing of the olives, has a stronger, purer flavor than virgin olive oil. Since it is more expensive, most cooks prefer to use it only for salad and other uncooked dishes. Virgin olive oil is better for sautéing.

Serves 8.

Nineteen

Searching for a new look? Have your faith lifted!
                                        —Mrs. Miracle

Mickey stepped into the apartment, still holding Gabe, and extended his hand to Jake. "You must be Jake Finley."

"And you must be Holly's brother, Mickey."

"I am."

"What's in there?" Gabe asked, looking over his father's shoulder at the large box resting on the other side of the open door.

"That's a little something Santa asked me to deliver," Mickey told his son. Gabe squirmed out of his arms and raced back into the hallway. He stared at Holly and his grin seemed to take up his whole face. "I think I know what it is," he declared before pushing the box inside. "Aunt Holly told me Santa sometimes makes deliveries late."

No one needed to encourage him to unwrap the gift this time. He tore into the wrapping paper, which flew in all directions. As soon as he saw the picture of Intellytron on the outside of the box, Gabe gave a shout of exhilaration.

"It's my robot! It's my robot!"

"Wherever did you find one?" J.R. asked Mickey. The older man stepped forward and extended his hand. "J. R. Finley," he said.

"He bought it at Finley's," Jake answered in a confused tone.

"Our department store?" J.R. sounded incredulous. "When?"

"My guess is that it was late on Christmas Eve." Again, Jake supplied the answer.

"And how do you know all this?" Holly had a few questions of her own.

"Because that's the gift wrap Mrs. Miracle used."

"But…who sold it to him?" J.R. appeared completely befuddled by this latest development.

"Mrs. Miracle," Jake and Holly murmured simultaneously.

"He's right," Mickey said as he sat on the couch next to his son, who remained on the floor. "I remember her name badge. Mrs. Miracle. We talked for a few minutes."

Thankfully, Gabe was too involved with his robot to listen.

"I had a chance to go into the city yesterday," Mickey told them.

"Wait." Holly held up her hand. "You've got some splainin' to do, Lieutenant Larson. Why are you in New York in the first place?"

Mickey laughed. "Don't tell me you don't want me here?"

"No, no, of course I do! But you might've said something."

"I couldn't."

"Security reasons?" Holly asked.

"No, just that I wasn't sure I'd get the leave I was hoping for. I've been sent back for specialized training—I'll be at Fort Dix for the next six weeks. I didn't want to say anything to Gabe yet, in case it fell through. I could tell from his emails that he was starting to adjust to life here with you. It would've been cruel to raise his hopes, only to have Uncle Sam dash them. Turns out I was on duty until nine this morning…so here I am. I thought I'd bring Gabe his Christmas surprise."

"You might've mentioned it to *me,*" Holly said with more than a little consternation.

"True, but I had to take your poor track record with keeping secrets into consideration."

"I can keep a secret," she insisted.

"Oh, yeah? What about the time you told Candi Johnson I had a crush on her?"

"I was twelve years old!"

Jake chuckled and she sent him a stern look. If Mickey had asked her not to say anything about his possible visit, she wouldn't have uttered a word. Then it occurred to her that he'd hinted at it when he referred to the surprise he was sending Gabe. Fantastic, stupendous, *exhilarating* though this was, a Christmas visit was the last thing she'd expected.

"But why buy the robot?" Holly asked. "I told you I'd get it for Gabe."

"Yes, but you were going without lunches—"

"True," she interrupted, whispering so Gabe

wouldn't hear. "Then Lindy Lee had a change of heart and decided to give me a Christmas bonus, after all."

Mickey shrugged. "You didn't say anything to me. Not that it matters because *I* wanted to get this for Gabe."

"I didn't tell you I received my bonus?"

"You've done enough for the two of us," Mickey told her, his eyes warm with appreciation. "I didn't want to burden you with the added expense of Christmas."

"Hey, Holly, that means Finley's owes you two hundred and fifty dollars," Jake said. "Plus tax. By the way, Mickey, did you tell Mrs. Miracle who you were?" he asked, approaching the two of them. He slipped his arm around Holly's waist and she casually leaned against him.

Mickey shook his head. "Should I have?"

Jake and Holly exchanged a glance, but it was Jake who voiced their question. "How did she know?"

"Know what?" Mickey asked.

"That it was you," Holly said.

"Look, Dad!" Gabe cried out.

Mickey turned his attention to the robot, who walked smartly toward him, stopped and asked in a tinny voice, "When…do…you…go…back…to…Afghanistan?"

Mickey's eyes widened. "How'd you make him say that?"

J.R., who'd been working with Gabe, grinned at Mickey. "I programmed him," Gabe announced proudly. "Mr. Finley helped, but he said I can do it on my own now that I know how."

"You managed to get the robot to do that already?"

"He does all kinds of cool tricks, Dad. Watch."

While Mickey and Gabe were engaged in programming the robot, Jake and Holly stepped into the kitchen.

"She *couldn't* have known Mickey was Gabe's father." Jake's face was clouded with doubt. "Could she?"

Holly didn't have an answer.

Jake continued, still frowning. "I tried to reach her, but the phone number she listed with HR wasn't in service."

"Then ask her when you see her again," Holly said. Jake had mentioned that, as seasonal help, Emily Miracle would be working until after inventory had been completed in January.

"I won't be able to," Jake told her. "When I went to HR for her personal information, I discovered that she'd handed in her notice. Christmas Eve was her last day."

"But…" Holly wanted to argue. Surely Mrs. Miracle would've said *something* at dinner the night before. Things didn't quite add up…. And yet, this wonderful woman had done so much to brighten their Christmas.

Before she could comment, the doorbell rang again. Holly chuckled, not even daring to guess who it might be *this* time. Her apartment was turning into Grand Central Station. If she had to guess, the last person to cross her mind would've been…

"Lindy!" Her employer's name shot out of Holly's mouth the second she opened the door.

Lindy Lee smiled hesitantly. "I hope I'm not intruding."

"You came, you came." Gabe bounded up from the floor and raced to Lindy Lee's side, taking her hand.

Lindy gave Holly an apologetic look. "Gabe invited me and since I, uh, didn't have any commitments, I thought I'd stop by for a few minutes and wish you all a merry Christmas." She glanced about the room. "I see you already have a houseful."

"I'm Gabe's father," Mickey said, stepping forward. "Holly's brother." He set his hands on Gabe's shoulders.

"She's the lady I wrote you about," Gabe said, twisting around and looking up at his father. "Isn't she pretty?"

"Yes, she is…." Mickey seemed unable to take his eyes off Lindy Lee.

Holly wouldn't have believed it possible, but Lindy actually blushed.

"Thank you," the designer murmured.

"Make yourself at home," Holly said. "I was just about to serve some eggnog. Would you like a glass?"

"Are you sure it won't be any bother?"

"She's sure," Gabe said, dragging Lindy Lee toward the couch. "Here, sit next to my dad." He patted an empty space on the sofa. "Dad, you sit here."

Mickey smiled at Lindy Lee. "I guess we've got our orders."

"Yes, sir," Lindy joked, winking at Gabe.

"You know what she said to me, Dad?"

"What?"

"I said," Lindy Lee supplied, "that I need a little boy in my life. A little boy just like Gabe."

Holly wondered if she'd heard correctly. This woman who looked identical to her employer sounded nothing like the Lindy Lee she knew. Gone was the dictatorial, demanding tyrant who ran her fashion-design business with military precision. She'd either been taken over by aliens or Lindy Lee had a gentle side that she kept hidden and revealed only on rare occasions. Like Christmas…

An hour later, during a private moment in the kitchen, Jake gave Holly a gift—a cameo that had once belonged to his mother. He said J.R. had given it to him for this very purpose the night before. Holly was thrilled, honored, humbled. She held her breath as he put the cameo on its gold chain around her neck. Holly didn't have anything for him, but Jake said all he wanted was a kiss, and she was happy to comply.

Two hours after that, the small group gathered around the table laden with Christmas fare, including several bottles of exceptional wine brought by Jake and his father. Gabe sat between Mickey and Lindy Lee and chatted nonstop, while J.R. and Jake sat with Holly between them. They took turns saying grace, then took turns again, passing serving dishes to one another.

Amid the clinking of silverware on china and the animated conversation and laughter, Gabe's voice suddenly rose.

"Mrs. Miracle was right," he declared after his first bite of turkey. "This is the *best* Christmas ever."

Emily Merkle reached for her suitcase and started down the long road. Her job in New York was finished, and it had gone even better than she'd expected. Holly and Jake were falling in love. J.R. had more interest in anticipating the future than reliving the pain of the past. Mickey had met Lindy Lee, and Gabe had settled in nicely with his aunt Holly.

Emily hadn't walked far when she was joined by two others, a beautiful woman and a ten-year-old girl. Kaitlyn skipped gracefully at her mother's side, holding Helene's hand.

"All is well," Emily told the other woman. "J.R. and

Jake will celebrate Christmas from now on. It was a big leap for J.R., but once the grandchildren arrive, he will lavish them with love."

"Jake will marry Holly?" she asked.

Emily nodded. "They'll have many years together."

"You chose well for my son."

Emily nodded in agreement. Jake and Holly were a good match and they'd bring out the best in each other.

The other woman smiled contentedly. "Thank you," she whispered.

"It was my pleasure," Emily told her.

And it truly was.

* * * * *

THE CHRISTMAS BASKET

To Laurie and Jaxon Macomber
And in memory of our son Dale

NOELLE McDOWELL'S JOURNAL

December 1

I did it. I broke down and actually booked the flight to Rose. I have a ticket for December 18—Dallas to San Francisco to Portland and then the commuter flight to Rose.

All my excuses are used up. I always figured there was no going back, and yet that's exactly what I'm doing. I'm going home when I swore I never would. Not after what happened... Not after Thom Sutton betrayed me. I know, I know, I've always been dramatic. I can't help that—it's part of my nature.

When I was a teenager I made this vow never to return. I spoke it in the heat of passion, and no one believed me. For that matter, I didn't believe me, not really. But it proved to be so easy to stay away.... I hardly had to invent excuses. While I was in college I had an opportunity to travel to Europe two years in a row. Then in my junior year I had a summer job and was a bridesmaid in a Christmas wedding. And when my senior year rolled around, I was working as an intern for the software company, and it was impossible to get time off. After that...well, it was just simpler to stay away. Without meaning to, my family made it convenient.

I didn't need to visit them; they seemed willing enough to come to Dallas.

All of that is about to end. I'm prepared to face my past. I joined Weight Watchers. If I happen to see Thom Sutton, I want him to know exactly what he's missing. I've already lost five of the ten pounds I need to get rid of, and by next week he'll hardly recognize me—if we even run into each other. We won't, of course, but just on the off chance, I plan to be prepared.

Good ol' Thom Sutton. I wonder what he's doing now. Naturally I could ask, but no one dares mention the name Sutton to my family. It's the Hatfields and McCoys or the Montagues and Capulets all over again. Except that it's our mothers who started this ridiculous feud.

If I really wanted to know about Thom, I could ask Megan or Stephanie. They're the only two girls out of my entire high school class who still live in Rose. But I wouldn't do that. Inquiring about Thom would only invite questions from them about what happened between the two of us. As far as I'm concerned, the fewer people who know, the better.

He's bound to be married, anyway. Good. I want him to be happy.

No, I don't.

If I can't be honest in my journal, then I shouldn't keep one. Okay, I admit it—what I really want is for him to have suffered guilt and regret all these years. He should have pined for me. His life should be a bleak series of endless days filled with haunting memories of me. It's what he deserves.

On a brighter note, I'm thrilled for Kristen. I'll return home, help her plan her wedding, hold my head high and pray that Thom Sutton has the opportunity to see me from afar, gorgeous and thin. Then I want him to agonize over all the might-have-beens.

One

It would be the wedding of the year. No—the wedding of the century.

Sarah McDowell intended to create the most exquisite event possible, a wedding worthy of *Vogue* magazine (or at least a two-page spread in the Rose, Oregon, *Gazette*). The entire town would talk about her daughter's wedding.

The foundation for Sarah's plans rested squarely on booking the Women's Century Club for the reception. It was why she'd maintained her association with the club after *that* woman had been granted membership. She was outraged that such a fine institution would lower itself to welcome the likes of Mary Sutton.

Sarah refused to dwell on the sordid details. She couldn't allow herself to get upset over something that had happened almost twenty years ago. Although it didn't hurt any to imagine Mary hearing—second- or third-hand, of course—about Kristen's wedding. As Sarah understood it, Mary's daughter had eloped. Eloped, mind you, with some riffraff hazelnut farmer. Sarah didn't know that for sure because it was her

Christian duty not to gossip or think ill of others. However, sometimes information just happened to come one's way….

Pulling into the parking lot of the Women's Century Club, Sarah surveyed the grounds. Even this late in the year, the rose garden was breathtaking. Many of the carefully tended bushes still wore their blooms, and next June, when the wedding was scheduled, the garden would be stunning. The antique roses with their intoxicating scents and the more recent hybrids with their gorgeous shapes and colors would make a fitting backdrop for the beautiful bride and her handsome groom. It would be *perfect,* she thought with satisfaction. Absolutely perfect.

Sarah had stopped attending the Women's Century Club meetings three years ago. Well, there wasn't any need to obsess over the membership committee's sorry lapse in judgment. For many years Sarah had chaired that committee herself. The instant she stepped down, Mary Sutton had applied for membership to the prestigious club—and received it. Now the only social event Sarah participated in was the annual Christmas Dance. Mary Sutton had robbed her of so much already, but Sarah wasn't letting her ruin that, too.

Sarah did continue to meet with other friends from the club and managed to keep up with the news. She understood that Mary had become quite active in the association. Fine. Good for her. It gave the woman something to write about in her column for the weekly *Rose Gazette.* Not that Sarah read "About Town." Someone had told her it was fairly popular, though. Which didn't bother her in the least. Mary was a good writer; Sarah would acknowledge that much. But then, what one lacked in certain areas was often compensated in others. And Mary was definitely lacking in the areas of generosity, fairness, ethics…. She could go on.

With a click of her key chain, Sarah locked her car and headed toward the large, two-story stone structure. There was a cold wind blowing in from the ocean, and she hurried up the steps of the large veranda that surrounded the house. A blast of warm air greeted her as she walked inside. Immediately in front of her was the curved stairway leading to the ballroom on the second floor. She could already picture Kristen moving elegantly down those stairs, her dress sweeping grandly behind her. Today, evergreen garlands were hung along the mahogany railing, with huge red velvet bows tied at regular intervals. Gigantic potted poinsettias lined both sides of the stairway. The effect was both festive and tasteful.

"Oh, how lovely," she said to Melody Darrington, the club's longtime secretary.

"Yes, we're very pleased with this year's Christmas decorations." Melody glanced up from her desk behind the half wall that overlooked the entry. The door to the office was open and Sarah heard the fax machine humming behind her. "Are you here to pick up your tickets for the Christmas dance?"

"I am," Sarah confirmed. "And I'd like to book the club for June seventh for a reception." She paused dramatically. "Kristen's getting married."

"Sarah, that's just wonderful!"

"Yes, Jake and I are pleased." This seriously understated her emotions. Kristen was the first of her three daughters to marry, and Sarah felt as if the wedding was the culmination of all her years as a caring, involved mother. She highly approved of Kristen's fiancé. Jonathan Clark was not only a charming and considerate young man, he held a promising position at an investment firm and had a degree in business. His parents were college professors who lived in Eugene; he was their only son. Whenever she'd spoken with Jonathan's mother, Louise Clark had sounded equally delighted.

Melody flipped the pages of the appointment book to June. "It's a good idea to book the club early."

Holding her breath, Sarah leaned over the half wall and stared down at the schedule. She relaxed the instant she saw that particular Saturday was free. The wedding date could remain unchanged.

"It looks like June seventh is open," Melody said.

"Fabulous." Sarah's cell phone rang, and she reached inside her purse to retrieve it. She sold real estate, but since entering her fifties, she'd scaled back her hours on the job. Jake, who was head of the X-ray department at Rose Hospital, enjoyed traveling. Sarah no longer had the energy to accompany Jake and also maintain her status as a top-selling agent. The number displayed on her phone was that of her husband's office. She'd call him back shortly. He was probably asking about the time of their eldest daughter's flight. Jake and Sarah were going to meet Noelle at the small commuter airport later in the day. What a joy it would be to have all three of their girls home for Christmas, not to mention Noelle's birthday, which was December twenty-fifth. This would be the first time in ten years that Noelle had returned to celebrate *anything* with her family. Sarah blamed Mary Sutton and her son for that, too.

"Should I give you a deposit now?" she asked, removing her checkbook.

"Since you're a member of the club, that won't be necessary."

"Great. Then that's settled and I can get busy with my day. I've got a couple of houses to show. Plus Jake and I are driving to the airport this afternoon to pick up Noelle. You remember our daughter Noelle, don't you?"

"Of course."

"She's living in Dallas these days, and has a high-powered job with one of the big computer companies." What Sarah didn't add was the Noelle had become a workaholic. Getting her twenty-eight-year-old daughter to take time off work was nearly impossible. Sarah and Jake made a point of visiting her once a year and sometimes twice, but this couldn't go on. Noelle had to get over her phobia about returning to Rose—and the risk of seeing Thom Sutton. Oh, yes, those Suttons had done a lot of damage to the McDowells.

With Kristen announcing her engagement and inviting the Clarks to share their Christmas festivities, Sarah had strongly urged Noelle to come home for the celebration. This was an important year for their family, and it was absolutely necessary that Noelle be there with them. After some back-and-forth discussion, she'd finally capitulated.

"Before you leave, there's something you should know," Melody said hesitantly. "There's been a rule change about members using the building."

"Yes?" Sarah tensed, anticipating a roadblock.

"The new rule states that only members who have completed a minimum of ten hours' community service approved by the club will be permitted to lease our facilities."

"But I'm an active part of our community already,"

Sarah complained. She provided plenty of services to others.

"I realize that. Unfortunately, the service project in question must be determined by the club and it must be completed by the end of December to qualify for the following year."

Sarah gaped at her. "Do you mean to say that in addition to everything else I'm doing in the next two weeks, I have to complete some club project?"

"You haven't been reading the newsletters, have you?" Melody asked, frowning.

Obviously not. Sarah refused to read about Mary Sutton, whose name seemed to appear in every issue these days.

"If you attended the meetings, you'd know it, too." Melody added insult to injury by pointing out Sarah's intentional absence.

Despite her irritation, Sarah managed a weak smile. "All right," she muttered. "What can I do?"

"Actually, you've come at an opportune moment. We need someone who's willing to pitch in on the Christmas baskets."

Sarah was trying to figure out how she could squeeze in one more task before the holidays. "Exactly what would that entail?"

"Oh, it'll be great fun. The ladies pooled the money they raised from the cookbook sale to buy gifts for these baskets. They've made up lists, and what you'd need to do is get everything on your list, arrange all the stuff inside the baskets and then deliver them to the Salvation Army by December twenty-third."

That didn't sound unreasonable. "I think I can do that."

"Wonderful." A smile lit up Melody's face. "The woman who's heading up the project will be grateful for some help."

"The woman?" That sounded better already. At least she wouldn't be stuck doing this alone.

"Mary Sutton."

Sarah felt as though Melody had punched her. "Excuse me. For a moment I thought you said *Mary Sutton*."

"I did."

"I don't mean to be catty here, but Mary and I have… a history."

"I'm sure you'll be able to work something out. You're both adults."

Sarah was stunned by the woman's lack of sensitivity. She wanted to argue, to explain that this was unacceptable, but she couldn't think of exactly what to say.

"You did want the club for June seventh, didn't you?"

"Well, yes, of course, but—"

"Then be here tomorrow morning at ten to meet with Mary."

Numb and speechless, Sarah slowly turned and trudged toward the door.

"Sarah," Melody called. "Don't forget the dance tickets."

Dance. How could she think about the dance when she was being forced to confront a woman who detested her? The feeling might be mutual but that didn't make it any less awkward.

One across. A four-letter word for fragrant flower. Rose, naturally. Noelle McDowell penciled in the answer and moved to the next clue. A prickly feeling crawled up her spine and she raised her head. She disliked the short commuter flights. This one, out of Portland, carried twenty-four passengers. It saved having to rent a vehicle or asking her parents to make the long drive into the big city to pick her up.

The feeling persisted and she glanced over her shoulder. She instantly jerked back and slid down in her seat as far as the constraints of the seat belt allowed. It couldn't be. *No, please,* she muttered, closing her eyes. *Not Thom.* Not after all these years. Not now. But it was, it had to be. No one else would look at her with such complete, unadulterated antagonism. He had some nerve after what he'd done to her.

Long before she was ready, the pilot announced that the plane was preparing to land in Rose. On these flights, no carry-on bags were permitted, and Noelle hadn't taken anything more than her purse on board. Her magazines would normally go in her briefcase, but that didn't fit in the compact space beneath her seat, so the flight attendant had stowed it. She had a *Weight Watchers* magazine and a crossword puzzle book marked *EASY* in large letters across the top. She wasn't going to let Thom see her with either and stuffed them in the outside pocket of her purse, folding one magazine over the other.

Her pulse thundered like crazy. The man who'd broken her heart sat only two rows behind her, looking as sophisticated as if he'd stepped off the pages of *GQ.* He'd always been tall, dark and handsome—like a twenty-first century Cary Grant. Classic features that were just rugged enough to be interesting and very, very masculine. Dark eyes, glossy dark hair. An impeccable sense of style. Surely he was married. But finding out would mean asking her sister or one of her friends who still lived in Rose. Coward that she was, Noelle didn't want to know. Okay, she did, but not if it meant having to ask.

The plane touched down and Noelle braced herself against the jolt of the wheels bouncing on tarmac. As soon as they'd coasted to a stop, the Unfasten Seat Belt sign went off, and the people around her instantly leaped to their feet. Noelle took her time. Her hair was a fright. Up at three that morning to catch the 6:00 a.m. out of Dallas/Ft. Worth, she'd run a brush through the dark tangles, forgoing the usual routine of fussing with mousse. As a result, large ringlets fell like bedsprings about her face. Normally, her hair was shaped and controlled and coerced into gentle waves. But today she had the misfortune of looking like Shirley Temple in one of her 1930s movies—and in front of Thom Sutton, no less.

When it was her turn to leave her seat, she stood, looking staunchly ahead. If luck was with her, she could slip away unnoticed and pretend she hadn't seen him. Luck, however, was on vacation and the instant she stepped into the aisle, the handle of her purse caught on the seat arm. Both magazines popped out of the outside pocket and flew into the air, only to be caught by none other than Thom Sutton. The crossword puzzle magazine tumbled to the floor and he was left holding the *Weight Watchers* December issue. As his gaze slid over her, she immediately sucked in her stomach.

"I read it for the fiction," she announced, then added, "Don't I know you?" She tried to sound indifferent—and to look thin. "It's Tim, isn't it?" she asked, frowning as though she couldn't quite place him.

"Thom," he corrected. "Good to see you again, Nadine."

"Noelle," she said bitterly.

He glared at her until someone from the back of the line called, "Would you two mind having your reunion when you get off the plane?"

"Sorry," Thom said over his shoulder.

"I barely know this man." Noelle wanted her fellow passengers to hear the truth. "I once thought I did, but I was wrong," she explained, walking backward toward the exit.

"Whatever," the guy behind them said loudly.

"You're a fine one to talk," Thom said. His eyes were as dark and cold as those of the snowman they'd built in Lions' Park their senior year of high school—like glittering chips of coal.

"You have your nerve," she muttered, whirling around just in time to avoid crashing into the open cockpit. She smiled sweetly at the pilot. "Thank you for a most pleasant flight."

He returned the smile. "I hope you'll fly with us again."

"I will."

"Good to see you, Thom," the pilot said next.

Placing her hand on the railing of the steep stairs that led to the ground, Noelle did her best to keep her head high, her shoulders square—and her eyes front. The last thing she wanted to do was trip and make an even worse fool of herself by falling flat on her face.

She was shocked by a blast of cold air. After living in Texas for the last ten years, she'd forgotten how cold it could get in the Pacific Northwest. Her thin cashmere wrap was completely inadequate.

"One would think you'd know better than to wear a sweater here in December," Thom said, coming down the steps directly behind her.

"I forgot."

"If you came home more often, you'd have remembered."

"You keep track of my visits?" She scowled at him. A thick strand of curly hair slapped her in the face and she tossed it back with a jerk of her head. Unfortunately she nearly put out her neck in the process.

"No, I don't keep track of your visits. Frankly, I couldn't care less."

"That's fine by me." Having the last word was important, no matter how inane it was.

The luggage cart came around and she grabbed her briefcase from the top and made for the interior of the small airport. Her flight had landed early, which meant that her parents probably hadn't arrived yet. At least her luck was consistent—all bad. One thing was certain: the instant Thom caught sight of her mother and father, he'd make himself scarce.

He removed his own briefcase and started into the terminal less than two feet behind her. Because of his long legs, he quickly outdistanced her. Refusing to let him pass her, Noelle hurried ahead, practically trotting.

"Don't you think you're being a little silly?" he asked.

"About what?" She blinked, hoping to convey a look of innocence.

"Never mind." He smiled, which infuriated her further.

"No, I'm serious," she insisted. "What do you mean?"

He simply shook his head and turned toward the

baggage claim area. They were the first passengers to get there. Noelle stood on one side of the conveyor belt and Thom on the other. He ignored her and she tried to pretend he'd never been born.

That proved to be impossible because ten years ago Thom Sutton had ripped her heart right out.

For most of their senior year of high school, Thom and Noelle had been in love; they'd also managed to hide that fact from their parents. Sneaking out of her room at night, meeting him after school and passing notes to each other had worked quite effectively.

Then they'd argued about their mothers and the ongoing feud between Sarah and Mary. They'd soon made up, however, realizing that what really mattered was their love. Because they were both eighteen and legally entitled to marry without parental consent, they'd decided to elope. It'd been Thom's suggestion. According to him, it was the only way they could get married, since the parents on both sides would oppose their wishes and try to put obstacles in their path. But once they were married, he said, they could bring their families together.

Noelle felt mortified now to remember how much she'd trusted Thom. But their whole "engagement" had turned out to be a ploy to humiliate and embarrass her. It seemed Thom was his mother's son, after all.

She'd been proud of her love for Thom, and before she left to meet him that fateful evening, she'd boldly announced her intentions to her family. Her stomach twisted at the memory. Her parents were shocked as well as appalled; she and Thom had kept their secret well. Her mother had burst into tears, her father had shouted and her two younger sisters had wailed in protest. Undeterred, Noelle had marched out the door, suitcase in hand, to meet the man she loved. The man she'd defied her family to marry. Except that he didn't show up.

At first she'd assumed it was a misunderstanding—that she'd mistaken the agreed-upon time. Then, throwing caution to the wind, she'd phoned his house and asked to speak to him, only to learn that Thom had gone bowling.

He'd gone *bowling?* Apparently some friends from school had phoned and off he'd gone, leaving her to wait in doubt and misery. The parking lot at the bowling alley confirmed his father's words. There was Thom's car—and inside the Bowlerama was Thom, carousing with his friends. Noelle had peered through the window and seen the waitress sitting on his lap and the other guys gathered around, joking and teasing. Before she went home, Noelle had placed a nasty note on his windshield, in which she described him as a scum-of-the-earth bastard. Their supposed elopement, their so-called love had all been a fraud, a cruel joke. She figured it was revenge what for her mother had done, losing Thom's grandmother's precious tea service. Not *losing* it, actually. She'd borrowed it to display at an open house for another real estate agent—and someone had taken it. That was how the feud started and it had escalated steadily after that.

To make matters worse, she'd had to return home in humiliation and admit that Thom had stood her up. Like the heroine of an old-fashioned melodrama, she'd been jilted, abandoned and forsaken.

For days she'd moped around the house, weeping and miserable. Thom hadn't phoned or contacted her again.

It was difficult to believe he could be so heartless, but she had all the evidence she needed. She hadn't seen or talked to him since. For ten years she'd avoided returning to the scene of her shame.

The grinding sound of the conveyor belt gearing up broke Noelle from her reverie. Luggage started to roll out from the black hole behind the rubber curtain. Thom stepped forward, in a hurry to claim his suitcase and leave, or so it seemed. Noelle was no less eager to escape. She'd rather wait in the damp cold outside the terminal than stand five feet across from Thomas Sutton.

The very attractive Thomas Sutton. Even better-looking than he'd been ten years ago. Life just wasn't fair.

"I would've thought your wife would be here to pick you up," she said without looking at him. She shouldn't have spoken at all, but suddenly she had to know.

"Is that your unsubtle way of asking if I'm married?"

She ground her teeth. "Stood up any other girls in the last ten years?" she asked.

His eyes narrowed. "Don't do it, Noelle."

"You're the one who shouldn't have done it."

The man from the back of the plane waltzed past Noelle and reached for his suitcase. "Why don't you two just kiss and make up," he suggested, winking at Thom.

"I don't think so," Noelle said, sending Thom a contemptuous glare. She was astonished to see his anger, as though *he* had something to be angry about. *She* was the injured party here.

"On that I'll agree with you," Thom said. He caught hold of a suitcase and yanked it off the belt with enough force to topple a second suitcase. Without another word, he turned and walked out the door.

No sooner had he disappeared than the glass doors opened and in walked Noelle's parents.

Noelle's youngest sister held a special place in her heart. Carley Sue was an unexpected surprise, born when Noelle was fifteen and Kristen twelve. She'd only been three when Noelle left for college. Nevertheless, all three sisters remained close. Or as close as email, phone calls and the occasional visit to Dallas allowed.

Sitting on Noelle's bed, Carley rested her chin on one hand as Noelle unpacked her suitcase. "You don't mind that I have your old room, do you?" she asked anxiously.

"Heavens, no. It's only right that you do."

Some of the worry disappeared from Carley's eyes. "Are you really going to be home for two whole weeks?"

"I am." Noelle had tentatively planned a discounted cruise with a couple of friends. Instead, she was vacationing with her parents, planning her sister's wedding and trying not to think about Thom Sutton.

"You're going to the Christmas dance, aren't you?"

"Not if I can get out of it." Her mother was the one who insisted on these social outings, but Noelle would live the rest of her life content if she never attended another dance. They reminded her to much of those long-ago evenings with Thom....

"Mom says you're going."

Noelle sat down on the end of the bed and sighed. "I'll tell her I don't have anything to wear."

"Don't do that," Carley advised. "She'll buy you a pink dress. Mom loves pink. Not just any old pink, either, but something that looks exactly like Pepto-Bismol. She actually wanted Kristen to choose pink for her wedding colors." She grimaced. Reaching down for her feet, Carley curled her fingers over her bare toes and nodded vigorously. "You'd better come to the dance."

This was one of the reasons Noelle found excuse after excuse to stay away from Rose. Admittedly it wasn't the primary reason—Thom Sutton and his mother were responsible for that. But as much as she loved her family, she dreaded being dragged from one social event to the next. She could see her mother putting her on display—in Pepto-Bismol pink, according to Carley. If that wasn't bad enough, Sarah had an embarrassing tendency to speak as though Noelle wasn't in the room, bragging outrageously over every little accomplishment.

"Hey, you want to go to the movies tomorrow?" Noelle asked her sister.

Carley's eyes brightened. "Sure! I was hoping we'd get to do things together."

The doorbell chimed and Carley rolled onto her stomach. "That's Kristen. She's coming over without Jonathan tonight."

"You like Jonathan?" Noelle asked.

"Yeah." Carley grinned happily. "He danced with me once and no one asked him to or anything."

This was encouraging. Maybe he'd dance with her, too.

"Noelle!" Kristen called from the far end of the hallway. She burst into the room, full of energy and spirit. Instantly Noelle was wrapped in a tight embrace. "I can't believe you're here—oh sis, it's so good to see you."

Noelle hugged her back. She missed the chats they used to have; discussions over the phone just weren't the same as hugs and smiles. "Guess who I ran into on the plane?" Noelle had been dying to talk about the chance encounter with Thom.

Some of the excitement faded from Kristen's eyes. "Don't tell me. Thom Sutton?"

Noelle nodded.

"Who's Thom Sutton?" Carley asked, glancing from one sister to the other.

"A guy I once dated."

"Were you lovers?"

"Carley!"

"Just curious." She shrugged as if this was information she was somehow entitled to.

"Where?" Kristen demanded.

"He was on the same flight as me."

"He still lives here, you know. He's some kind of executive for a mail-order company that's really taken off in the last few years. Apparently he does a lot of traveling."

"How'd you know that?" They'd always avoided the topic of Thom Sutton in their telephone and email communications.

"Jon told me about him. I think Thom might be one of his clients."

"Oh." Not only was Thom Sutton gorgeous, he was successful, too. "I suppose he's engaged to someone stunningly beautiful." That was to be expected.

"I hear—again from Jon—that he dates quite a bit, but there's no one serious."

Noelle shouldn't be pleased, but she couldn't help it. She didn't want to examine that reaction too closely.

"I want to know what happened," Carley demanded, rising to her knees. "I'm not a kid anymore. Tell me!"

"He was Noelle's high school sweetheart," Kirsten explained.

"The guy who left you at the altar?"

"Who told you that?" Noelle asked, although the answer was obvious. "And he didn't leave me at the altar." *Just being accurate,* she told herself. *I'm not defending him.*

"Mom told me 'cause she wants me to keep away from those Suttons. When I asked her why, she said you learned your lesson the hard way. She said a Sutton broke your heart and jilted you."

"There's more to it than that," Kristen told her.

"I want to know *everything,*" Carley pleaded. "How can I hate them if I don't know what they did that was so awful?"

"You shouldn't hate anyone."

"I don't, not really, but if our family doesn't like their family, then I should know why."

"It's a long story."

Carley sat back on her heels. "That's what Mom said."

"God help me," Kristen murmured, covering her eyes with one hand. "Don't tell me I already sound like Mom. I didn't think this would happen until I turned thirty."

Noelle laughed, although she wasn't sure how funny it was, since she herself was only days from her twenty-ninth birthday.

"Did you love him terribly?" Carley asked with a faraway look in her eyes.

Noelle wasn't sure how to respond. She felt a distant and remembered pain but refused to let it take hold. "I thought I did."

"It was wildly romantic," Kristen added. "They were madly in love, but then they had a falling-out—"

"That's one way to put it," Noelle said, interrupting her sister. Thom had apparently fallen out of love with her. He'd certainly fallen out of their plans to elope.

"This is all so sad," Carley said with an exaggerated sigh.

"Our parents not getting along is what started this in the first place."

"At least you and Thom didn't kill yourselves, like Romeo and Juliet—"

"No." Noelle shook her head. "I've always been the sane, sensible sister. Remember?" But even as she spoke, she recognized her words for the lie they were. Staying away for ten years was a pretty extreme and hardly "sensible" reaction. Even she knew that. The fact was, though, something that had begun as a protest had simply become habit.

"Oh, sure," Kristen teased. "Very sensible. You work too hard, you don't date nearly enough and you avoid Rose as though we've got an epidemic of the plague."

"Guilty, guilty, not guilty." She wasn't *purposely* avoiding Rose, she told herself, at least not anymore and not to the extent that Kristen implied. Noelle's job was demanding and it was difficult to take off four or five days in a row.

"I've never met Thom, and already I don't like him," Carley announced. "Anyone who broke your heart is a dweeb. Besides, if he married you the way he said he would, you'd be living in Rose now and I could see you anytime I wanted."

"Well put, little sister," Kristen said. She shrugged off her coat, then joined Carley at the foot of the bed.

Noelle smiled at her two sisters and realized with a pang how much she missed them. Back in Texas it was all too easy to let work consume her life—to relegate these important relationships to fifteen-minute conversations on the phone.

"Look," Kristen said and stretched out her arm so Noelle could see her engagement ring. It was a solitaire diamond, virtually flawless, in a classic setting. A perfect choice for Kristen. "Jon and I shopped for weeks. He wanted the highest-quality stone for the best price." Her eyes softened as she studied the ring.

"It's beautiful," Noelle whispered, overcome for a moment by the sheer joy she saw in her sister's face.

"You'll be my maid of honor, won't you?"

"As long as I don't have to wear a dress the color of Pepto-Bismol."

"You're safe on that account."

"If you ask me to be the flower girl, I think I'll scream," Carley muttered. "Why won't anyone believe me when I tell them I'm not a little kid anymore? I'm almost fourteen!"

"Not for ten months," Noelle reminded her.

"But, I'm *going* to be fourteen."

Kristen brushed the hair away from Carley's face. "Actually, I intended to ask you to be a bridesmaid."

"You did?" Carley shrieked with happiness. "Well, then, I'll tell you what I overheard Mom tell Dad." Her voice dropped to a whisper as she detailed a conversation between their parents regarding Christmas baskets.

"Mom's meeting with *Mrs. Sutton* tomorrow morning?" Noelle repeated incredulously.

"That's what she said. She didn't sound happy about it, either."

"I'll just bet she didn't."

"This should be interesting," Kristen murmured.

Yes, it should, Noelle silently agreed. *It should be very interesting, indeed.*

NOELLE McDOWELL'S JOURNAL

December 19
(2:00 a.m.)

So I saw him before I even got back to town. Of all the flights I could've taken...

Seeing Thom after all these years was probably the most humbling experience of my life, except for the last time I was with him. Correction. Wasn't with him. Why did this have to happen to me? Or did I bring it on myself because of my obsession over seeing him again?

Okay, the thing to do is look at the positive aspect of this. It's over. I saw him, it was worse than I could have imagined, but now I don't need to worry about it anymore. Thom made it clear that he wasn't any happier to see me than I was about running into him. At least the feeling's mutual. Although I'm kind of confused by that, since I'm the offended one. He jilted me. Unfortunately, after this latest run-in, he doesn't have any reason to regret that. I behaved like an idiot.

On a brighter note—and I'm always looking for brighter notes!—it's good to be home. I shouldn't have stayed away for ten years. That was foolish and I'm sorry about it. I walked all through the house, stopping in each room. After a while, I got all teary as I looked around. Nothing's really changed and yet everything's different. I didn't realize how much I've missed my home. Mom's got the house all decorated for Christmas, including those funny-looking cotton-ball snowmen I made at camp a thousand years ago. When I commented on that, she told me it was tradition. She puts them out every Christmas. She got all choked up and I did, too. We hugged, and I promised I'd never stay away this long again. And I won't.

Carley Sue (she hates it when I use her middle name) is so much fun. Seeing her here, in her own space (even if it is my old room), is like discovering an entirely different side of her. She's freer, more relaxed, and so eager to share the camaraderie between me and Kristen.

Speaking of Kristen—she's on cloud nine. We sat up and talked for hours, and she told me all about meeting and falling in love with Jonathan. I'd heard it before, but the story felt brand-new as I listened to her tell it in person. It's so romantic, meeting her future husband in a flower shop when he's there to pick up a dozen red roses for another woman. I give him credit, though; Jonathan knew a real flower when he saw one. It was Kristen who walked out with those roses.

Carley warned me that Mom's going to be looking for company when she has to meet Mrs. Sutton in the morning. We've already thwarted her. We sisters have our ways....

Two

Sarah would have preferred a root canal to meeting with Mary Sutton. A root canal without anaesthetic.

Her husband lingered over his morning coffee before leaving for the hospital. "You're really stressed about this, aren't you?"

"Yes!" Sarah wasn't afraid to admit it. "The last time I spoke to Mary was the day she wrote that dreadful article about me in her column."

"You think that article was only about you," Jake said. "But it could've been about any real estate agent. Maybe even a bunch of different ones." His voice drifted off.

Sarah didn't understand why her husband was arguing when they both knew the entire dreadful piece titled *The Nightmare Real Estate Agent,* was directed solely at *her.* Although she hadn't committed any of sins Mary had described, she'd been guilty of the one crime Mary hadn't mentioned. Never once had she misrepresented a home or hidden a defect. Nor had she ever low-balled a client. But Sarah had borrowed something she couldn't return.

"Was that *before* or *after* you planted the *OPEN HOUSE* sign in her front yard?" Jake asked.

"Before, and she deserved it."

Her husband chuckled. "Go on, meet with her and don't for a moment let her know you're upset."

"You sound like a commercial for deodorant."

"Yes, dear." He kissed her cheek and headed out the door to work.

Tightening the belt of her housecoat, Sarah gazed out the front window as he drove away. *Meet with her...* Easy for him to say. He wasn't the one coming face-to-face with Mary after all these years.

Yawning, Noelle wandered into the kitchen and poured a cup of coffee. Sarah's spirits lifted immediately. It was so good to have her daughter home—and even better that she'd arrived at such an opportune moment. Noelle could act as a buffer between her and that demented newspaper writer who'd once been her friend. True, there was the business with the Sutton boy, but if nothing else, that unfortunate bit of history would distract them all from this current awkwardness. She felt a twinge of guilt at the idea of involving her daughter. Still, she needed reinforcements, and surely Noelle was long over her infatuation with Thom.

"Good morning, dear," Sarah said, mustering a cheerful greeting. "I was wondering if you'd like to come with me this morning." Try as she might, she couldn't keep the plea out of her voice.

Her daughter leaned against the kitchen counter, holding the mug with both hands. "I promised to take Carley shopping and to the movies."

"Oh. That won't be until later, will it?"

"Mom," Noelle said, sighing loudly. "I'm *not* going to let you use me as a buffer when you meet Mrs. Sutton."

"Who told you I was meeting…" She didn't bother to finish the question, since the answer was obvious. Jake! Dumping the rest of her coffee down the sink, she reluctantly went to her room to dress. She'd be entering the lion's den alone, so she wanted to look her best.

"I don't think she's nearly the monster you make her out to be," Noelle called after her

That her own daughter, her oldest child—the very one who'd been jilted by Thom Sutton—could say such a thing was beyond Sarah. As far as she was concerned, there was too much forgiveness going on here. And if Noelle thought Mary was so wonderful, then she should be willing to come along.

Didn't Noelle grasp the unpleasantness of this situation? Clearly not. Even Jake didn't take it seriously. He seemed to think this was some kind of joke! Well, she, for one, wasn't laughing.

Despite her bad feelings about the meeting with Mary Sutton, Sarah arrived at the Women's Century Club twenty minutes early. This was the way she'd planned it. As she recalled, Mary possessed a number of irritating habits, one of which was an inability to ever show up on time. Therefore, Sarah considered it advantageous to be early, as though that would highlight Mary's lack of responsibility and basic courtesy.

"Good morning, Melody," she said as she stepped briskly into the entry.

"Morning," came Melody's reply. The phone rang just then, and she reached for it, still standing in front of the copy machine.

While she waited, Sarah checked her appearance in

the lobby restroom. She'd taken an inordinate amount of time with her makeup that morning. Her hair was impeccably styled, if she did say so herself, and her clothes looked both businesslike and feminine. Choosing the right outfit was of the utmost importance; in the end, after three complete changes, she'd chosen navy-blue wool slacks, a white cashmere sweater and a silk scarf with a pattern of holly and red berries.

Melody finished with the phone. "Sorry, it's crazy around here this morning. Everyone's getting ready for the dance."

Of course. In her dread, she'd nearly forgotten about the annual dance.

The door opened, and with a dramatic flair—all swirling scarves and large gestures—Mary Sutton entered the building. Did the woman think she was on stage, for heaven's sake? "Hello Melody," she said, her voice light and breezy. Then—as if she'd only now noticed Sarah—she turned in her direction, frowned slightly and then acknowledged her with a curt nod.

"Good to see you, too," Sarah muttered.

"I'm here for the list. The Christmas basket list," Mary said, walking over to the half wall behind which Melody stood.

"That's why I'm here," Sarah said and forced herself into the space between Mary and the wall.

The two jockeyed for position, elbowing each other until Melody stared at them aghast. "What's *wrong* with you two?" she asked.

"As I explained earlier, we have a *history,*" Sarah said, as though that should account for everything.

"A very long and *difficult* history," Mary added.

"You'll have to work together on this." Melody

frowned at them both. "I'd hate to see these needy families deprived because you two can't get along." The phone rang again and Melody scooped up the receiver.

"You're impossible to work with," Mary said, practically shoving Sarah aside.

"I won't stand here and be insulted by the likes of you," Sarah insisted. Talk about impossible!

"This isn't going to work."

"You're telling me!" She was ready to walk out the door. But then she realized that was exactly what Mary wanted her to do. She'd been provoking Sarah from the moment she'd made that stagy entrance. This was a low, underhanded attempt to prevent her from holding Kristen's wedding reception at the club. Somehow Mary had found out about the wedding and hoped to thwart the McDowells' plans. That had to be it. But Sarah refused to let a Sutton—especially *this* Sutton—manipulate her.

"There are ways of doing what needs to be done without tripping over each other's feet," Sarah murmured, trying to sound conciliatory. She could only hope that Kristen truly appreciated the sacrifice she was making on her behalf. If it wasn't for the wedding, she wouldn't be caught dead working on a project with Mary Sutton, charity or not!

"What do you mean?"

"There *must* be a way." She personally didn't have any ideas, but perhaps the club secretary could think of something. "Melody?"

Another line rang, and Melody put the first caller on hold in order to answer the second. She placed her palm over the mouthpiece and said, "Why don't you two go talk this out in the lobby?" She waved them impatiently away. "I'll be with you as soon as I can."

Sarah took a few steps back, unwilling to voluntarily give up hard-won territory. This was more of a problem than she'd expected. For her part, she was willing to make the best of it, but she could already tell that Mary had her own agenda.

"The Christmas decorations are lovely this year, aren't they?" Sarah said, making an effort to start again. After all, she was stuck with the woman.

"Yes," came Mary's stilted reply. "I'm the chair of the decorating committee."

"Oh." She studied the staircase again and noticed a number of flaws apparent on closer inspection. Walking to the bottom step, she straightened a bow.

"Leave my bows alone!"

"A little possessive, are we?" Sarah murmured.

"You would be, too, if you'd spent twenty minutes making each of those velvet bows."

"I could have done it in ten."

"Next year, I'll let you." Then, as if she was bored with the subject, Mary said, "I understand Noelle's in town."

"Yes, and I'd appreciate if you'd keep your son away from her."

"My son!" Mary cried. "You don't need to worry about *that*. Thom learned his lesson as far as your daughter's concerned a long time ago."

"On the contrary, I believe your son broke my daughter's heart."

"Ladies!" Melody came out from behind the counter, shaking her head. "I thought we were discussing ways you two can work together to fill those Christmas baskets."

"I don't think I *can* work with her," Mary said, crossing her arms. She presented Sarah with a view of her back.

"Then divide the list," Melody suggested. "One of

you can shop for the gifts and the other can buy the groceries. Arrange a day to meet and assemble the baskets, and then you'll be done with it."

Sarah didn't know why she hadn't thought of that earlier. It made perfect sense and would allow them to maintain a healthy distance from each other.

"Divide the list," Mary instructed with a dramatic wave of her hand.

"By all means, divide the list," Sarah said and mimicked Mary's gesture.

"All right," Melody said. She went back to her office, with the two women following, and slipped the list into the photocopier. The phone rang again, and she answered it, holding the receiver between her shoulder and ear. Melody retrieved the original and the copy, reached for the scissors and cut both lists in two. Still talking, she dropped the papers, then picked them up and handed half of the original list to Mary and half to Sarah. The copies of each woman's list went into a file on her desk.

Sarah glanced over her list and tucked it inside her purse. "When do you suggest we meet to assemble the baskets?"

"The twenty-third before noon. That way, we'll be able to drop them off at the Salvation Army in plenty of time. They'll distribute the baskets on Christmas Eve."

"Fine." That settled, Sarah charged out the door without a backward glance. This wasn't the best solution, but it was manageable. She'd do her share of the work, and she wasn't about to let anyone suggest otherwise.

"This is so cool," Carley said as they left the mall late Thursday afternoon, their arms loaded with bags and packages. Noelle smiled fondly at her youngest sister. That summer, Carley had spent two weeks with her in Texas while their parents were on a cruise. She'd matured noticeably in the six months since then.

"Mom's not selling much real estate anymore," her sister told her as they climbed into the car. "I think she's bored with it, but she won't admit it."

"Really?"

"She's totally involved in Kristen's wedding. It's all she thinks about. She's read a whole bunch of books and magazine articles and has everything set in her mind. Just the other day, she said that what this town really needs is a wedding planner."

"And you think Mom would enjoy that?"

"Are you kidding?" Carley said. "She'd *love* it."

Their mother was extremely sociable, which was one of the reasons she was such a successful real estate agent, Noelle mused. Sarah knew nearly everyone in town and had wonderful connections. Perhaps Carley was right.

"The Admiral really hasn't changed," Noelle murmured. She'd spent a lot of time at the old downtown theater, back in high school. It was there, in the balcony, that Thom had first kissed her. To this day—as much as she wanted to forget it—she remembered the thrill of that kiss.

The Admiral was a classic theater built sixty years earlier. The screen was huge and the second-floor balcony held the plush loge seats—always Noelle's favorite place to sit.

They purchased the tickets, a large bucket of popcorn and drinks.

"Do you want to go up to the balcony?" Carley asked.

"Where else would we sit?" Noelle was already half-way up the winding staircase that led to the second floor. She went straight to the front row and plopped down on a cushioned seat. Carley plopped down beside her. The main feature was a Christmas release, an animated film starring the voices of Billy Crystal and Nathan Lane.

"I'm not a kid anymore, but I'm glad you wanted to see this movie, too," her sister confided.

Noelle placed the bucket of popcorn between them. "Thanks for giving me the excuse." She leaned forward and looked at the audience below. The theater was only half-full and she wondered if she'd recognize anyone.

"Oh, my goodness," she whispered. This couldn't be happening! Thom Sutton sat almost directly below her. If that wasn't bad enough, a blonde sat in the seat beside him and—to Noelle's disgust—had her hands all over him.

"What?" Carley demanded.

"It's Thom." Heaven help her, Noelle couldn't keep from watching. The blonde's hand lingered at the base of his neck; she was stroking his hair with all the tenderness of a longtime lover.

"Not Thom Sutton? The son of the enemy?" Carley asked.

Noelle nodded. Sad and shocking though it was, he obviously still had the power to hurt her. No, not hurt her—infuriate her!

Carley reached for a kernel of popcorn and tossed it down.

Noelle gasped, grabbing her sister's hand. The last thing she wanted was to call attention to the balcony. "Don't do that!"

"Why not? He jilted you and now he's here with

another woman." She hurled another kernel in his direction.

Noelle glanced down and saw the blonde nibbling on his earlobe. That did it. She scooped out a handful of popcorn and threw it over the balcony railing. Noelle and her sister leaned back and smothered their giggles. A few minutes later, unable to resist, Noelle looked down again.

"Oh, no," Carley muttered under her breath as she sent a fresh shower of popcorn over the edge. She jerked back instantly.

"What?" Noelle asked.

"I think we're in trouble. He just turned around and looked up here and I don't think he's pleased."

Fine, the management could throw her out of the theater if he complained. Noelle didn't care.

"I want to know about you and him," Carley said. "I wasn't even born when his mom and our mom had their big fight."

Noelle was reluctant to describe all this old history, but she supposed her sister had a right to know. "Well, Mom had just started selling real estate and was making new friends. She claims Mary was jealous of those friends, especially one whose name was Cheryl. Cheryl had been working at the agency for a while and was kind of showing Mom the ropes. She was holding an open house and wanted something elegant to set off the dining room. Mom knew that Mary had this exquisite silver tea service—the perfect thing. But Mom also knew that if she asked Mary to lend it to Cheryl, Mrs. Sutton would turn her down. Instead, Mom asked to borrow it for herself, which was a fib."

Carley frowned. "So that's why Mrs. Sutton blamed

Mom? Because Mom lied—I mean fibbed—and then the expensive silver tea service got stolen? Oh, I bet Mom was just sick about it."

"She felt awful. According to Mrs. Sutton, the tea service had belonged to her grandmother and was a family heirloom. It was irreplaceable."

"What did Mom do?"

"She called the police and offered a reward for its return, but the tea service didn't turn up. She went to every antique store in the area, looking for something similar. Finally there was nothing more she could do. She tried to repair the damage to the friendship, but Mrs. Sutton was angry—and really, you can't blame her. She was hurt because Mom had misled her. They got into this big argument about it and everything escalated from there. Mrs. Sutton did some petty things and Mom retaliated. Next thing you know, a grudge developed that's gone on to this day."

"Retaliated?" Carley asked. "How?"

"When it became clear that Mrs. Sutton wasn't going to forgive and forget, Mom tried another tactic. She thought she'd be funny." Noelle smiled at the memory. "Mrs. Sutton got her hair cut, and Mom sent her flowers and a sympathy card. Then Mrs. Sutton ordered pizza with double anchovies and had it delivered to Mom. You know how Mom hates anchovies—and furthermore she had to pay for it." She shook her head. "It's sad, isn't it? That a good friendship should fall apart for such a silly reason."

"Yeah," Carley agreed. "They acted pretty childish."

"And my relationship with Thom was one of the casualties."

"When did you fall in love with him?" Carley wanted to know.

"We became good friends when we were kids. For a long time, our families got along really well. We often went on picnics and outings together. Thom and I were the closest in age, and we were constant companions—until the argument."

"What happened after the argument?"

"Mrs. Sutton sent Thom and his older sister to a private school, and I didn't see him again for about six years. He came back to public school when we were sophomores. We didn't have a lot in common anymore and hardly had anything to do with each other until we both were assigned to the same English class in our senior year."

"That was when you fell in love?" Carley's voice rose wistfully.

Noelle nodded, and the familiar pain tightened her stomach. "Apparently I fell harder than Thom."

Noelle carefully glanced down again. Talking about Thom and her romance—especially while she was sitting in this theater—brought up memories she'd prefer to forget. Why wouldn't the stupid movie start? It was two minutes past the scheduled time.

The boy who'd rung up the popcorn order marched down the side aisle toward Noelle and Carley. He wore a bored but determined look. "There's been a complaint from the people down below about you throwing popcorn," he said accusingly.

Noelle could feel the heat build up in her cheeks. "I'm sorry—that was, uh, an accident."

The kid's expression said he'd heard it all before. "Make sure it doesn't happen again, okay?"

"It won't," Noelle promised him.

"Sorry," Carley said in a small voice as the boy left.

"It was my fault. I encouraged you."

"But I started it."

"You think you're the one who invented throwing popcorn? Hey, I've got fifteen years on you."

"I want to fall in love one day, too," Carley said, leaning back in her seat, which rocked slightly.

"You will," Noelle said, hoping her sister had better luck in that department than she'd had.

The lights dimmed then and with a grand, sweeping motion the huge velvet curtains hanging over the screen slowly parted. Soon, they were watching previews for upcoming features. Noelle absently nibbled on popcorn and let her mind wander.

Thom had changed if the blonde down below was the type of woman he found attractive. That shouldn't surprise her, though. Time changed a lot of things in life. Some days, when she felt lonely and especially sorry for herself, she tried to imagine what would've happened if she *had* married Thom all those years ago. Getting married that young rarely worked out. They might've been divorced, she might've ended up a single mother, she might never have completed her education.... All kinds of difficult outcomes were possible. In all honesty, she told herself, it was for the best that they hadn't run off together.

Carley slid forward and peeked over the railing. Almost immediately she flopped back. "You wouldn't *believe* what they're doing now."

"Probably not."

"They're—"

Noelle gripped her sister's elbow. "I don't want to know."

Carley's eyes were huge. "You don't want me to tell you?"

"No."

Her sister stared at her in utter amazement. "You really don't care?"

Noelle shook her head. That wasn't the whole truth—or even part of it. But she didn't want to know if Thom had his arm around the blonde or if he was kissing her—or anything else. It was a lot less painful to keep her head buried in a popcorn bucket. Forget Weight Watchers. Sometimes fat grams were the only source of comfort.

"Are you going to confront him after the movie?" Carley asked excitedly.

Noelle snickered. "Hardly."

"Why not?"

"Just watch the movie," she advised.

Carley settled in her seat and and began to rock back and forth. Another time, the action might have annoyed Noelle, but just then she found it oddly comforting. She wanted a special someone to put his arm around her and gently rock her. To create a private world for the two of them, the way Thom had once done in this very theater, on this very balcony. He'd kissed her here and claimed her heart. It'd been a pivotal moment in their fledgling romance. From that point onward, they knew—or at least Noelle had known. She was in love and willing to make whatever sacrifices love demanded.

All too soon, the feature had ended and the lights came back on. "That was great," Carley announced.

Caught up in wistful memories, Noelle got to her feet, gathering her coat and purse. She took pains not to glance below, although her curiosity was almost overwhelming.

"We meet again," an all-too-familiar voice said from behind her.

"Thom?" She turned to see him two rows back, with a four- or five-year-old boy at his side.

Noelle's reaction was instantaneous. She looked below and discovered the blonde beauty with her male friend, who just happened *not* to be Thom Sutton. "I thought—"

"*You're* Thom?" Carley asked, glowering with righteous indignation.

"Don't tell me you're Carley," he returned, ignoring the girl's outrage. "My goodness, you've grown into a regular beauty."

Carley's anger died a quick death. "Do you really think so?"

"I sure do. Oh, this is my nephew Cameron."

"Hello, Cameron," Noelle said. "Did you enjoy the movie?"

The boy nodded. "Yeah, but the best part was when the man came up and told you not to throw any more popcorn. Uncle Thom said you got in trouble." The kid sounded far too smug for Noelle's liking.

So Thom had heard and seen the whole thing.

Oh, great.

Friday morning, Sarah dressed for her Christmas basket shopping adventure. She felt as though she was suiting up for an ordeal, some test or rite of passage. The hordes of shoppers were definitely going to try her patience; she'd finished her own shopping months ago and failed to see why people waited until the very last week. Well, the sooner she purchased the things on her half of the list, the better. With Christmas only five days away, she didn't have a minute to waste.

She wasn't getting any help from her family—not that she'd really expected it. Jake was at work, and Noelle was driving Carley to her friend's house and then meeting Kristen for lunch.

She was on her own.

Wanting to get the most for her buying dollar, Sarah drove to the biggest discount store in Rose. The Value-X parking lot was already filled. After driving around repeatedly, she finally found a space. She locked her car and hunched her shoulders against the wind as she hurried toward the building. The sound of the Salvation Army bell-ringer guided her to the front entrance. She paused long enough to stick a dollar bill in his bucket, then walked into the store.

Sarah grabbed a cart and used the booster seat to prop up her purse. The list was in the side pocket of her bag, and she searched for the paper as she walked. She hadn't gone more than a few feet from the entrance when she nearly collided with another woman obtaining a cart.

"I'm sorry," she said automatically. "I—" The words froze on her lips.

"I should've known anyone that rude must be you," Mary Sutton muttered sarcastically.

Although her heart was pounding, Sarah made a relatively dignified escape and steered the cart around Mary. With purpose filling every step, she pushed her cart toward the toy department. Her list was gifts, which meant Mary had the grocery half. Hmph. It didn't surprise her that Mary Sutton bought her family's Christmas gifts at a discount store—or that she waited until the last minute.

The first part of the list directed her to purchase gifts for two girls, ages six and seven. The younger girl had requested a doll. Having raised three daughters, Sarah knew that every little girl loved Barbie. This late in the season, she'd be fortunate to find the current Barbie.

Almost right away she saw that the supplies were depleted, just as she'd suspected. But one lone Firefighter Barbie stood on the once-crowded shelf. Sarah reached for it at the precise moment someone else did.

"I believe I was first," she insisted. Far be it from her to allow some other person to deprive a poor little girl longing for a Barbie on Christmas morning.

"I believe you're wrong."

Mary Sutton. Sarah glared at her with such intensity that Mary must have realized she was not about to be dissuaded.

"Fine," Mary said after a moment and released her death grip on the Barbie.

"Thank you." Sarah could be gracious when called upon.

With her nose so high in the air she was in danger of hitting a light fixture, Mary stomped off in the opposite direction. Feeling satisfied with herself, Sarah studied the list again and noticed the name of a three-year-old boy. A small riding toy would do nicely, she decided and headed for that section of the department.

As she turned the corner she ran into Mary Sutton a third time. Mary stopped abruptly, her eyes narrowed. "Are you following me?" she demanded.

"Following *you*?" Sarah faked a short, derisive laugh. "You've got to be joking. I have no desire to be within ten feet of you."

"Then I suggest you vacate this aisle."

"You can't tell me where to shop or in what aisle!"

"Wanna bet?" Mary leaned forward and, intentionally or not, her cart rammed Sarah's.

Refusing to allow such an outrage to go unanswered, Sarah retaliated by banging her cart into Mary's.

Mary pulled back and hit her again, harder this time.

Soon they were throwing stuffed French poodles at each other, hurling them off the shelves. A German shepherd sailed over Sarah's head. That was when she reached for the golden retriever, the largest of the stuffed animals.

"Ladies, ladies." A man in a red jacket hurried toward them, his arms outstretched. His name badge read Michael and identified him as the store manager.

"I'm so sorry, Michael," Sarah said, pretending to recognize him. "This little, uh, misunderstanding got completely out of hand."

"You're telling me!" Mary yelled.

"This woman is following me."

"Oh, puh-leeze." Mary groaned audibly. "This woman followed *me*."

"I don't think it's important to know who followed whom," the manager said in a conciliatory voice. "But we need to—"

"She took the last Barbie," Mary broke in, pointing an accusing finger at Sarah. "I got it first—the doll was *mine*. Any jury in the land would rule in my favor. But I kindly offered it to her."

"Kindly, nothing. I had that Barbie and you know it!"

"Ladies, please…" The manager stood between them in an effort to keep them apart.

"There's only so much of this I can take," Mary said, sounding close to tears. "I'm here—"

"It isn't important why you're here," Sarah interrupted. She wasn't about to let Mary Sutton come off looking like the injured party. The woman had purposely rammed her cart. "She assaulted me."

"I most certainly did not!"

"You should check the front of my cart for damage, and if there is any, I suggest that you, as manager, charge this woman," Sarah said.

Two security officers arrived then, dressed in blue uniforms.

"Officer, officer…"

Mary turned soft and gentle. "Thank you for coming."

"Oh, give me a break," Sarah muttered. "Is it within your power to arrest this woman?" she demanded.

"Ladies," the manager said, trying once more, it seemed, to appeal to their better natures. "This is the season of goodwill toward men—and women. Would it be possible for you to apologize to each other and go about your business?"

Mary crossed her arms and looked away.

Sarah gestured toward the other woman as if to say Mary's action spoke for itself. "I believe you have your answer."

"Then you leave me no choice," the manager said. "Officers, please escort these two ladies from the store."

"What?" Mary cried.

"I beg your pardon?" Sarah said, hands on hips. "What is this about?"

The larger of the two security guards answered. "You're being kicked out of the store."

Sarah's mouth fell open.

The only person more shocked was Mary Sutton. "You're evicting me from Value-X?"

"You heard the manager, lady," the second officer said. "Now, come this way."

"Could I pay for the Barbie doll first?" Sarah asked, clutching the package to her chest. "It's for a little girl and it's all she wants for Christmas."

"You should've thought of that before you threw the first poodle," the manager said.

"But—"

Dramatically, he pointed toward the front doors. "Out."

Mortified to the marrow of her bones, Sarah turned, taking her cart with her. One wheel was now loose and it squeaked and squealed. Just when she figured things couldn't get any worse, she discovered that a crowd had gathered in the aisle to witness her humiliation.

"Merry Christmas," she said with as much bravado as she could manage.

The officer at her side raised his hand. "We're asking that everyone return to their shopping. What happened here is over."

With her dignity intact but her pride in shreds, Sarah made her way to the parking lot, still accompanied by the officer.

She could see the "About Town" headline already. *Manager Expels Sarah McDowell From Value-X After Cat Fight.* Although technically, she supposed, it should be Dog Fight.

She had no doubt that Mary Sutton would use the power of the press to complete her embarrassment.

NOELLE McDOWELL'S JOURNAL

December 19
11:30 p.m.

I can't believe it! Even now, when it's long past time for bed, I'm wide-awake and so furious, any chance of falling asleep is impossible. I doubt if anyone could do a better job of looking like a world-class idiot. Right there in the theater, with my little sister at my side, I behaved like a juvenile.

I've worked hard to be a positive influence on Carley. I take my role as oldest sister very seriously. Then I go and pull a stunt like this. Adding insult to injury is the fact that I then had to face Thom, knowing he was completely aware of what a fool I'd made of myself.

Speaking of Thom...no, I don't want to think about him. First the airplane and now this! I'd sincerely hoped he'd be married with a passel of kids. I wanted him to be so completely out of the picture that I'd never need to think about him again. Instead—just my luck—he's single, eligible and drop-dead handsome. Life can be brutally unfair.

One good thing that came from all this is the long conversation I had with Carley after the movie. She's young and idealistic, much the same way I was at her age. We talked some more about Mom and Mrs. Sutton. It's really a very sad feud. I told her what good friends our two families used to be. The telling brought up a lot of memories. At one time, our families did everything together.

Thom was the first boy ever to kiss me. We were both sixteen. Wow! I still remember how good it felt. I don't remember what movie was playing and I doubt Thom does, either. That kiss was really something, even though we had no idea what we were doing. There was a purity to it, an innocence. His lips stayed on mine for mere seconds, but somehow we knew. I certainly did, and I thought Thom did, too.

It's funny how much it hurts to think about the way he deceived me. I try not to dwell on it. But I can't help myself, especially now....

Three

"I've never been so humiliated in my life!" Thom's mother sagged into the chair across from his desk as if she were experiencing a fainting spell. The back of her hand went to her forehead and she closed her eyes. "I'll never be able to look those people in the eye again," she wailed. "Never!"

"Mother, I'm sure no one recognized you," Thom said, hoping to calm her down before she caused a second scene by retelling the first. He hadn't really appreciated his mother's flair for drama until now. This was quite a performance, and he could only imagine the show she'd put on at the store.

"Of *course* I was recognized," Mary insisted, springing to life. "My picture's right there by my news column each and every week. Why, I could be fired from the newspaper once the editor gets wind of this." She swooned again and slumped back in the chair. "Where's your father, anyway? He should've known something like this was bound to happen. It seems every time I need him, he's conveniently in court." Greg Sutton was the senior partner in a local law firm.

Thom managed to hold back a smile. As far as he was concerned, his father possessed impeccable timing. Unfortunately, that meant his mother had sought solace from him.

"I'll sue Sarah McDowell," his mother said, as if she'd suddenly come to that decision. "Assault and besmirching my reputation and…and—"

"Mother," Thom pleaded. He stood and leaned forward, his hands on the edge of his desk. "Take a couple of deep breaths and try to calm down." Dragging a lawyer—most likely someone from his father's firm—into the middle of this feud would only complicate things.

"Do you believe it's remotely possible to calm down after this kind of humiliation?"

Perhaps she was right. "Why don't I take you to lunch and we can talk about it," Thom suggested. It was the Friday before Christmas and he could spare the time.

"The Rose Garden?" His mother raised pleading eyes to him. The Rose Garden was the most elegant dining room in town.

"If you like." It was more a "ladies who lunch" kind of place, but if that was what it took to make his mother listen to reason, then he'd go there.

"At least the day won't be completely ruined," she mumbled, opening her purse. "Let me put on some lipstick and I'll be ready to go." She took out her compact and gasped when she saw her reflection in the mirror.

"What?" Thom asked.

"My hair." Her fingers worked feverishly to repair the damage. "Why didn't you say something?"

Mainly because he hadn't been able to get a word in edgewise from the moment she'd stormed into his office. At first, Thom had assumed she'd been in some kind of accident. His mother had spoken so fast it was hard to understand what she was saying—other than the fact that she'd been kicked out of the Value-X because of Sarah McDowell.

"This must have happened when she hurled a French poodle at me."

"Mrs. McDowell threw a dog at you?" He gazed at her in horror.

"A stuffed one," she qualified. "It hit me on the head." Her hand went back to her hair, which she'd more or less managed to straighten.

Thom could picture the scene—two grown women acting like five-year-olds fighting in a schoolyard. Once again, he struggled to hide his amusement. His mother had tried to give him the impression that she was an innocent victim in all this, but he strongly suspected she'd played an equal role.

"I think I might be getting a bruise on my cheek," she said, peering closely into the small compact mirror. She lowered it and angled her face for him to get a better look.

"I don't see anything," he told her.

"Look harder," she said.

To appease her, he did but saw nothing. "Sorry," he said and reached for his overcoat. "Ready for lunch?"

"I'm starving," his mother told him. "You know how hungry I get when I'm angry."

He didn't, and felt this was information he could live without. The Rose Garden was only a block from his office, so they decided to walk. His mother chattered the whole way, reliving the incident and her outrage all over again, embellishing it in the retelling. Thom listened politely and wondered what Noelle would think when she heard *her* mother's version of the incident. He quickly pulled himself up. He didn't want to think about Noelle; that was something his self-esteem could do without.

As he'd expected, The Rose Garden bustled with activity. Christmas was only a few days away, and shoppers taking a welcome lunch break now filled the restaurant. Thom glanced about the room as they were waiting to be seated. He recognized a few associates, who acknowledged him with nods. Two women sitting by the window gave him an appreciative glance and he warmed to the attention. That was when he caught sight of another pair of women.

Noelle and her younger sister, Kristen. Wouldn't you know it? He nearly groaned aloud. He hadn't seen or heard from her in ten years and yet in the last three days she seemed to turn up every place he went.

This wasn't good. In fact, if his mother were to see them, she might very well consider it her duty to create a scene and walk out of the restaurant. Worse yet, she might find it necessary to make some loud and slanderous comment about their mother. Staring in their direction was a dead giveaway, but for the life of him, he couldn't stop. Noelle. The years had matured her beauty. He'd been in love with her as a teenager and she'd become the greatest source of pain in his life. For a long time, he'd convinced himself that he hated her. Eventually he'd realized it wasn't true. If anything, he was as strongly drawn to her now as he had been back then. More so, and he detested his own weakness. The woman had damn near destroyed him. In spite of that, he couldn't look away.

"I can seat you now," the hostess said.

Thom hesitated.

"Thom," his mother said, nudging him, "we can be seated now."

"Yes, sorry." He could only hope it wouldn't be anywhere close to Noelle.

The hostess escorted them to a table by the window. He pulled out his mother's chair, making sure her back was to Noelle and Kristen. Unfortunately, that meant *he* was facing them. Kristen had her back to him, which left him with an excellent view of Noelle. She apparently noticed him for the first time because her fork froze halfway to her mouth. For the longest moment, she stared at him, then caught herself and averted her eyes.

"Do you see someone you know, dear?" his mother asked, scrutinizing the menu.

"Yes…no," he corrected. He lifted the rather large menu and pretended to read over the offerings. The strategy of entertaining his mother in order to get her mind off the events of that morning was about to backfire.

In the years since Noelle, Thom had been in several relationships, two of which had grown serious. Both times he'd come close to suggesting marriage and then panicked. It was little wonder after what Noelle had done to him, but he couldn't blame her entirely.

When the moment came to make a commitment, he couldn't. He simply couldn't. And he knew why—although the reason baffled and frustrated him. He didn't love either Caroline or Brenda with the same intensity he'd loved Noelle. Perhaps it was impossible to recapture the emotional passion of that youthful episode; he didn't know. What he did know was that the feelings he'd had for other women hadn't been enough. He'd found them attractive, enjoyed their company…but he needed more than that.

He needed what he'd had with Noelle.

As he thought about the scene at the theater, he started to grin. It couldn't have worked out better had he planned it. Just thinking about her tossing popcorn at some poor, unsuspecting moviegoer's head was enough to keep him laughing for years. He'd listened in while she talked about their mothers—and about them. But the most priceless part of all was the astonished look on her face when she'd realized he was sitting right behind her and had heard every word.

"What is so amusing?" his mother asked.

"Oh, I was just thinking about something that happened recently."

"What? Trust me, after the morning I've had, I could use a good laugh."

Thom shook his head. "It'll lose something in the translation."

"Oh." She sounded disappointed, then sighed. "I do feel better. This was an excellent idea."

The waitress came by and his mother ordered a glass of wine. "For my nerves," she explained to the woman. "Ordinarily I don't drink during the day, but…well, suffice it to say I've had a very difficult morning."

"I understand," the waitress told her in a sympathetic voice. She glanced at Thom and gave him a small coy smile.

"What a nice young woman," his mother commented as the waitress walked off.

"I suppose so," he said with little interest. He looked up, straight into Noelle's steady gaze.

"Perhaps now isn't the right moment to broach the

subject, but both your father and I think it's time you considered settling down."

She was right; the timing could be better. However, a little appeasement seemed in order. "I've been thinking the same thing myself," he said, forcing himself to focus on his mother.

"Really?" Her face lit up. "Is there someone special?"

"Not yet." Involuntarily he stared at Noelle again. As if against her will, her eyes met his and held. Then she looked away—but she quickly looked back.

Kristen turned around and glanced at him over her shoulder.

"Did you know Kristen McDowell is getting married?" his mother said.

Thom nearly choked on his glass of water. "Now that you mention it, I remember hearing something about that." It also explained why his mother had brought up the subject of his settling down. She didn't want Sarah McDowell to outdo her in the married children department.

"Now," his mother said, eagerly leaning forward, "tell me about your lady friend."

"What lady friend?"

"The one you're going to propose to."

"Propose?" He'd only proposed to one woman, the one watching him from two tables away. "I told you already—I'm not seeing anyone."

"You were never able to keep a secret from me, Thomas. I'm your mother."

He stared at her blankly, not knowing how to respond. "What makes you think I've met someone?"

"It isn't *think,* Thom, I know. I told your father, too.

Ask him if you don't believe me. I noticed it the day you came home from your business trip to California. It was the sparkle in your eyes."

"California?" Thom tried to recall the trip. It had been a quick one, and strictly business. But on the return flight, he'd bumped into Noelle McDowell.

Noelle got home after lunch with Kristen to discover her mother sitting in the family room, stocking feet propped up on the ottoman. She leaned back against the sofa cushion and held an icepack to her forehead.

"Mom?" Noelle whispered. "Are you ill?"

"Thank goodness someone's finally home," her mother said, lowering the bag of ice.

"What's wrong?"

"Never in all your life could you guess the kind of morning I had." She clutched Noelle's arm as she spoke.

"What happened?"

Sarah closed her eyes. "I can't even tell you about it. I have never been more humiliated."

"Does this have something to do with Mrs. Sutton?"

Her mother's eyes sprang open in sheer terror. "You heard about it? Who told you?"

"Ah…"

"She's going to report it in the newspaper, I just know she is. I wouldn't put it past her to use her news column to smear my good name. It was *her* fault, you know. She followed me, and then purposely rammed her cart into mine. And that was only the beginning."

An ugly picture began to take shape in Noelle's mind. A Sutton/McDowell confrontation would explain the fierce looks Thom had sent her way during lunch. The fact that he'd showed up at The Rose Garden—with his mother in tow—was a coincidence she could have done without.

Kristen had invited her to lunch, and then after a few minutes of small talk, her sister had immediately turned to the subject that happened to be on Noelle's mind: Thom Sutton. Noelle had described the disaster at the movies the day before and reluctantly confessed her part. To her consternation, Kristen had thought the incident downright hilarious. Noelle, however, had yet to recover from the embarrassment of knowing that Thom had seen her resort to such childish behavior.

Now their mother had been involved in another confrontation with Mary Sutton. If her present state of mind was anything to go by, Sarah had come out of it badly. Judging by what Noelle had seen of Mrs. Sutton at the restaurant, *she* wasn't the least bit disturbed.

"The police took down our names and—"

"The *police?*"

"Value-X Security, but they wear those cute blue uniforms and look just like regular policemen."

"They took your names? What for?"

Her mother covered her face with both hands. "I can't talk about it."

The door off the garage opened and in walked Noelle's father. "Dad," she said, hoping to prepare him. "Something happened to Mom this morning."

"Oh, Jake…" Her mother languished in her seat as though she lacked the energy to even lift her head.

"Sarah?"

"Apparently Mom and Mrs. Sutton tangled with security at the Value-X this morning."

"We more than tangled," her mother insisted, her voice rising, "we were…banished. The officer who escorted me out told me I won't be allowed inside the store for three months." She bit her lip and swallowed a loud sob. "I don't know if I misunderstood him, but I think I might be permanently banned from all blue-light specials."

"No!" Her father feigned outrage.

"Jake, this is serious."

"Of course it is," he agreed. "I take it this is Mary's doing?"

Her mother's fist hit the sofa arm. "I swear to you she started it!"

"You don't need to tell me what happened," Jake said. "I can guess."

So could Noelle.

"From here on out, I absolutely refuse to be in the same room as that woman." She sat straighter, jaw firm, head back. "For years I've had to deal with her…her malice, and I won't put up with it anymore!"

Jake reached for Sarah's hand and gently patted it. "You're absolutely right—you shouldn't."

Her mother's eyes narrowed suspiciously. "How do you mean? Are you being sarcastic?"

"Of course not, dear," he said reassuringly. "But there's no need to rehash old history, is there?"

"No-o-o." Noelle heard her mother's hesitation.

"Not going to the Christmas dance will show Mary Sutton that she won't have you to kick around anymore."

As far as Noelle was concerned, missing the Century Club Christmas dance was far from a tragedy. The only reason she'd agreed to attend was to placate her mother. This mysterious incident at the Value-X was a blessing in disguise; it seemed her father saw it in the same light.

She just hoped he hadn't overplayed his hand with that last ringing pronouncement.

"Who said anything about not going to the dance?" her mother demanded.

"You did." Her father turned to Noelle for agreement, which she offered with a solemn nod.

"Yes, Mom, you just said you won't be in the same room with that woman ever again."

"I did?"

"Yes, sweetheart," Noelle's father said. "And I agree wholeheartedly. Missing the dance is a small price to pay if it means protecting your peace of mind."

"We aren't going to the dance?" Carley asked, entering the room. She looked disappointed, but then Noelle's little sister was too young to understand what a lucky escape she'd just had.

"No," Jake said. "We're going to skip the dance this year, and perhaps every year from now on. We won't let Mary Sutton hurt your mother's feelings or her reputation again!"

"We're going," her mother insisted.

"But sweetheart—"

"You're absolutely right, Jake, Mary Sutton's done enough to me. I refuse to allow her to ruin my Christmas—and Noelle's birthday—too. We're going to show up at the dance and hold our heads high. We have nothing to be ashamed of."

"But…" Her father cleared his throat. "What if Mary mentions the incident at the Value-X?" He lowered his voice, sounding as though that would be a horrible embarrassment to them all. Noelle had to give her father credit; he was good at this.

"She won't say a word," her mother said with complete confidence. "Mary wouldn't dare bring up the subject, seeing that she was tossed out on her ear, right along with me."

Her resolve clearly renewed, Sarah stood and placed her hands on her hips. Nothing would thwart her now. "We're attending the dance tomorrow night, and that's all there is to it."

Her father made a small protesting noise that echoed Noelle's sentiments. She was stuck going to this dance when it was the very last thing she wanted.

Dressed in a floor-length pink formal that had once been worn by Kristen in high school, Noelle felt like last year's prom queen. Her enthusiasm for this dance was on a par with filing her income tax return.

"You look positively lovely," her mother told her as they headed out the door.

How Noelle looked had little to do with how she felt. Her father brought the car out of the garage and held open the doors for Noelle and Carley, then helped their mother into the front seat beside him.

"How did I get so lucky—escorting three beautiful women to the biggest dance of the year?"

"Clean living," Noelle's mother said with authority. "And a clear conscience." Noelle didn't know whether to laugh at that remark or shrug in bewilderment. Leaning forward in order to look out the front window, Sarah added, "I think it's going to snow."

Hearing "Jingle Bells" on the car radio, Noelle suspected her mother was being influenced by the words of the song.

"We're more prone to ice storms than snow this time of year," her father said mildly.

Noelle had forgotten about the treacherous storms, although she'd experienced a number of them during the years she'd lived in Rose. They created astonishing beauty—and terrible dangers.

"Kristen and Jonathan are meeting us at the dance, aren't they?" Carley asked.

"That's what she said," Noelle answered. Carley was dressed in a full-length pale blue dress with cap sleeves and she wore matching low-heeled shoes. She looked lovely and so mature it was all Noelle could do not to cry. Her baby sister was growing up.

"Do you think *she'll* be there?" her mother asked, lowering her voice.

"Mrs. Sutton's probably asking the same thing about you," Noelle said.

Her mother gave an exaggerated sigh. "I'll say one thing about Mary Sutton—she never did lack nerve."

The Century Club was festive, with Christmas music and evergreen swags and large red bows. The ballroom was on the second floor, the cloakroom, a bar and buffet on the first. Couples lingered on the wide staircase, chatting and sipping champagne.

Noelle glanced toward the upstairs, and her stomach tensed. Thom was there. She didn't need to see him to feel his presence. Why did he have to show up everywhere she did? Was this some kind of cosmic joke?

"Kristen!" her mother called. "Yoo hoo!" Anyone might think it'd been weeks since she'd last spoken to her daughter. "Hello, Jonathan." She hugged her soon-to-be son-in-law.

"Hi, Mom. Hi, Dad." Kristen paused in front of Carley, feigning shock. "This isn't my little sister, is it? It can't be."

Carley rolled her eyes, but couldn't hide her pleasure. "Of course it's me. Don't be ridiculous."

"Shall we go upstairs?" her mother suggested.

Noelle recognized the order disguised as a request. They were to mount the stairs on guard, as a family, in case they ran into the dreaded Mary Sutton.

Kristen cozied up to Noelle. "He's here," she whispered in her ear.

"I know."

"Who told you?"

"No one." She couldn't explain how she'd recognized Thom's presence. She just did. Like it or not.

The ballroom was crowded, and although this wasn't the kind of social activity Noelle would have attended on her own, she couldn't help getting caught up in the spirit of the evening. A six-piece orchestra was playing a waltz, the chandeliers glittered and she saw that it had indeed begun to snow; flakes drifted gently past the dark windows. On the polished dance floor, the women in their long shimmery gowns whirled around in the arms of their dashing partners. The scene reminded her of a Victorian Christmas card.

"Would you care to dance?" Jonathan asked.

Surprised, Noelle nodded. She'd only spoken once or twice to this man who was marrying her sister, and was anxious to know him better. "Thank you. That would be very nice."

Just as Noelle and Jonathan stepped onto the dance floor, Kristen's gaze met her fiancé's. Noelle could have sworn some unspoken message passed between them. She didn't have time to question her sister before Jonathan loosely wrapped her in his arms.

"I assume you heard what happened at the Value-X store," she said, searching for a subject of conversation.

"Did you have as much trouble not laughing as I did?"

"More," Noelle confessed with a grin.

"I've done business with the Suttons. They're good people."

"This feud between our mothers is ridiculous." Out of the corner of her eye, she noticed Kristen, who was dancing, too—her partner none other than Thom Sutton. It didn't take a genius to put two and two together, especially when she noticed that Kristen was steering Thom in her direction. Noelle marveled at her sister's courage in asking Thom to dance with her. And of course she had. Thom would never have sought Kristen out, especially for a dance in the Women's Century Club Ballroom with both mothers present.

The two couples made their way toward the center of the polished floor. When they were side by side, Jonathan stopped.

"I believe you're dancing with the wrong partner," he said.

Noelle didn't need to look over her shoulder to guess Jonathan was speaking to Thom.

"I believe you're with the wrong woman," Noelle heard Kristen tell her partner.

Jonathan released Noelle, and Kristen stepped out of Thom's embrace and sailed into her fiancé's waiting arms, leaving Thom and Noelle standing alone in the middle of the crowded dance floor.

Slowly, dread dictating every move, Noelle turned and came face-to-face with Thom. He didn't look any happier than she felt at this sudden turn of events. "I didn't plan this," she said in clear, even tones.

His expression implied that he didn't consider her comment worthy of a response.

"Are you two going to dance or are you just going to stand there and stare at each other all night?" Jonathan asked.

Thom shrugged, implying that he could do this if he had to. Reluctantly Noelle stepped into his arms. She wasn't sure what to expect. Actually, she hadn't expected to feel anything, certainly not this immediate deluge of emotion. He kept her at arm's length and gazed into the distance.

To Noelle's horror, tears filled her eyes as all the old feelings came flooding back. She was about to turn and walk off the dance floor when his fingers dug into her upper arms.

"You're not running away from me again."

"Me?" she cried, furious at the accusation.

"Yes, you."

His words made no sense, she thought grimly, but said nothing. The dance would be over soon and she could leave him behind. Or try to. Kristen would answer for this.

No, she decided, she had only herself to blame. Over lunch, Noelle had confided in her sister. Kristen, being idealistic and in love, had plotted to bring Noelle and Thom back together. She didn't understand that reconciliation wasn't always possible.

"I'd like to ask you a question," she said when she could tolerate the silence no longer.

"Fine."

"Why'd you do it? Did you want revenge for your mother so badly it was worth using me to get it?"

He stopped dancing and frowned at her. "What?"

"You heard me." She couldn't keep the pain out of her voice.

He continued to frown, as if he still didn't understand the question.

"Don't give me that injured look," she said, clenching her jaw. "Too many years have passed for me to be taken in by that."

"You were the one who stood *me* up."

"Yeah, right," she said with a mocking laugh. "After I made an idiot of myself in front of my parents, too. That must've given you a real kick."

"I don't know what you're talking about."

"Thom, I waited in that park for two miserable hours and you didn't show."

Not an inch separated them now as his icy glare cut into her. Dancing couples swirled around them, but Noelle was barely conscious of anyone else. For all she knew or cared, they were alone on the dance floor.

"I waited hours for you, too."

His lying to her now was almost more than she could stand. "I beg to differ," she said stiffly.

"Noelle, listen to me! I was there."

"You most certainly were not." Then, to prove that she wasn't going to accept a lie, no matter how convenient, she added, "You think I just waited around? I was sure something had gone wrong, sure there was some misunderstanding, so I phoned your home."

"I wasn't there because I was waiting for you!"

He persisted with the lie and that irritated her even more.

"You were gone, all right," she said, spitting out the words. "You were with your buddies bowling."

His eyes narrowed and he began to speak.

But the music stopped just then, which was all the excuse Noelle needed to get away from him. He reached for her hand and pulled her back. "We need to talk."

"No. It happened years ago. Some things are better left alone."

"Not this time," he insisted, unwilling to budge.

"What do you hope to accomplish by going through all of this now? It's too late." They'd gain nothing more than the pain of opening old wounds. Any discussion was futile. It'd been a mistake to let herself get drawn into this silly drama—just one very big mistake.

"I'm not hoping to accomplish one damn thing," he told her coldly.

"I didn't think so."

Thom released her hand. "Just a minute," he said as she turned from him.

Noelle hesitated.

"I *was* there. I stood there for two hours and waited. You were the one who never showed."

"That's not true!"

They stood glowering at each other, both refusing to give in. Noelle wasn't going to let him lie his way out of this, though—not after what his deception had cost her.

"Hey, you two, this is Christmas," someone called out.

The voice ended Noelle's resolve. Whatever had happened in the past didn't matter anymore. Certainly not after all these years.

"If you find comfort in believing a lie, then do so,"

he said, "but don't involve me." He walked away, his face hard and impassive.

Left alone in the middle of the dance floor, Noelle stared at him in amazement. Of all the nerve! He'd stopped her from leaving and now *he'd* taken off!

Picking up her skirt, she raced after him. "All right! You want to talk this out, then we will."

"When?" He continued walking, tossing the question over his shoulder.

With Christmas so close, her time was booked solid. "I...soon."

"Tonight."

"All right." She swallowed hard. "When and where?"

"After the dance. In the park, same place as before."

That seemed fitting, since it was where they were originally going to meet the day they'd planned to elope.

"What time is the dance over?"

"Midnight." He glanced at his watch. "So make it one."

"I'll be there."

He shot her a look. "That was what you said the *last* time."

NOELLE McDOWELL'S JOURNAL

December 21
5:00 p.m.

Everyone's getting ready for the big dance, but my head's still spinning and I've learned that it helps me sort through my emotions if I write everything down. I ran into Thom again. It's as though we're being drawn together, as though we're trapped in some magnetic field and are being pulled toward each other from opposite directions. I can tell he doesn't like it any better than I do.

It happened yesterday when I met Kristen for lunch at The Rose Garden. No sooner had our order arrived when in walked Thom and his mother.

Try as I might, I couldn't keep my eyes off him. He apparently suffered from the same malady. Every time I glanced up, he was staring at me—and frowning. His mother was with him and I could see that he was trying to keep her distracted so she wouldn't notice Kristen and me. I didn't completely understand why until we arrived home and discovered that Mom and Mrs. Sutton had had another run-in while shopping for the Christmas baskets. That must have been something to see, although I'm grateful I didn't!

After we left the restaurant, Kristen and I had a long talk about Thom. I told her far more than I meant to. I don't think I've thought or talked this much about Thom in years, and I found myself experiencing all those pathetic emotions all over again. Kristen confessed that she's been hurt and upset with me for staying away, and now that I'm home, I can understand her disappointment. It's ironic, because after I told her how devastated I was when Thom and I broke up, she said she could understand why I'd stayed away. She even said she'd probably have done the same thing.

When I got back to the house, Mom was in quite a state. For a moment I thought she might have talked herself out of attending the dance, but our hopes were quickly dashed. Dad and I should've realized Mom has far too much pride to let Mary Sutton get the upper hand.

This Christmas-basket project is driving her nuts, but Mom's determined to make Kristen's wedding one this town will long remember, and she's willing to make whatever sacrifice is necessary. I do admire her determination.

It's time to get ready for the dance. Wouldn't you know it? Mom came up with a dress, and just as Carley predicted, it's pink. Pepto-Bismol pink. I can only hope Thom doesn't show up, but at the rate my luck is running...

Four

The rest of the Christmas dance passed in a blur for Noelle. She danced with a constant stream of attractive men. She greeted longtime family friends and socialized the evening away, but not once did she stop thinking about Thom. They were finally going to settle this. Only she wasn't a naive eighteen-year-old anymore and she wouldn't allow his lies to go unchallenged. Thom claimed he'd been waiting for her in the park, but she knew otherwise.

At the end of the evening, the families trooped down the wide sweeping staircase. Noelle, Carley and their mother waited while Jake stood in line to collect their coats. No more than three feet away from them was Mary Sutton, who also appeared to be waiting for her coat. Noelle had to hand it to the woman; she did a marvelous job of pretending not to see them.

"Good evening, Mrs. Sutton," Noelle greeted her, refusing to ignore Thom's mother.

Sarah's onetime friend opened and then closed her mouth, as if she didn't know how to respond.

"Noelle." Her mother elbowed her sharply in the ribs. "What's the matter with you?"

"Nothing. I'm greeting an old family friend."

"*Former* friend," her mother insisted. "We haven't been friends in almost twenty years."

"But you once were."

Her mother sighed wearily. "I was younger then, and I didn't have the discretion I have now. You see, back then I took friendship at face value. I trusted in goodwill and forgiveness."

"Hello, Noelle," Mary Sutton said, moving closer. "I, too, was once young and I, too, believed in the power of friendship. But I was taught a painful lesson when the woman I assumed was my dearest friend lied and deceived me and entrusted a priceless family heirloom to another. But that was a very long time ago. Tell me," she said, turning a cold shoulder to Noelle's mother. "How are *you*?"

"Very well, thank you."

Her mother clasped Carley's arm and stepped back as though to protect her youngest daughter.

"You're looking lovely," Thom's mother said, and her eyes were kind.

"Thank you," Noelle said, although she could feel her mother's gaze burning into her back.

Mary Sutton lowered her voice. "I couldn't help overhearing your mother's comments just now about friendship. I probably should've stayed out of it—but I couldn't."

"It's so sad that the two of you have allowed this nonsense to go on for all these years."

"Let me assure you, my grandmother's tea service is not nonsense. It was all I had to remind me of her.

Your mother lied to me about using it, and then lost it forever." Her downcast eyes clearly said that the loss of her grandmother's legacy still caused her pain. "You're right, though. It's unfortunate this has dragged on as long as it has."

That sounded encouraging, and Noelle was ready to leap on what she considered a gesture of peace.

"However," Mrs. Sutton continued, "there are certain things no friendship can overcome, and I fear your mother has crossed that line too many times to count. Regrettably, our friendship is unsalvageable."

"But—"

"Another thing," Mrs. Sutton said, cutting Noelle off. "I saw you dancing with Thom this evening. You two were once sweet on each other, but you hurt him badly. I hope for both your sakes that you're not thinking of renewing your acquaintance."

"I…I…" Noelle faltered, not knowing how to answer.

Noelle's mother stepped forward. "I suggest your son stay away from our daughter."

"Mom, keep out of this, please," Noelle cried, afraid of what would happen if the two women started in on each other—particularly after the Value-X incident. This was the town's biggest social event of the year, and a scene was the last thing either family needed.

Mr. Sutton returned with the coats, and Noelle's father followed shortly afterward. The McDowells headed immediately for the parking lot, careful to avoid any and all Suttons. Everyone was silent on the drive home, but Noelle knew she'd upset her mother.

Fifteen minutes later as they walked into the house, she decided she should be the one to compromise. "Mom, I wish now that I hadn't spoken to Mrs. Sutton," she said quietly. And she meant it; she should have restricted her remarks to "Hello" and maybe "Merry Christmas."

"I do, too," her mother said. "I know your intentions were good, but it's best to leave things as they are. I tried for a long time to make up with her, but she refused to accept a replacement set and she refused my apology." Sadness crept into her voice. "Mary did make one good point, though."

Noelle mentally reviewed the conversation.

"She said it's a good idea for you to stay away from Thom, and she's right." She sighed, then briefly placed her palm against Noelle's cheek. Her eyes were warm with love. "The two of you have a history you can't escape."

"Mom, it isn't like that. We—"

"Sweetheart, listen please. I know you once had strong feelings for that young man, and it hurt me deeply."

"It hurt *you?*"

Her mother nodded. "Very much so, because I knew you'd be forced to make a choice between your family and Thom. I couldn't bear the thought of you married to him or sharing my grandchildren with Mary Sutton. You saw for yourself how she feels about me. There's no forgiveness in her. Really, is this the kind of woman you want in your life and the lives of your children? That's the history I mean." She kissed Noelle on the cheek and headed down the hallway to her room. "Good night now."

Noelle shut her eyes and sagged against the wall. She'd been just a moment away from explaining that she was going to meet Thom in order to talk things out.

Her mother sounded as though she'd consider it a personal affront if Noelle so much as looked at him. It was like high school all over again.

The only thing left to do now was sneak out the same way she had as a teenager. She couldn't leave him waiting in the cold, that was unthinkable. Besides, this might be her one and only chance to sort out what had really happened, and she wasn't going to throw it away. She didn't intend any disrespect toward her mother or his, but she *had* to be there. If she didn't show up, she'd confirm every negative belief he already had about her.

Carley was in bed asleep as Noelle passed her room. She went in to drop a kiss on her sister's forehead, then softly closed the door. Noelle changed out of her party dress, choosing wool slacks and a thick sweater to wear to the park. Sitting on the edge of the bed, she waited for the minutes to tick past. With luck, her parents would be exhausted and both go directly to bed. Then Noelle could slip away undetected.

Finally the house was dark and quiet. The only illumination came from the flashing Christmas lights that decorated the roofline.

Opening her bedroom door, Noelle was horrified by the way it creaked. On tiptoe, she carefully, silently crept down the narrow corridor.

"Jake." Her mother was instantly awake. "I heard something."

"Go to sleep, honey."

"There's someone in the house," her mother insisted.

Noelle froze. She could hardly breathe. Just imagining what her mother would say was enough to paralyze her.

"Jake, I'm serious."

"I don't hear anything," her father mumbled.

"I did. We could all be murdered in our beds."

"Sarah, for the love of heaven."

"Think of the children."

Noelle nearly groaned aloud. She was trapped. She'd have to pass her parents' bedroom in order to steal back into her own. They were sure to see her. She couldn't go forward and she couldn't go back.

"All right, all right," her father muttered as he climbed out of bed.

"Take something with you," her mother hissed.

"Like what?"

"Here, take a wooden hanger."

"So I can hang him out to dry if I happen on a burglar?"

"Just do it, Jake."

"Yes, dear."

Noelle had made it safely into the kitchen by the time her father came upon her. "Dad," she whispered, hiding in the shadows, "it's me."

"Why didn't you say so?" he whispered back.

"I couldn't. I'm sneaking out of the house."

"This late? Where are you going?"

He wouldn't like the answer, but she refused to lie. "I'm meeting Thom Sutton in the park. We're going to talk."

Her father didn't say anything for a long moment. Then it sounded as if he was weeping.

Noelle felt dreadful. "Dad? I'm sorry if this upsets you."

"Upsets me?" he repeated. "I think it's hilarious."

"You…do?"

"Go ahead and meet your young man and talk all you

want. This thing is between Sarah and Mary. Greg and I have been friends for years."

This was news to Noelle. "You're still friends?"

"Of course. He's the best golfing partner I ever had."

"You and Mr. Sutton are golf partners?" Noelle thought perhaps she'd slipped into another dimension.

"Shhh." Her father raised a finger to his lips. "Your mother doesn't know."

"Mom doesn't know." This was more unbelievable by the moment.

"Scoot," her father ordered, and reaching for the keys on the peg outside the garage door, he said, "Here, take my car. It's parked on the street."

Noelle clutched the set of keys and leaned forward to kiss his cheek. "Thanks, Dad."

He coughed loudly as she opened the back door. "You're hearing things, Sarah," he called out. "There's nothing." He gave her a small wave and turned back toward the hallway.

As soon as she was out the door, Noelle sprinted toward her dad's car. It took her a moment to figure out which key she needed and then another to adjust the mirror and the seat. When she glanced at her watch, she was shocked to see the time. It was already ten minutes past one.

Thom would assume she wasn't coming. He'd think she'd stood him up…when nothing could be further from the truth.

Thom expelled his breath into the cold, and it came out looking like the snort of a cartoon bull. An *angry* cartoon bull. That was exactly how he felt. Once again, he'd allowed his heart to rule his head and he'd fallen prey to Noelle McDowell.

He should have known better. Everything he'd learned about heartache, Noelle had taught him. And now, fool that he was, he'd set himself up to be taken again. Noelle McDowell was untrustworthy. He knew it and yet he'd still risked disappointment and worse.

Slapping his hands against his upper arms to ward off the cold, he paced the area beneath the trees across from the pool at Lions' Park. This had been their special meeting place. It was here that Thom had kissed Noelle for the second time. Here, they'd met and talked and shared their secrets. Here, he'd first confessed his love.

A car door slammed in the distance. Probably the police coming to check out his vehicle, which was parked in a lot that was closed to the public at this time of night. He deserved to get a ticket for being enough of an idiot to trust Noelle.

He didn't know why he'd hung around as long as he had. Looking at his watch he saw that it was twenty after one. She'd kept him waiting nineteen minutes too long. Her non-appearance was all the proof he'd ever need.

"Thom...Thom!" Noelle called out as she ran across the lawn.

Angry and defiant, he stepped out from beneath the shadow of the fifty-foot cedar tree.

"Thank goodness you're still here," she cried and to her credit, she did sound relieved. She was breathless when she reached him. "I had to sneak out of the house."

"Sneak out? You're almost thirty years old!"

"I know, I know. Listen, I'm so sorry." She pushed back the sleeve of her coat and squinted at her watch.

"You waited—I can't believe you stayed for twenty extra minutes. I prayed you would, but I wouldn't have blamed you if you'd left."

The anger that had burned in him moments earlier evaporated so fast it shocked him.

"When did they turn Walnut into a dead-end street?"

"Years ago." Of course she'd drive down the same street they'd used as teenagers. He'd forgotten the changes made over the last decade; it hadn't occurred to him that she wouldn't know. "You're here now."

"Yes…listen, I know I shouldn't do this, but I can't help myself." Having said that, she slipped her arms around his waist and hugged him hard. His own arms went around her, too, tentatively and then with greater strength.

Closing his eyes and savoring the feel of her was a mistake, the first of many he knew he'd be making. She smelled like Christmas, somehow, and her warmth wrapped itself around him.

"Why'd you do that?" he asked gruffly as she released him and took a step back. He was trying to hide how damn good it'd felt to hold her.

"It's the only way I could think of to thank you for staying, for believing in me enough to wait."

"I wasn't exactly enumerating your good points while I stood here freezing."

"I know, I wouldn't either—I mean, well, you know what I mean."

He did.

Clearing off a space on the picnic table, Noelle climbed up and sat there just as she had when they were teenagers. "All right," she said, drawing in a deep breath. "Let's talk. Since you were the one to suggest we do this, you should go first."

So she'd become a take-charge sort of woman. That didn't surprise him. She'd displayed leadership qualities in high school, as well, serving on the student council and as president of the French Club. "All right, that's fair enough." She might be able to sit, but Thom couldn't. He had ten years of anger stored inside and that made it impossible to stand still for long. "We argued, remember?"

"Of course I do. The argument had to do with our mothers. You said something derogatory about mine and I defended her."

"As I recall, you had a less-than-flattering attitude toward *my* mother."

"But you were the first…" She paused. "None of that's important now. What we should be discussing is what happened afterward."

Once again she was right. "We made up, or so I thought."

"We made up because we refused to allow the ongoing feud between our mothers to come between us. Later that day, you wrote me a note and suggested we elope."

Her voice caught just a little. He wanted so badly to believe her. It was a struggle not to. "I loved you, Noelle."

She smiled, but he saw pain in her eyes and it shook him. For years he'd assumed that she'd used his love against him. That she'd stood him up just to hurt him. To humiliate him. He'd never really understood why. Was it vindication on behalf of her mother?

"We were going to confront our parents, remember?" Noelle said.

"Yes. I made a big stand, claiming how much I loved you and how I refused to let either of our mothers interfere in our lives. You should've heard me."

"I did, too!" she declared. "I spilled out my guts to them. Can you imagine how humiliating it was to have to go back and confess that you'd tricked me—that you'd jilted me?"

"Me!" he shouted. "You were the one—"

Noelle held up both hands and he let his anger fade. "Something happened. It must have." She pressed one hand to her heart. "I swear by all I consider holy that I've never lied to you."

"You're assuming I did?" he challenged.

"Yes. I mean no," she cried, confused now. "Something *did* happen, but what?"

"I don't know," he said. "I was here at three, just like I wrote you in the note."

She frowned, and he wondered if she was going to try to tell him she hadn't gotten his note. He knew otherwise because he'd personally seen Kristen hand it to her at school.

"The note said eight."

"Three," he insisted. Now it was his turn to look perplexed. "I wrote down three o'clock."

"The note said…" She brought her hand to her mouth. "No, I refuse to believe it."

"You think Kristen changed the time?"

"She wouldn't do that." She shook her head. "I know my sister, and she'd never hurt me like that."

"How do you explain the discrepancy then?"

"I have no idea." She squeezed her eyes shut. "I remember it vividly. You'd sent it to me after your math class."

His defenses were down. Time rolled back, and the events of that day were starting to focus in his mind. The fog of his pain dissipated. Finally he was able to look at the events with a clear head and an analytical eye.

"Kristen spilled soda on it," Noelle said thoughtfully. "Do you think that might have smudged the number?"

"It might explain part of it—but not the nasty note you left on my windshield."

She had the grace to blush at the reminder. "After waiting until after ten o'clock, I didn't know what to do. It was pretty dark by then, and I couldn't believe you'd just abandon me. I was positive something must've happened, so I phoned your house."

He nodded, encouraging her to go on.

"Your father said you were out with your friends bowling. I went to the alley to see for myself." Her voice tightened. "Sure enough, you were in there, boozing it up with your buddies."

"Don't tell me you actually thought I was having a good time?"

"Looked like it to me."

"Noelle, I was practically crying in my beer. I felt… I felt as if I'd just learned about some tragedy that was going to change my whole life."

"Why didn't you call me? How could you believe I'd stand you up? If you loved me as much as you said, wouldn't you make some effort to find out what happened?"

"I did." To be fair, it'd taken him a day, but he had to know, had to discover how he could've been so mistaken about Noelle. "I waited until the following afternoon.

Your mother answered the phone and said I'd already done enough damage. She hung up on me."

"She never told me," Noelle whispered. "She never said a word."

"Why would she?" Thom murmured. "Your mother assumed I'd done you wrong, just the way everyone else in your family did."

"I left that horrible note on your car and you still phoned me?"

He nodded.

"I can only imagine what you must have thought."

"And you," he said.

They both grew quiet.

"I'm so sorry, Thom," she finally said. "So very sorry."

"So am I." He was afraid to touch her, afraid of what would happen if she came into his arms.

Noelle brushed the hair back from her face and when he glanced at her, he saw tears glistening in her eyes.

"It all worked out for the best, though, don't you think?" he asked. He had to say *something*.

She nodded. Then after a moment she spoke in a voice so low he had to lean closer to hear. "Do you really believe that?"

"No." He reached for her then, crushing her in his arms, lifting her from the picnic table and holding her as if his very life depended on keeping her close to his heart.

His mouth found hers, and her lips were moist and soft, her body melting against his. Their kisses were filled with hunger and passion, with mingled joy and discovery. This sense of *rightness* was what had been missing from every relationship he'd had since his breakup with Noelle. Nothing had felt right with any other woman. He loved Noelle. He'd always loved her.

She buried her face in his shoulder and he kissed the top of her head. Her arms circled his neck and he ran his fingers through her hair, gathering it in his hands as he closed his eyes and let his emotions run free— from anger to joy. From joy to fear. From fear to relief.

"What happens now?" he asked. They didn't seem to have many options. Each had made a life without the other.

She didn't answer him for a long time, but he knew she'd heard the question.

"Noelle," he said as she raised her head. "What do we do now?"

She blinked back tears. "Do we have to decide this minute? Can't you just kiss me again?"

He smiled and lowered his mouth to hers. "I think that could be arranged."

Fresh from Sunday services—where she'd been inspired by a sermon on giving—Mary Sutton drove to the local Walmart store. She refused to show up the following day and not have the items on her list. No doubt Sarah McDowell assumed she'd arrive at the club empty-handed, but Mary fully intended to prove otherwise.

As soon as Greg had settled in front of the television set watching the Seahawks' play-off game, she was out the door. Shopping this close to Christmas went against every dictate of common sense. Usually she was the organized one. Christmas gifts had been purchased, wrapped and tucked away soon after Thanksgiving. But, with these six Christmas baskets, she had no choice. She had to resort to last-minute shopping.

The parking lot at Walmart was packed. Finding a space at the very rear of the lot, Mary trudged toward the busy store. She dreaded dealing with the mob of shoppers inside. On the off-chance she might have a repeat of that horrible scene in Value-X, she surveyed the lot—looking up one row and down the next—in search of Sarah's vehicle. She sighed with relief when she didn't see the other woman's car.

List in hand, Mary grabbed a cart and headed straight for the toy section. She hoped the store would have Barbie dolls left on the shelf. She hated the thought of a single child being disappointed on Christmas morning. Fortunately, the shelves appeared to have been recently restocked.

Reaching for a Firefighter Barbie doll, she set it inside her basket. With a sense of accomplishment, she wheeled the cart around the corner to the riding toys. To her horror and dismay, she discovered Sarah McDowell reading the label on a toddler-sized car. This was her worst nightmare.

"No," she muttered, not realizing Sarah would hear her.

Her bitterest enemy turned and their eyes locked. "What are *you* doing here?" Sarah demanded.

"The same thing you are."

Sarah gripped her cart with both hands, as if she was prepared to engage in a second ramming session. Frankly, Mary had suffered all the humiliation she could stand and had no desire to go a second round.

"Can't you buy your grandson's gifts some other time?"

"How dare you tell me when I can or cannot shop." Mary couldn't believe the gall. She would shop when and where she pleased without any guidance from the likes of Sarah McDowell.

"Mary, hello."

Mary wanted to groan out loud. Janice Newhouse, the pastor's wife, was easing her cart toward them. "This must be Sarah McDowell. I've seen your photo on a real estate brochure." She smiled warmly at the woman who had caused Mary so much pain. "I'm Janice Newhouse."

"Hello." Sarah's return greeting was stiff.

"I've heard so much about you," Janice said, apparently oblivious to the tension between the two women.

"I'll just bet you have." Sarah said this as though to suggest that Mary was a gossipmonger, when nothing could be further from the truth. For years, she'd quietly refused to get drawn into any discussion involving Sarah. It wouldn't do either of them any good. The same could not be said for Sarah McDowell. She'd taken delight in blackballing Mary's membership in the Women's Century Club. She'd dragged Mary's name and reputation through the mud. Mary, on the other hand, had chosen the higher ground—with the exception, perhaps, of that newspaper column on the perfidy of real estate agents, and that certainly hadn't been a personal attack.

"I understand the Willis family bought their home through you," Janice said, making polite conversation.

"You know the Willises?"

"Yes, they're members of our church. So are Mary and her husband."

Sarah's expression was glacial. "Oh."

"Sarah and I are buying gifts for the charity baskets," Mary said.

"We divided the list and now we're each getting half," Sarah went on to explain. "Tomorrow we're assembling the baskets and taking them to Salvation Army headquarters."

That was much more than Janice needed to know, Mary thought irritably. Sarah was just showing off.

"That's wonderfully charitable of you both," Janice murmured.

"Thank you." Sarah added a pull toy to her basket. Mary reached for one herself.

Next Sarah took down a board game; Mary took two.

Sarah grabbed a skateboard.

"How generous you are," Janice commented, eyes widening as she observed their behavior. "Both of you appear to be very…zealous."

"I believe in giving back to the community," Mary said.

"As do I," Sarah insisted. By now her cart was so full she couldn't possibly cram anything else into it.

"Leave something for me to buy," Mary challenged, doing her best to keep the smile on her face from turning into a scowl.

"I'm the one who has the little girl who wants a Firefighter Barbie on my list," Sarah said, staring pointedly at the doll in Mary's cart.

"*I'm* the one with the gift list," Mary countered. "Besides, there are plenty of Barbie dolls."

"You aren't even supposed to be buying toys. That was *my* job." Sarah's eyes narrowed menacingly.

"Ladies, I don't think there's any reason to squabble

here." Janice raised both hands in a calming gesture. "Let me look at your lists."

"Fine," Sarah snapped.

"Good idea," Mary added in a far more congenial tone. She opened her purse and dug out the list Melody Darrington had given her.

Janice examined both pages. She ran down Sarah's first and then Mary's. She frowned. "Here's the problem," she said, handing them back. "You have the same list."

"That's impossible," Mary protested.

"Let me see." Sarah snatched Mary's from her hand with such speed it was a wonder Mary didn't suffer a paper cut.

"That's what I think happened," Janice said. "You were accidentally given one list instead of two."

Sarah glanced over each page. "She's right."

Mary wanted to weep with frustration. "Do you mean to say we're actually working from the same list?" It made sense now that she thought about it. Melody had been so busy that morning, and the phone was ringing off the hook. It was no wonder the secretary had been distracted.

"You were supposed to pick up the grocery items," Mary said.

"I most certainly was not. That was *your* job."

If Sarah was trying to be obtuse and irritating, she was succeeding.

Janice glanced from one to the other. "Ladies, this is for the Christmas baskets, remember?"

Mary smiled benevolently at the pastor's wife, who was new to the area. Janice couldn't know. But then, a twenty-year-old feud wasn't something Mary was inclined to brag about.

"She's right," Sarah said again. "We're both behaving a bit childishly, don't you think?"

Mary was staying away from that question.

"I'll call Melody in the morning and pick up the second half of the list."

"No, you won't," Mary told her. "I'll do it."

"I said I would," Sarah said from between clenched teeth.

"You don't need to, I will."

"Would you ladies prefer that I do it?" Janice volunteered.

"No way," Sarah muttered.

"Thank you, but no," Mary said more politely.

Janice looked doubtful. "You're sure?"

"Yes."

"Yes." Sarah's voice blended with Mary's.

"All right, ladies, I'll leave you to your good works then."

Out of the corner of her eye, Mary watched Janice stroll away.

As soon as the pastor's wife was out of earshot, Sarah said, "You can pick up the list if you want." She made it sound as though she was making a big concession.

Naturally, she'd agree now. Mary sighed; this problem with the list complicated everything. "I'll need time to shop for the groceries."

"And your point is?"

"Shouldn't it be obvious?" Clearly it wasn't. "We'll need to meet on the morning of the twenty-fourth now."

"Christmas Eve?"

"Yes, the twenty-fourth is generally known as Christmas Eve," Mary told her a bit sarcastically.

"Fine. Let's meet at the club at nine and deliver the baskets to the Salvation Army from there."

"Fine."

"In the meantime," Sarah suggested, "let's do the sensible thing and divide up the toys on this list. Why don't I get the girls' stuff and you get the boys'?"

Wordlessly, they each returned half of their purchases. Mary hated to follow Sarah's lead, but for once the woman had come up with a reasonable idea. "I'll see you Tuesday morning at nine," she finally said.

Sarah gave a curt nod.

Mary wheeled her cart to the front of the store. All the cashiers were busy, so she found the shortest line and waited her turn. Not until a few moments later did she notice that Sarah stood in the line beside hers.

Mary took a magazine from the stand, leafed through it and tossed it into her cart.

Sarah placed two magazines in hers.

Mary decided to splurge and buy a candy bar. As she put it in the cart, she glanced at Sarah. The other woman grabbed one of every candy bar on the rack. Refusing to be outdone, Mary reached for two.

Sarah rolled her eyes and then emptied the entire container of candy into her cart.

Mary looked over and saw two men staring at them. A woman was whispering to her companion, pointing in her and Sarah's direction.

Once again, they'd managed to make spectacles of themselves.

NOELLE McDOWELL'S JOURNAL

December 22

I just got back from church, and it was lovely to attend services with Mom and Dad and Carley. The music was stirring and brought back so many memories of Christmases spent in Rose. I wish I'd paid closer attention to the sermon, but my mind refused to remain focused on the pastor's message. All I could think about was Thom.

Now that we've talked, I think we've actually created more problems than we've solved. We're going to get together again later in the day, but that's not until one. We both realize we can't leave things as they are, yet neither one of us knows where to go from here.

Still, it's wonderful to know my faith in him was justified. That makes this decision even harder, though. I'm afraid I'm falling in love with him again—if I ever stopped!—but there are so many complications. In fact, I wonder if our best choice would be simply to call it quits. But I'm not sure we can, because we made a mistake last night. We kissed.

If we hadn't done that, I might've found the courage to shake Thom's hand, claim there were no hard feelings and walk away. But we did kiss and now. . .well, now we're in *a quandary. I wish his kisses didn't affect me, but they do. Big time. Oh boy, nothing's changed in that department. It's as if I was sixteen all over again, and frankly, that's a scary feeling.*

I felt Thom's kisses all the way through me, from head to toe. Thom felt them, too, and I think he's just as confused as I am. Things got intense very quickly, and we both recognized we had to stop. Now it's decision time.

Thom withdrew from me, physically and emotionally, and I did from him, too. We both tried to play it cool—as if this was all very nice and it was good to clear the air. He acted as if we should just get on with our lives. I played along and was halfway back to the car when he stopped me. He wanted to know if we could meet at the mall today to talk again.

God help me, I jumped at the invitation. Maybe I should've been more nonchalant, but I couldn't do it. I was just happy for the chance to see him again.

Five

Shopping was the perfect excuse to get out of the house on Sunday afternoon, and Noelle used it. Her mother was gone, her father was absorbed in some televised football game and Carley was in her room checking "Buffy" websites on her computer.

"I'm going out for a while," Noelle said casually.

Her father's eyes didn't waver from the television screen. "Are you meeting Thom?"

"Ah…"

Her father raised his hand. "Say no more. What do you want me to tell your mother if she asks?"

"That I've gone shopping… We're meeting at the mall."

"That's all she needs to know."

Noelle kissed her father on the cheek. His eyes didn't leave the screen as he reached inside his pants pocket and handed her his car keys. "Why don't you take my car again?"

"Thanks, Dad."

"Don't mention it." Then her father did look away

from the television and his gaze sought hers. "You have feelings for this young man?"

Noelle nodded. It was the truth, much as she hated to acknowledge it, even to herself.

Her father nodded, too. "I was afraid of that."

His words lingered in Noelle's mind as she drove to the Rose Mall on the west side of town. She'd lived for this moment ever since she and Thom had parted the night before. They'd resolved what both had considered a deception, but so many questions were still unanswered. They needed time to think, to consider the consequences of becoming involved a second time. Nothing had changed between their families—or more specifically, their mothers—but other things *were* different. Noelle wasn't the naive eighteen-year-old she'd been ten years ago; neither was Thom.

It took a good twenty minutes to find a parking space, and the mall was equally crowded. Carolers dressed in Victorian costumes stood in front of the JCPenney store, cheerfully singing "Silver Bells." Noelle wished she could listen for a while, but fearing she might be late, she paused only a moment to take in the sights and the sounds of the holiday season.

She hurried through the overheated mall and found Thom at a table in the food court, just the way they'd agreed. He stood as she approached.

"I haven't kept you waiting, have I?" she asked.

"No, no. It occurred to me that with Christmas this close we might have trouble finding a table so I grabbed one early."

He'd always been thoughtful. As he put down his coffee and pulled out her chair, she shrugged out of her coat and threw it on the back of the seat. "Would you like to get some lunch?"

She shook her head. "You should have something, though." Her stomach had been upset all morning.

"Are you ill?"

"No—it's guilt." He might as well know. She'd been anxious since last night, since their first moonlit kiss... All through church services and afterward, she'd repeatedly told herself how ridiculous it was to sneak around behind her mother's back. Her father had apparently been doing it for years, but secretive actions truly bothered Noelle.

"Guilt?"

"I don't like being dishonest."

"Then tell your mother." Thom made it sound so easy, but he didn't need an excuse every time he stepped out the front door. He didn't even live at home, and he wasn't visiting his family for Christmas the way she was. He wasn't accountable to his parents for every minute spent outside their presence.

"Did you let your parents know we were meeting?" she asked.

He half grinned, looking sheepish. "No."

"That's what I thought."

"How about coffee?" he asked in an all-too-obvious effort to change the subject. "I could use a refill."

She gave a quick nod. She'd been counting the minutes until they could talk again. After their meeting in the park, she'd barely slept. She'd relived their conversation—and their kisses—over and over. It seemed a miracle that they'd finally learned what must have happened that day ten years ago. Truly a Christmas miracle. Now, if only their mothers would miraculously reconcile…

Thom left and returned a few minutes later with two steaming cups of coffee.

Noelle held her cup with both hands, letting the heat warm her palms. She hadn't felt chilled before, but she did now. "I—I don't know where to start."

"Why didn't you ever come home?" he asked bluntly. "Start by telling me that."

"It was just too painful to come back here. I made excuses at first and it got easier after a while. Plus, Mom and Dad and my sisters were always willing to visit Texas. It's beautiful in a way that's completely different from the Northwest. Oh, and the shopping is excellent."

He laughed. "Is there anyone special in your life?"

"I have a number of good friends."

"Male or female?"

She hesitated. "Female."

Thom visibly relaxed. "You don't date much, then?"

"Of course I date—I've gone out lots. Well, maybe not as much as I'd like, but I *was* engaged for a while. How about you?"

"I came close to getting engaged. Twice."

Without knowing a single detail, Noelle was instantly jealous. "Who?"

He seemed pleased by her reaction. He leaned back in his chair, stretched out his legs and crossed his ankles. "No one you know. Besides, I'm the one asking the questions here. You can drill me later."

"No way! In other words, you became some kind of ladies' man after you dumped me?"

His face suddenly grew serious and he reached

across the table for her hand. "I didn't dump you, No-elle."

She'd meant to tease him but realized her remark was insensitive—not to mention plain wrong. "I know. I apologize. Chalk it up to a bad choice of words."

Thom squeezed her hand. "Do you think that's what happened with our mothers?" he asked. "A bad choice of words?"

"How do you mean?"

"Think about it. Just now, you reverted to your old thought pattern—your assumption that you'd been betrayed. It wasn't until after you spoke that you remembered what had really happened."

He was right. The words had slipped out easily, thoughtlessly.

"Our mothers are probably behaving in the same way. After all these years, they're caught in this pattern of disparaging each other, and they can't break the habit."

Noelle wasn't sure she agreed with him. For one thing, she knew her mother had desperately tried to end the feud. Every attempt had been rebuffed. "I don't think it's a good idea to discuss our mothers."

"Why not?"

"Because we argue. You want to defend your mother and I want to defend mine, and the two of us end up fighting. Besides, weren't we talking about the women in your life after I left Rose?"

He chuckled. "You make it sound like there were hordes of them."

"There weren't?" She pretended to be shocked.

He shook his head. "Not really. Two I considered

marrying and a few others I saw for a while. What about you?"

"You keep asking. All right, I was serious once. Paul was a computer programmer, and we both worked for the same company, developing new software. It was an exciting time in the business and we got caught up in the thrill of it all." Paul was actually very sweet and very brilliant, but their romance wasn't meant to be. Noelle had been the first to realize it. She'd ended their brief engagement, and they'd parted on good terms, remaining friends to this day. "After the launch of Curtains, our new operating system, well…it was curtains for our marriage plans, too," she said, smiling at her own feeble pun.

"Just one guy?" Thom asked.

"Don't sound so disappointed." Noelle had told him far more than necessary. He hadn't said a word about either of the women he'd loved.

"Listen, what I said earlier regarding our mothers— I wonder if—"

"I don't want to discuss our mothers, Thom."

"We can't avoid it forever."

"Maybe not," she agreed, "but does it have to be the first thing we talk about?"

"It's not," he argued.

"Look at us," she said. "I haven't been with you fifteen minutes and already we're both on the defensive. This isn't going to work." She was ready to give up and go home, but Thom stopped her.

"Okay, we'll leave our mothers out of the conversation."

Now it seemed neither one had anything to say.

"I kept waiting to hear that you were married," she

said after a silence. "But I refused to ask. That's silly I suppose." It was like waiting for the dentist's drill; when it happened there'd be pain and she hadn't been in a hurry to experience it.

"I assumed you'd get married first," he said.

Noelle grinned, shaking her head. "There's something else we need to talk about," she murmured. "What are we going to do now?" She began with the least palatable option—which was also the easiest. "I mean, we could shake hands and say it's great to have this cleared up, then just go back to our respective lives." She waited, watching for a response from him.

His face revealed none of his thoughts. "We could do that," he said. "Or…" He looked at her.

"Or we could renew our friendship."

Thom leaned back in his chair. "I like that option."

So did Noelle. "But, as you said, there's still the situation with our mothers." Now she was the one bringing it up, although she'd hoped to avoid any mention of their mothers' feud. It was futile, she realized. They *couldn't* avoid it, no matter how hard they tried.

"If your mother hadn't borrowed my great-grandmother's tea service," Thom began, "she—"

"My mother?" Noelle cried. "I agree she made a mistake, but she was the first to admit it. Your mother refused to forgive her, and that says a lot about the kind of person she is."

Thom's eyes were flinty with anger. "Don't paint *your* mother as the one who was wronged because—"

Noelle was unwilling to listen to any more. "Listen, Thom, this isn't going to solve anything. I think it'd be best if we dropped the subject entirely."

"That isn't the only thing you want to drop, is it?"

It was a question she didn't want to answer. A question that implied it would be best for all concerned if they simply walked away from each other right now. Their circumstances hadn't changed, not really; the business with their mothers would always be an obstacle between them. They could ignore it, but it would never disappear.

She stood and gathered her purse, pulled on her coat. This time Thom didn't try to stop her.

"So, you're walking away at the first sign of difficulty," he said.

"No. As a teenager my heart was open to you and your family, but I'm older now."

"What's that got to do with anything?" he demanded.

"This time, my eyes are open, too."

He looked as if he wanted to continue their argument. But she didn't have the heart for it. Obviously Thom didn't, either, because he let her go without another word.

"Help me carry everything in, Greg," Mary Sutton said as she stepped into the house. Her arms were loaded with plastic bags bursting at the seams.

Mary had never understood or appreciated football, and she didn't mind saying so. Her husband's gaze reluctantly left the television screen, where a bunch of men in tight pants and large helmets chased after an oddly shaped ball. As far as she was concerned, it was ridiculous the way they grunted and called out a few numbers now and then and groped their privates right on national television.

"Greg, are you going to help me or not?"

Her husband slowly stood up, his eyes still on the TV. "Honey, it's third down and inches."

He might as well be speaking Greek, but she wasn't going to argue with him. From the sudden reaction of the crowd, something had happened. Greg muttered, shaking his head in a disparaging manner. Mary pretended not to hear and walked back out to the car.

A moment later, he met her in the garage. "We're losing."

"Sorry, darling." She hoped she sounded sympathetic, but she didn't try very hard. Men and their football.

"What on earth did you buy?" he complained, lifting the last of the blue plastic bags from the car's trunk.

"Oh, various things," she said dismissively. "This Christmas basket project hasn't been a positive experience," she went on, following her husband into the house.

"Why not?"

Distressed and angry, she blurted out, "You won't believe this. Sarah McDowell was there!"

"At Walmart?" Even Greg sounded surprised. "Don't tell me we've lost our shopping privileges there, too?"

"Very funny." The incident at the Value-X would haunt her forever.

"So you got along better?"

"I wouldn't say that, but I did discover the problem. We had the same list."

"For the Christmas baskets?"

"Yes." Mary set her load on top of the kitchen counter.

The football game ended, and Greg reached for the remote control to turn off the television set. He opened the first sack and seemed pleasantly surprised to find a stash of candy bars. "For me?" he asked. Without waiting for her to respond, he peeled the wrapper halfway down a Baby Ruth bar and took a bite.

"You can have them all." She threw herself onto the sofa.

Her husband walked into the family room and sat down. "You'd better tell me exactly what happened."

"What makes you think anything did?"

Greg chortled. "I haven't been married to you all these years without knowing when something's bothering you."

"Oh, Greg," she moaned. "I behaved like such an idiot." She longed to cover her face with her hands.

"What went wrong this time?"

She shook her head, unwilling to reveal how low she'd sunk. One thing she'd discovered years ago was still true: Sarah McDowell brought out the very worst in her. It never failed. Mary became another person whenever Sarah was around—a person she didn't like.

"Do you want to talk about it?"

"No. I want to crawl into bed and hide my head in shame." The most embarrassing part of all was that the pastor's wife had seen the whole thing.

"Tomorrow morning, I need to go back to the Club."

"For what?"

"I need the second half of the list."

"What's on the list?"

"I won't know until I see it, now will I?" She didn't mean to be short-tempered, but this afternoon hadn't been one of her best.

"I don't know if I want you driving. There's an ice storm forecast."

"Greg, I have to get that list. I told Sarah I'd take care of this. It's my responsibility."

"Then I'll drive you."

"You will?" Mary felt better already.

"Of course. Can't have you out on icy roads." Her husband finished off the candy bar and returned to the kitchen, where he rummaged through the bags on the counter. "You never did say why you bought all this candy."

Mary looked over at the ten plastic bags that lined her kitchen counter and shuddered. Half of them were filled with candy bars. "You don't want to know."

Greg didn't respond, but she caught him sneaking more Baby Ruth bars into his pockets and the sleeves of his sweater. He wasn't fooling her, but some things were best ignored.

On the other hand, certain things had to be faced. "Greg," she said thoughtfully. "I'm worried about Thom."

"Why?"

"Did you see him with Noelle last night? The two of them were dancing."

"Yes, dear, I saw them."

"Doesn't that concern you?" she asked.

"No." He added a couple of candy bars to his pants pockets, as though she wasn't going to see them protruding.

"Well, it should. Noelle is a sweet girl, but she's her mother's daughter. She's not to be trusted."

"Thom is an adult. He's fully capable of making his own decisions. My advice is to stay out of it."

Mary couldn't believe her husband would say such

a thing to her. "You don't mean that! After what happened the last time—"

"You heard me. Stay out of it."

"But Thom is—"

Greg just shook his head. She wanted to say more but swallowed the words. Fathers weren't nearly as caring and concerned about matters of the heart; they lacked sensitivity. Greg hadn't spent time with Thomas the way she had that fateful summer ten years earlier. The McDowell girl had crushed him.

Her husband started toward the garage.

"Greg," she said.

"Yes, dear?"

"Put the candy bars back. I'm adding them to the charity baskets."

He muttered something under his breath, then said, "Yes, dear."

When Thom returned from the mall, he was suffering a full-blown case of the blues. His apartment had never seemed emptier. The small Christmas tree he'd purchased already decorated looked pitiful in the middle of his coffee table. Some Christmas this was turning out to be.

The light on his answering machine blinked, demanding his attention, and for half a heartbeat he thought it might be Noelle. But even as he pressed the Play button, he realized she wouldn't phone.

"Hey, Thom, this is Jonathan Clark," the message said. "Give me a call when you've got a moment."

Thom reached for the phone and punched in the number the investment broker had left. He knew Jonathan but didn't consider him a close friend. He was a business associate and Kristen McDowell's fiancé. This was the first time Jonathan had sought him out socially; Thom hoped it had something to do with Noelle.

After a brief conversation, they agreed to meet at a local pub. Jonathan didn't say why, but it didn't matter. The way Thom felt, he was grateful for any excuse to get out of the house. The walls were closing in around him. Some jovial guy-talk and loud music was exactly what he needed. Although Jonathan was about to marry into the other camp, Thom knew he'd be objective.

Jon was sitting at the bar nursing a dark ale when Thom joined him. The music in the background was Elvis Presley's "Blue Christmas"—appropriate under the circumstances. They exchanged pleasantries and then Jonathan got right to the point.

"I wanted to make sure there weren't any hard feelings about last night."

"You mean finagling it so I ended up dancing with Noelle? No problem."

"I didn't really want to do it, but Kristen seemed to think it was important."

Thom pulled out his wallet and paid for his beer when the bartender delivered it. "Like I said, it wasn't a big deal."

"So you and Kristen's sister were once an item?"

"Once."

"But no more?"

Thom took a deep swallow of the cold beer. "There's trouble between our families."

"Kristen told me about it."

"You're lucky, you know." Jonathan faced none of the challenges he did.

"Very," Jonathan agreed.

There was a pause, not an uncomfortable one. Jon seemed willing to discuss the situation further, but he wouldn't force it. He'd left it up to Thom.

"Noelle and I talked after the dance," he finally ventured.

Jonathan swiveled around on his stool in order to get a better look at Thom. "How'd it go?"

"Last night? Good." His blood warmed at the memory of their kisses. It'd taken every ounce of self-control he'd possessed to let her go. That was one of the reasons he'd suggested they meet at the mall today; it was neutral ground.

"Did you two work everything out?"

"We tried." He waited, half hoping Jonathan would question him about it. Jonathan didn't. Thom sighed, feeling a little discouraged. Now that he'd started, he wanted to talk. "I think we're both leery of getting involved a second time," he continued. "Her home's in Texas now and I live here."

"Right, got ya."

"But it's more than logistics." He tipped back the mug and took another swallow of beer. "We have… this situation. She wants to defend her mother. I want to defend mine."

"Only natural." Jonathan glanced at his watch.

Thom shut up. He had the feeling he was boring the other man. Perhaps he had someplace he needed to be.

Jonathan's next remark surprised him. "Kristen and I were making out our guest list and I put down your name. You'll come, won't you?"

"Sure," Thom answered almost flippantly, and then it occurred to him that if he accepted the invitation, he'd see Noelle again. He found himself eager for the opportunity. "Speaking of the wedding—" well, not really, but he didn't know how else to introduce the topic "—did Kristen ever mention her sister being involved with a guy named Paul?"

Jonathan considered it for a moment, then shook his head. "Not that I can remember. Why?"

"Just curious." And jealous. And worried. Noelle had said it was over between her and this Paul character, but Thom had to wonder. She seemed far too willing to walk away from their conversation this afternoon. Maybe the relationship with Paul wasn't as dead as she'd led him to believe.

"Paul," Jonathan repeated slowly. "Did she give you a surname?"

Thom shook his head.

The door to the pub opened, and Kristen McDowell walked inside. Jonathan glowed like a neon light, he was so pleased to see her. "Over here, sweetheart," he called, waving his hand.

Kristen walked to the bar and slipped her arm around her fiancé's waist. "Hello, Thom," she said as naturally as if they saw each other every day. "How's it going?"

"All right. I understand congratulations are in order."

Kristen smiled up at Jonathan and nodded.

Thom felt like an intruder. Reaching for his overcoat, he was getting ready to go when Kristen stopped him.

"There's no need to rush off."

He was about to pretend he had people to see, places to go, but then decided not to lie. "You sure?"

"Of course I'm sure."

Thom was eager to learn what he could about Noelle, so he lingered and ordered another beer. Jon did, too; Kristen had a glass of red wine.

Thom paid for the second round. The three of them sat on bar stools with Kristen in the middle, talking about Christmas plans for a few minutes. "She had me call you," Jonathan confessed suddenly.

Kristen elbowed her fiancé in the ribs. "You weren't supposed to tell him."

The second beer had loosened Thom's tongue. "She damn near knocked me off my feet when I first saw her."

"Kristen?" Jonathan asked, sounding worried.

"No, Noelle."

"Really?" This appeared to please Noelle's younger sister. "So you're still stuck on her, after all these years."

"Damned if I know," Thom muttered. He did know but he wasn't willing to admit it. "We decided it's not going to work."

"Why not?" Kristen sounded outraged.

"We met and talked this afternoon," Thom informed them both.

Jonathan frowned. "I thought you met last night after the dance."

"We did."

"So you've talked twice in the past twenty-four hours."

"Yeah, and like I said, we both realized there are too many complications."

Kristen raised her hand for the bartender. "We need another round."

"I think we've already done enough damage," Jonathan protested.

"Coffee here," she said, pointing at her fiancé. "Same as before over here." She made a sweeping gesture that included Thom.

The bartender did as requested. As soon as the wine and beer arrived, Kristen turned to face Thom. "I thought you loved my sister."

"I did once." He was still working on his second beer.

"But not now?"

Thom didn't want to answer her. Hell, the last time he'd admitted to loving Noelle he was just a kid. But he'd stood up to his parents and been willing to relinquish everything for Noelle. To say he'd loved her was an understatement. He'd been crazy about her.

"Well?" Kristen pressed. "Don't you have an answer?"

"I do," Thom said, picking up his beer. "I just don't happen to like it."

"What's that mean?" Jonathan asked Kristen.

"I think it means he still has feelings for Noelle." Then, as though she'd suddenly remembered, she said, "Hey! Her birthday's on Christmas Day, you know."

Like he needed a reminder. Not a Christmas passed that Thom forgot.

"She doesn't feel the same way about me," he murmured.

"Yeah, right," Kristen said, exaggerating the words. It took only two beers for him to bare his soul—and it was all for nothing because Noelle didn't love him anymore. It took only two beers to make him maudlin, he thought sourly.

"Yeah, right," Kristen said again.

"It's true," Thom argued. "Did you ask her?"

"Did you?" Kristen asked.

NOELLE McDOWELL'S JOURNAL

December 22
Afternoon

I blew it. I had the perfect chance to have a rational conversation with Thom. We had a chance to settle this once
and for all without the angst and emotion. It didn't happen. Instead I let the opportunity slip through my fingers.
Naturally I have a wealth of excuses, the first one being
that I didn't sleep more than a couple of hours all night.
This situation between Thom and me was on my mind and
I couldn't seem to let it go. My feelings swung from happiness to dread and from joy to fear, and then the whole
cycle repeated itself. I kept thinking about what I wanted
to say when we saw each other again. Then I started wor-
rying what would happen if he kissed me.

How is it that I can develop complicated software programs used all over the world, but when it comes to Thom
Sutton I'm hopeless?

Mom's home from shopping, and when Carley asked if
she'd gotten everything she needs for the Christmas baskets, it looked as if Mom was about to burst into tears. She
said she had a headache, and went to bed. Apparently I
wasn't the only one suffering from too little sleep. I have a

feeling that something happened with Mrs. Sutton again, which is bad news all the way around.

Kristen wasn't home when I tried to phone, although she hadn't said she was going out. I'd hoped to discuss this with her, get her perspective. She's heard just about everything else that's gone on between Thom and me since I arrived. I could use a sympathetic ear and some sisterly advice.

Everything fell into place so naturally between her and Jonathan, but it sure hasn't been that way with me. I actually considered talking to Carley, which is a sign of how desperate I'm beginning to feel.

I'm not going to see Thom again. We left the mall and nothing more was said. It's over, even though I don't want it to be. It was within my power to change things, and I didn't have the courage to do it. I could've run after him and begged him not to let our relationship end this way, not after we'd come so far. But I didn't, and I'm afraid this is something I'm going to regret for a long time to come.

Six

"**Y**ou don't need to worry about the dishes," Sarah McDowell protested.

Noelle continued to load the dishwasher. "Mom, quit treating me like a guest in my own home." The menial task gave her something to do. Furthermore, she hoped it would help take her mind off her disastrous meeting with Thom at the mall. She'd reviewed their conversation a dozen times and wished so badly it had taken a different course. Their second attempt at a relationship had staggered to a halt before it had really begun, she thought with regret as she rinsed off the dinner plates and methodically set them inside the dishwasher.

"Thank you, dear. This is a real treat," her mother said, walking into the family room to join her dad.

Sarah had returned from her shopping trip in a subdued mood. Noelle didn't ply her with questions, mainly because she wasn't in a talkative mood herself. Even Carley Sue seemed to be avoiding the rest of the family. Except for dinner, her sister had spent most of the day in her room, first on her computer, and then wrapping Christmas presents.

As Noelle finished wiping the counters, her youngest sister entered the kitchen. Carley glanced into the family room, where her parents sat watching television. Their favorite courtroom drama was on, and they seemed to be absorbed in it.

"Wanna play a game of Yahtzee?" Noelle asked. It was one of Carley's favorites.

Her sister shook her head, then motioned for Noelle to come into her room. Carley nodded toward their parents, then pressed her finger to her lips.

"What's going on?" Noelle asked, drying her hands on a kitchen towel.

"Shh," Carley said, tiptoeing back toward her room.

"What?" Noelle asked impatiently.

Carley opened her bedroom door, grabbed Noelle's hand and pulled her into the bedroom. To her shock, Thom stood in the middle of the room, wearing his overcoat.

"Thom!"

"Shh," both Thom and Carley hissed at her.

"What are you *doing* here?" she whispered.

"When did you trade bedrooms with your sister?" he asked.

"A long time ago." She couldn't believe he was in her family's home. Years ago, he'd come to the house and tapped on her bedroom window, and she'd leaned out on the sill and they'd kissed. Amazingly, her parents hadn't heard—and the neighbors hadn't reported him. "Why are you here?"

"I came to see you."

Okay, that much was obvious. But she still didn't understand why he'd come.

"It was a bit of a surprise to bump into your little sister."

"I didn't mind," Carley said. "But he scared me like crazy when he knocked on the window."

"Sorry," Thom muttered.

"You said he broke your heart," Carley said, directing her remarks at Noelle. "We threw popcorn at him, remember? At least, we thought it was him, but then it wasn't."

Noelle didn't need any further reminders of that unfortunate incident. "I broke his heart, too. It was all a misunderstanding."

"Oh." Carley clasped her hands behind her back and leaned against the door, waiting. She was certainly in no hurry to leave and seemed immoderately interested in what Thom had to say.

Thom glanced at her sister, who refused to take the hint, and then said, "We need to talk."

"Now? Here?"

He nodded and touched her face in the gentlest way. "Listen, I'm sorry about this afternoon. We didn't even talk about what's most important—and that's you and me."

"I'm sorry, too." Unable to resist, Noelle slipped her arms around his waist and they clung to each other.

"This is *so-o-o* romantic," Carley whispered. "Why don't you two sit down and make yourselves comfortable. Can I get you anything to drink?"

Her little sister was as much of a hostess as their mother, Noelle thought with amusement. "No, but thanks."

Thom shrugged. "I should leave, but—"

"No, don't," Noelle pleaded with him. It might make more sense to meet Thom later, but she didn't want him out of her sight for another second.

Thom sat on the edge of the bed and Noelle sat beside him. He took both her hands in his. "I've been doing a lot of thinking about us."

"I have, too," she said hurriedly.

"I don't want it to end."

"Oh, Thom, I don't either! Not the way it did this afternoon—and for all the wrong reasons." Noelle was acutely aware of her sister, listening in on their conversation, but she didn't care.

"Noelle, I know what I want, and that's you back in my life."

"Oh, Thom." She bit her lower lip, suddenly on the verge of tears.

Carley sighed again. "This is better than any movie I've ever seen."

Noelle ignored her. "What are we going to do about our families?" They couldn't pretend their relationship wouldn't cause problems.

"I've been thinking about that, but I'm just not sure." Thom stroked the side of her face, and his hand lingered there.

"Oh, this *is* difficult," Carley agreed.

Her little sister was absorbing every word. Had Carley left the room, Noelle was sure Thom would be kissing her by now. Then they'd be lost in the kissing and oblivious to anything else.

"Is there a solution for us? One that doesn't involve alienating our families. Or our mothers, at any rate." Thom didn't look optimistic.

"What about the tea service?" Noelle said, mulling over an idea. "You said there's no replacing it, but maybe if we found a similar one, your mother would be willing to accept it."

"I don't know," he said. "This wasn't just any tea service. It was a family heirloom that belonged to my great-grandmother. We'll never find one exactly like it."

"I know, but finding one even remotely similar would be a start toward rebuilding the relationship, don't you think?"

He didn't seem convinced. "Perhaps."

"Could you find out the style and type?"

Thom shook his head doubtfully. "I could try."

"Please, Thom. And see if there are any photos."

They hugged again and Noelle closed her eyes, savoring the feel of his strong arms around her, inhaling his clean, outdoorsy scent.

Everything had changed for her. The thought of returning to Texas and her life there held little appeal. For years, she'd stayed away from her hometown because it represented a past that had brought her grief, and now—now she knew this was where her future lay.

There was a knock on Carley's door.

Noelle and Thom flew apart and a look of panic came into Carley's eyes.

"The closet," Noelle whispered, quickly ushering Thom inside. No sooner had she shut the door than her little sister admitted their mother into the room.

Noelle figured they must look about as guilty as any two people could. Carley stared up at the bedroom ceiling and Noelle was tempted to hum a catchy Yuletide tune.

"I thought I'd turn in for the night," her mother said. She obviously hadn't noticed anything out of the ordinary.

"Good idea," Carley told her mother.

"You don't want to wear yourself out," Noelle added,

letting her arms swing at her sides. "With Christmas and all…"

Her mother gave them a soft smile. "It does my heart good to see the two of you together. You were like a second mother to Carley when she was a baby."

"Mom!" her little sister wailed.

"I always thought you'd have a house full of your own children one day," she said nostalgically. "Don't you remember how you used to play with all your dolls?"

Noelle wanted to groan, knowing that Thom was listening in on the conversation.

"You'd make a wonderful mother."

"Thank you, Mom," she said. "'Night now. See you in the morning."

"'Night." She stepped out the door.

Noelle sighed with relief and so did Carley. She was about to open the closet when her mother stuck her head back inside the room. "Noelle, do you have plans for the morning?"

"No, why?" she asked, her voice higher than normal.

"I might need some help."

"I'll be glad to do what I can."

"Thank you, sweetheart." And with that she was gone. For good this time.

After a moment, Thom opened the closet door and peered out. "Is it safe?"

"I think so."

"Do you want me to keep watch?" Carley asked. "You know, so you guys can have some privacy." She smiled at Thom. "He's been wanting to kiss you ever since you got here." She lowered her voice. "I think he's kinda cute."

"So do I," Noelle confessed. "And yes, some privacy would be greatly appreciated."

Carley winked at Thom. "I think I'll go out and see what Dad's doing."

The instant the door closed, Thom took her in his arms and lowered his mouth to hers. Noelle groaned softly, welcoming him. Together, they created warm, moist kisses, increasing in intensity and desire. Other than the brief episode in the park, it'd been years since they'd kissed like this. Yet his touch felt so familiar....

"It's always been you," he whispered.

She heard the desperation in his voice. "I know—it's always been you," she echoed.

He kissed her again with a hunger and a need that reflected her own.

"Oh, Thom, what are we going to do?"

"We're going to start with your suggestion and find a silver tea service," he said firmly. "Then we're going to give it to my mother and tell her it's time to mend fences."

"What if we *can't* find one?" She frowned. "Or what if we do and they still won't forgive each other?"

"You worry too much." He kissed the tip of her nose. "And you ask too many questions."

Sarah was sitting up in bed reading a brand-new and highly touted mystery when her husband entered their room.

"You've been quiet this evening," Jake commented as he unbuttoned his shirt.

"Have I?" She gazed at the novel, but her attention kept wandering. She'd read this paragraph at least six times and she couldn't remember what it said. Every word seemed to remind her of a friend she'd lost twenty years ago.

"You haven't been yourself since you got back from shopping."

Sarah decided to ignore his words. "I stopped in and said good-night to the girls before I went to bed. Isn't it nice that Noelle and Carley get along so well?"

"You're changing the subject," Jake said. "And not very subtly."

Sarah set aside the book. In her present frame of mind, she was doing the author and herself a disservice. She reached for the light, but instead of flicking it off, she fell back against her pillows.

"I ran into Mary this afternoon," she told her husband.

"Again?"

"Again," she confirmed. "This meeting didn't go much better than the one at Value-X."

"That bad?"

"Almost. I can't even begin to tell you how horribly the two of us behaved."

Jake chuckled, shaking his head. "Does this have anything to do with the two hundred or so candy bars I found in the back of the big freezer?"

"You saw?"

He nodded. "What is it with you two?"

"Oh, honey, I wish I knew. I *hate* this. I've always hated this animosity. It would've been over years ago if Mary had listened to reason."

Her husband didn't respond.

"Everything was perfectly fine until we were forced to work on this Christmas project. Until then, she ignored me and I ignored her."

"Ignored her, did you?" he asked mildly.

Sarah pretended not to hear his question. "I think Melody Darrington might have planned this." The scheme took shape in her mind. "Melody *must* have."

"Isn't she the club secretary?"

"You know Melody," Sarah snapped. "She's the cute blonde who sold me the tickets to the dance."

"I wasn't there when you picked up the tickets," Jake reminded her as he climbed into bed.

"But you know who I mean."

"If you say so."

"You do. Now listen, because I think I'm on to something here. Melody's the one who told me we couldn't rent the hall for Kristen's wedding unless I performed a community service for the club."

"Yes, I remember, and that's how you got involved in the Christmas basket thing."

"Melody's also the one who assigned me to that project," she went on. "There had to be dozens of other projects I could've done. Plus, she insisted I had to fulfill those hours this year. That makes no sense whatsoever."

"Why would Melody do anything like that?"

"How would I know?"

Her husband looked skeptical. "I think you might be jumping to conclusions here."

"Melody gave us half of the same list, too." Outrage simmered just below the surface as Sarah sorted through the facts. She tossed aside the covers and leaped out of bed. Hands on hips, she glared at her husband. Of course. It all added up. Melody definitely had a role in this, and Sarah didn't like it.

"Hey, I didn't do anything," Jake protested.

"I'm not saying you did." Still not satisfied, she

started pacing the area at the foot of the bed. "This is the lowest, dirtiest trick anyone's ever played on me."

"Now, Sarah, you don't have any real proof."

"Of course I do! Why did Melody make a copy of that list, anyway? All she had to do was divide it."

"Sounds like an honest mistake to me. Didn't you tell me the office was hectic that morning? Melody was dealing with you, the phones and everything else when she gave you and Mary the lists."

"Yes, but that's no excuse for what happened."

"You're angrier with yourself than Melody."

Sarah knew the truth when she heard it. The outrage vanished as quickly as it had come, and she climbed back into bed, next to her husband.

For a long time neither spoke. Finally Jake turned on their bedside radio and they listened to "Silent Night" sung by a children's choir. Their pure, sweet voices almost brought tears to Sarah's eyes.

"In two days, it'll be Christmas," she said in a soft voice.

"And Noelle's birthday." Her husband smiled. "Remember our first year? We could barely afford a Christmas tree, let alone gifts. Yet you managed to give me the most incredible present of all, our Noelle."

"Remember the next Christmas, when I'd just found out I was pregnant with Kristen?" she said fondly. "Our gift to each other was a secondhand washer." In the early years of their marriage, they'd struggled to make ends meet. Yet in many ways, those had been the very best.

Jake smiled. "We were poor as church mice."

"But happy."

"Very happy," he agreed, sliding his arm around her shoulders. "I thought it was clever of you to knit Christmas stockings for the girls the year Noelle turned four. Or was it five?"

"I didn't knit them," Sarah said sadly. "Mary did."

"Mary?"

"Don't you remember? She knit all the kids stockings, and I baked the cookies and we exchanged?"

"Ah, yes. You two had quite a barter system worked out."

"If we hadn't traded babysitting, none of us would've been able to afford an evening out." Once a month, they'd taken the girls over to their dearest friends' home for the night; Mary and Greg had done the same. It'd been a lifesaver in those early years. She and Jake had never been able to afford anything elaborate, but a night out, just the two of them, had been heaven. Mary and Greg had cherished their nights, as well.

"I miss her," Sarah admitted. "Even after all these years, I miss my friend."

"I know." Jake gently squeezed her shoulder.

"I'd give anything never to have borrowed the silver tea service."

"You were trying to help someone out."

"That's how it started, but I should've been honest with Mary. I should've told her the tea service wasn't for my open house, but for Cheryl's."

"Why didn't you?"

She'd had years to think about the answer to that question. "Because Mary didn't like Cheryl. I assumed she was jealous. Now…I don't know."

Sarah remembered the circumstances well. She'd recently begun selling real estate and Cheryl Carlson had given her suggestions and advice. Cheryl had wanted something to enhance the look of the dining room for her open house, and Sarah had volunteered to bring in the tea service. When she'd asked Mary, her friend had hesitated, but then agreed. Sarah had let Mary assume it was for her own open house.

"You were so upset when you found out the tea service had been stolen."

To this day her stomach knotted at the memory of having to face Mary and confess what had happened. Soon afterward, Cheryl had left the agency and hired on with another firm, and Sarah had lost touch with her.

"I'd always hoped that one day Mary would find it in her heart to forgive me."

"I did, too."

"I'm so sorry, sweetheart," Sarah whispered, resting her head against her husband's shoulder.

"Why are you apologizing to me?"

"Because you and Greg used to be good friends, too."

"Oh."

"Remember how you used to golf together."

"Yes."

"I wonder if Greg still plays."

"I see him out at the club every now and then," Jake told her.

"Does he speak to you?"

"Yes."

Sarah was comforted knowing that. "I'm glad."

"So am I," her husband said, then kissed her goodnight.

On December twenty-third, Thom's office was running on a skeleton crew. His secretary was in for half a day and he immediately handed her the assignment of locating every antique store in a hundred-mile radius.

He'd called his father before eight that morning. "Tell me what you know about Mom's old tea service."

"Tell you what I know?" he repeated. "It was stolen, remember?"

"I realize that," Thom said impatiently.

"What makes you ask?"

"I thought I'd buy her a replacement for Christmas."

"Don't you think you're leaving your shopping a little late?"

"Could be." Thom didn't feel comfortable sharing what this was really about, but he was going to do whatever he could to replace that damn tea service.

"I think we might have a picture of it somewhere."

Thom perked up.

"For years your mother looked for a replacement, you know. We hadn't actually taken a picture of the tea set, but it was in the background of another photograph."

Thom remembered now. His parents had the photo enlarged in order to get as much detail as possible.

"Do you still have the photograph? Or better yet, the enlargement?"

"I think it might be around here somewhere. I assume you need this ASAP."

"You got it."

"Well, I promised to drive your mother out to the Women's Century Club this morning and then to the grocery store. You're welcome to stop by the house and look."

"Where do you figure it might be?"

His father considered that for a moment. "Maybe the bottom drawer of my desk. There are a few old photographs there. That's my best suggestion."

"Anyplace else I should look?"

"Your mother's briefcase. Every once in a while she visits an antique store, but for the most part she's given up hope. She's still got her name in with several of the bigger places. If anything even vaguely similar comes in, the stores promised to give her a call."

"Has she gotten many calls?"

"Only two in all these years," his father told him. "Both of them excited her so much she could barely sleep until she'd checked them out. They turned out to be completely the wrong style."

Thom didn't know if he'd have any better success, but he had to try.

"Good luck, son."

"Thanks, Dad."

As soon as he hung up, Thom called Noelle's cell phone. She answered right away.

"Morning," he said, warming to the sound of her voice. "I hope you're free to do a bit of investigating."

"I am. I canceled out on Mom—told her I was meeting an old friend."

"Did she ask any questions?"

"No, but I could tell she was disappointed. I do so hope we're successful."

"Me, too. Listen, I've got news." Thom told her about the old photograph and what his father had said earlier. He hoped it would encourage Noelle, but she seemed disheartened when she spoke again.

"If your parents searched all these years, what are the chances of us finding a replacement now?"

"We'll just keep working on it. I'm not giving up, and I'm guessing you feel the same way."

"I do—of course."

"Good. How soon before we can meet?"

"Fifteen minutes."

"I'll wait for you at my parents' place."

On his way out the door, Thom grabbed the list Martha, his secretary, had compiled and when he read it over, he knew why he paid this woman top dollar. Not only had she given him the name and address of every store in the entire state, she'd also listed their websites and any other internet information.

"Merry Christmas," he said, then gave her the rest of the day off with pay.

Noelle was already parked outside his parents' house when Thom arrived. She got out of her car and joined him as he pulled into the driveway.

"Hi," she said softly.

Thom leaned over and kissed her. "Hi." The key to the house was under a decorative rock. He unlocked the door and turned off the burglar alarm. Holding Noelle's hand, he led her into his parents' home.

Noelle stopped in the entryway and glanced around. It'd been many, many years since she'd walked into this house. It wasn't really familiar—everything had been redecorated and repainted since she was a little girl— but the place had a comfortable relaxed feel. Big furniture dominated the living room, hand-knit stockings hung on the fireplace and the mantel was decorated with holly. The scent of the fresh Christmas tree filled the air.

"Your mother has a wonderful eye for color and design," she commented, taking in the bright red bows on the tree and all the red ornaments.

Still holding her hand, Thom led her into his father's den. The oak rolltop desk sat in the corner, and Thom immediately started searching through the bottom drawer. He found the stack of photographs his father had mentioned and sorted through them with Noelle looking over his shoulder. She leaned against him, and he wondered if she realized how good it felt to have her pressed so close to him. Or how tempting it was to turn and kiss her...

"That's it," she cried triumphantly when he flipped past a black-and-white picture. She grabbed it before he had a chance to take a second look. Examining the print, she murmured, "It really was exquisite, wasn't it?" She passed it back to him.

"It *is* beautiful," he said, emphasizing the present tense. Thom wasn't sure why he insisted on being this optimistic about finding a replacement. He suspected that wanting it so badly had a lot to do with it.

Reaching into his coat pocket, he pulled out the list Martha had compiled for him.

"Now that we have a picture," Noelle said, "I'll go home and scan it into Carley's computer. Then I'll send it out to these addresses and see what comes back."

"Great. But before you do, I'll get a copy of this photograph and start contacting local dealers. They might be able to steer me in a different direction."

"Oh, Thom, it'd mean so much to me if we could bring our mothers back together."

They kissed, and it would've been the easiest thing in the world to become immersed in the wonder of having found each other again. Her mouth was warm, soft to the touch. She enticed him, fulfilled him and tempted him beyond any woman he'd ever known or loved. He didn't know much about her present life. They'd spoken very little of their accomplishments, their friends, their jobs. It wasn't necessary. Thom *knew* her. The girl he'd loved in high school had matured into a capable, beautiful and very desirable adult.

"It's hard to think about anything else when you kiss me," she whispered.

"It is for me, too."

Before leaving the Sutton home, Thom put everything back as it was, and remembered to reset the burglar alarm.

After making a photocopy at his office, Thom gave her the original, thinking that would scan best.

"I'll go back to the house now and plead with Carley to let me on the computer," she told him.

"Okay, and I'll see what a little old-fashioned footwork turns up."

Noelle started to get into her car, then paused. "What'll happen if we don't find a replacement before I return to Texas?"

Thom didn't want to think about that yet. "I don't know," he had to admit.

"Want to meet in the park at midnight?" she asked.

Thom chuckled. "I'm a little old to be sneaking around to meet my girlfriend."

"That didn't stop you from climbing in my bedroom window last night."

True, but his need to see her had overwhelmed his caution, not to mention his good sense.

"I love you, Noelle." There, he'd said it. He'd placed his heart in her hands, to accept or reject.

Tears glistened in her eyes. "I love you, too—I never stopped loving you."

"Even when you hated me?"

She laughed shakily. "Even then."

NOELLE MCDOWELL'S JOURNAL

December 23
11:00 a.m.

I feel as if I'm on an emotional roller coaster. One moment I'm feeling as low as I can get, and the next I'm soaring into the clouds. Just now, I'm in the cloud phase. Thom found the picture of the tea set! We're determined to locate one as close to the original as possible. As I said to Thom, I'm hoping for a Christmas miracle. (I never knew I was such a romantic.) Normally I scoff at things like miracles, but that's what both Thom and I need. We've already had one miracle—we have each other back.

Before we parted this morning, Thom said he loved me. I love him, too. I've always loved Thom, and that's what made his deception—or what I believed was his deception—so terribly painful.

Now all we've got to do is keep our mothers out of the picture until we can replace the tea service. I know it's a challenging task, but we're up to it.

As of right now, we each have our assignments. Carley's using the computer for ten more minutes and then it's all mine. My job is to scan in the picture he found at his parents' house and send it to as many online antique dealers as I can. Thom is off checking local dealers and has some errands to run. We're going to meet up again later.

I had to cancel a lunch date with Kristen and Jonathan, but my sister understood. She's excited about Thom and me getting back together. Apparently she's had more of a hand in this than I realized. I really owe her.

Finding a tea service to replace the one that was stolen is turning out to be even harder than I expected—but we have to try. I believe in miracles. I was a doubter less than a week ago, but now I'm convinced.

Seven

"How many turkeys did you say we had to buy?"

"Six," Mary said, checking the list to make sure she was correct. December twenty-third, and the grocery store was a nightmare. The aisles were crowded, and many of the shelves needed restocking. The last thing Mary wanted to do was fight the Christmas rush, but that couldn't be helped. Next year, she'd leave the filling of these Christmas baskets to someone else.

"Get six bags of potatoes while you're at it," she told her husband as they rolled past a stack of ten-pound bags.

"Getting a little bossy, aren't you?" Greg muttered.

"Sorry, it's just that there are a hundred other things I'd rather be doing right now."

"Then you should've given the task to Sarah McDowell. Didn't you tell me she offered?"

Mary didn't want to hear the other woman's name. "I don't trust her to see that it's done properly."

"Don't you think you're being a little harsh?"

"No." That should be plain enough. The more she thought about her last encounter with Sarah McDowell, the more she realized how glad she'd be when they'd completed this project. "Being around Sarah has dredged up a whole slew of bad memories," she informed her husband.

Greg dutifully loaded sixty pounds of potatoes into the cart. As soon as he'd finished, Mary headed down the next aisle.

"My Christmas has been ruined," she said through gritted teeth.

"How's that?"

"Greg, don't be obtuse." She reached for several cans of evaporated milk and added them to the food piled high in their cart. "I've had to deal with *her*."

"Yes, but—"

"Never mind," Mary said, cutting him off. She didn't expect Greg to understand. Her husband had never really grasped the sense of loss she'd felt when Sarah destroyed their friendship with her deception. The silver tea service was irreplaceable; so was the friendship its disappearance had shattered.

"Hello, Mary." Jean Cummings, a friend who edited the society page, pulled her cart alongside Mary's. "Merry Christmas, Greg."

Her husband had the look of a deer caught in the headlights. He no more knew who Jean was than he would a stranger, although he'd attended numerous social functions with the woman.

"You remember Jean, don't you?" she said, hoping to prompt his memory.

"Of course," he lied. "Good to see you again."

"It looks like you're feeding a big crowd," Jean said, surveying the contents of Mary's cart.

Mary didn't bother to explain about the Christmas

baskets. "Is your family coming for the holidays?" she asked.

"Oh, yes, and yours too, I imagine?"

"Of course." Mary was eager to get about her business. She didn't have time to dillydally. As soon as she was finished with the shopping, she could go back to planning her own family's Christmas dinner. Greg would need to order the fresh Dungeness crabs they always had on Christmas Eve; he could do that while they were here.

"Tell me," Jean said, leaning close to Mary and talking in a stage whisper. "Am I going to get the scoop on Thom?"

"Thom?" Mary didn't know what she was talking about.

"I saw him just now in Mendleson's."

It was well known that the jeweler specialized in engagement rings.

"Thom's one of the most eligible bachelors in town. I know plenty of hearts will be broken when he finally chooses a bride."

Mary was speechless. She'd had lunch with her son on Friday and although he'd hinted, he certainly hadn't said anything that suggested he was on the verge of proposing. She didn't even know who he was currently seeing.

"I'm sure Thom would prefer to do his own announcing," Greg said coolly, answering for Mary.

"Oh, drat," Jean muttered. "I was hoping you'd let the cat out of the bag."

"My lips are sealed," Mary said, recovering. "Have a wonderful Christmas."

"You, too." Jean pushed her cart past them.

As soon as the society page editor was out of earshot, Mary gripped her husband's forearm. "Has Thom spoken to you lately?"

"This morning," Greg told her. "But he didn't say anything about getting engaged."

"Who could it be?" Mary cried, aghast that she was so completely in the dark. As his mother, she should know these things.

"If he was serious about any woman, we'd know."

Mary wasn't buying it.

"Let's not leap to conclusions just because our son happened to walk into a certain jewelry store. I'm sure there's a perfectly logical reason Thom was in Mendleson's and I'll bet it hasn't got a thing to do with buying an engagement ring."

"This is all Sarah's fault," she murmured.

Her husband looked at her as though she were speaking in a foreign language.

"I mean it, Greg. I've been so preoccupied with the whole mess Sarah's created about these baskets, I haven't had time to pay attention to my son. Why, just on Friday when we had lunch..." Suddenly disheartened, Mary let her words fade.

"What's wrong?" Greg asked.

All the combativeness went out of her. "I can't blame Sarah entirely—I played a role in this, too."

"What role?"

Once again, she was amazed by her husband's obliviousness. "This business with Thom. Now that I think about it, I'm convinced he wanted to talk over his engagement with me, only I was so rattled by the Value-X incident I didn't give him a chance. Oh, Greg, how could I have been so self-absorbed?"

"What makes you think he was going to tell you he was getting engaged? Why don't we call and ask him when we get home?" Greg suggested.

"And let him think we're interfering in his life? We can't do that!"

"Why not?"

"We'd ruin his surprise, if indeed there is one."

Greg merely sighed as they wheeled the cart to the checkout counter.

Ten minutes later, once everything was safely inside the trunk, Mary turned to him. "I just don't know what I'll do if *she's* the one he's interested in. I couldn't stand it if he married into *that* family."

"I don't think we need to worry about it," he told her as they started back to the house. "There's no evidence whatsoever."

"He *danced* with Noelle McDowell!"

"He danced with lots of girls."

The engine made a coughing sound as they approached the first intersection. "What's that?" Mary asked.

"It's time for an oil change," her husband said. "I'll have the car looked at after the holidays."

She nodded. She trusted the upkeep of their vehicles to her husband and immediately put the thought out of her mind. Car troubles were minor in the greater scheme of things.

By the end of the day, when clouds thickened the sky and the cold swept in, fierce and chilling, Thom finally had to admit that replacing the silver tea service wasn't going to be easy.

He'd tried everything he could think of, called

friends and associates who might know where he could find an antique dealer who specialized in silver—anyone who might lead him to his prize. Far more than a gift lay in the balance. It was possible that his and Noelle's entire future hinged on this.

At seven, after an exhaustive all-day search, he went home. The first thing he did was check his answering machine, hoping to hear from Noelle. Sure enough, the message light was flashing. Without waiting to remove his coat, he pushed the button and grabbed paper and a pen.

A female voice, high and excited, spilled out. "It's Carley Sue. Remember me? I'm Noelle's sister. Anyway, Noelle asked me to call you. She'd call you herself, but I asked if I could do it, 'cause it was my bedroom window you knocked on. And my computer Noelle used."

Thom laughed out loud, almost missing the second half of the message.

"Anyway, Noelle wanted to know if you could meet her at the park tomorrow morning. She said you should be there early. She said six o'clock 'cause you have to drive all the way to Portland. She said you'd know why, but she wouldn't tell me. When you see Noelle, please tell her it's not nice to keep secrets from her sister, will you?" She giggled. "Never mind, I could get it out of her if I really wanted to. Bye."

Thom smiled, feeling a surge of energy. Obviously Noelle had had better luck than he did.

A second message followed the first.

"Thom, it's me. I wasn't sure Carley got the entire message to you. When we meet at the park, come with a full tank of gas. If this conflicts with your Christmas Eve plans, call me on my cell phone." There was a short pause. "I don't want you to get your hopes up. I found a tea service that's not *exactly* like your grandmother's, but I'm looking for a Christmas miracle. We'll need to compare it to the picture. The dealer's only keeping his store open until noon, which is why we need to leave here so early. I'm sorry I can't see you tonight. I wish I could, but I've got family obligations. I know you understand."

He did understand—all too well. A third message started; he was certainly popular today. It was his mother and she sounded worried.

"It's Mom… I ran into a friend from the newspaper this morning and she mentioned seeing you at Mendleson's Jewelers. Were you…buying an engagement ring? Thom, it isn't that McDowell girl, is it? Call me, will you? I need reassurance that you're not about to make a big mistake."

This was what happened when you lived in a small town. Everyone knew your business. So, his mother had heard, and even with the wrong facts, she'd put together the right answer. Yes, he'd been at Mendleson's. And yes, it *was* "that McDowell girl."

Thom decided he had to talk about all of this with someone who understood the situation and knew all the people involved. Someone discreet, who had his best interests at heart. Someone with no agenda, hidden or otherwise.

The one person he could trust was his older sister. Suzanne was three years his senior, married and living ten miles outside of town; she and her husband, Rob, owned a hazelnut orchard. Thom didn't see Suzanne often, but he was godfather to his five-year-old nephew, Cameron.

A brief phone call assured him that his sister was available and eager to see him. Off he went, grabbing a chunk of cheese and an apple to eat on the way. Maybe his sister would have some wisdom to share with him…. How quickly life can change, he mused, and never more so than at Christmas.

Suzanne had a mug of hot cider waiting when he arrived. Rob was out, dealing with some late deliveries. His family owned the orchard and leased it to him. Rob worked long hours making a success of their business, and so did Suzanne. Both his sister and brother-in-law were honest, hardworking people, and he trusted their advice.

"This is a surprise," Suzanne said, pulling out a chair at the large oak table in the center of her country kitchen.

"Cameron's in bed already?" Thom asked, disappointed to miss seeing his nephew.

"He thinks if he goes to bed early Santa will come sooner." She gave a shrug. "Never mind that this is only the twenty-third. I guess he's hoping he can make time speed up," she said with a smile. "By the way, he had a ridiculous tale about you and some woman at the movies the other day. Throwing popcorn was a big theme in this story."

"I don't know what he told you, but more than likely it's true. We bumped into Noelle McDowell and her little sister at the theater."

"Noelle. Oh, no." Suzanne was instantly sympathetic. "That must've been uncomfortable."

"Yes and no." He hesitated, wondering to what extent his sister's attitude was a reflection of their parents'. "It was difficult at first, because we didn't exactly part on the best of terms."

"At first?"

His sister had picked up on that fast enough. "We've talked since and resolved our difficulties."

"Resolved them, did you?" Suzanne raised her eyebrows.

"I love Noelle." There, he'd said it.

"Who's Noelle?" Rob asked as he walked in through the kitchen door, shedding hat, scarf and gloves.

"I'll explain later," Suzanne promised, ladling a cup of cider from the pot on the stove. "Here, honey."

"Our families don't get along," Thom explained.

"Do Mom and Dad know?" his sister asked.

"Not yet, but Mom got wind of me going to Mendleson's. She must have her suspicions, since she left a message on my machine practically begging me to tell her I'm not seeing Noelle."

"Did you buy a ring?"

"That's not the point."

"Okay," his sister said slowly. "What *do* you plan to tell Mom and Dad?"

"I don't know."

Suzanne sipped her cider, then put down the mug to focus on him. "You're going to wait until Christmas's over before you say anything, right?"

Thom didn't know if he could. His mother was already besieging him with questions and she'd keep at him until she got answers—preferably the answers she wanted. He needed an ally and he hoped he could count on Suzanne.

"Let me play devil's advocate here a moment," his sister suggested.

"Please."

"Put yourself in Mom's place. Noelle's family has hurt our family. And now you're asking Mom to welcome Noelle into our lives and our hearts."

"Noelle is already in my heart."

"I know," Suzanne told him, "but there's more than one person involved in this. How does her family feel about you, for instance?"

That was a question Thom didn't want to consider. This wouldn't be easy for Noelle, either. Kristen and Carley were obviously supportive, but Sarah McDowell—well, she was another matter.

"We were ready to defy everyone as teenagers," he said, reminding his sister of the difficult stand he'd taken at eighteen.

"You were a kid."

"I was in love with her then, and I'm still in love with her."

"Yes," Suzanne said, "but you're more responsible now."

"I can't live my life to suit everyone else," he said, frustrated by her response.

"He's got a point," Rob said. "I don't understand the family dynamics here, but I have a fairly good idea what you're talking about. I say if Thom feels this strongly about Noelle after all these years, he should go for it. He should live his own life."

Thom felt a rush of gratitude for his brother-in-law's enouragement.

"That's what you wanted to hear, isn't it?" Suzanne said, smiling. "For what it's worth, I agree with my husband."

"Thanks," Thom said. "That means a lot, you guys."

He shook his head. "Noelle and I are well aware of the problems we face as a couple. We'd hoped to come to our parents with a solution."

"What kind of solution?"

"I've been pounding the pavement all day, checking out antique stores and jewelry stores for a replacement tea service. Noelle's been doing an internet search."

His sister frowned. "I don't want to discourage you, but you're not going to find one."

She certainly had a way of cutting to the chase. "Thank you for that note of optimism. Anyway, how can you be so sure? Noelle thinks she might have a lead."

"Hey, that's good," Rob said. "It's worth trying to find...whatever this thing is that you're looking for."

"An antique silver tea service—I'll fill you in later, Rob." She turned to her brother. "I don't want to be pessimistic. It's just that Mom and Dad looked for years. They've given up now, but for a long time they left no stone unturned."

"If we find one, we'll consider it a Christmas miracle."

"Definitely," Suzanne agreed. "And I'd consider it a lucky omen, too."

"But you don't think we'll succeed."

"No," his sister told him. "I don't think so, but who knows?"

"If I ask Noelle to be part of my life, will you accept her?"

"Of course." Suzanne didn't hesitate. "But I'm not the one whose opinion matters. However, Rob's right, you've got to live your own life, and we'll support you in whatever choice you make."

He visited with his sister a while longer and assured

her that no matter what he decided, he'd meet the family for the annual Christmas Eve dinner, followed by church services.

The next morning Noelle was waiting in the park at the appointed time and place when he got there. His heart reacted instantly to the sight of her. She looked like an angel in her long white wool coat and cashmere scarf. A Christmas angel. He smiled at the thought— even if he *was* getting sentimental in his old age.

"Merry Christmas," he said.

"Merry Christmas, Thom." Her eyes brightened as he approached.

Thom folded her in his arms and their kisses were deep and urgent. His mouth lingered on hers, gradually easing into gentler kisses. Finally he whispered, "Ready to go?"

"I hope this isn't a wild-goose chase," Noelle told him as she leaned her head against his shoulder.

"I do, too." But if it was, at least he'd be spending the day with her.

If they couldn't carry out their quest, they'd simply have to find some other way to persuade both mothers to accept the truth—that Thomas Sutton and Noelle McDowell were in love.

It was Christmas Eve, nine in the morning, and Sarah McDowell was eager to finish with the Christmas baskets. She'd skillfully wrapped each gift to transport to the Salvation Army.

"You're coming with me, aren't you?" she asked her husband.

Jake glanced up from the morning paper, frowning. "I can't."

"Why not?" Sarah didn't know if she could face Mary alone—not again. She'd assumed Jake would drive with her.

"I've got errands of my own. It's Christmas Eve."

"What about you, Carley?" she said, looking hopefully toward her daughter.

"Can't, Mom, sorry."

But not nearly sorry enough, Sarah thought. Her family was abandoning her in this hour of need. "Where's Noelle?" she asked. Surely she could count on Noelle.

"Out," Carley informed her.

"She's left already?"

Carley nodded.

Sarah thought she saw Jake wink at Carley. Apparently those two were involved in some sort of conspiracy against her.

At least Jake helped her load up the car, shifting his golf clubs to the backseat, but he disappeared soon afterward. Grumbling under her breath, Sarah drove out to the Women's Century Club.

Mary's car was already in the lot when she arrived. So, Mary Sutton was breaking a lifelong habit of tardiness in her eagerness to finish this charity project. For that, Sarah couldn't blame her. She, too, had reached her limit.

The cold air cut through her winter coat the instant she climbed out of the car. The radio station had mentioned the possibility of an ice storm later in the day. Sarah only hoped it wouldn't materialize.

"Merry Christmas," Melody called out as Sarah struggled through the front door, carrying the largest and most awkward of the boxes.

Sarah muttered a reply. Her Christmas Eve was *not* getting off to a good start.

"Mary's waiting for you," Melody told her. "I understand there was a mix-up with the lists. I'm so sorry. It was crazy that morning, wasn't it?"

Sarah wasn't fooled by the other woman's cheerful attitude. Melody Darrington had done her utmost to manipulate the two of them into working on this project together, and Sarah, for one, didn't take kindly to the interference. It was clear that Mary hadn't realized anything was amiss, but then Mary Sutton wasn't the most perceptive person in the world. Still, Sarah wasn't going to make a federal case of it, on the off-chance that it *had* all been an innocent mistake as Melody was implying.

Sarah made her way into the meeting room, where Mary had the six baskets set up on a long table, as well as six large boxes, already filled with the makings for Christmas dinner.

"Is that everything you've got?" Mary asked, peering into Sarah's carton. Her tone insinuated that Sarah had contributed less than required.

"Of course not," she snapped. "I have two more boxes in the car."

Neither woman leaped up to help her carry them inside, although Melody did make a halfhearted offer when Sarah headed out the front door.

"No thanks—you've already done enough," she said pointedly.

"You're sure you don't need the help?" Melody asked.

Shaking her head, Sarah brought in the second of the boxes and set it on the table.

"I thought you'd bring one of the girls with you," Mary said in that stiff way of hers.

"They're busy." She started back for the last of the cartons.

"Noelle isn't with Thom, is she?"

The question caught her off guard. No one had said where Noelle had gone, but it couldn't be to meet Thom Sutton. Could it? No, she wouldn't do that. Not her daughter.

"Absolutely not," Sarah insisted. Noelle had already learned her lesson when it came to the Suttons.

"Good," Mary said.

"Noelle's with friends," Sarah returned and then, because she had to know, she asked a question of her own. "What makes you ask?"

"Oh—no reason."

Sarah didn't believe that for a moment. "You tell your son Noelle's under no illusions about him. She won't be so easily fooled a second time."

"Now just one minute—"

"We both know what he did."

"You're wrong, Sarah—but then you often are."

Melody stepped into the meeting room and stopped abruptly. With a shocked look, she regarded both women. "Come on, you two! It's Christmas."

"And your point is?" Sarah asked.

"My point is that the least you can do is work together on this. These baskets need to get to the Salvation Army right away. They're late already, and my husband just phoned and said there's definitely an ice storm coming, so you shouldn't delay."

"I'll get them there in time," Mary promised. "If we could get the baskets filled…"

"Fine," Sarah said. "I'll bring in the last box."

"We wouldn't be this late if you'd—"

Sarah ignored her and hurried out the door, only to hear Melody mutter something about an ice storm developing right in this room.

She knew that the minute she left, Melody and Mary would talk about her. However, she didn't care. Right after Kristen's wedding, she was letting her membership in the Women's Century Club lapse.

Once the third box was safely inside, Sarah placed the gifts in the correct baskets. Then both women sorted through the family names by checking the tag on each present. Sarah had spent a lot of time wrapping her gifts, wanting to please the recipients…and, to be honest, impress Mary and Melody with her talents. Given the opportunity, she could have decorated the clubhouse to match Mary's efforts. No, to exceed them.

"You did get that Firefighter Barbie doll, didn't you?" Mary asked.

"Of course I did," she answered scornfully.

They attached ribbons to each basket, then prepared everything—gifts and groceries—for transport.

"Would you like help loading up your car?" Sarah asked. Since Mary was driving and this was a joint project, she felt constrained to offer.

Mary seemed surprised, then shook her head. "I can manage. But…thanks."

Sarah had wanted to make a quick getaway, but Melody stopped her at the door, appointment book in hand.

"I have a few questions about Kristen's wedding."

"What do you need to know?"

Melody flipped open the book. "Will you require the use of our kitchen?"

"I'm not sure because we haven't picked the caterer yet, but we'll do that right after the first of the year."

"I have a list, if you'd like to look at it."

"I would." Sarah wanted to make her daughter's day as special as she could. But as she answered Melody's questions, her mind drifted to Noelle. Mary had brought up a frightening possibility. Noelle had been absent from the house quite a bit since the dance on Saturday night. She was at the mall on Sunday, and then on Monday—oh, yes, she'd worked on Carley's computer most of the day. Reassured now, Sarah relaxed. Mary's fears about her son and Noelle were unfounded.

She glanced around the lot; Mary's car was gone. She'd apparently left for the Salvation Army already. She must have moved her vehicle to the side entrance in order to load up the baskets and boxes more easily and Sarah hadn't seen her drive off. That was just fine. Maybe this was the last she needed to see of Mary Sutton.

Now she could enjoy Christmas.

"Merry Christmas, Melody," she said. "I'm sorry for the way I snapped at you earlier."

Melody accepted her apology. "I realize this was hard on both of you but what's important are the Christmas baskets."

"I couldn't agree with you more."

Sarah's spirits lifted considerably as she walked to her car or rather, Jake's. He'd insisted she take his SUV, and she was glad of it. If possible, it seemed even colder out; she drew her coat more closely around her and bent her head as she trudged toward the car.

As she turned out of the parking lot, she saw that the roads were icing over. The warning of an ice storm had become a reality, and even earlier than expected. This weather made her nervous, and Sarah drove carefully, hoping she wouldn't run into any problem.

She hadn't gone a mile when she noticed a car pulled off to the side of the road. She slowed down and was surprised to see Mary Sutton in the driver's seat. Mary was on her cell phone; she looked out the passenger window as Sarah slowed down. Mary's eyes met hers, and then she waved her on, declining help before Sarah could even offer it.

A NOTE FROM NOELLE McDOWELL

Christmas Eve

Dear Carley Sue,
Good morning. I'll be gone by the time you read this. I'm meeting Thom in the park and we're driving to an antique store outside Portland to check out a tea service. Kristen knows I'm with Thom, but not why.

I'm asking you to keep my whereabouts a secret for now. No, wait—you can mention it to Dad if you want. Mom's the only one who really can't know. I don't think she'll ask, because she's got a lot to do this morning delivering the Christmas baskets.

This whole mix-up with those baskets has really got her in a tizzy. I find it all rather humorous and I suspect Dad does, too.

I'm trusting you with this information, little sister. I figured you (and your romantic heart) would want to know.

Love,
Noelle

Eight

The car had made a grinding noise as soon as Mary started it—the same sound as the day before. Greg had said he'd look into it after the holidays, but she'd assumed it was safe to drive. Apparently not.

The car had slowed to a crawl, sputtered and then died. That was just great. The Salvation Army was waiting for these Christmas baskets, which, according to Melody, were already late. If Mary didn't hurry up and deliver them to the organization's office before closing time, six needy families would miss out on Christmas. She couldn't let that happen.

Reaching for her cell phone, she punched in her home number and hoped Greg was home. She needed rescuing, and soon. Greg would know what to do. The phone had just begun to ring when Sarah McDowell drove past.

Mary bit her lip hard. Pride demanded that she wave her on. She didn't need that woman's help. Still, she felt Sarah should've stopped; it was no less than any decent human being would do.

Well, she should know better than to expect compas-

sion or concern from Sarah McDowell. Good Christian
that she professed to be, Sarah had shown not the slight-
est interest in Mary's safety.

Mary clenched her teeth in fury. So, fine, Sarah
didn't care whether *she* froze the death, but what about
the Christmas baskets? What about the families, the
children, whose Christmas depended on them? The
truth was, Sarah simply didn't care what happened to
Mary *or* the Christmas baskets.

The phone was still ringing—where on earth was
Greg? Suddenly an operator's tinny voice came on with
a recorded message. "I'm sorry, but we are unable to
connect your call at this time."

"*You're* sorry?" Mary cried. She punched in Thom's
number and then Suzanne's and got the same response.
She tossed the phone back in her purse and waited. The
Women's Century Club was on the outskirts of Rose.
On Christmas Eve, with an ice storm bearing down,
the prospect of a Good Samaritan was highly unlikely.

"Great," she muttered. She might be stuck here for
God knows how long. Surely *someone* would realize
she wasn't where she was supposed to be. Still, it might
take hours before anyone came looking for her. And
even more hours before she was found.

With the engine off, the heater wasn't working, and
Mary was astonished by how quickly the cold seeped
into the car's interior. She tried her cell phone again
and got the same message. There was obviously trouble
with the transmitters; maybe it would clear up soon. She
struggled to remain optimistic, but another depressing
thought overshadowed the first. How long could she
last in this cold? She could imagine herself still sitting

in the car days from now, frozen stiff, abandoned and forgotten on Christmas Eve.

Trying to ward off panic, she decided to stand on the side of the road to see if that would help her cell phone reception. That way, she'd also be ready to wave for assistance if someone drove by.

She retrieved her phone, climbed out of the car and immediately became aware of how much colder it was outside. Hands shaking, she tried the phone. Same recorded response. She tucked her hands inside her pockets and waited for what seemed like an eternity. Then she tried her cell phone again.

Nothing. Just that damned recording.

Resigned to waiting for a passerby, she huddled in her coat.

Five minutes passed. The icy wind made it feel more like five hours. The air was so frigid that after a few moments it hurt to breathe. Her teeth began to chatter, and her feet lost feeling, but that was what she got for wearing slip-on loafers instead of winter boots.

A car appeared in the distance and Mary was so happy she wanted to cry. Greg was definitely going to hear about this! Once she got safely home, of course.

Stepping into the middle of the road, she raised her hand and then groaned aloud. It wasn't some stranger coming to her rescue, but Sarah McDowell. Desperate though she was, Mary would rather have seen just about anyone else.

Sarah pulled up alongside her and rolled down the window. "What's wrong?"

"Wh-what does it l-look like? M-my car broke down." She wished she could control the chattering of her teeth.

"Is someone coming for you?"

"N-not yet…I c-can't get through on my cell phone."

"I'm here now. Would you like me to deliver the Christmas baskets?"

Mary hesitated. If the gifts were to get to the families in time, she didn't really have much choice. "M-maybe you should."

Sarah edged her vehicle closer to Mary's and with some difficulty they transferred the six heavy baskets and the boxes of groceries from one car to the next.

"Thanks," Mary said grudgingly.

Sarah nodded curtly. "Go ahead and call Greg again," she suggested.

"Okay." Mary punched out the number and waited, hoping against hope that the call would connect. Once again, she got the "I'm sorry" recording.

"Won't go through."

"Would you like to use my phone?" Sarah asked.

"I doubt your phone will work if mine doesn't." It was so irritating—Sarah always seemed to believe that whatever she had was better.

"It won't hurt to try."

"True," Mary admitted. She accepted Sarah's phone and tried again. It gave her no satisfaction to be right.

"Go ahead and deliver the baskets," Mary said, putting on a brave front.

"I'm not going to leave you here."

Mary hardened her resolve. "Someone will come by soon enough."

"Don't be ridiculous!" Sarah practically shouted.

"Oh, all right, you can drive me back to the Club. And then deliver the baskets."

Sarah glared at her. "Aren't you being a little stubborn? I could just as easily drive you home."

Mary didn't answer. She intended to make it clear that she preferred to wait for Greg to rescue her rather than ride to town with Sarah.

"Fine, if that's what you want," Sarah said coldly.

"I'm grateful you came back," Mary told her—and she was. "I don't know how long I could've stood out here."

This time Sarah didn't respond.

"What's most important is getting these baskets to the families."

"At least we can agree on that," Sarah told her.

Mary climbed into the passenger side of Sarah's SUV and nearly sighed aloud when Sarah started the engine. A blast of hot air hit her feet and she moaned in pleasure.

Sarah was right, she decided. She *was* being unnecessarily stubborn. "If you don't mind," she said tentatively, "I would appreciate a ride home."

Sarah glanced at her as she started down the winding country road. "That wasn't so hard, now was it?"

"What?" she asked, pretending not to understand.

Just then, Sarah hit a patch of ice and the vehicle slid scarily into the other lane. With almost no traction, Sarah did what she could to keep the car on the road. "Hold on!" she cried. She struggled to maintain control but the tires refused to grip the asphalt.

"Oh, no," Mary breathed. "We're going into the ditch!" At that instant the car slid sideways, then swerved and went front-first into the irrigation ditch.

Mary fell forward, bracing her hands against the console. The car sat there, nose down. A frozen turkey rolled out of its box and lodged in the space between the two bucket seats, tail pointed at the ceiling. Sarah's eyes were wide as she held the steering wheel in a death grip.

Neither spoke for several moments. Then in a slightly breathless voice, Sarah asked, "Are you hurt?"

"No, are you?"

"I'm okay, but I think I broke three nails clutching the steering wheel."

Mary couldn't keep from smiling. Sarah had always been vain about her fingernails.

"Do you think we should try to climb out of the car?" Sarah murmured.

"I don't know."

"One of us should."

"I will," Mary offered. After all, Sarah would've been home by now if she hadn't come back to help.

"No, I think I should," Sarah said. "You must be freezing."

"I've warmed up—some. Listen, I'll go get Melody."

"It's at least a mile to the club."

"I know how far it is," Mary snapped. Sarah argued about everything.

"Why can't you just accept my help?"

"I'm in your car, aren't I?" She resisted the urge to remind Sarah that she hadn't actually been much help. Now they were both stuck, a hundred feet from where she'd been stranded. The charity baskets were no closer to their destination, either.

"Maybe another car will come by."

"Don't count on it," Mary told her.

"Why not?"

"Think about it. We're in the middle of an ice storm.

It's Christmas Eve. Anyone with half a brain is home in front of a warm fireplace."

"Oh. Yes."

"I'll walk to the club."

"No," Sarah insisted.

"Why not?"

Sarah didn't say anything for a moment. "I don't want to stay here alone," she finally admitted.

Mary pondered that confession and realized she wouldn't want to wait in the car by herself, either. "Okay," she said. "We'll both go."

"Tell me what you found out about the tea service," Thom said as they headed toward the freeway on-ramp.

"The internet was great. Your secretary's list was a big help, too. I scanned in the photograph you gave me and got an immediate hit with the man we're going to see this morning."

"Hey, you did well."

"I have a good feeling about this." Noelle's voice rose with excitement.

Thom didn't entirely share her enthusiasm. "I don't think we should put too much stock in this," he said cautiously.

"Why not?"

"Don't forget, my mom and dad searched for years. It's unrealistic to think we can locate a replacement after just one day."

"But your parents didn't have the internet."

She was right, but not all antique stores were online. Under the circumstances, it would be far too easy to build up their expectations only to face disappointment. "You said yourself this could be a wild-goose chase."

"I know." Noelle sounded discouraged now.

Thom reached out and gently clasped her fingers. "Don't worry—we're going to keep trying for as long as it takes." The road was icy, so he returned his hand to the steering wheel. "Looks like we're in for a spell of bad weather."

"I heard there's an ice storm on the way."

Thom nodded. The roads were growing treacherous, and he wondered if they should have risked the drive. However, they were on their way and at this point, he wanted to see it through as much as Noelle did.

What was normally a two-and-a-half-hour trip into Portland took almost four. Fortunately, the roads seemed to improve as they neared the city.

"I'm beginning to wonder if we should've come," Noelle said, echoing his thoughts as they passed an abandoned car angled off to the side of the road.

"We'll be fine." They were in Lake Oswego on the outskirts of Portland already—almost there.

"It's just that this is so important."

"I know."

"Maybe we should discuss what we're going to do if we don't find the tea service," Noelle said as they sought out the Lake Oswego business address.

"We'll deal with that when we have to, all right?"

She nodded.

The antique store was situated in a strip mall between a Thai restaurant and a beauty parlor. Thom parked the car. "You ready?" he asked, turning to her.

Noelle smiled encouragingly.

They held hands as they walked to the store. A bell above the door chimed merrily when they entered, and they found themselves in a long, narrow room crammed with glassware, china and polished wood furniture. Every conceivable space and surface had been put to use. A slightly moldy odor filled the air, competing with the piney scent of a small Christmas tree. Thom had to turn sideways to get past a quantity of comic books stacked on a chest of drawers next to the entrance. He led Noelle around the obstacles to the counter, where the cash register sat.

"Hello," Noelle called out. "Anyone here?"

"Be with you in a minute," a voice called back from a hidden location deep inside the store.

While Noelle examined the brooches, pins and old jewelry beneath the glass counter, Thom glanced around. A collection of women's hats filled a shelf to the right. He couldn't imagine his mother wearing anything with feathers, but if she'd lived in a different era...

He studied a pile of old games next, but they all seemed to be missing pieces. This looked less and less promising.

"Sorry to keep you waiting." A thin older man with a full crop of white hair ambled into the room. He was slightly stooped and brushed dust from his hands as he walked.

"Hello, my name is Noelle McDowell," she said. "We spoke yesterday."

"Ah, yes."

"Thom Sutton." Thom stepped forward and offered his hand.

"Peter Bright." His handshake was firm, belying his rather frail appearance. "I didn't know if you'd make it or not, with the storm and all."

"We're grateful you're open this close to Christmas," Noelle told him.

"I don't plan on staying open for long. But I wanted to escape the house for a few hours before Estelle found an excuse to put me to work in the kitchen." He chuckled. "Would you like to take a look at the tea service?"

"Please."

"I have it back here." He started slowly toward the rear of the store; Thom and Noelle followed him.

Noelle reached for Thom's hand again. Although he'd warned her against building up their expectations, he couldn't help feeling a wave of anticipation.

"Now, let me see…" Peter mumbled as he began shifting boxes around. "You know, a lot of people tell me they're coming in and then never show up." He smiled. "Like I said, I didn't really expect you to drive all the way from Rose in the middle of an ice storm." He removed an ancient Remington typewriter and set it aside, then lifted the lid of an army-green metal chest.

"I've had this tea service for maybe twenty years," Peter explained as he extracted a Navy sea bag.

"Do you remember how you came to get it?"

"Oh, sure. An English lady sold it to me. I displayed it for a while. People looked but no one bought."

"Why keep it in the chest now?" Noelle asked.

"I didn't like having to polish it," Peter said. "Folks have trouble seeing past the tarnish." He straightened and met Thom's gaze. "Same with people. Ever notice that?"

"I have," Thom said. Even on short acquaintance, he liked Peter Bright.

Nodding vigorously, Peter extracted a purple pouch from the duffel bag and peeled back the cloth to display a creamer. He set it on the green chest for their examination.

Noelle pulled the photograph from her purse and handed it to Thom, who studied the style. The picture wasn't particularly clear, so he found it impossible to tell if this was the same creamer, but there was definitely a similarity.

The sugar bowl was next. Peter set it out, waiting for Thom and Noelle's reaction. The photograph showed a slightly better view of that.

"This isn't the one," Noelle said. "But it's close, I think."

"Since you drove all this way, it won't hurt to look at all the pieces."

Thom agreed, but he already knew it had been a futile trip. He tried to hide his disappointment. Against all the odds, he'd held high hopes for this. Like Noelle, he'd been waiting for a Christmas miracle but apparently it wasn't going to happen.

Bending low, Peter thrust his arm inside the canvas bag and extracted two more objects. He carefully unwrapped the silver teapot and then the coffeepot and offered them a moment to scrutinize his wares.

The elaborate tray was last. Carefully arranging each piece on top of it, Peter stepped back to give them a full view of the service. "It's a magnificent find, don't you think?"

"It's lovely," Noelle said.

"But it's not the one we're looking for."

He accepted their news with good grace. "That's a shame."

"You see, this service—" she held out the picture "—was stolen years ago, and Thom and I are hoping to replace it with one that's exactly the same. Or as much like it as possible."

Peter reached for the photograph and studied it a moment. "I guess I should've looked closer and saved you folks the drive."

"No problem," Thom said. "Thanks for getting back to us."

"Yes, thank you for your trouble," Noelle said as they left the store. "It's a beautiful service."

"I'll give you a good price on it if you change your mind," the old man said, following them to the front door. "I'll be here another hour or so if you want to come back."

"Thank you," Thom said, but he didn't think there was much chance they'd be back. It wasn't the tea service they needed.

"How about lunch before we head home," he suggested. The Thai restaurant appeared to be open.

"Sure," Noelle agreed.

Thom shared her discouragement, but he was determined to maintain her optimism—and his own. "Hey, we've only started to look. It's too early to give up."

"I know. You're right, it was foolish of me to think we'd find it so quickly. It's just that…oh, I don't know, I guess I thought it *would* be easy because everything else fell into place for us."

They were the only customers in the restaurant. A charming waitress greeted them and escorted them to a table near the window.

Thom waited until they were seated before he spoke. "I guess this means we go to Plan B."

"What about pad thai and—" Noelle glanced up at him over the menu. "What exactly is Plan B?"

Thom reached inside his coat pocket and set the jeweler's box in the middle of the table.

"Thom?" Noelle put her menu down.

This wasn't the way he'd intended to propose, but—as the cliché had it—there was no time like the present. "I love you, Noelle, and I'm not going to let this feud stand between us. Our parents will have to understand that we're entitled to our own happiness."

Tears glistened in her eyes. "Oh, Thom."

"I'm asking you to be my wife."

She stretched her arm across the table and they joined hands. "And I'm telling you it would be the greatest honor of my life to accept. I have a request, though."

"Anything."

"I want to buy that tea service. Not you. Me."

Thom frowned. "Why?"

"I want to give it to your mother. From me to her. I can't replace the original, but maybe I can build a bridge between our families with this one."

Thom's fingers tightened around hers. "It's worth a try."

"I think so, too," she whispered.

"I'm going to try my phone again," Sarah said. Technology had betrayed them, but surely it would come to their rescue. Eventually. Walking a mile in the bitter cold was something she'd rather avoid.

"Go ahead," Mary urged. She didn't seem any more eager than Sarah to make the long trek.

Sarah got her phone and speed dialed her home number. Hope sprang up when the call instantly connected, but was dashed just as quickly when she heard the recording once again.

"Any luck?" Mary asked, her eyes bright and teary in the cold.

She shook her head.

"Damn," Mary muttered. "I guess that means there's no option but to hoof it."

"Appears that way."

"I think we should have a little fortification first, though," Sarah said. Her husband's golf bags were in the backseat, and she knew he often carried a flask.

"Fortification?"

"A little Scotch might save our lives."

Mary's look was skeptical. "I'm all for Scotch, but where are we going to find any out here?"

"Jake." She opened the back door and grabbed the golf bag. Sure enough, there was a flask.

"I don't remember you liking Scotch," Mary said.

"I don't, but at this point I can't be choosy."

"Right."

Sarah removed the top and tipped the flask, taking a sizable gulp. Wiping her mouth with the back of her hand, she swallowed, then shook her head briskly. "Oh my, that's strong." The liquor burned all the way down to her stomach, but as soon as it hit bottom, a welcoming warmth spread through her limbs.

"My turn," Mary said.

Sarah handed her the flask and watched as Mary rubbed the top, then tilted it back and took a deep swallow. She, too, closed her eyes and shook her head. Soon, however, she was smiling. "That wasn't so bad."

"It might ward off hypothermia."

"You're right. You'd better have another."

"You think?"

Mary nodded and after a moment, Sarah agreed. Luckily Jake had refilled the flask. The second swallow didn't taste nearly as nasty as the first. It didn't burn this time, either. Instead it enhanced the warm glow spreading through her system.

"How do you feel?"

"Better," Sarah said, giving Mary the flask.

Mary didn't need encouragement. She took her turn with the flask, then growled like a grizzly bear.

Sarah didn't know why she found that so amusing, but she did. She laughed uproariously. In fact, she laughed until she started to cough.

"What?" Mary asked, grinning broadly.

"Oh, dear." She coughed again. "I didn't know you did animal impressions."

"I do when I drink Scotch."

Then, as if they'd both become aware that they were having an actual conversation, they pulled back into themselves. Sarah noticed that Mary's expression suddenly grew dignified, as though she'd realized she was laughing and joking with her enemy.

"We should get moving, don't you think?" Mary said in a dispassionate voice.

"You're right." Sarah put the flask back in the golf bag and wrapped her scarf more tightly around her neck and face. Fortified in all respects, she was ready to face the storm. "It's a good thing we're walking together. Anything could happen on a day like this."

They'd gone about the length of a football field when Mary said, "I'm cold again."

"I am, too."

"You should've brought along the Scotch."

"We'll have to go back for it."

"I think we should," Mary agreed solemnly. "We could freeze to death before we reach the club."

"Yes. The Scotch might make the difference between survival and death."

Back at the car, they climbed in and shared the flask again. Soon, for no apparent reason, they were giggling.

"I think we're drunk," Mary said.

"Oh, hardly. I can hold my liquor better than this."

Mary burst into peals of laughter. "No, you can't. Don't you remember the night of our Halloween party?"

"That was—what?—twenty-two years ago!"

"I know, but I haven't forgotten how silly those margaritas made you."

"You were the one who kept filling my glass."

"You were the one who kept telling me how good they were."

Sarah nearly doubled over with hysterics. "Next thing I knew, I was standing on the coffee table singing 'Guantanamera' at the top of my lungs."

"You sounded fabulous, too. And then when you started to dance—"

"I *what?*" All Sarah recalled was the blinding headache she'd suffered the next morning. When she woke and could barely lift her head from the pillow without stabbing pain, she'd phoned her dearest, best friend in the world. Mary had dropped everything and rushed over. She'd mixed Sarah a tomato-juice concoction that had saved her life, or so she'd felt at the time.

Both women were silent. "I miss those days," Sarah whispered.

"I do, too," Mary said.

Sarah sniffled. It was the cold that made her eyes water. Digging through her purse, she couldn't find a single tissue. Mary gave her one.

"I've missed you," Sarah said and loudly blew her nose.

"I've missed you, too."

The cold must have intensified, because her eyes began to water even more. Using her coat sleeve, she wiped her nose.

"Here," she said to Mary, handing her the flask. "I want you to have this. Take the rest."

"The Scotch?"

Sarah nodded. "If we're not found until it's too late— I want you to have the liquor. It might keep you alive long enough for the rescue people to revive you."

Mary looked as though she was close to bursting into tears. "You'd die for—me?" She hiccuped on the last word.

Sarah nodded again.

"That's the most beautiful thing anyone's ever said to me."

"But before I die, I need to ask you something."

"Anything," Mary told her. "Anything at all."

Sarah sniffled and swallowed a sob. Leaning her forehead against the steering wheel, she whispered, "Forgive me."

Mary placed her hand on Sarah's shoulder. "I do forgive you, but first you have to forgive *me* for acting so badly. You were right—I *was* jealous of Cheryl. I thought you liked her better than me."

"Never. She's one of those people who move in and out of a person's life, but you—you're my...my soul sister. I've missed you so much."

"We're idiots." Mary returned the flask. "I can't accept this Scotch. If we freeze, we freeze together."

Sarah was feeling downright toasty at the moment.

The world was spinning, but that was probably because she was drunker than a skunk. The thought made her giggle.

"What's so funny?" Mary wanted to know.

"We're drunk," she muttered. "Drunk as skunks. Drunk as skunks," she recited in a singsong voice.

"Isn't it wonderful?"

They laughed again.

"Jake always insists I eat something when I've had too much to drink."

"We have lots of food," Mary said, sitting up straight.

"Yes, but most of it's half-frozen by now."

Mary's eyes gleamed bright. "Not everything. I'm sure the families would want us to take what we need, don't you think?"

"I'm sure you're right," Sarah said as Mary climbed over the front seat and into the back, her coat flipping over her head.

Sarah laughed so hard she nearly peed her pants.

Women's Century Club
Rose, Oregon

December 24

Dear Mary and Sarah,

Just a note to let you know how much the Women's Century Club appreciates the effort that went into preparing these Christmas baskets. You two did a splendid job. I could see from the number of gifts filling the baskets that you went far beyond the items listed on the sheet I gave you. Both of you have been generous to a fault.

Sarah, I realize it was difficult to come into this project at the last minute, but you are to be commended for your cooperation.

Mary, you did a wonderful job making all the arrangements, and I'm confident the baskets will reach the Salvation Army in plenty of time to be distributed for the holidays.

If you're both willing to take up the task again next year, I'd be happy to recommend you for the job.

Sincerely,

Melody Darrington

Nine

Jake McDowell glanced at the kitchen clock and frowned. "What time did your mother say she'd be home?"

"I don't know." His youngest daughter was certainly a fount of information. Carley lay flat on her stomach in front of the Christmas tree, her arms outstretched as she examined a small package.

"She should be back by now, don't you think?" Jake asked, looking at the clock again.

"I suppose."

"When will Noelle be home?"

Unconcerned, Carley shrugged.

Jake decided he wasn't going to get any answers here and tried Sarah's cell for perhaps the fiftieth time. Whenever he punched in the number, he received the same irritating message. "I'm sorry. We are unable to connect your call…."

Not knowing what else to do, he phoned his golfing partner. Greg Sutton answered on the first ring.

"I thought you were Mary," he said, sounding as worried as Jake was.

"You haven't heard from Mary?"

"Not a word. Is Sarah back?"

"No," Jake said. "That's why I was calling you."

"What do you think happened?"

"No idea. I could understand if one of them was missing, but not both."

Greg didn't say anything for a moment. "Did you phone the Women's Century Club?"

"I did. Melody said they were there and left two hours ago. She told me the ice storm's pretty bad in her area. She's going to stay put until her husband can come and get her this afternoon."

"What did she say about Mary and Sarah?"

"Not much. Just that they got the baskets all sorted and loaded into Mary's vehicle. Melody did make some comment about Sarah and Mary being pretty hostile toward each other. According to her, they left at different times."

"That doesn't explain why they're both missing."

"What if one of them had an accident and the other stopped to help?" Greg suggested.

Jake hadn't considered that. "But wouldn't they have been back by now?"

"Unless they got stuck."

"Together?"

"I wouldn't know."

Jake laughed grimly. "If that's the case, God help us all."

"What do you think we should do?"

"We can't leave them out there."

"You're right," Greg said. "But I have to tell you the idea is somewhat appealing. If they *are* stuck with each other for a while, they just might settle this mess."

"They could murder each other, too." Jake knew his wife far too well. When it came to Mary Sutton, she could be downright unreasonable. "I say we go after them—together."

Jake had no objection to that. Greg owned a large four-wheel drive truck that handled better on the ice than most vehicles. "You want to pick me up?"

"I'm on my way," Greg said.

Sarah reached for another Christmas cookie. "What did you call these again?" she asked, studying the package. Unfortunately, the letters wouldn't quite come into focus.

"Pfeffernusse."

"Try to say *that* three times when you're too drunk to stand up."

Mary giggled and helped herself to one of the glazed ginger cookies. "They're German. One family on the list had a German-sounding name and I thought they might be familiar with these cookies."

Sarah was touched. Tears filled her eyes. "You're so thoughtful."

"Not really," Mary said with a sob. "I…I was trying to outdo you." She was weeping in earnest now. "How could I have been so silly?"

"I did the same thing." Sarah wrapped her arm around Mary's shoulders. "I was the one who got us thrown out of Value-X."

Mary sniffled and dried her eyes. "I'm never going to let anything come between us again."

"I won't, either," Sarah vowed. "I think this has been the best Christmas of my life."

"Christmas!" Mary jerked upright. "Oh, Sarah, we've got to get these baskets to the Salvation Army!"

"But how? We can't carry all this stuff."

"True, but we can't just sit here, either." She looked

into the distance, in the direction of the Women's Century Club. "We're going to have to walk, after all."

Her friend was right. They had to take matters into their own hands and work together. "We can do it."

"We can. We'll walk to the club and send someone to get the baskets. Then we'll call Triple A. See? We have a plan. A good plan. There isn't anything we can't do if we stick together."

Sarah felt the tears sting her eyes again. "Is there any Scotch left?"

"No," Mary said, sounding sad. "We're going to have to make it on our own."

Clambering out of the car, Sarah was astonished by how icy the road had become in the hour or so they'd dawdled over their comforting Scotch. Luckily, she was wearing her boots, whereas Mary wore loafers.

Her friend gave a small cry and then, arms flailing, struggled to regain her balance. "My goodness, it's slippery out here."

"How are we going to do this?" Sarah asked. "You can't walk on this ice."

"Sure I can," Mary assured her, straightening with resolve. But she soon lost her balance again and grabbed hold of the car door, just managing to save herself.

"It's like you said—we'll do it together," Sarah declared. "We have to, because I'm not leaving you behind."

With Mary's arm around Sarah's waist and Sarah's arm about Mary's shoulder, they started walking down the center of the road. The treacherous ice slowed them down, and their progress was halting, especially since both of them were drunk and weepy with emotion.

"I wonder how long it'll take Greg to realize I'm not home," Mary said. Her husband was in trouble as it was, leaving her a defective vehicle to drive.

"Probably a lot longer than Jake. I told him I wouldn't be more than an hour."

"I'm sure there's some football game on TV that Greg's busy staring at. He won't notice I'm not there until Suzanne and Thom arrive for dinner." Mary went strangely quiet.

"Are you okay?" Sarah asked, tightening her hold on her friend.

"Yes, but…Thom. I was thinking about Thom. He's in love with Noelle, you know."

"Noelle's been in love with Thom since she was sixteen. It broke her heart when he dumped her."

"Thom didn't dump her. She dumped him."

Sarah bristled. "She did not!"

"You mean to say something else happened?"

"It must have, because I know for a fact that Noelle's always loved Thom."

"And Thom feels the same about her."

"We have to do something," Sarah said. "We've got to find a way to get them back together."

"I think they might've been secretly seeing each other," Mary confessed.

Sarah shook her head, which made her feel slightly dizzy. "Noelle would've told me. We're this close." She attempted to cross two fingers, but couldn't manage it. Must be because of her gloves, she decided. Yes, that was it.

"We're drunk," Mary said. "Really and truly drunk. The cookies didn't help one bit."

"I don't care. We're best friends again and this time it's for life."

"For life," Mary vowed.

"We're on a mission."

"A mission," Mary repeated. She paused "What's our mission again?"

Sarah had to stop and think about it. "First, we need to deliver the Christmas baskets."

Mary slapped her hand against her forehead. "Right! How could I forget?"

"Then…"

"There's more?" Mary looked confused.

"Yes, lots more. Then we need to convince Noelle and Thom that they were meant to be together."

"Poor Thom," Mary said. "Oh no." She covered her mouth with her hand.

"What?"

"I left a message on his answering machine. I may not remember much right now, but I remember that. I told him I didn't think he should marry Noelle…."

"Why would you do that?"

"Well, because—oh dear, Sarah, I might have ruined everything."

"We'll deal with it as soon as we're home," Sarah said firmly.

A car sounded from behind them. "Someone's coming," Mary cried, her voice rising with excitement.

"We've got to hitch a ride." Sarah whirled around and held out her thumb as prominently as she could.

"That's not going to work," Mary insisted, thrusting out her leg. "Don't you remember that old Clark Gable movie?"

"Clark Gable got a ride by showing off his ankle?"

"No… Claudette Colbert did."

The truck turned the corner; Sarah wasn't willing to trust in either her thumb or Mary's leg, so she raised both hands above her head and waved frantically.

"It's Greg," Mary cried in relief.

"And Jake's with him." Thank God. Sarah had never been happier to see her husband.

To their shock and anger, the two men drove directly past them.

"Hey!" Mary shouted after her husband. "I am in no mood for games."

The truck stopped, and the driver and passenger doors opened at the same time. Greg climbed down and headed over to Mary, while Jake hurried toward Sarah.

"We're friends for life," Mary told her husband, throwing her arm around Sarah again.

"You're drunk," Greg said. "Just what have you been drinking?"

"I know exactly what I'm doing," she answered with offended dignity.

"Do *you?*" Jake asked Sarah.

"Of course I do."

"We're on a mission," Mary told the two men.

Jake frowned. "What happened to the car?"

"I'll tell you all about it later," Sarah promised, enunciating very carefully.

"What mission?" Jake asked.

Sarah exchanged an exasperated look with Mary. "Why do we have to explain everything?"

"Men," Mary said in a low voice. "Can't live with 'em, can't live without 'em."

Her friend was so wise.

The drive back to Rose took even longer than the trip into Portland. The roads seemed to get icier and more slippery with every mile. Keeping her eyes on the road, Noelle knew how tense Thom must be.

"Would you rather wait until after Christmas?" she asked as they neared her family's home. It might be better if they got through the holidays before making their announcement and throwing their families into chaos. Noelle hated the thought of dissension on Christmas Day.

"Wait? You mean to announce our engagement?" Thom clarified. "I don't think we should. You're going to marry me, and I want to tell the whole world. I refuse to keep this a secret simply because our mothers don't happen to get along. They'll just have to adjust."

"But   "

"I've waited all these years for you. I'm not waiting any longer. All right?"

"All right." Noelle was overwhelmed by contradictory emotions. Love for Thom—and love for her family. Excitement and nervousness. Happiness and guilt.

"Do you know what I like most about Christmas?" Thom asked, breaking into her thoughts.

"Tell me, and then I'll tell you what I like."

"Mom has a tradition she started when Suzanne entered high school. On Christmas Eve, she serves fresh Dungeness crab. We all love it. She has them cooked at the market because she can't bear to do it herself, then Dad brings them home. Mom's got the butter melted and the bibs ready and we sit around the table and start cracking."

"Oh, that sounds delicious."

"It is. Does your family have a Christmas Eve tradition?"

"Bingo."

"Bingo?"

"Christmas Bingo. We play after the Christmas Eve service at church. The prizes aren't worth more than five dollars, but Mom's so good at getting neat stuff. I haven't been home for Christmas in years, but Mom always makes up for it by mailing me three or four little Bingo gifts."

"My favorite carol is 'What Child Is This,'" he said next.

"Mine's 'Silent Night.'"

"What was your favorite gift as a kid?"

"Hmm, that's a toss-up," she said. "There was a Christmas Barbie I adored. Another year I got a set of classic Disney videos that I watched over and over."

Thom smiled. "As a little boy, I loved my Matchbox car garage. I got it for Christmas when I was ten. Mom's kept it all these years. She has Dad drag it out every year and tells me she's saving it to give to my son one day."

She sighed, at peace with herself and this man she loved. "I want to have your babies, Thom," she said in a soft voice.

His eyes left the street to meet hers. The sky had darkened and he looked quickly back at the road. "You make it hard to concentrate on driving."

"Tell me some of the other things you love about Christmas. It makes me feel good to hear them."

"It's your turn," he said.

"The orange in the bottom of my stocking. Every year there's one in the toe. It's supposed to commemorate the Christmases my great-grandparents had—an orange was a pretty special thing back then."

"I like Christmas cookies. Especially meringue star ones."

"Mexican tea cakes for me," she said. "I'll ask your mother for the recipe for star cookies and bake you a batch every Christmas."

"That sounds like a very wifely thing to do."

"I want to be a good wife to my husband." Noelle suddenly realized that she was genuinely grateful they hadn't married so young. Yes, the years had brought pain, but they'd brought wisdom and perspective, too.

The love she and Thom felt for each other would deepen with time. They were so much more capable now of valuing what they had together.

"What's it like to be born on Christmas Day?" Thom asked.

"It's not so bad," Noelle said. "First, I share a birthday with Jesus—that's the good part. The not-so-good is having the two biggest celebrations of the year fall on the same day. When I was a kid, Mom used to throw me a party in June to celebrate my half-year birthday."

"I remember that."

"Do you remember teasing me by saying it really wasn't my birthday so you didn't need to bring a gift?"

Thom chuckled. "What I remember is getting my ears boxed for saying it."

Twenty minutes later, they were almost at her family's house. They'd decided to confront her parents first. Their laughter, which had filled the car seconds earlier, immediately faded.

"You ready?" Thom asked as he stopped in front of the house.

Noelle nodded and swallowed hard. "No matter what happens, I want you to remember I love you."

His hand squeezed hers.

Glancing at her family's home, Noelle noticed a truck parked outside. "Looks like we have company." She didn't know whether to feel relief or disappointment.

"Oh, no." Thom's voice was barely above a whisper.

"What is it?"

"That's my parents' truck."

Dread slipped over her. "They must've found out that we spent the day together. That's my fault—I left a note for Carley telling her I was with you." Noelle could imagine what was taking place inside. Her mother would be shouting at Thom's, and their fathers would be trying to keep the two women apart.

"Should we wait?" Noelle asked, just as she had earlier.

"For another time?" His jaw tensed. "No, we face them here and now, for better or worse. Agreed?"

Noelle nodded. "Okay…just promise me you won't let them change your mind."

He snorted inelegantly. "I'd like to see them try."

Thom parked behind the truck and turned off the engine. Together, holding hands, they approached the house. Never had Noelle been more nervous. If this encounter went wrong, she might alienate her mother, and that was something she didn't want to do. In high school, she'd self-righteously cast her family aside in the name of love. But if the years in Dallas had taught her independence, they'd also taught her the importance of home and family. Her self-imposed exile was over now, and she'd learned from it. Listening to Thom talk about his Christmas traditions, she'd realized that he'd find it equally hard to turn his back on his parents.

He was about to ring the doorbell when she stopped him. "Remember how I said I was looking for a Christmas miracle?"

Thom nodded. "You mean finding a tea service similar to my grandmother's?"

"Yes. But if I could be granted only one miracle this Christmas, it wouldn't be that. I'd want our families to rekindle the love and friendship they once had."

"That would be my wish, too." Thom gathered her in his arms and kissed her with a passion that readily found a matching fire in her. The kiss was a reminder of their love, and it sealed their bargain. No matter what happened once they entered the house, they would face it together.

"Actually, this is a blessing in disguise," Thom said. "We can confront both families at the same time and be done with it." He reached for the doorbell again, and again Noelle stopped him.

"This is my home. We don't need to ring the bell." Stepping forward, she opened the door.

Noelle wasn't sure what she expected, but certainly not the scene that greeted her. Her parents and two sisters, plus Thom's entire family, sat around the dining room table. Her mother and Mrs. Sutton, both wearing aprons, stood in the background, while her father and Thom's dished up whole Dungeness crabs, with Jonathan pouring wine.

"Thom!" his mother shouted joyfully. "It's about time you got here."

"What took you so long?" Sarah asked Noelle.

Stunned, Thom and Noelle looked at each other for an explanation.

"There's room here," Carley called out, motioning to the empty chairs beside her.

Noelle couldn't do anything other than stare.

"What...happened?" Thom asked.

"It's a long story. Sit down. We'll explain everything later."

"But..."

Thom put his arm around Noelle's shoulder. "Before we sit down, I want everyone to know that I've asked Noelle to be my wife and she's accepted."

"Nothing you say or do will make us change our minds," Noelle said quickly, before anyone else could react.

"Why would we want to change your minds?" her father asked. "We're absolutely delighted."

"You can fight and argue, threaten and yell, and it won't make any difference," Thom added. "We're getting married!"

"Glad to hear it," his father said.

A round of cheers followed his announcement.

Thom's mother and Noelle's mother embraced in joy.

"One thing this family refuses to tolerate anymore is fighting," his mother declared.

"Absolutely," her own mother agreed.

Both Thom and Noelle stared back at them, shocked into speechlessness.

"There's no reason to stand there like a couple of strangers," her mother said. "Sit down. You wouldn't believe the day we had."

Sarah and Mary put their arms around each other's shoulders. "At least the Christmas baskets got delivered on time," Mary said with a satisfied nod.

"And no one mentioned that the two of us smelled like Scotch when we got there," her mother pointed out.

They both giggled.

"What happened?" Noelle asked.

Her father waved aside her question. "You don't want to know," he groaned.

"I'll tell you later," her mother promised.

Thom leaned close to her and whispered, "Either we just walked into the middle of an *X-Files* episode or we got our Christmas miracle."

Noelle slipped an arm around his waist. "I think you must be right."

Sarah McDowell
9 Orchard Lane
Rose, Oregon

December 26

Dear Melody,

Mary and I found your note when we delivered the baskets on Christmas Eve. We did have a wonderful time, and Mary has agreed to head up the committee next year. I promised I'd be her cochair.

Now, about using the club for Kristen's wedding reception... Well, it seems there's going to be another wedding in the family, and fairly soon. Mary and I will be in touch with you about that right after New Year's.

Sincerely,

Sarah McDowell

* * * * *

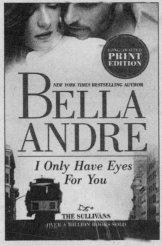

REQUEST YOUR FREE BOOKS!

2 FREE NOVELS
FROM THE ROMANCE COLLECTION
PLUS 2 FREE GIFTS!

YES! Please send me 2 FREE novels from the Romance Collection and my 2 FREE gifts (gifts are worth about $10). After receiving them, if I don't wish to receive any more books, I can return the shipping statement marked "cancel." If I don't cancel, I will receive 4 brand-new novels every month and be billed just $6.24 per book in the U.S. or $6.74 per book in Canada. That's a savings of at least 22% off the cover price. It's quite a bargain! Shipping and handling is just 50¢ per book in the U.S. and 75¢ per book in Canada.* I understand that accepting the 2 free books and gifts places me under no obligation to buy anything. I can always return a shipment and cancel at any time. Even if I never buy another book, the two free books and gifts are mine to keep forever.

194/394 MDN F4XY

Name	(PLEASE PRINT)

Address	Apt. #

City	State/Prov.	Zip/Postal Code

Signature (if under 18, a parent or guardian must sign)

Mail to the **Harlequin®** Reader Service:
IN U.S.A.: P.O. Box 1867, Buffalo, NY 14240-1867
IN CANADA: P.O. Box 609, Fort Erie, Ontario L2A 5X3

Want to try two free books from another line?
Call 1-800-873-8635 or visit www.ReaderService.com.

* Terms and prices subject to change without notice. Prices do not include applicable taxes. Sales tax applicable in N.Y. Canadian residents will be charged applicable taxes. Offer not valid in Quebec. This offer is limited to one order per household. Not valid for current subscribers to the Romance Collection or the Romance/Suspense Collection. All orders subject to credit approval. Credit or debit balances in a customer's account(s) may be offset by any other outstanding balance owed by or to the customer. Please allow 4 to 6 weeks for delivery. Offer available while quantities last.

Your Privacy—The Harlequin® Reader Service is committed to protecting your privacy. Our Privacy Policy is available online at www.ReaderService.com or upon request from the Harlequin Reader Service.

We make a portion of our mailing list available to reputable third parties that offer products we believe may interest you. If you prefer that we not exchange your name with third parties, or if you wish to clarify or modify your communication preferences, please visit us at www.ReaderService.com/consumerschoice or write to us at Harlequin Reader Service Preference Service, P.O. Box 9062, Buffalo, NY 14269. Include your complete name and address.

DEBBIE MACOMBER

32988	OUT OF THE RAIN	___ $7.99 U.S.	___ $9.99 CAN.
32970	8 SANDPIPER WAY	___ $7.99 U.S.	___ $9.99 CAN.
32969	74 SEASIDE AVENUE	___ $7.99 U.S.	___ $9.99 CAN.
32968	6 RAINIER DRIVE	___ $7.99 U.S.	___ $9.99 CAN.
32967	44 CRANBERRY POINT	___ $7.99 U.S.	___ $9.99 CAN.
32946	311 PELICAN COURT	___ $7.99 U.S.	___ $9.99 CAN.
32929	HANNAH'S LIST	___ $7.99 U.S.	___ $9.99 CAN.
32918	AN ENGAGEMENT IN SEATTLE	___ $7.99 U.S.	___ $9.99 CAN.
32911	THE MANNING SISTERS	___ $7.99 U.S.	___ $9.99 CAN.
32861	204 ROSEWOOD LANE	___ $7.99 U.S.	___ $9.99 CAN.
32858	HOME FOR THE HOLIDAYS	___ $7.99 U.S.	___ $9.99 CAN.
32828	ORCHARD VALLEY BRIDES	___ $7.99 U.S.	___ $9.99 CAN.
32798	ORCHARD VALLEY GROOMS	___ $7.99 U.S.	___ $9.99 CAN.
32783	THE MAN YOU'LL MARRY	___ $7.99 U.S.	___ $9.99 CAN.
32743	THE SOONER THE BETTER	___ $7.99 U.S.	___ $9.99 CAN.
32702	FAIRY TALE WEDDINGS	___ $7.99 U.S.	___ $9.99 CAN.
32701	WYOMING BRIDES	___ $7.99 U.S.	___ $8.99 CAN.
32602	THE MANNING GROOMS	___ $7.99 U.S.	___ $7.99 CAN.
32569	ALWAYS DAKOTA	___ $7.99 U.S.	___ $7.99 CAN.
32474	THE MANNING BRIDES	___ $7.99 U.S.	___ $7.99 CAN.
32362	COUNTRY BRIDES	___ $7.99 U.S.	___ $9.50 CAN.
31688	16 LIGHTHOUSE ROAD	___ $7.99 U.S.	___ $9.99 CAN.
31457	HEART OF TEXAS VOLUME 3	___ $7.99 U.S.	___ $8.99 CAN.
31441	HEART OF TEXAS VOLUME 2	___ $7.99 U.S.	___ $8.99 CAN.
31426	HEART OF TEXAS VOLUME 1	___ $7.99 U.S.	___ $9.99 CAN.
31424	MONTANA	___ $7.99 U.S.	___ $9.99 CAN.
31413	LOVE IN PLAIN SIGHT	___ $7.99 U.S.	___ $9.99 CAN.
31395	GLAD TIDINGS	___ $7.99 U.S.	___ $9.99 CAN.
31390	1225 CHRISTMAS TREE LANE	___ $7.99 U.S.	___ $9.99 CAN.
31299	YOU...AGAIN	___ $7.99 U.S.	___ $9.99 CAN.
31251	1105 YAKIMA STREET	___ $7.99 U.S.	___ $9.99 CAN.
28810	BACK ON BLOSSOM STREET	___ $7.99 U.S.	___ $9.99 CAN.
28803	A GOOD YARN	___ $7.99 U.S.	___ $9.99 CAN.
28629	50 HARBOR STREET	___ $7.99 U.S.	___ $9.99 CAN.

(limited quantities available)

TOTAL AMOUNT	$	_____
POSTAGE & HANDLING	$	_____
($1.00 for 1 book, 50¢ for each additional)		
APPLICABLE TAXES*	$	_____
TOTAL PAYABLE	$	_____

(check or money order—please do not send cash)

To order, complete this form and send it, along with a check or money order for the total above, payable to Harlequin MIRA, to: **In the U.S.:** 3010 Walden Avenue, P.O. Box 9077, Buffalo, NY 14269-9077; **In Canada:** P.O. Box 636, Fort Erie, Ontario, L2A 5X3.

Name: _____

Address: _____ City: _____

State/Prov.: _____ Zip/Postal Code: _____

Account Number (if applicable): _____

075 CSAS

*New York residents remit applicable sales taxes.
*Canadian residents remit applicable GST and provincial taxes.

HARLEQUIN® MIRA®
™ www.Harlequin.com

MDM1013BL

Don't miss any of New York Times
*bestselling author Debbie Macomber's
celebrated NAVY series!*

* * *

"If you think it would be best to leave, go now," Carol whispered. "The choice is yours."

His gaze locked with hers, Steve wordlessly
lifted Carol into his arms and carried her down the
hallway to the bedroom that had once been theirs.
For one crazy second Carol thought he meant to
drop her on the mattress and march right on out
of the house. Instead, he continued to hold her,
the look in his eyes wild and uncertain.

Nearly choking on the emotions that threatened
to overwhelm her, Carol tentatively raised her
hand to his face. To her surprise, Steve lowered
her gently onto the bed and leaned over her.

"We aren't married," he said, his voice rough.
"Not a damn thing has been settled between us."

Carol said nothing, but slid her hand to the back
of his head, urging his mouth down to hers.

She met with no resistance.

DEBBIE
MACOMBER

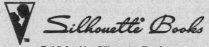

Published by Silhouette Books

America's Publisher of Contemporary Romance

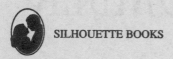

SILHOUETTE BOOKS

NAVY BLUES

ISBN 0-373-21845-1

Copyright © 1989 by Debbie Macomber

Visit Silhouette at www.eHarlequin.com

Printed in U.S.A.

Dedicated to
Mary Magdalena Lanz,
July 2, 1909 to May 1, 1988
Beloved Aunt

Special thanks to:
Rose Marie Harris, wife of MMCM Ralph Harris,
retired U.S. Navy; Debbie Korrell,
wife of Chief Steven Korrell, USS *Alaska;*
Jane McMahon, RN

Dear Reader,

I live in a navy town, across Sinclair inlet from the navy shipyard in Bremerton. Aircraft carriers, diesel submarines and destroyers are all part of the water view. Growing up in eastern Washington, I didn't know many navy folks. My dad was an army man who fought in WWII, and when he talked about his war experiences, it had to do with the land battles.

I know I'll never forget the first time I saw an aircraft carrier. I stood agog watching all 1092 feet of this huge flattop sail toward Bremerton. Wives, daughters, girlfriends, sons and daughters lined the wharf. The inlet was filled with sailboats and small watercraft that zigzagged across the wake, bouncing over the swelling waves the *Nimitz* created. As I stood on a hillside in Port Orchard and watched the scene below, I could feel the excitement and joy from both carrier and land. It'd been six long months since these men had been with their loved ones.

For the first time in my life I understood why my father would tear up when he saluted an American flag. In witnessing the *Nimitz* homecoming, I experienced such a surge of patriotism that I covered my heart with my hand and started to sing "God Bless America." My friend who was with me at the time asked, "What's with you?" What, my friends, were five navy books. The second of these books is titled *Navy Blues*. I wrote them all back in the late 1980s before we ever thought about e-mail or cell phones, which are in common use today.

Over the years I've been repeatedly asked when my navy books will be published again. I'm very excited to see them reissued now. May you read them and appreciate the men and the women of our military who've dedicated themselves to our national defense. I hope you experience that surge of patriotism the way I did that bright summer's afternoon when I first laid eyes on the *Nimitz*.

God Bless America and the United States Navy.

Sincerely,

Debbie Macomber

P.S. I love hearing form my readers. You can write me at P.O. Box 1458, Port Orchard, WA 98366 or visit my Web site at www.debbiemacomber.com.

Chapter 1

Seducing her ex-husband wasn't going to be easy, Carol Kyle decided, but she was determined. More than determined—resolute! Her mind was set, and no one knew better than Steve Kyle how stubborn she could be when she wanted something.

And Carol wanted a baby.

Naturally she had no intention of letting him in on her plans. What he didn't know wouldn't hurt him. Their marriage had lasted five good years, and six bad months. To Carol's way of thinking, which she admitted was a bit twisted at the moment, Steve owed her at least one pregnancy.

Turning thirty had convinced Carol that drastic

measures were necessary. Her hormones were jumping up and down, screaming for a chance at moth-
erhood. Her biological clock was ticking away, and
Carol swore she could hear every beat of that blasted
timepiece. Everywhere she turned, it seemed she was
confronted with pregnant women, who served to remind her that her time was running out. If she picked
up a magazine, there would be an article on some
aspect of parenting. Even her favorite characters on
television sitcoms were pregnant. When she found
herself wandering through the infant section of her
favorite department store, Carol realized drastic measures needed to be taken.

Making the initial contact with Steve hadn't been
easy, but she recognized that the first move had to
come from her. Getting in touch with her ex-husband
after more than a year of complete silence had required two weeks of nerve building. But she'd managed to swallow her considerable pride and do it.
Having a woman answer his phone had thrown her
for a loop, and Carol had visualized her plans swirling down the drain until she realized the woman was
Steve's sister, Lindy.

Her former sister-in-law had sounded pleased to
hear from her, and then Lindy had said something
that had sent Carol's spirits soaring to the ceiling:
Lindy had claimed that Steve missed her dreadfully.
Lordy, she hoped that was true. If so, it probably

meant he wasn't dating yet. There could be complications if Steve was involved with another woman. On the other hand, there could also be problems if he wasn't involved.

Carol only needed him for one tempestuous night, and then, if everything went according to schedule, Steve Kyle could fade out of her life once more. If she failed to get pregnant…well, she'd leap that hurdle when she came to it.

Carol had left a message for Steve a week earlier, and he hadn't returned her call. She wasn't overly concerned. She knew her ex-husband well; he would mull it over carefully before he'd get back to her. He would want her to stew a while first. She'd carefully figured the time element into her schedule of events.

Her dinner was boiling on the stove, and Carol turned down the burner after checking the sweet potatoes with a cooking fork. Glaring at the orange-colored root, she heaved a huge sigh and squelched her growing dislike for the vegetable. After she became pregnant, she swore she would never eat another sweet potato for as long as she lived. A recent news report stated that the starchy vegetable helped increase the level of estrogen in a woman's body. Armed with that information, Carol had been eating sweet potatoes every day for the last two weeks. There had to be enough of the hormone floating around in her body by now to produce triplets.

Noting the potatoes were soft, she drained the water and dumped the steaming roots into her blender. A smile crowded the edges of her mouth. Eating sweet potatoes was a small price to pay for a beautiful baby…for Steve's baby.

"Have you called Carol back yet?" Lindy Callaghan demanded of her brother as she walked into the small kitchen of the two-bedroom apartment she shared with her husband and Steve.

Steve Kyle ignored her until she pulled out the chair and plopped down across the table from him. "No," he admitted flatly. He could see no reason to hurry. He already knew what Carol was going to tell him. He'd known it from the minute they'd walked out of the King County Courthouse, the divorce papers clenched in her hot little hands. She was remarrying. Well, more power to her, but he wasn't going to sit back and blithely let her rub his nose in the fact.

"Steve," Lindy insisted, her face tight with impatience. "It could be something important."

"You told me it wasn't."

"Sure, that's what Carol said, but…oh, I don't know, I have the feeling that it really must be. It isn't going to do any harm to call her back."

Methodically Steve turned the page of the evening newspaper and carefully creased the edge before folding it in half and setting it aside. Lindy and Rush, her husband, couldn't be expected to understand his reluctance to phone his ex-wife. He hadn't told either of them the details that had led to his and Carol's divorce. He preferred to keep all thoughts of the disastrous relationship out of his mind. There were plenty of things he could have forgiven, but not what Carol had done—not infidelity.

As a Lieutenant Commander aboard the submarine USS *Atlantis*, Steve was at sea for as long as six months out of a year. From the first Carol hadn't seemed to mind sending him off on a three-to-four month cruise. She even used to joke about it, telling him all the projects she planned to complete when he was at sea, and how pleased she was that he would be out of her hair for a while. When he'd returned she'd always seemed happy that he was home, but not exuberant. If anything had gone wrong in his absence—a broken water pipe, car repairs, anything—she'd seen to it herself with barely more than a casual mention.

Steve had been so much in love with her that the little things hadn't added up until later—much later. He'd deceived himself by overlooking the obvious. The physical craving they had for each other had diluted his doubts. Making love with Carol had been so hot it was like a nuclear meltdown. Toward the end she'd been eager for him, but not quite as enthusiastic as in the past. He'd been trusting, blind and incredibly stupid when it came to his ex-wife.

Then by accident he'd learned why she'd become so blasé about his comings and goings. When he left their bed, his loveless, faithless wife had a built-in replacement—her employer, Todd Larson.

It was just short of amazing that Steve hadn't figured it out earlier, and yet when he thought about it, he could almost calculate to the day when she'd started her little affair.

"Steve?"

Lindy's voice cut into his musings, and he lifted his gaze to meet hers. Her eyes were round and dark with concern. Steve experienced a small twinge of guilt for the way he'd reacted to his sister and Rush's marriage. When he'd learned his best friend had married his only sister after a dating period of a mere two weeks, Steve had been furious. He'd made no bones about telling them both the way he felt about their hurry-up wedding. Now he realized his own bitter experience had tainted his reasoning, and he'd long since apologized. It was obvious they were crazy about each other, and Steve had allowed his own misery to bleed into his reaction to their news.

"Okay, okay. I'll return Carol's call," he answered in an effort to appease his younger sibling. He understood all too well how much Lindy wanted him to settle matters with Carol. Lindy was happy, truly happy, and it dismayed her that his life should be at such loose ends.

"When?"

"Soon," Steve promised.

The front door opened, and Rush let himself into the apartment; his arms were loaded with Christmas packages. He paused just inside the kitchen and exchanged a sensual look with his wife. Steve watched the heated gaze and it was like throwing burning acid on his half-healed wounds. He waited a moment for the pain to lessen.

"How'd the shopping go?" Lindy asked, her silky smooth voice eager and filled with pleasure at the sight of her husband.

"Good," Rush answered and faked a yawn, "but I'm afraid it wore me out."

Steve playfully rolled his eyes toward the ceiling and stood, preparing to leave the apartment. "Don't tell me you two are going to take another nap!"

Lindy's cheeks filled with crimson color and she looked away. In the past few days the two of them had taken more naps than a newborn babe. Even Rush looked a bit chagrined.

"All right, you two," Steve said good-naturedly, reaching for his leather jacket. "I'll give you some privacy."

One glance from Lindy told him she was grateful. Rush stopped Steve on his way out the door and his eyes revealed his appreciation. "We've decided to look for a place of our own right away, but it doesn't look like we'll be able to move until after the first of the year." He paused and lowered his gaze, looking almost embarrassed. "I know this is an inconvenience for you to keep leaving, but..."

"Don't worry about it," Steve countered with a light chuckle. He patted his friend on the back. "I was a newlywed once myself."

Steve tried to sound casual about the whole matter, but doubted if he'd succeeded. Being constantly exposed to the strong current of love flowing between his friend and his sister was damn difficult, because he understood their need for each other all too well. There'd been a time when a mere look was all that was required to spark flames between him and Carol. Their desire seemed to catch fire and leap to brilliance with a single touch, and they couldn't get to bed fast enough. Steve had been crazy in love with her. Carol had appealed to all his senses and he'd ached with the desire to possess her completely. The only time he felt he'd accomplished that was when he was making love to her. Then and only then was Carol utterly his. And those times were all too brief.

Outside the apartment, the sky was dark with thick gray clouds. Steve walked across the street and headed toward the department stores. He didn't have much Christmas shopping to do, but now appeared to be as good a time for the task as any.

He hesitated in front of a pay phone and released a long, slow breath. He might as well call Carol and be done with it. She wanted to gloat, and he would let her. After all, it was the season to be charitable.

The phone rang just as Carol was coming in the front door. She stopped, set her purse on the kitchen counter and glared at the telephone. Her heart rammed against her rib cage with such force that she had to stop and gather her thoughts. It was Steve. The phone might as well have been spelling out his name in Morse code, she was that sure.

"Hello?" she answered brightly, on the third ring.

"Lindy said you phoned." His words were low, flat and emotionless.

"Yes, I did," she murmured, her nerves clamoring.

"Do you want to tell me why, or are you going to make me guess? Trust me, Carol, I'm in no mood to play twenty questions with you."

Oh Lord, this wasn't going to be easy. Steve sounded so cold and uncaring. She'd anticipated it, but it didn't lessen the effect his tone had on her. "I...I thought we could talk."

A short, heavy silence followed.

"I'm listening."

"I'd rather we didn't do it over the phone, Steve," she said softly, but not because she'd planned to make her voice silky and smooth. Her vocal chords had tightened and it just came out sounding that way. Her nerves were stretched to their limit, and her heart was pounding in her ear like a charging locomotive.

"Okay," he answered, reluctance evident in every syllable.

"When?" Her gaze scanned the calendar—the timing of this entire venture was of primary importance.

"Tomorrow," he suggested.

Carol's eyes drifted shut as the relief worked its way through her stiff limbs. Her biggest concern was that he would suggest after the Christmas holidays, and then it would be too late and she would have to reschedule everything for January.

"That would be fine," Carol managed. "Would you mind coming to the house?" The two bedroom brick rambler had been awarded to her as part of the divorce settlement.

Again she could feel his hesitation. "As a matter of fact, I would."

"All right," she answered, quickly gathering her wits. His not wanting to come to the house shouldn't have surprised her. "How about coffee at Denny's tomorrow evening?"

"Seven?"

Carol swallowed before answering. "Fine. I'll see you then."

Her hand was still trembling a moment later when she replaced the telephone receiver in its cradle. All along she'd accepted that Steve wasn't going to fall into her bed without some subtle prompting, but from the brusque, impatient sound of his voice, the whole escapade could well be impossible...this month. That bothered her. The one pivotal point in her plan was that everything come together quickly. One blazing night of passion could easily be dismissed and forgotten. But if she were to continue to invite him back one night a month, several months running, then he just might catch on to what she was doing.

Still, when it had come to interpreting her actions in the past, Steve had shown a shocking lack of insight. Thankfully their troubles had never intruded in the bedroom. Their marriage relationship had been a jumbled mess of doubts and misunderstandings, accusations and regrets, but their love life had always been vigorous and lusty right up until the divorce, astonishing as it seemed now.

At precisely seven the following evening, Carol walked into Denny's Restaurant on Seattle's Capitol Hill. The first year she and Steve had been married, they'd had dinner there once a month. Money had been tight because they'd been saving for a down payment on the house, and an evening out, even if it was only Saturday night at Denny's, had been a real treat.

Two steps into the restaurant Carol spotted her former husband sitting in a booth by the window. She paused and experienced such a wealth of emotion that advancing even one step more would have been impossible. Steve had no right to look this good— far better than she remembered. In the thirteen months since she'd last seen him, he'd changed considerably. Matured. His features were sharper, clearer, more intense. His lean good looks were all the more prominent, his handsome masculine features vigorous and tanned even in December. A few strands of gray hair streaked his temple, adding a distinguished air.

His gaze caught hers and Carol sucked in a deep, calming breath, her steps nearly faltering as she advanced toward him. His eyes had changed the most, she decided. Where once they had been warm and caressing, now they were cool and calculating. They narrowed on her, his mistrust shining through as bright as any beacon.

Carol experienced a moment of panic as his gaze seemed to strip away the last shreds of her pride. It took all her willpower to force a smile to her lips.

"Thank you for coming," she said, and slipped into the red upholstered seat across from him.

The waitress came with a glass coffeepot, and Carol turned over her cup, which the woman promptly filled after placing menus on the table.

"It feels cold enough to snow," Carol said as a means of starting conversation. It was eerie that she could have been married to Steve all those years and feel as if he were little more than a stranger. He gave her that impression now. This hard, impassive man was one she didn't know nearly as well as the one who had once been her lover, her friend and her husband.

"You're looking fit," Steve said after a moment, a spark of admiration glinting in his gaze.

"Thank you." A weak smile hovered over her lips. "You, too. How's the Navy treating you?"

"Good."

"Are you still on the *Atlantis*?"

He nodded shortly.

Silence.

Carol groped for something more to say. "It was a surprise to discover that Lindy's living in Seattle."

"Did she tell you she married Rush?"

Carol noted the way his brows drew together and darkened his face momentarily when he mentioned the fact. "I didn't realize Lindy even knew Rush," Carol said, and took a sip of the coffee.

"They were married two weeks after they met. Lord, I can't believe it yet."

"Two weeks? That doesn't sound anything like Rush. I remember him as being so methodical about everything."

Steve's frown relaxed, but only a little. "Apparently they fell in love."

Carol knew Steve well enough to recognize the hint of sarcasm in his voice, as if he were telling her what a mockery that emotion was. In their instance it had certainly been wasted. Sadly wasted.

"Are they happy?" That was the important thing as far as Carol was concerned.

"They went through a rough period a while back, but since the *Mitchell* docked they seem to have mended their fences."

Carol dropped her gaze to her cup as reality cut sharply into her heart. "That's more than we did."

"As you recall," he said harshly, under his breath, "there wasn't any fence left to repair. The night you started sleeping with Todd Larson, you destroyed our marriage."

Carol didn't rise to the challenge, although Steve had all but slapped her face with it. There was nothing she could say to exonerate herself, and she'd given up explaining the facts to him more than a year ago. Steve chose to believe what he wanted. She'd tried, God knew, to set the record straight. Todd had been her employer and her friend, but never anything more. Carol had pleaded with Steve until she was blue with exasperation, but it hadn't done her any good. Rehashing the same argument now wasn't going to help either of them.

Silence stretched between them and was broken by the waitress who had returned to their booth, pad and pen in hand. "Have you decided?"

Carol hadn't even glanced at the menu. "Do you have sweet-potato pie?"

"No, but pecan is the special this month."

Carol shook her head, ignoring the strange look Steve was giving her. "Just coffee then."

"Same here," Steve added.

The woman replenished both their cups and left.

"So how is good ol' Todd?"

His question lacked any real interest, and Carol had already decided her former boss was a subject they'd best avoid. "Fine," she lied. She had no idea how Todd was doing, since she hadn't worked for Larson Sporting Goods for over a year. She'd been offered a better job with Boeing and had been employed at the airplane company since before the divorce was final.

"I'm glad to hear it," Steve said with a soft snicker. "I suppose you called this little meeting to tell me the two of you are finally going to be married."

"No. Steve, please, I didn't call to talk about Todd."

He arched his brows in mock consternation. "I'm surprised. What's the matter, is wife number one still giving him problems? You mean to tell me their divorce hasn't gone through?"

A shattering feeling of hopelessness nearly choked Carol, and she struggled to meet his gaze without flinching. Steve was still so bitter, so intent on making her suffer.

"I really would prefer it if we didn't discuss Todd or Joyce."

"Fine. What do you want to talk about?" He checked his watch as if to announce he had plenty of other things he could be doing and didn't want to waste precious time with her.

Carol had carefully planned everything she was going to say. Each sentence had been rehearsed several times over in her mind, and now it seemed so trite and ridiculous, she couldn't manage a single word.

"Well?" he demanded. "Since you don't want to rub my nose in the fact that you're marrying Todd, what could you possibly have to tell me?"

Carol gestured with her hand, her fingers trembling. "It's Christmastime," she murmured.

"Congratulations, you've glanced at a calendar lately." He looked straight through her with eyes as hard as diamond bits.

"I thought…well, you know, that we could put

our differences aside for a little while and at least be civil to each other.''

His eyes narrowed. ''What possible reason could there be for us to have anything to do with each other? You mean nothing to me, and I'm sure the feeling is mutual.''

''You were my husband for five years.''

''So?''

She rearranged the silverware several times, choosing not to look at Steve. He wore his anger like a tight pair of shoes and sitting across from him was almost too painful to bear.

''We loved each other once,'' she said after a drawn-out, strained moment.

''I loved my dog once, too,'' he came back. One corner of his mouth was pulled down, and his eyes had thinned to narrow slits. ''What does having cared about each other have to do with anything now?''

Carol couldn't answer his question. She knew the divorce had made him bitter, but she'd counted on this long time apart to have healed some of his animosity.

''What did you do for the holidays last year?'' she asked, refusing to argue with him. She wasn't going to allow him to rile her into losing her temper. He'd played that trick once too often, and she was wise to his game.

"What the hell difference does it make to you how I spent Christmas?"

This wasn't going well, Carol decided—not the least bit as she'd planned. Steve seemed to think she wanted him to admit he'd been miserable without her.

"I...I spent the day alone," she told him softly, reluctantly. Their divorce had been final three weeks before the holiday and Carol's emotions had been so raw she'd hardly been able to deal with the usual festivities connected with the holiday.

"I wasn't alone," Steve answered with a cocky half smile that suggested that whoever he was with had been pleasant company, and he hadn't missed her in the least.

Carol didn't know how anyone could look so damned insolent and sensuous at the same moment. It required effort to keep her chin up and meet his gaze, but she managed.

"So *you* were alone," he added. The news appeared to delight him. "That's what happens when you mess around with a married man, my dear. In case you haven't figured it out yet, Todd's wife and family will always come first. That's the other woman's sad lot in life."

Carol went still all over. She felt as though her entire body had turned to stone. She didn't breathe, didn't move, didn't so much as blink. The pain

spread out in waves, circling first her throat and then
her chest, working its way down to her abdomen,
cinching her stomach so tightly that she thought she
might be sick. The whole room seemed to fade away
and the only thing she was sure about was that she
had to get out of the restaurant. Fast.

Her fingers fumbled with the snap of her purse as
she opened her wallet. Her hands weren't any more
steady as she placed several coins by the coffee cup
and scooted out of her seat.

Mutely Steve watched Carol walk out of the restaurant and called himself every foul name that he
could come up with from his extensive Navy vocab-
ulary. He hadn't meant to say those things. Hadn't
intended to lash out at her. But he hadn't been able
to stop himself.

He'd lied, too, in an effort to salvage his pride.
Lied rather than give her the satisfaction of knowing
he'd spent last Christmas Day miserable and alone.
It had been the worst holiday of his life. The pain of
the divorce had still ached like a lanced boil, while
everyone around him had been celebrating and exchanging gifts, their happiness like a ball and chain
shackling his heart. This year didn't hold much prospect for happiness, either. Lindy and Rush would
prefer to spend the day alone, although they'd gone
out of their way to convince him otherwise. But

Steve wasn't stupid and had already made other plans. He'd volunteered for watch Christmas Day so that a fellow officer could spend time with his family.

Gathering his thoughts about Carol, Steve experienced a healthy dose of regret about the way he'd behaved toward his ex-wife.

She'd looked good, he admitted reluctantly—better than he'd wanted her to look for his own peace of mind. From the moment they'd met, he'd felt the vibrant energy that radiated from her. Thirteen months apart hadn't diminished that. He'd known the minute she walked into Denny's; he'd felt her presence the instant the door opened. She wore her thick blond hair shorter than he remembered so that it fell forward and hugged the sides of her face, the ends curling under slightly, giving her a Dutch-boy look. As always, her metallic blue eyes were magnetic, irrevocably drawing his gaze. She looked small and fragile, and the desire to protect and love her had come at him with all the force of a wrecking ball slamming against his chest. He knew differently, but it hadn't seemed to change the way he felt—Carol needed him about as much as the Navy needed more salt water.

Sliding out of the booth, Steve laid a bill on the table and left. Outside, the north wind sent a chill racing up his arms and he buried his hands into his pants pockets as he headed toward the parking lot.

Surprise halted his progress when he spied Carol leaning against the fender of her car. Her shoulders were slumped, her head hanging as though she were burdened by a terrible weight.

Once more Steve was swamped with regret. He had never learned the reason she'd phoned. He started walking toward her, not knowing what he intended to say or do.

She didn't glance up when he joined her.

"You never said why you phoned," he said in a wounded voice after a moment of silence.

"It isn't important...I told Lindy that."

"If it wasn't to let me know you're remarrying, then it's because you want something."

She looked up and tried to smile, and the feeble effort cut straight through Steve's resolve to forget he'd ever known or loved her. It was useless to try.

"I don't think it'll work," Carol said sadly.

"What?"

She shook her head.

"If you need something, just ask!" he shouted, using his anger as a defense mechanism. Carol had seldom wanted anything from him. It must be important for her to contact him now, especially after their divorce.

"Christmas Day," she whispered brokenly. "I don't want to spend it alone."

Chapter 2

Until Carol spoke, she hadn't known how much she wanted Steve to spend Christmas Day with her—and not for the reasons she'd been plotting. She sincerely missed Steve. He'd been both lover and friend, and now he was neither; the sense of loss was nearly overwhelming.

He continued to stare at her, and regret worked its way across his features. The success of her plan hinged on his response and she waited, almost afraid to breathe, for his answer.

"Carol, listen…" He paused and ran his hand along the back of his neck, his brow puckered with a condensed frown.

Carol knew him well enough to realize he was carefully composing his thoughts. She was also aware that he was going to refuse her! She knew it as clearly as if he'd spoken the words aloud. She swallowed the hurt, although she couldn't keep her eyes from widening with pain. When Steve had presented her with the divorce papers, Carol had promised herself she would never give him the power to hurt her again. Yet here she was, handing him the knife and exposing her soul.

She could feel her heart thumping wildly in her chest and fought to control the emotions that swamped her. "Is it so much to ask?" she whispered, and the words fell broken from her lips.

"I've got the watch."

"On Christmas..." She hadn't expected that, hadn't figured it into the scheme of things. In other words, the excuse of Christmas wasn't going to work. Ultimately her strategy would fail, and she would end up spending the holiday alone.

"I'd do it if I could," Steve told her in a straightforward manner that convinced her he was telling the truth. She felt somewhat less disappointed.

"Thank you for that," she said, and reached out to touch his hand, in a small gesture of appreciation. Amazingly he didn't draw away from her, which gave her renewed hope.

A reluctant silence stretched between them.

There'd been a time when they couldn't say enough to each other, and now there was nothing.

"I suppose I'd better get back." Steve spoke first.

"Me, too," she answered brightly, perhaps a little too brightly. "It was good to see you again...you're looking well."

"You, too." He took a couple of steps backward, but still hadn't turned away. Swallowing down her disappointment, Carol retrieved the car keys from the bottom of her purse and turned to climb into her Honda. It dawned on her then, hit her square between the eyes. If not Christmas Day then...

"Steve," she whirled back around, her eyes flashing.

"Carol." He called her name at the same moment.

They laughed and the sound fell rusty and awkward between them.

"You first," he said, and gestured toward her. The corner of his mouth was curved upward in a half smile.

"What about Christmas Eve?"

He nodded. "I was just thinking the same thing."

Carol felt the excitement bubble up inside her like fizz in a club soda. A grin broke out across her face as she realized nothing had been lost and everything was yet to be gained. Somewhere in the distance, Carol was sure she could hear the soft, lilting strains of a Brahms lullaby. "Could you come early enough for dinner?"

Again, he nodded. "Six?"

"Perfect. I'll look forward to it."

"I will, too."

He turned and walked away from her then, and it was all Carol could do to keep from doing a war dance, jumping up and down around the car. Instead she rubbed her bare hands together as though the friction would ease some of the excitement she was feeling. Steve hadn't a clue how memorable this one night would be. Not a clue!

"Your mood has certainly improved lately," Lindy commented as Steve walked into the kitchen whistling a lively Christmas carol.

His sister's words stopped him. "My mood has?"

"You've been downright chipper all week."

He shrugged his shoulders, hoping the action would discount his cheerful attitude. "'Tis the season."

"I don't suppose your meeting with Carol has anything to do with it?"

His sister eyed him skeptically, seeking his confidence, but Steve wasn't going to give it. This dinner with his ex-wife was simply the meeting of two lonely people struggling to make it through the holidays. Nothing less and certainly nothing more. Although he'd been looking for Carol to deny that she was involved with Todd, she hadn't. Steve considered her refusal to talk about the other man as good as an admission of guilt. That bastard had left her alone for Christmas two years running.

If Lindy was right and his mood had improved, Steve decided, it was simply because he was going to be out of his sister and Rush's hair for the evening; the newlyweds could spend their first Christmas Eve together without a third party butting in.

Steve reached for his coat, and Lindy turned around, her dark eyes wide with surprise. "You're leaving."

Steve nodded, buttoning the thick wool jacket.

"But...it's Christmas Eve."

"I know." He tucked the box of candy under his arm and lifted the bright red poinsettia he'd purchased on impulse earlier in the day.

"Where are you going?"

Steve would have liked to say a friend's house, but that wouldn't be true. He didn't know how to classify his relationship with Carol. Not a friend. Not a lover. More than an acquaintance, less than a wife.

"You're going to Carol's, aren't you?" Lindy prompted.

The last thing Steve wanted was his sister to get the wrong impression about this evening with Carol, because that's all there was going to be. "It's not what you think."

Lindy raised her hands in mock consternation. "I'm not thinking a single thing except that it's good to see you smile again."

Steve's frown was heavy with purpose. "Well, don't read more into it than there is."

"Are the two of you going to talk?" Lindy asked, and her dark eyes fairly danced with deviltry.

"We're going to eat, not talk," Steve explained with limited patience. "We don't have anything in common anymore. I'll probably be home before ten."

"Whatever you say." Lindy answered, but her lips twitched with the effort to suppress a knowing smile. "Have a good time."

Steve chose not to answer that comment and left the apartment, but as soon as he was outside, he discovered he was whistling again and stopped abruptly.

Carol slipped the compact disk into the player and set the volume knob so that the soft Christmas music swirled festively through the house. A small turkey was roasting in the oven, stuffed with Steve's favorite sage dressing. Two pies were cooling on the kitchen counter—pumpkin for Steve, mincemeat for her. To be on the safe side a sweet-potato-pecan pie was in the fridge.

Carol chose a red silk dress that whispered enticingly against her soft skin. Her makeup and perfume had been applied with a subtle hand. Everything was ready.

Well, almost everything.

She and Steve were two different people now, and there was no getting around the fact. Regretting the past was an exercise in futility, and yet Carol had been overwhelmed these past few days with the realization that the divorce had been wrong. Very wrong. All the emotion she'd managed to bury this past year had seeped to the surface since her meeting with Steve and she couldn't remember a time when she'd been more confused.

She wanted a child, and she was using her ex-husband. More than once in the past week, she'd been forced to deal with twinges of guilt. But there was no going back. It would be impossible to recapture what had been between them before the divorce. There could be no reconciliation. Even more difficult than the past, Carol had trouble dealing with the present. They couldn't come in contact with each other without the sparks igniting. It made everything more difficult. They were both too stubborn, too temperamental, too obstinate.

And it was ruining their lives.

Carol felt they couldn't go back and yet they couldn't step forward, either. The idea of seducing

Steve and getting pregnant had, in the beginning, been entirely selfish. She wanted a baby and she considered Steve the best candidate…the only candidate. After their one short meeting at the restaurant, Carol knew her choice of the baby's father went far beyond the practical. A part of her continued to love Steve, and probably always would. She wanted his child because it was the only part of him she would ever be able to have.

Everything hinged on the outcome of this dinner. Carol pressed her hands over her flat stomach and issued a fervent prayer that she was fertile. Twice in the past hour she'd taken her temperature, praying her body would do its part in this master plan. Her temperature was slightly elevated, but that could be caused by the hot sensation that went through her at the thought of sharing a bed with Steve again. Or it could be sheer nerves.

All day she'd been feeling anxious and restless with anticipation. She was convinced Steve would take one look at her and instantly know she intended for him to spend the night. The crux of her scheme was for Steve to think their making love was *his* idea. Again and again, her plans for the evening circled her mind, slowly, like the churning blades of a windmill stirring the air.

The doorbell chimed, and inhaling a calming breath, Carol forced a smile, walked across the room and opened the door for her ex-husband. "Merry Christmas," she said softly.

Steve handed her the poinsettia as though he couldn't get rid of the flower fast enough. His gaze didn't quite meet hers. In fact, he seemed to be avoiding looking at her, which pleased Carol because it told her that the red dress was having exactly the effect she'd hoped for.

"Thank you for the flower," she said and set it in the middle of the coffee table. "You didn't need to do that."

"I remembered how you used to buy three and four of those silly things each year and figured one more couldn't hurt."

"It was thoughtful of you, and I appreciate it." She held out her hand to take his coat.

Steve placed a small package under the tree and gave her a shy look. "Frangos," he explained awkwardly. "I suppose they're still your favorite candy."

"Yes. I have a little something for you, too."

Steve peeled off his heavy jacket and handed it to her. "I'm not looking for any gifts from you. I brought the flowers and candy because I wanted to contribute something toward dinner."

"My gift isn't much, Steve."

"Save it for someone else. Okay?"

Her temper nearly slipped then, but Carol managed

to keep it intact. Her smile was just a little more forced when she turned from hanging his jacket in the hall closet, but she hoped he hadn't noticed.

"Would you like a hot-buttered rum before we eat?" she offered.

"That sounds good."

He followed her into the kitchen and brought the bottle of rum down from the top cupboard while she put water on to boil.

"When did you cut your hair?" he asked unexpectedly.

Absently Carol's fingers touched the straight, thick strands that crowded the side of her head. "Several months ago now."

"I liked it better when you wore it longer."

Gritting her teeth, she managed to bite back the words to inform him that she styled her hair to suit herself these days, not him.

Steve saw the flash of irritation in his ex-wife's eyes and felt a little better. The comment about her hair wasn't what she'd wanted to hear; she'd been waiting for him to tell her how beautiful she looked. The problem was, he hadn't been able to take his eyes off her from the moment he entered the house. The wisecrack was a result of one flirtatious curl of blond hair that swayed when she moved. He hadn't been able to look past that single golden lock. Nei-

ther could he stop staring at the shape of her lips nor
the curve of her chin, nor the appealing color of her
china blue eyes. When he'd met her at Denny's the
other night he'd been on the defensive, waiting for
her to drop her bombshell. All his protective walls
were lowered now. He would have liked to blame it
on the Christmas holidays, but he realized it was
more than that, and what he saw gave him cause to
tremble. Carol was as sensuous and appealing to him
as she'd always been. Perhaps more so.

Already he knew what was going to happen. They
would spend half the evening verbally circling each
other in an anxious search for common ground. But
there wasn't one for them...not anymore. Tonight
was an evening out of sequence, and when it had
passed they would return to their respective lives.

When Carol finished mixing their drinks, they
wandered into the living room and talked. The al-
cohol seemed to alleviate some of the tension. Steve
filled the silence with details of what had been happening in Lindy's life and in his career.

"You've done well for yourself," Carol admitted,
and there was a spark of pride in her eyes that
warmed him.

Steve didn't inquire about her career because it
would involve asking about Todd, and the man was
a subject he'd sworn he would avoid at all costs.

Carol didn't volunteer any information, either. She knew the unwritten ground rules.

A half hour later, Steve helped her carry their meal to the table.

"You must have been cooking all day."

She grinned and nodded. "It gave me something to do."

The table was loaded with sliced turkey, creamy potatoes, giblet gravy, stuffing, fresh broccoli, sweet potatoes and fruit salad.

Carol asked him to light the candles and when Steve had, they sat down to eat. Sitting directly across the table from her, Steve found he was mesmerized by her mouth as she ate. With all his might he tried to remember the reasons he'd divorced Carol. Good God, she was captivating—too damn good to look at for his own peace of mind. Her hands moved gracefully, raising the fork from her plate to her mouth in motions as elegant as those of a symphony director. He shouldn't be enjoying watching her this much, and he realized he would pay the price later when he returned to the apartment and the loneliness overtook him once more.

When he'd finished the meal, he leaned against the shield-back dining-room chair and placed his hands over his stomach. "I can't remember when I've had a better dinner."

"There's pie…"

"Not now," he countered quickly and shook his head. "I'm too full to down another bite. Maybe later."

"Coffee?"

"Please."

Carol carried their dishes to the sink, stuck the leftovers in the refrigerator, and returned with the glass coffeepot. She filled both their cups, returned it to the kitchen and then took her seat opposite him. She rested her elbows on the table, and smiled.

Despite his best intentions through a good portion of the meal, Steve hadn't been able to keep his eyes away from her. The way she was sitting—leaning forward, her elbows on the tabletop—caused her breasts to push together and more than amply fill the bodice of her dress. His breath faltered someplace between his lungs and his throat at the alluring sight she made. He could have sworn she wasn't wearing a bra. Carol had fantastic breasts and Steve watched, captivated, as their tips beaded against the shiny material. They seemed to be pointing directly at him, issuing a silent invitation that asked him to fondle and taste them. Against his will, his groin began to swell until he was throbbing with painful need. Disconcerted, he dropped his gaze to the steaming cup of coffee. With his hands shaking, he took a sip of his coffee and nearly scalded the tender skin inside his mouth.

"That was an excellent dinner," he repeated, after a moment of silence.

"You're not sorry you came, are you?" she asked unexpectedly, studying him. The intent look that crowded her face demanded all Steve's attention. Her skin was pale and creamy in the muted light, her eyes wide and inquiring, as though the answer to her question was of the utmost importance.

"No," he admitted reluctantly. "I'm glad I'm here."

His answer pleased her and she smiled, looking tender and trusting, and Steve wondered how he could ever have doubted her. He knew what she'd done—knew that she'd purposely destroyed their marriage—and in that moment, it didn't matter. He wanted her again. He wanted to hold her warm and willing body in his arms. He wanted to bury himself so deep inside her that she would never desire another man for as long as they both lived.

"I'll help you with the dishes," he said, and rose so abruptly that he nearly knocked over the chair.

"I'll do them later." She got to her feet as well. "But if you want to do something, I'd appreciate a little help with the tree."

"The tree?" The words sounded as foreign as an obscure language.

"Yes, it's only half decorated. I couldn't reach the tallest limbs. Will you help?"

He shrugged. "Sure." He could have sworn that
Carol was relieved, and he couldn't imagine why.
The Christmas tree looked fine to him. There were a
few bare spots, but nothing too noticeable.

Carol dragged a dining-room chair into the living
room and pulled a box of ornaments out from underneath the end table.

"You're knitting?" Steve asked, hiding a smile as
his gaze fell on the strands of worsted yarn. Carol
had to be the worst knitter in the world, yet she tack-
led one project after another, seeming oblivious of
any lack of talent. There had been a time when he
could tease her about it, but he wasn't sure his insight
would be appreciated now.

She glanced away as though she feared his comment.

"Don't worry, I'm not going to tease you," he
told her, remembering the time she'd proudly presented him with a sweater she'd made herself—the
left sleeve had been five inches longer than the right.
He'd tried it on and she'd taken one look at him and
burst into tears. It was one of the few times he could
ever remember Carol crying.

Carol dragged the chair next to the tree and raised
her leg to stand on it.

Steve stopped her. "I thought you wanted me to
do that?"

"No, I need you to hand me the ornaments and then stand back and tell me how they look."

"Carol...if I placed the ornaments on the tree, you wouldn't need the chair."

She looked at him and sighed. "I'd rather do it. You don't mind, do you?"

He didn't know why she was so determined to hang the decorations herself, but it didn't make much difference to him. "No, if you want to risk your fool neck, feel free."

She grinned and raised herself so that she was standing on the padded cushion of the chair. "Okay, hand me one," she said, tossing him a look over her shoulder.

Steve gave her a shiny glass bulb, and he noted how good she smelled. Roses and some other scent he couldn't define wrapped gently around him. Carol stretched out her arms and reached for the tallest branch. Her dress rose a solid five inches and exposed the back of her creamy smooth thighs and a fleeting glimpse of the sweet curve of her buttocks. Steve knotted his hands into fists at his sides to keep from touching her. It would be entirely plausible for him to grip her waist and claim he was frightened she would tumble from her perch. But if he allowed that to happen, his hands would slip and soon he would be cupping that cute rounded bottom. Once he touched her, Steve knew he would never be able to stop. He clenched his teeth and inhaled deeply through his nose. Having Carol standing there, exposing herself in this unconscious way, was more than a mere man could resist. At this point, he was willing to use any excuse to be close to her once more.

Carol lowered her arms, her dress fell back into place and Steve breathed normally again. He thought he was safe from further temptation until she twisted around. Her ripe, full breasts filled the front of her dress, their shape clearly defined against the thin fabric. If he'd been guessing about the bra before, he was now certain. She wasn't wearing one.

"I'm ready for another ornament," she said softly.

Like a blind man, Steve turned and fumbled for a second glass bulb. He handed it to her and did everything within his power to keep his gaze away from her breasts.

"How does that one look?" Carol asked.

"Fine," Steve answered gruffly.

"Steve?"

"Don't you think that's enough decorations, for God's sake?"

His harsh tone was as much a surprise to him as it obviously was to Carol.

"Yes, of course."

She sounded disappointed, but that couldn't be helped. Steve moved to her side once more and offered her his hand to help her down. His foot must have hit against one leg of the chair because it jerked forward. Perhaps it was something she did, Steve wasn't sure, but whatever happened caused the chair to teeter on the thick carpet.

With a small cry of alarm, Carol threw out her arms.

With reflexes born of years of military training, Steve's hands shot out like bullets to catch her. The chair fell sideways onto the floor, but Steve's grip on Carol's waist anchored her firmly against his torso. Their breathing was labored, and Steve sighed with relief that she hadn't fallen. It was on the tip of his tongue to berate her, call her a silly goose for not letting him place the glass bulbs on the tree, chastise her for being such a fool. She shouldn't put herself at risk over something as nonsensical as a Christmas tree. But none of the words made it to his lips.

Their gazes were even, her haunting eyes stared into his and said his name as clearly as if it were spoken. Carol's feet remained several inches off the floor, and still Steve held on to her, unable to release her. His heart was pounding frantically with wonder as he raised a finger and touched her soft throat. His gaze continued to delve into hers. He wanted to set her back on the carpet, to free them both from this invisible grip before it maimed them, but he couldn't seem to find the strength to let her go.

Slowly she slid down his front, between his braced feet, crimping the skirt of her dress between them. Once she was secure, he noted that her lower abdomen was tucked snugly in the joint between his thighs. The throbbing in his groin began again, and he held in a groan that threatened to emanate from deep within his chest.

He longed to kiss her more than he'd ever wanted anything in his life, and only the greatest strength of will kept him from claiming her sweet mouth with his own.

She'd betrayed him once, crippled him with her deceit. Steve had sworn he would never allow her to use him again, yet his arguments burned away like dry timber in a forest fire.

His thumb found her moist lips and brushed back and forth as though the action would be enough to satisfy either of them. It didn't. If anything, it created an agony even more powerful. His heart leaped into a hard, fast rhythm that made him feel breathless and weak. Before he could stop himself, his finger lifted her chin and his mouth glided over hers. Softly. Moistly. Satin against satin.

Carol sighed.

Steve groaned.

She weakened in his arms and closed her eyes. Steve kissed her a second time and thrust his tongue deep into her mouth, his need so strong it threatened to consume him. His hand was drawn to her breast, as if caught by a vise and carried there against his will. He cupped the rounded flesh, and his finger teased the nipple until it beaded and swelled against his palm. Carol whimpered.

He had to touch her breasts again. Had to know for himself their velvet smoothness. Releasing a ragged sigh, he reached behind her and peeled down her zipper. She was as eager as he when he lowered the top of her dress and exposed her naked front.

Her hands were around his neck, and she slanted her mouth over his, rising to her tiptoes as she leaned her weight into his. Steve's mouth quickly abandoned hers to explore the curve of her neck and then lower to the rosy tips of her firm, proud breasts. His moist tongue traced circles around the pebbled nipples until Carol shuddered and plowed her fingers through his hair.

"Steve...oh, I've missed you so much." She repeated the sentence over and over again, but the words didn't register in his clouded mind. When they did, he went cold. She may have missed him, may have hungered for his touch, but she hadn't been faithful. The thought crippled him, and he went utterly still.

Carol must have sensed his withdrawal, because she dropped her arms. Her shoulders were heaving as though she'd been running in a heated race. His own breathing wasn't any more regular.

Abruptly Steve released her and stumbled two paces back.

"That shouldn't have happened," he announced in a hoarse whisper.

Carol regarded him with a wounded look but said nothing.

"I've got to get out of here," he said, expelling the words on the tail end of a sigh.

Carol's gaze widened and she shook her head.

"Carol, we aren't married anymore. This shouldn't be happening."

"I know." She lowered her gaze to the carpet.

Steve walked to the hall closet and reached for his jacket. His actions felt as if they were in slow motion—as if every gravitational force in the universe was pulling at him.

He paused, his hand clenching the doorknob. "Thank you for dinner."

Carol nodded, and when he turned back, he saw that her eyes had filled with tears and she was biting her bottom lip to hold them back. One hand held the front of her dress across her bare breasts.

"Carol…"

She looked at him with soft, appealing eyes and held out her hand. "Don't go," she begged softly. "Please don't leave me. I need you so much."

Chapter 3

Carol could see the battle raging in Steve's tight features. She swallowed down the tears and refused to release his gaze, which remained locked with her own.

"We're not married anymore," he said in a voice that shook with indecision.

"I...don't care." Swallowing her pride, she took one small step toward him. If he wouldn't come to her, then she was going to him. Her knees felt incredibly weak, as though she were walking after being bedridden for a long while.

"Carol..."

She didn't stop until she was standing directly in

front of him. Then slowly, with infinite care, she released her hold on the front of her dress and allowed it to fall free, baring her breasts. Steve rewarded her immediately with a swift intake of breath, and then it seemed as if he stopped breathing completely. Carol slipped her flattened hands up his chest and leaned her body into his. When she felt his rock-hard arousal pressing against her thigh, she closed her eyes to disguise the triumph that zoomed through her blood like a shot of adrenaline.

Steve held himself stiffly against her, refusing to yield to her softness; his arms hung motionless at his sides. He didn't push her away, but he didn't welcome her into his embrace, either.

Five years of marriage had taught Carol a good deal about her husband's body. She knew what pleasured him most, knew what would drive him to the edge of madness, knew how to make him want her until there was nothing else in their world.

Standing on the tips of her toes, she locked her arms tightly around his neck and raised her soft lips to gently brush her mouth over his. Her kiss was as moist and light as dew on a summer rose. Steve's lashes dropped and she could feel the torment of the battle that raged in his troubled mind.

Slightly elevating one foot, she allowed her shoe to slip off her toes. It fell almost silently to the floor. Carol nearly laughed aloud at the expression that

came over Steve's contortcd features. He knew what
was coming, and against his will, Carol could see
that he welcomed it. In a leisurely exercise, she
raised her nylon-covered foot and slid it down the
backside of his leg. Again and again her thigh and
calf glided over his, each caressing stroke moved
higher and higher on his leg, bringing her closer to
her objective.

When Steve's hand closed, almost painfully, over
her thigh, Carol knew she'd won. He held her there
for a timeless moment, neither moving nor breathing.

"Kiss me," he ordered, and the words seemed to
be ground out from between clenched teeth.

Although Carol had fully intended to comply with
his demand, she apparently didn't do it fast enough
to suit her ex-husband. He groaned and his free hand
locked around the back of her head, compelling her
mouth to his. Driven by urgency, his kiss was force-
ful and demanding, almost grinding, as if he sought
to punish her for making him want her so much.
Carol allowed him to ravage her mouth, giving him
everything he wanted, everything he asked for, until
finally she gasped for breath and broke away briefly.
Steve brought her mouth back to his, and gradually
his kisses softened until Carol thought she was sure
her whole body would burst into flames. Sensing this,
Steve moved his hand from the back of her head and
began to massage her breast in a leisurely circular

motion, his palm centering on her nipple. Her whole torso started to pulsate under his gentle touch.

Carol arched her spine to grant him easier access, and tossed back her head as his fingers worked their magic. Then his hand left her breast, and she wanted to protest until she felt his fingers slip around her other thigh and lift her completely off the carpet, raising her so that their mouths were level, their breath mingling, moist and excited.

They paused and gazed into each other's eyes. Steve's were filled with surprise and wonder. Carol met that look and smiled with a rediscovered joy that burst from deep within her. An inner happiness that had vanished from her life the moment Steve had walked away from her, returned. She leaned forward and very gently rubbed her mouth across his, creating a moist, delicious friction. Gently her tongue played over the seam of his lips, sliding back and forth, teasing him, testing him in a love game that had once been familiar between them.

Carol gently caught his lower lip between her teeth and sucked on it, playing with it while darting the tip of her tongue in and out of his mouth.

The effect on Steve was electric. His mouth claimed hers in an urgent kiss that drove the oxygen from her lungs. Then, with a strength that astonished her, he lifted her even higher until his mouth closed over her left breast, rolling his tongue over her nipple, then sucking at it greedily, taking in more and more of her breast.

Carol thought she was going to go crazy with the tidal wave of sensation that flooded her being. She locked her legs around his waist and braced her hands against his shoulders. His mouth and tongue alternated from one breast to the other until she was convinced that if he didn't take her soon, she was going to faint in his arms.

Braced against the closet door, Steve used what leverage he could to inch his hand up the inside of her thigh. His exploring fingers reached higher and higher, then paused when he encountered a nylon barrier. He groaned his frustration.

Carol was so weak with longing that if he didn't carry her voluntarily into the bedroom soon, she was going to demand that he make love to her right there on the entryway floor.

"You weren't wearing a bra," he chastised her in a husky thwarted voice. "I was hoping…"

He didn't need to finish for Carol to know what he was talking about. When they were married, she'd often worn a garter belt with her nylons instead of panty hose so their lovemaking wouldn't be impeded.

"I want you," she whispered, her hands framing his face. "But if you think it would be best to leave…go now. The choice is yours."

His gaze locked with hers, Steve marched wordlessly across the living room and down the long hallway to the bedroom that had once been theirs.

"Not here," she told him. "I sleep there now," she explained, pointing to the room across the hall.

Steve switched directions and marched into the smaller bedroom, not stopping until he reached the queen-size bed. For one crazy second, Carol thought he meant to drop her on top of the mattress and storm right out of the house. Instead he continued to hold her, the look in his eyes wild and uncertain.

Carol's eyes met his. She was nearly choking on the sadness that threatened to overwhelm her. Tentatively she raised one hand and pressed it to the side of his face, her eyes wide, her heart pounding so hard she was sure the sound of it would soon bring down the walls.

To her surprise, Steve tenderly placed her on the bed, braced one knee against the edge of the mattress and leaned over her.

"We aren't married.... Not a damn thing has been settled between us," he announced, as though this should be shocking news.

Carol said nothing, but she casually slipped her hand around the side of his neck, urging his mouth down to hers. She met with no resistance.

"Make love to me," she murmured.

Steve groaned, twisted around and dropped to sit

on the side of the bed, granting her a full view of his solid back. The thread of disappointment that wrapped itself around Carol's heart was followed by a slow, lazy smile that spread over her mouth as she recognized his frantic movements.

Steve was undressing.

Feeling deliciously warm and content, Carol woke two hours later to the sound of Steve rummaging in the kitchen. No doubt he was looking for something to eat. Smiling, she jerked her arms high above her head and stretched. She yawned and arched her back, slightly elevating her hips with the action. She felt marvelous. Stupendous. Happy.

Her heart bursting with newfound joy, she reached for Steve's shirt and purposely buttoned it just enough to be provocative while looking as if she'd made some effort to cover herself.

Semiclothed, she moved toward the noise emanating from her kitchen. Barefoot, dressed only in his slacks, Steve was bent over, investigating the contents of her refrigerator.

Carol paused in the doorway. "Making love always did make you hungry," she said from behind him.

"There's hardly a damn thing in here except sweet potatoes. Good grief, woman, what are you doing with all these leftover yams?"

Carol felt sudden heat rise in her cheeks as hurried excuses crowded her mind. "They were on sale this week because of Christmas."

"They must have been at rock-bottom price. I counted six containers full of them. It looks like you've been eating them at every meal for an entire week."

"There's some pie if that'll interest you," she said, a little too quickly. "And plenty of turkey for a sandwich, if you want."

He straightened, closed the refrigerator and turned to face her. But whatever he'd intended to say apparently left him when he caught sight of her seductive pose. She was leaning against the doorjamb, hands behind her back and one foot braced against the wall, smiling at him, certain he could read her thoughts.

"There's pumpkin, and the whipped topping is fresh."

"Pumpkin?" he repeated.

"The pie."

He blinked, and nodded. "That sounds good."

"Would you like me to make you a sandwich while I'm at it?"

"Sure." But he didn't sound sure of anything at the moment.

Moving with ease around her kitchen, Carol brought out the necessary ingredients and quickly put together a snack for both of them. When she'd finished, she carried their plates to the small table across from the stove.

"Would you like something to drink?" she asked, setting their plates down.

"I'll get it," Steve said, apparently eager to help. "What would you like?"

"Milk," she responded automatically. She'd never been overly fond of the beverage but had recently made a habit of drinking a glass or two each day in preparation for her pregnancy.

"I thought you didn't like milk."

"I...I've acquired new tastes in the past year."

Steve grinned. "There are certain things about you that haven't changed, and then there's something more, something completely unexpected. Good God, woman, you've turned into a little she-devil, haven't you?"

Carol lowered her gaze and felt the heated blush work its way up her neck and spill into her cheeks. It wasn't any wonder Steve was teasing her. She'd been as hot as a stick of dynamite. By the time he'd undressed, she'd behaved like a tigress, clawing at him, driven by mindless passion.

Chuckling, Steve delivered two glasses of milk to the table. "You surprised me," he said. "You used to be a tad more timid."

Doing her best to ignore him, Carol brought her

feet up to the edge of the chair and pulled the shirt down over her legs. With feigned dignity, she reached for half of her sandwich. "An officer and a gentleman wouldn't remind me of my wicked ways."

Still grinning, Steve lounged against the back of the chair. "You used to be far more subtle."

"Steve," she cried, "stop talking about it. Can't you see you're embarrassing me?"

"I remember one time when we were on our way to an admiral's dinner party and you casually announced you'd been in such a rush that you'd forgotten to put on any underwear."

Carol closed her eyes and looked away, remembering the time as clearly as if it had been last week instead of several years ago. She remembered, too, how good the lovemaking had been later that same evening.

"There wasn't time for us to go back to the house, so all night while you strolled around, sipping champagne, chatting and looking sedately prim, only I knew differently. Every time you looked at me, I about went crazy."

"I wanted you to know how much I longed to make love. If you'll recall, you'd just returned from a three-month tour."

"Carol, if *you'll* recall, we'd spent the entire day in bed."

She took a sip of her milk, then slowly raised her gaze to meet his. "It wasn't enough."

Steve closed his eyes and shook his head before grudgingly admitting, "It wasn't enough for me, either."

As soon as it had been socially acceptable to do so, Steve had made their excuses to the admiral that night and they'd hurriedly left the party. The entire way home, he'd been furious with Carol, telling her he was certain someone must have known what little trick she was playing. Just as heatedly, Carol had told Steve she didn't care who knew. If some huffy admiral wanted to throw a dinner party he shouldn't do it so soon after his men return from deployment.

They'd ended up making love twice that evening.

"Steve," Carol whispered with ragged emotion.

"Yes?"

"Once wasn't enough tonight, either." She dared not look at him, dared not let him see the way her pulse was clamoring.

Abruptly he stopped eating, and when he swallowed, it looked as if he'd downed the sandwich whole. A full minute passed before he spoke.

"Not for me, either."

Their lovemaking was different this time. Unique. Unrepeatable. Earlier, it'd been like spontaneous combustion. This time was slow, easy, relaxed. Steve led her into the bedroom, unfastened the buttons of

the shirt that she was wearing and let it drop un-
heeded to the floor.

Carol stood before him tall and proud, her taut
nipples seeming to beg for his lips. Steve looked at
her naked body as if seeing her for the first time.
Tenderly he raised his hand to her face and brushed
back a wisp of blond hair, his touch light, gentle.
Then he lowered his hands and cupped the under-
sides of her breasts, as though weighing them in a
delicate measure. The velvet stroke of his thumbs
worked across her nipples until they pebbled to a
throbbing hardness. From there he slid the tips of his
fingers down her rib cage, grazing her heated flesh
wherever he touched her.

All the while, his dark, mesmerizing gaze never
left hers, as though he half expected her to protest
or to stop him.

Carol felt as if her hands were being manipulated
like a puppet's as she reached for his belt buckle. All
she knew was that she wanted him to make love to
her. Her fingers fumbled at first, unfamiliar with the
workings of his belt, then managed to release the
clasp.

Soon Steve was nude.

She studied him, awed by his strength and beauty.
She wanted to tell him all that she was feeling, all
the good things she sensed in him, but the words

withered on her tongue as he reached out and
touched her once more.

His hand continued downward from her rib cage,
momentarily pausing over her flat, smooth stomach,
then moving lower until it encountered her pelvis.
Slowly, methodically, he braced the heel of his hand
against the apex of her womanhood and started a
circling, gyrating motion while his fingers explored
between her parted thighs.

Hardly able to breathe, Carol opened herself more
to him, and once she had, he delicately parted her
and slipped one finger inside. Her eyes widened at
the stab of pleasure that instantly sliced through her
and she bit into her lower lip to keep from panting.

She must have made some kind of sound because
Steve paused and asked, "Did I hurt you?"

Carol was incapable of any verbal response. Frantically she shook her head, and his finger continued
its deft movements, quickly bringing her to an exploding release. Wave upon wave of seething
spasms, each one stronger, each one more intense,
overtook every part of her. Whimpering noises escaped from deep within her throat as she climaxed,
and the sound propelled Steve into action.

He wrapped his arms around her and carried her
to the bed, laying her on top of the rumpled sheets.
Not allowing her time to alter her position or rear-

range the sheets, Steve moved over her, parted her thighs and quickly impaled her.

His breathing was ragged, barely under control.

Carol's wasn't any more even.

He didn't move, torturing her with an intense longing she had never experienced. Her body was still tingling in the aftermath of one fulfillment and reaching, striving toward another. Her whole person seemed to be filled with anxious expectancy…waiting for something she couldn't define.

Taking her hands, Steve lifted them above her head and held them prisoner there. He leaned over her, bracing himself on his arms on either side of her head. The action thrust him deeper inside Carol. She moaned and thrashed her head against the mattress, then lifted her hips, jerking them a couple of times, seeking more.

"Not yet, love," he whispered and placed a hand under her head, lifting her mouth to his. Their kiss was wild and passionate, as though their mouths couldn't give or take enough to satisfy their throbbing need.

Steve shifted his position and completely withdrew his body from hers.

Carol felt as if she'd suddenly gone blind; the whole world seemed black and lifeless. She started to protest, started to cry out, but before the sound escaped her throat, Steve sank his manhood back inside her. A shaft of pure light filled her senses once more and she sighed audibly, relieved. She was whole again, free.

"Now," Steve told her. "Now." He moved eagerly then, in deep, calculated strokes, plunging into her again and again, gifting her with the sun, revealing the heavens, exploring the universe. Soon all Carol knew was this insistent warm friction and the sweet, indescribable pangs of pleasure. Her body trembled as ripple after ripple of deep, pure sensation pulsed over her, driving her crazy as she remembered what had nightly been hers.

Breathless, Steve moved to lie beside her, bringing her into the circle of his arms. An hour passed, it seemed, before he spoke. "Was it always this good?"

The whispered question was so low Carol had to strain to hear him. "Yes," she answered after a long, timeless moment. "Always."

He pressed his forehead against the top of her head and moaned. "I was afraid of that."

The next thing Carol was aware of was a muffled curse and the unsettling sound of something heavy crashing to the floor.

"Steve?" she sat up in bed and reached for a sheet to cover her nakedness. The room was dark and still. Dread filled her—it couldn't be morning. Not yet, not so soon.

"I'm sorry. I didn't mean to wake you."

"You're leaving?" She sent her hand searching for the lamp on the nightstand. It clicked and a muted light filled the room.

"I've got the watch today," he reminded her.

"What time is it?"

"Carol, listen," he said gruffly, "I didn't mean for any of this to happen." All the while he was speaking, Steve's fingers were working the buttons of his shirt and having little success in getting it to fasten properly. "Call what happened last night what you will—the holiday spirit, a momentary slip in my better judgment...whatever. I'm sure you feel the same way." He paused and turned to study her.

She leaned forward, resting her chin on her raised knees. Her heart was in her throat, and she felt shaken and miserable. "Yes, of course."

His mouth thinned and he turned his back to her once more. "I thought as much. The best thing we can do is put the entire episode out of our minds."

"Right," she answered, forcing some enthusiasm into her voice. It was working out exactly as she'd planned it: they would both wake up in the morning, feel chagrined, make their apologies and go their separate ways once more.

Only it didn't feel the way she'd anticipated. It felt wrong. Very wrong.

Steve was in the living room before she moved

from the bed. Grabbing a thin robe from her closet, she slipped into it as she rushed after him.

He seemed to be waiting for her, pacing the entryway. He combed his fingers through his hair a couple of times before turning to look at her.

"So you want to forget last night?" he asked.

"I...if you do," she answered.

"I do."

Carol's world toppled for a moment, then quickly righted itself. She understood—it was better this way. "Thank you for the poinsettia and candy." It seemed inappropriate to mention the terrific lovemaking.

"Right." His answer was clipped, as though he was eager to be on his way. "Thanks for the dinner...and everything else."

"No problem." Stepping around him, Carol opened the door. "It was good to see you again, Steve."

"Yeah, you, too."

He walked out of the house and down the steps, and watching him go did crazy things to Carol's equilibrium. Suddenly she had to lean against the doorjamb just to remain upright. Something inside her, something strong and more powerful than her own will demanded that she stop him.

"Steve," she cried frantically. She stood on tiptoe. "Steve."

He turned around abruptly.

They stared at each other, each battle scarred and weary, each hurting. Each proud.

"Merry Christmas," she said softly.

"Merry Christmas."

Three days after Christmas, Carol was convinced her plan had worked perfectly. Thursday morning she woke feeling sluggish and sick to her stomach. A book she'd been reading on pregnancy and childbirth stated that the best way to relieve those early bouts of morning sickness was to nibble on soda crackers first thing—even before getting out of bed.

A burning sense of triumph led her into the bathroom, where she stared at herself in the mirror as though her reflection would proudly announce she was about to become a mother.

It had been so easy. Simple really. One tempestuous night of passion and the feat was accomplished. Her hand rested over her abdomen, and she patted it gently, feeling both proud and awed. A new life was being nurtured there.

A baby. Steve's child.

The wonder of it produced a ready flow of emotion and tears dampened her eyes.

Another symptom!

The book had explained that her emotions could

be affected by the pregnancy—that she might be more susceptible to tears.

Wiping the moisture from the corners of her eyes, Carol strolled into the kitchen and searched the cupboard for saltines. She found a stale package and forced herself to eat two, but she didn't feel any better than she had earlier.

Not bothering to dress, she turned on the television and made herself a bed on the sofa. Boeing workers were given the week between Christmas and New Year's off as part of their employment package. Carol had planned to spend the free time painting the third bedroom—the one she planned to use for the baby. Unfortunately she didn't have any energy. In fact, she felt downright sick, as though she were coming down with a case of the flu.

A lazy smile turned up the edges of her mouth. She wasn't about to complain. Nine months from now, she would be holding a precious bundle in her arms.

Steve's and her child.

Chapter 4

With his hands cupped behind his head, Steve lay in bed and stared blindly at the dark ceiling. He couldn't sleep. For the past hour he hadn't even bothered to close his eyes. It wouldn't do any good; every time he did, the memory of Christmas Eve with Carol filled his mind.

Releasing a slow breath, he rubbed his hand down his face, hoping the action would dispel her image from his thoughts. It didn't work. Nothing did.

He had never intended to make love to her, and even now, ten days later, he wasn't sure how the hell it had happened. He continued to suffer from a low-grade form of shock. His thoughts had been in utter chaos since that night, and he wasn't sure how to respond to her or where their relationship was headed now.

What really distressed him, Steve realized, was that after everything that had happened between them, he could still want her so much. More than a week later and the memory of her leaning against the doorjamb in the kitchen, wearing his shirt—and nothing else—had the power to tighten his loins. Tighten his loins! He nearly laughed out loud; that had to be the understatement of the year.

When Carol had stood and held out her arms to him, he'd acted like a starving child offered candy, so eager he hadn't stopped to think about anything except the love she would give him. Any protest he'd made had been token. She'd volunteered, he'd accepted, and that should be the end of it.

But it wasn't.

Okay, so he wasn't a man of steel. Carol had always been his Achilles' heel, and he knew it. She knew it. In thinking over the events of that night, it was almost as though his ex-wife had planned everything. Her red dress with no bra, and that bit about placing decorations on the tree. She'd insisted on standing on the chair, stretching and exposing her thigh to him…his thoughts came to a skidding halt.

No.

He wasn't going to fall into that familiar trap of

thinking Carol was using him, deceiving him. It did no good to wade into the muddy mire of anger, bitterness, regret and doubt.

He longed to repress the memory of Carol's warm and willing body in his arms. If only he could get on with his life. If only he could sleep.

He couldn't.

His sister, Lindy, had coffee brewed by the time Steve came out of his bedroom. She sat at the table, cradling a cup in one hand while holding a folded section of the *Post-Intelligencer* in the other.

"Morning." She glanced up and greeted him with a bright smile. Lately it seemed his sister was always smiling.

Steve mumbled something unintelligible as a means of reply. Her cheerfulness grated against him. He wasn't in the mood for good humor this morning. He wasn't in the mood for anything...with the possible exception of making love to Carol again, and that bit of insight didn't suit him in the least.

"It doesn't look like you had a good night's sleep, brother dearest."

Steve's frown deepened, and he gave his sister another noncommittal answer.

"I don't suppose this has anything to do with Carol?" She waited, and when he didn't answer, added, "Or the fact that you didn't come home Christmas Eve?"

"I came home."

"Sure, sometime the following morning."

Steve took down a mug from the cupboard and slapped it against the counter with unnecessary force. "Drop it, Lindy. I don't want to discuss Carol."

A weighted silence followed his comment.

"Rush and I've got almost everything ready to move into the new apartment," she offered finally, and the light tone of her voice suggested she was looking for a way to put their conversation back on an even keel. "We'll be out of here by Friday."

Hell, here he was snapping at Lindy. His sister didn't deserve to be the brunt of his foul mood. She hadn't done anything but mention the obvious. "Speaking of Rush, where is he?" Steve asked, forcing a lighter tone into his own voice.

"He had to catch an early ferry this morning," she said, and hesitated momentarily. "I'm happy, Steve, really happy. I was so afraid for a time that I'd made a dreadful mistake, but I know now that marrying Rush was the right thing to do."

Steve took a sip of coffee to avoid looking at his sister. What Lindy was actually saying was that she wanted him to find the same contentment she had. That wasn't possible for him now, and wouldn't be until he got Carol out of his blood.

And making love to her Christmas Eve hadn't helped.

"Well, I suppose I should think about getting dressed," Lindy said with a heavy dose of feigned enthusiasm. "I'm going to get some boxes so Rush and I can finish up the last of the packing."

"Where's your new apartment?" Steve had been so preoccupied with his own troubles that he hadn't thought to inquire until now.

As Lindy rattled off the address Steve's forehead furrowed into a brooding frown. His sister and Rush were moving less than a mile away from Carol's place. Great! That was the last thing he needed to hear.

Steve's day wasn't much better than his sleepless night had been. By noon he'd decided he could no longer avoid the inevitable. He didn't like it, but it was necessary.

He had to talk to Carol.

He was thankful the apartment was empty when he arrived home shortly after six. Not willing to test his good fortune, and half expecting Lindy or Rush to appear at any minute, he walked directly to the phone and punched out Carol's number as though punishing the telephone would help relieve some of his nervousness.

"Hello?" Carol's soft, lilting voice clawed at his abdomen.

"It's Steve."

A pregnant pause was followed by a slightly breathless "Hi."

"I was thinking we should talk."

"All right." She sounded surprised, pleased, uncertain. "When?"

Steve rotated his wrist and looked at the time. "What are you doing right now?"

She hesitated. "I ...nothing."

Although slightly awkward, their conversation to this point had felt right to Steve. But the way she paused, as though searching for a delaying tactic, troubled him. Fiery arrows of doubt hit their mark and he said, "Listen, Carol, if you're 'entertaining' Todd, I'd prefer to stop by later."

The ensuing silence was more deafening than jungle drums pounding out a war chant.

It took her several seconds to answer him, and when she did, the soft voice that had greeted him was racked with pain. "You can come now."

Steve tightened his hold on the phone receiver in a punishing grip. He hated it when he talked to her like that. He didn't know who he was punishing: Carol or himself. "I'll be there in fifteen minutes."

Carol replaced the telephone in its cradle and battled down an attack of pain and tears. How dare Steve suggest Todd was there. Suddenly she was so furious with him that she could no longer stand in one place. She started pacing the living room floor like a raw recruit, taking five or six steps and then doing an abrupt about-face. And yet she was excited—even elated.

Steve had taken the initiative to contact her, and it proved that he hadn't been able to stop thinking about her, either.

Nothing had been right for her since Christmas Eve. Oh, she'd reached her objective—exceeded it. Everything had gone according to plan. Only Carol hadn't counted on the doubts and bewilderment that had followed their night of loving. Their short hours together brought back the memory of how good their lives had once been, how much they'd loved each other and how happy those first years were.

Since Christmas Eve, Carol had been crippled with "if onlys" and "what ifs," tossing around those weak phrases as though she expected them to alter reality. Each day it became more difficult to remember that Steve had divorced her, that he believed her capable of the worst kind of deception. One night in his arms and she was fool enough to be willing to forget all the pain of the past thirteen months.

Almost willing, she amended.

It took vindictive, destructive comments like the one he'd just made to remind her that they had a rocky road to travel if they hoped to salvage their relationship.

Before Steve arrived, Carol had time to freshen her

makeup and run a brush through her thick blond hair. She paused to study her reflection in the mirror and wondered if he would ever guess her secret. She doubted it. If he couldn't read the truth in her eyes about Todd, then he wasn't likely to recognize her joy, or guess the cause.

Thinking about the baby helped lighten the weight of Steve's bitterness. Briefly she closed her eyes and imagined holding that precious bundle in her arms. A little girl, she decided, with dark brown eyes like Steve's and soft blond curls.

The mental picture of her child made everything seem worthwhile.

When the doorbell chimed, Carol was ready. She held the door open for Steve and even managed to greet him with a smile.

"I made coffee."

"Good." His answer was gruff, as though he were speaking to one of his enlisted men.

He followed her into the kitchen and stood silently as she poured them each a cup of coffee. When she turned around, she saw Steve standing with his hands in his pockets, looking unsettled and ill at ease.

"If you're searching for traces of Todd, let me tell you right now, you won't find any."

He had the good grace to look mildly chagrined. "I suppose I should apologize for that remark."

"I suppose I should accept." She pulled out a chair and sat.

Steve claimed the one directly across from her.

Neither spoke, and it seemed to Carol that an eternity passed. "You wanted to talk to me," she said, after what felt like two lifetimes.

"I'm not exactly sure what I want to say."

She smiled a little at that, understanding. "I'm not sure what I want to hear, either."

A hint of a grin bounced from his dark eyes. "Forgiving you for what happened with Todd…"

Carol bolted to her feet with such force that her chair nearly fell backward. "Forgiving me!" she demanded, shaking with outrage.

"Carol, please, I didn't come here to fight."

"Then don't start one. Don't come into my home and hurl insults at me. The one person in this room who should be seeking forgiveness is *you*!"

"Carol…"

"I should have known this wouldn't work, but like a lovesick fool I thought…I hoped you…" She paused, jerked her head around and rubbed the heels of her hands down her cheeks, erasing the telltale tears.

"Okay, I apologize. I won't mention Todd again."

She inhaled a wobbly breath and nodded, not trusting her voice, and sat back down.

Another awkward moment followed.

"I don't know what you've been thinking, or how you feel about...what happened," Steve said, "but for the past ten days, I've felt like a leaf caught in a windstorm. My emotions are in turmoil...I can't stop remembering how good it was between us, and how right it felt to have you in my arms again. My instincts tell me that night was a fluke, and best forgotten. I just wish to hell I could."

Carol bowed her head, avoiding eye contact. "I've been thinking the same thing. As you said when you left, we should chalk it up to the love and goodwill that's synonymous with the season. But the holidays are over and I can't stop thinking about it, either."

"The loving always was terrific, wasn't it?"

He didn't sound as though he wanted to admit even that much, as if he preferred to discount anything positive about their lives together. Carol understood the impulse. She'd done the same thing since their divorce; it helped ease the pain of the separation.

Grudgingly she nodded. "Unfortunately the lovemaking is only a small part of any marriage. I think Christmas Eve gave me hope that you and I might be able to work everything out. I'd like to resolve the past and find a way to heal the wounds." They'd been apart for over a year, but Carol's heart felt as bloodied and bruised as if their divorce had been decreed yesterday.

"God knows, I want to forget the past..."

Hope clamored in her breast and she raised her eyes to meet Steve's, but his gaze was as weary and doubtful as her own.

His eyes fell. "But I don't think I can. I don't know if I'll ever be able to get over finding Todd in our bedroom."

"He was in the shower," Carol corrected through clenched teeth. "And the only reason he was there was because the shower head in the other bathroom wasn't working properly."

"What the hell difference does it make?" Steve shouted. "He spent the night here. You've never bothered to deny that."

"But nothing happened...if you'd stayed long enough to ask Todd, he would have explained."

"If I'd stayed any longer, I would have killed him."

He said it with such conviction that Carol didn't doubt him. Long before, she'd promised herself she wouldn't defend her actions again. Todd had been her employer and her friend. She'd known Todd and his wife, Joyce, were having marital troubles. But she cared about them both and didn't want to get caught in the middle of their problems. Todd, however, had cast her there when he showed up on her doorstep, drunk out of his mind, wanting to talk. Alarmed, Carol had brought him inside and phoned Joyce, who suggested Todd sleep it off at Carol's house. It had seemed like a reasonable solution, although she wasn't keen on the idea. Steve was away and due back to Seattle in a couple of days.

But Steve had arrived home early—and assumed the worst.

The sadness that settled over her was profound, and when she spoke, her voice was little more than a whisper. "You tried and found me guilty on circumstantial evidence, Steve. For the first couple of weeks, I tried to put myself in your place...I could understand how you read the scene that morning, but you were wrong."

It looked for a moment as though he was going to argue with her. She could almost see the wheels spinning in his mind, stirring up the doubts, building skyscrapers on sand foundations.

"Other things started to add up," he admitted reluctantly, still not looking at her.

Carol could all but see him close his mind to common sense. It seemed that just when they were beginning to make headway, Steve would pull something else into their argument or make some completely ridiculous comment that made absolutely no sense to her. The last time they'd tried to discuss this in a reasonable, nonconfrontational manner, Steve had hinted that she'd been Todd's lover for months. He'd suggested that she hadn't been as eager to welcome· him home from his last cruise, which was ridiculous. They may have had problems, but none had extended to the bedroom.

"What 'other things' do you mean now?'' she asked, defeat coating her words.

He ignored her question. His mouth formed a cocky smile, devoid of amusement. "I will say one thing for ol' Todd—he taught you well."

She gasped at the unexpected pain his words inflicted.

Steve paled and looked away. "I shouldn't have said that—I didn't mean it."

"Todd did teach me," she countered, doing her best to keep her bottom lip from quivering. "He taught me that a marriage not based on mutual trust isn't worth the ink that prints the certificate. He taught me that it takes more than a few words murmured by a man of God to make a relationship work."

"That's not what I meant."

"I know what you meant. Your jealousy has you tied up in such tight knots that you're incapable of reasoning any of this out."

Steve ignored that comment. "I'm not jealous of Todd—he can have you if he wants."

Carol thought she was going to be sick to her stomach. Indignation filled her throat, choking off any possible reply.

Steve stood and walked across the kitchen, his hands knotted into fists at his sides. He closed his eyes briefly, and when he opened them, he looked like a stranger, his inner torment was so keen.

"I didn't mean that," he said unevenly. "I don't know why I say such ugly things to you."

Carol heard the throb of pain in her voice. "I don't know why you do, either. If you're trying to hurt me, then congratulations. You've succeeded beyond your expectations."

Steve stood silently a few moments, then delivered his untouched coffee to the sink. His hesitation surprised Carol. She'd assumed he would walk out—that was the way their arguments usually ended.

Instead he turned to face her and asked, "Are Todd and Joyce still married?"

She'd gotten a Christmas card from them a couple of weeks earlier. Until she'd seen both their names at the bottom of the greeting, she hadn't been sure if their marriage had weathered better than hers and Steve's. "They're still together."

Steve frowned and nodded. "I know that makes everything more difficult for you."

"Stop it, Steve!" This new list of questions irritated her almost as much as his tireless insinuations. "All the years we were married, not once did I accuse you of being unfaithful, even though you were gone half the time."

"It's difficult to find a woman willing to fool around 400 feet under water."

"That's not my point. I trusted you. I always did, and I assumed that you trusted me, too. That's all I've ever asked of you, all I ever wanted."

He was quiet for so long that Carol wondered if he'd chosen to ignore her rather than come up with an appropriate answer.

"You didn't discover another woman lounging around in a see-through nightie while I showered, either. You may be able to explain away some of what happened, but as far as I'm concerned there are gaping holes in your story."

Carol clenched her teeth so tightly that her jaw ached. She'd already broken a promise to herself by discussing Todd with Steve. When the divorce was final, Carol had determined then that no amount of justifying would ever satisfy her ex-husband. Discussing Todd had yet to settle a single problem, and in the end she only hurt herself.

"I don't think we're going to solve anything by rehashing this now," she told him calmly. "Unless our love is firmly grounded in a foundation of trust, there's no use even trying to work things out."

"It doesn't seem to be helping, does it? I wanted us—"

"I know," she interrupted softly, sadly. "I wanted

it, too. The other night only served to remind us how much we'd loved each other.''

They shared a discouraged smile, and Carol felt as though her heart was breaking in half.

He took a few steps toward the front door. ''I'll be leaving in less than three weeks.''

''How long will you be away?'' For a long time she hadn't felt comfortable asking him this kind of question, but he seemed more open to discussion now.

''Three months.'' He buried his hands in his pockets and Carol got the impression that the action was to keep him from reaching for her and kissing her goodbye. He paused, turned toward her and said, ''If you need anything...''

''I won't.''

Her answer didn't appear to please him. ''No, I don't suppose you will. You always could take care of yourself. I used to be proud of you for being so capable, but it intimidated me, too.''

''What do you mean?''

He hedged, as if searching his reserve of memories to find the perfect example, then shook his head. ''Never mind, it isn't important now.''

Carol walked him to the front door, her heart heavy. ''I wish it could be different for us.''

''I do, too.''

Steve stood, unmoving, in the entryway. Inches

from him, Carol felt an inner yearning more potent than anything she'd ever experienced engulf her, filling her heart with regret. Once more she would have to watch the man she loved walk away from her. Once more she must freely allow him to go.

Steve must have sensed the intense longing, because he gently rested his hands on the curve of her shoulders. She smiled and tilted her chin toward him, silently offering him her mouth.

Slowly, without hurry, Steve lowered his face to hers, drawing out each second as though he were relaxing a hold on his considerable pride, admitting his need to kiss her. It was as if he had to prove, if only to himself, that he had control of the situation.

Then his mouth grazed hers. Lightly. Briefly. Coming back for more when it became apparent the teasing kisses weren't going to satisfy either of them.

What shocked Carol most was the gentleness of his kiss. He touched and held her as he would a delicate piece of porcelain, slipping his arms around her waist, drawing her close against him.

He broke off the kiss and Carol tucked her forehead against his chest. "Have a safe trip." Silently she prayed for his protection and that he would come back to her.

"If you want, I'll phone when I return. That is…if you think I should?"

Maybe she could tell him about the baby then,

depending on how things went between them. "Yes, by all means, phone and let me know that you made it back in one piece."

His gaze centered on her mouth and again he bent his head toward her. This time his kiss was hungry, lingering, insistent. Carol whimpered when his tongue, like a soft flame, entered her mouth, sending hot sparks of desire shooting up her spine. Her knees weakened and she nearly collapsed when Steve abruptly released her.

"For once, maybe you could miss me," he said, with a sad note of bitterness.

The following morning, Carol woke feeling queasy. It'd been that way almost since Christmas morning. She reached for the two soda crackers on the nightstand and nibbled on them before climbing out of bed. Her hand rested lovingly on her flat stomach.

She'd wanted to schedule an appointment with the doctor, but the receptionist had told her to wait until her monthly cycle was a week late. She was only overdue by a day, but naturally she wouldn't be having her period. As far as Carol was concerned, another week was too long to wait, even if she was certain she bore the desired fruit from her night with Steve.

In an effort to confirm what she already knew, Carol had purchased a home-pregnancy test. Now she climbed out of bed, read the instructions through twice, did what the package told her and waited.

The waiting was the worst part. Thirty minutes had never seemed to take so long.

Humming a catchy tune, she dressed for work, poured herself a glass of milk, then went back to the bathroom to read the test results.

She felt so cocky, so sure of what the test would tell her that her heart was already pounding with excitement.

The negative reading claimed her breath. She blinked, certain she'd misread it.

Stunned, she sat on the edge of the bathtub and took several deep breaths. She started to tremble, and tears of disappointment filled her eyes. She must be pregnant—she had to be. All the symptoms were there—everything she'd read had supported her belief.

Once more she examined the test results.

Negative.

After everything she'd gone through, after all the sweet potatoes she'd forced down her throat, after the weeks of planning, the plotting, the scheduling...

There wasn't going to be any baby. There never had been. Her plan had failed.

There was only one thing left to do.

Try again.

Chapter 5

It took courage for Carol to drive to Steve's apartment. Someone should award medals for this brand of lionheartedness, she murmured to herself—although she was more interested in playing the role of a tigress than a lion. If this second venture was anything like the first, Steve wouldn't know what hit him. At least, she hoped he wouldn't guess.

She straightened her shoulders, pinched some color into her cheeks and pasted on a smile. Then she rang the doorbell.

To say Steve looked surprised to see her when he opened the door would be an understatement, Carol acknowledged. His eyes rounded, his mouth relaxed and fell open, and for a moment he was utterly speechless. "Carol?"

"I suppose I should have phoned first..."

"No, come in." He stepped aside so that she could enter the apartment.

Beyond his obvious astonishment, Carol found it difficult to read Steve's reaction. She stepped inside gingerly, praying that her plastic smile wouldn't crack. The first thing she noticed was the large picture window in the living room, offering an unobstructed view of the Seattle waterfront. It made Elliott Bay seem close, so vivid that she could almost smell the seaweed and feel the salty spray in the air. A large green-and-white ferry boat plowed its way through the dark waters, enhancing the picture.

"Oh...this is nice." Carol turned around to face him. "Have you lived here long?"

He nodded. "Rush had the apartment first. I moved in after you and I split and sort of inherited it when Rush and Lindy moved into their own place recently."

The last thing Carol wanted to remind him of was their divorce, and she quickly steered the conversation to the reason for her visit. "I found something I thought might be yours," she said hurriedly, fumbling with the snap of her eel-skin purse to bring out the button. It was a weak excuse, but she was desperate. Retrieving the small gray button from inside her coin purse, she handed it over to him.

Steve's brow pleated into a frown and he stiffened. "No...this isn't mine. It must belong to another man," he said coldly.

A bad move, Carol realized, taking back the button. "There's only been one man at my house, and that's you," she said, trying to stay calm. "If it isn't yours, then it must have fallen off something of my own."

Hands in his pockets, Steve nodded.

An uneasy pause followed.

Steve didn't suggest she take off her coat, didn't offer her any refreshment or any excuse to linger. Feeling crestfallen and defeated, Carol knew there was nothing more to do but leave.

"Well, I suppose I should think about getting myself some dinner. There's a new Mexican restaurant close to here I thought I might try," she said with feigned enthusiasm, and glanced up at him through thick lashes. Steve loved enchiladas, and she prayed he would take the bait. God knew, she couldn't have been any more obvious had she issued the invitation straight out.

"I ate earlier," he announced starkly.

Steve rarely had dinner before six. He was either wise to her ways or lying.

"I see." She took a step toward the exit, wonder-

ing what else she could do to delay the inevitable.
"When does the *Atlantis* leave?"

"Monday."

Three days. She had only three days to carry out
her plan. Three days to get him into bed and convince him it was all his idea. Three miserable days.
Her fingers curled into impotent fists of frustration
inside her coat pocket.

"Have a safe trip, Steve," she said softly.
"I'll...I'll be thinking of you."

It had been a mistake to come to his place, a mistake not to have plotted the evening more carefully.
It was apparent from the stiff way Steve treated her,
he couldn't wait to get her out of his apartment.
Since it was Friday night, he might have a date. The
thought of Steve with another woman produced a
gut-wrenching pain that she did her best to ignore.
Dropping by unexpectedly like this wasn't helping
her cause.

She'd hoped they could make love tonight. Her
temperature was elevated and she was as fertile as
she was going to get this month.

Swallowing her considerable pride, she paused,
her hand on the door handle. "There's a new spy
thriller showing at the Fifth Avenue Theater.... You
always used to like espionage films."

Steve's eyes narrowed as he studied her. It was
difficult for Carol to meet his heated gaze and not

wilt from sheer nerves. She was sure her cheeks were hot pink. Coming to his apartment was the most difficult thing she'd done in years. Her heart felt as if it was going to hammer its way right out of her chest, and her fingers were shaking so badly that she didn't dare remove them from her pockets.

"Why are you here?" His question was soft, suspicious, uncertain.

"I found the button." One glance told her he didn't believe her, as well he shouldn't. That excuse was so weak it wouldn't carry feathers.

"What is it you *really* want, Carol?"

"I...I..." Her voice trembled from her lips, and her heart, which had been pounding so furiously a second before, seemed to stop completely. She swallowed and forced her gaze to meet his before dropping it. When she finally managed to speak, her voice was low and meaningful. "I thought with you going away...." Good grief, woman, her mind shouted, quit playing games. Give him the truth.

She raised her chin, and her gaze locked with his. "I'm not wearing any underwear."

Steve went stock-still, holding his jaw tight and hard. The inner conflict that played over his face was as vivid as the picturesque scene she'd viewed from his living-room window. The few feet of distance between them seemed to stretch wider than a mile.

It felt as if an eternity passed as Carol waited for

his reaction, and she felt paralyzed with misgivings. She'd exposed her hand and left her pride completely vulnerable to him.

She saw it then—a flicker of his eyes, a movement in the line of his jaw, a softening in his tightly controlled facial features. He wanted her, too—wanted her with a desperation that made him as weak as she was. Her heart leaped wildly with joy.

Steve lifted his hand and held it out to her, and Carol thought she would collapse with relief as she hurried toward him. He crushed her in his arms and his mouth hungrily came down on hers. His eager lips smothered her cry of happiness. Equally greedy, Carol returned his kiss, reveling in his embrace. She twined her arms around his neck, her softness melding against the hardened contours of his body.

His hands tightened around her possessively, stroking her spine, then lowered over the rounded firmness of her buttocks. He gathered her pelvis as close to him as was humanly possible.

"Dear God, I've gone crazy."

Carol raised her hands to frame his face and gazed lovingly into his eyes. "Me, too," she whispered before spreading a circle of light kisses over his forehead, chin and mouth.

"I shouldn't be doing this."

"Yes, you should."

Steve groaned and clasped her tighter. He kissed

her, plunging his tongue into the sweet softness of her mouth, exploring it with a desperate urgency. Carol met his tongue with her own in a silent duel that left them both exhausted.

While they were still kissing, Steve unfastened the buttons of her coat, slipped it from her shoulders and dropped it to the floor. His hands clawed at the back of her skirt, lifting it away from her legs, then settled once again, cupping her bare bottom.

He moaned, his breath seemed to jam in his throat, and his eyes darkened with passion. "You weren't kidding."

Carol bit her lower lip as a wealth of sensation fired through her from the touch of his cool hands against her heated flesh. She rotated her lower body shamelessly against the rigid evidence of his desire.

His hands closed over her breasts and her nipples rose as though to greet him, to welcome him. His eager but uncooperative fingers fiddled with the fastenings of her blouse. Smiling, content but just as eager, Carol gently brushed his hands aside and completed the task for him. He pulled the silk material free of her waistline and disposed of it as effectively as he had her coat. Her breasts sprang to life in his hands and when he moaned, the sound of it excited her so much that it throbbed in her ears.

The moist heat of his mouth closed over her nipple and she gasped. The exquisite pleasure nearly caused her knees to buckle. Blood roared through her veins, and liquid fire scorched her until she was certain she would soon explode. She lifted one leg and wrapped it around his thigh, anchoring her weight against him.

Steve's fingers reached for her and instinctively she opened herself to him. He teased her womanhood, toyed with her, tormented her with delicate strokes that drove her over the brink. Within seconds, she tossed back her head and groaned as the pulsating climax rocked through her, sending out rippling waves of release.

By the time Steve carried her into his bedroom, Carol was panting. He didn't waste any time, discarding his clothes with an urgency that thrilled her. When he moved to the bed, his features were keen with desire.

Carol lifted her arms to welcome him, loving him with a tenderness that came from the very marrow of her bones.

Steve shifted his weight over her and captured her mouth in a consuming kiss that sent Carol down into a whirlpool of the sweetest oblivion. Anxious and eager, she parted her thighs for him and couldn't hold back a small cry as he sheathed himself inside her, slipping the proud heat of his manhood into her moist softness.

He waited, as though to prolong the pleasure and soak in her love before he started to move. The feelings that wrapped themselves around her were so incredible that Carol had to struggle to hold back the tears. With each delicious stroke the tension mounted and slowly, methodically began to uncurl within her until she was thrashing her head against his pillow and arching her hips to meet each plunging thrust.

Steve groaned and threw back his head, struggling to regain control, but soon he, too, was over the edge. When he cried out his voice harmonized with hers in a song that was as ageless as mankind.

Breathless, he collapsed on top of her. Her arms slipped around his neck and she buried her face in the hollow of his throat, kissing him, hugging him, needing him desperately. Tears slipped silently from the corners of her eyes. They spoke the words that she couldn't, eloquently telling him of all the love buried in her heart—words Carol feared she would never be able to voice again.

When Steve moved to lift himself off of her, she wouldn't let him. She held him tightly, her fingers gripping his shoulders.

"I'm too heavy," he protested.

"No...hold me."

With his arms wrapped around her, he rolled over, carrying her with him in one continuous motion until their positions were reversed.

Content for the moment, Carol pressed her ear

over his chest, listening to the strong, steady beat of his heart.

Neither spoke.

His hand moved up and down her spine in a tender caress as though he had to keep touching her to know she was real. Her tears slid onto his shoulder, but neither mentioned it.

In her soul, Carol had to believe that something this beautiful would create a child. At this moment everything seemed perfect and healed between them, the way it had been two years before.

Gently Steve kissed her forehead, and she snuggled closer, flattening her hands over his chest.

He wrapped his arms around her and his thumb tenderly wiped the moisture from her cheek. Tucking his finger under her chin, he lifted it enough to find her mouth and kiss her. Sweetly.

"I tried, but I never could stop loving you," he whispered in a voice raw with emotion. "I hated myself for being so weak, but I don't anymore."

"I'll always love you," she answered. "I can't help myself. This year has been the worst of my entire life. I've felt as if I was trapped in a freezer, never able to get warm."

"No more," he said, his eyes trapping hers.

"No more," she agreed, and her heart leaped with unleashed joy.

They rested for a full hour, their legs entwined,

their arms wrapped around each other. Every now and again, Steve would kiss her, his lips playing over hers. Then Carol would kiss him back, darting her tongue in and out of his mouth and doing all the things she knew he enjoyed. She raised herself up on her elbows and brushed a thick swatch of dark hair from his brow. It felt so good to be able to touch him this freely.

"What's the name of that Mexican restaurant you mentioned earlier?" Steve asked.

Carol smiled smugly. "You are so predictable."

"How's that?"

"Making love never fails to make you hungry!"

"True," he growled into her ear, "but often my appetite isn't for food." His index finger circled her nipple, teasing it to a rose-colored pebble. "I've got a year's worth of loving stored up for you, and the way you make me feel tonight, we may never leave this bedroom."

And they didn't.

Carol woke when Steve pressed a soft kiss on her lips.

"Hmm," she said, not opening her eyes. She smiled up at him, sated and unbelievably happy. She wore the look of a woman who loves wisely and who knows that her love is returned. "Is it morning yet?"

"It was morning the last time we made love."

Steve laughed and leaned over to kiss her again, as if one sample wasn't nearly enough to satisfy him.

"It was?" she asked lazily. They'd slept intermittently, waking every few hours, holding and kissing each other. While asleep, Carol would roll over and forget Steve was at her side. Their discovery each time was worth far more than a few semiprecious hours of sleep. And Steve seemed equally excited about her being there with him.

"Currently," he said, dragging her back to reality, "it's going on noon."

"Noon!" She bolted upright. She'd been in her teens the last time she'd slept this late.

"I'm sorry to wake you, honey, but I've got to get to the sub."

Carol was surprised to see that he was dressed and prepared to leave. He handed her a fresh cup of coffee, which she readily took from him. "You'll be back, won't you?"

"Not until tomorrow morning."

"Will you...could you stop off and see me one more time, before you leave?"

His dark gaze caressed her. "Honest to God, Carol, I don't think I could stay away."

As Steve walked away from his parked car at the Navy base in Bangor, less than ten miles north of

Bremerton, he was convinced his strut would put a rooster to shame. Lord, he felt good.

Carol had come to him, wanted him, loved him as much as he'd always loved and wanted her. All the world felt good to him.

For the first time since they'd divorced, he felt whole. He'd been a crazed fool to harp on the subject of Todd Larson to Carol. From this moment on, he vowed never to mention the other man's name again. Obviously whatever had been between the two was over, and she hadn't wanted Todd back. Okay, so she'd made a mistake. Lord knew, he'd committed his share, and a lot of them had to do with Carol. He'd been wrong to think he could flippantly cast her out of his life.

In his pain, he'd lashed out at her, acted like a heel, refused to have anything to do with her because of his foolish pride. But Carol had been woman enough to forgive him. He couldn't do anything less than be man enough to forget the past. The love they shared was too precious to muddy with doubts. They'd both made mistakes, and the time had come to rectify those and learn from them.

Dear God, he felt ready to soar. He shouldn't be on a nuclear submarine—a feeling this good was meant for rockets.

Carol found herself humming as she whipped the cream into a frothy topping for Steve's favorite dessert: French pudding. She licked her index finger, grinned lazily to herself and leaned her hip against the kitchen counter, feeling happier than she could remember being in a long time.

Friday night had been incredible. Steve had been incredible. The only cost had been her bruised pride when she'd arrived at his apartment with such a flimsy excuse. The price had been minor, the rewards major.

Not once during the entire evening had Steve mentioned Todd's name. Maybe, just maybe, he was ready to put that all behind them now.

If she was pregnant from their Friday night lovemaking, which she sincerely prayed she was, it would be best for the baby to know "her" father. Originally Carol had intended to raise the child without Steve. She wasn't sure she would ever have told him. Now the thought of suppressing the information seemed both childish and petty. But she wasn't going to use the baby as a convenient excuse for a reconciliation. They would settle matters first—then she would tell him.

Steve would make a good father; she'd watched him around children and had often been amazed by his patience. He'd wanted a family almost from the first. Carol had been the one who'd insisted on waiting, afraid she wouldn't be able to manage her job, a home and a baby with her husband away so much of the time, although she'd never admitted it to Steve. She knew how important it was for him to believe in her strength and independence. But this past year had matured her. Now she was ready for the responsibility.

Naturally hindsight was twenty-twenty, and she regretted having put off Steve's desire to start a family. The roots of their marriage might have been strong enough to withstand what had happened if there'd been children binding them together. But it did no good to second-guess fate.

Children. Carol hadn't dared think beyond one baby. But if she and Steve were to get back together—something that was beginning to look like a distinct possibility—then they could plan on having a houseful of kids!

It was early afternoon by the time Steve made it to Carol's house. A cold wind from the north whistled through the tops of the trees and the sky was darkening with a brewing storm.

Carol tossed aside her knitting and flew across the room the minute she heard a car door close, knowing it had to be Steve. By the time he was to the porch, she had the front door open for him.

He wore his uniform, which told her he hadn't stopped off at his apartment to change. Obviously he was eager to see her again, Carol thought, immeasurably pleased.

"I'm glad to see you're waiting for me," he said, and his words formed a soft fog around his mouth. He took the steps two at a time and rubbed his bare hands together.

"I can't believe how cold it is." Carol pulled him inside the house and closed the door.

His gaze sought hers. "Warm me, then."

She didn't require a second invitation, and stood on the tips of her toes to kiss him, leaning her weight into his. Steve wrapped her in his embrace, kissing her back greedily, as if they had been apart six weeks instead of a single day. When he finished, they were both breathless.

"It feels like you missed me."

"I did," she assured him. "Give me your coat and I'll hang it up for you."

He gave her the thick wool jacket and strolled into the living room. "What's this?" he asked, looking at her knitting.

Carol's heart leaped to her throat. "A baby blanket."

"For who?"

"A...friend." She considered herself a friend, so that was at least a half-truth. She'd been working on the blanket in her spare time since before Christmas. It had helped her feel as if she was doing something constructive toward her goal.

Suddenly she felt as if she had a million things to tell him. "I got energetic and cleaned house. I don't know what's wrong with me lately, but I don't have the energy I used to have."

"Have you been sick?"

She loved him for the concern in his voice. "No, I'm in perfect health...I've just been tired lately...not getting enough vitamins, I suppose. But it doesn't matter now because I feel fantastic, full of ambition—I even made you French pudding."

"Carol, I think you should see a doctor."

"And if he advises bed rest, do you promise to, er...rest with me?"

"Good heavens, woman, you've become insatiable."

"I know." She laughed and slipped her arm around his waist. "I was always that way around you."

"Always?" he teased. "I don't seem to recall that."

"Then I'll just have to remind you." She steered him toward the bedroom, crawled onto the mattress and knelt there. "If you want French pudding, fellow, you're going to have to work for it."

* * *

The alarm went off at six. Carol blindly reached out and, after a couple of wide swipes, managed to hit the switch that would turn off the electronic beeping.

Steve stirred at her side. "It's time," she said in a small, sad voice. This would be their last morning together for three months.

"It's six already?" Steve moaned.

"I'm afraid so."

He reached for her and brought her close to his side. His hand found hers and he laced her fingers with his. "Carol, listen, we only have a little time left and there's so much I should have said, so much I wanted to tell you."

"I wanted to talk to you, too." In all the years they were married, no parting had been less welcome. Carol yearned to wrap her arms around him and beg him not to leave her. It was times like this that she wished Steve had chosen a career outside the Navy. In a few hours he would sail out of Hood Canal, and she wouldn't hear from him for the entire length of his deployment. Other than hearsay, Carol wasn't even to know where he would be sailing. For reasons of national security, all submarine deployments were regarded as top secret.

"When I return from this tour, Carol, I'd like us to have a serious talk about getting back together. I know I've been a jerk, and you deserve someone better, but I'd like you to think about it while I'm away. Will you do that for me?''

She couldn't believe how close she was to breaking into tears. "Yes," she whispered. "I'll think about it very seriously. I want everything to be right...the second time."

"I do, too." He raised her hand to his mouth and kissed her knuckles. "Another thing...make an appointment for a physical. I don't remember you being this thin."

"I lost fifteen pounds when we were divorced; I can't seem to gain it back." The tears broke through the surface and she sobbed out the words, ending in a hiccup. Embarrassed, she pressed her fingertips over her lips. "I've been a wreck without you, Steve Kyle...I suppose it makes you happy to know how miserable and lonely this past year has been."

"I was just as miserable and lonely," he admitted. "We can't allow anything to do this to us again. I love you too damn much to spend another year like the last one." His touch was so tender, so loving that she melted into his embrace.

"You have to trust me, Steve. I can't have you coming back and even suspecting I'd see another man."

"I know...I do trust you."

She closed her eyes at the relief his words gave her. "Thank you for that."

He kissed her then and, with a reluctance that tore at her heart, pulled away from her and started to dress.

She reached for her robe, not looking at him as she slipped her arms into the long sleeves. "If we do decide to make another go at marriage, I'd like to seriously think about starting a family right away. What would you say to that?"

Steve hesitated. Carol turned around to search out his gaze in the stirring light of early morning, and the tender look he wore melted any lingering doubts she harbored.

"Just picturing you with my child in your arms," he whispered hoarsely, "is enough to keep me going for the next three months."

Chapter 6

A week after Steve sailed, Carol began experiencing symptoms that again suggested she was pregnant. The early morning bouts of nausea returned. She found herself weeping over a rerun of *Magnum, P.I.* And she was continually tired, feeling worn-out at the end of the day. Everything she was going through seemed to point in one direction.

Self-diagnosis, however, had misled her a month earlier, and Carol feared her burning desire to bear a child was dictating her body's response a second time.

Each morning she pressed a hand over her stomach and whispered a fervent prayer that her weekend of lovemaking with Steve had found fertile ground. If she wasn't pregnant, then it would be April before they could try again, and that seemed like a thousand years away.

Carol was tempted to hurry out and buy another home pregnancy test. Then she would know almost immediately if her mind was playing tricks on her or if she really was pregnant. But she didn't. She couldn't explain—even to herself—why she was content to wait it out this time. If her monthly cycle was a week late, she decided, then and only then would she make an appointment with her doctor. But until that time she was determined to be strong—no matter what the test results said.

The one thing that astonished Carol the most was that in the time since Steve's deployment she missed him dreadfully. For months she'd done her utmost to drive every memory of that man from her mind, and sometimes she'd succeeded. Since Christmas, however, thoughts of Steve had dominated every waking minute. Until their weekend, Carol had assumed that was only natural. Steve Kyle did play a major role in her scheme to get pregnant. But she considered having a baby more of a bonus now. The possibility of rebuilding her marriage—which she had once considered impossible to do—claimed precedence.

Missing Steve wasn't a new experience. Carol had always felt at loose ends when he was aboard the

Atlantis. But never had she felt quite like this. Nothing compared to the emotion that wrapped itself around her heart when she thought about Steve on this tour. She missed him so much that it frightened her. For more than a year she'd lived in the house alone; now it felt like an empty shell because he wasn't there. In bed at night her longing for him grew even more intense. She lay with her eyes closed, savoring the memory of their last two nights together. A chill washed over her at how close they'd come to destroying the love between them. The only thing that seemed to lessen this terrible longing she felt for her ex-husband was constructing dreams that involved him to help ease the loneliness as she drifted off to sleep.

Friday morning Carol woke feeling rotten and couldn't seem to force herself out of bed. She pulled into the huge Boeing parking lot at the Renton plant ten minutes later than usual and hurriedly locked her car. She was walking toward her building, trying to find the energy to rush when she heard someone call out her name.

She turned, but didn't see anyone she recognized.

"Carol, is that you?"

"Lindy?" Carol could hardly believe her eyes. It was Steve's sister. "What are you doing here?"

"I was just about to ask you the same thing."

Lindy looked fantastic. It had been nearly two

years since Carol had last seen her former sister-in-law. Lindy had been a senior in college at the time, girlish and fun loving that summer she and Steve had visited his family. Had that been only two summers ago? It felt as though a decade had passed. Lindy had always held a special place in Carol's heart, and she smiled and hugged her close. When she drew back, Carol was surprised at the new maturity Lindy's eyes revealed.

"I work here," Lindy said, squeezing Carol's fingers. "I have since this past summer."

"Me, too—for over a year now."

Lindy tossed the sky a chagrined look. "You mean to tell me we've been employed by the same company, working at the same plant, and we didn't even know it?"

Carol laughed. "It looks that way."

They started walking toward the main entrance, still bemused, laughing and joking like long-lost sisters...which they were of sorts.

"I'm going to kick Steve," Lindy muttered. "He didn't tell me you worked for Boeing."

"He doesn't know. I suppose he assumes I'm still at Larson's Sporting Goods. I quit...long before the divorce was final. We haven't talked about my job, and I didn't think to mention it."

"How are you?" Lindy asked, but didn't give her more than a second to respond. "Steve growls at me every time I mention your name, which by the way, tells me he's still crazy about you."

Carol needed to hear that. She grinned, savoring the warm feeling Lindy's words gave her. "I'm still crazy about him, too."

"Oh, Carol," Lindy said with a giant sigh. "I can't tell you how glad I am to hear that. Steve never told any of us why the two of you divorced, but it nearly destroyed him. I can't tell you how happy I was when you phoned last Christmas. He hasn't been the same since."

"The divorce was wrong.... We should never have gone through with it," Carol said softly. Steve had been the one who had insisted on ending their marriage, and Carol had been too hurt, too confused to fight him the way she should have. Not wanting to linger on the mistakes of the past, Carol added, "Steve told me about you and Rush. Congratulations."

"Thanks." Lindy's eyes softened at the mention of Rush's name, and translucent joy radiated from her smile. "You met Paul didn't you?"

Carol nodded, recalling the time she had been introduced to Lindy's ex-fiance in Minneapolis. She hadn't been overly impressed by him and, as she recalled, neither had Steve.

"He married...someone else," Lindy explained. "I was devastated, convinced my life was over.

That's how I ended up in Seattle. I'm so happy I moved here. Paul did me the biggest favor of my life when he dumped me; I found Rush and we were meant to be together—we both know it.''

Hold on to that feeling, Carol mused, saddened that she'd been foolish enough to allow Steve to walk away from her. It had been a mistake, and one they'd both paid for dearly. ''I'm really pleased for you, Lindy,'' she said sincerely.

''Thank you…oh, Carol, I can't tell you how good it is to see you again.''

They paused once they passed the security gate, delaying their parting. ''What area are you working in?'' Carol asked, stopping. The others flooding through the entrance gate walked a wide circle around them.

''Section B.''

''F for me.'' Which meant they were headed in opposite directions.

''Perhaps we could meet for lunch one day,'' Lindy suggested, anxiously glancing at her watch.

''I'd like that. How about next Tuesday? I can't until then, I'm involved with a special project.''

''Great. Call me. I'm on extension 314.''

''Will do.''

Steve walked past the captain's quarters and through the narrow hallway to his stateroom. Tired, he sat on the edge of his berth and rubbed his hand across his eyes. This was his favorite time of day. His shift was complete, and he had about an hour to kill before he thought about catching some sleep. For the past several days, he'd been writing Carol. His letter had become a journal of his thoughts. Chances were that he would be home long before the letter arrived. Because submarines spent their deployment submerged, there were few opportunities for the pickup or delivery of mail. Any emergencies were handled by radio transmission. There were occasions when they could receive mail, but it wasn't likely to happen this trip.

Steve felt good. From the moment his and Carol's divorce had been declared final, he'd felt as if he'd steered his life off course. He'd experienced the first turbulent storm and, instead of riding it out as he should have, he'd jumped overboard. Ever since, he'd felt out of sync with his inner self.

In his letter, he'd tried to explain that to Carol, but putting it in words had been as difficult as admitting it had been.

He didn't know what had happened between Todd and Carol. Frankly he didn't want to know. Whatever had been between them was over and Steve could have her back. Lord knew he wanted her. He was destined to go to his grave loving that woman.

When he'd sailed out of Hood Canal and into the

Pacific Ocean, Steve had felt such an indescribable pull to the land. He loved his job, loved being a part of the Navy, but at that moment he would have surrendered his commission to have been able to stay in Seattle another month.

Although he'd told Carol that they should use this time apart to consider a reconciliation, he didn't need two seconds to know his own mind: he wanted them to remarry.

But first they had to talk, really talk, and not about Todd. There were some deep-rooted insecurities he'd faced the past couple of weeks that needed to be discussed.

One thing that had always bothered Steve was the fact that Carol had never seemed to need him. His peers continually related stories about how things fell apart at home while they were deployed. Upon their return, after the usual hugs and kisses, their wives handed them long lists of repairs needed around the house or relayed tales of horror they'd been left to deal with in their husband's absence.

Not Carol. She'd sent him off to sea, wearing a bright smile and greeted him with an identical one on his return. The impression she gave him was that it was great when he was home, but was equally pleasant if he wasn't.

Her easy acceptance of his life-style both pleased and irritated Steve. He appreciated the strength of her personality, and yet a small part of him wished she weren't quite so strong. He wasn't looking for a wife who was a clinging vine, but occasionally he wished for something less than Carol's sturdy oak-tree character. Just once he would have liked to hear her tell him how dreadful the weeks had been without him, or how she'd wished he'd been there to take care of the broken dryer or to change the oil in the car.

Instead she'd given him the impression that she'd been having a grand ol' time while he was at sea. She chatted about the classes she took, or how her herb garden was coming along. If he quizzed her about any problems, she brushed off his concern and assured him she'd already dealt with whatever turned up.

Steve knew Carol wasn't that involved in the Navy wife activities. He figured it was up to her whether or not she joined. He hadn't pressed her, but he had wished she would make the effort to form friendships with the wives of his close friends.

Carol's apparent strength wasn't the only thing that troubled Steve, but it was one thing he felt they needed to discuss. The idea of telling his ex-wife that the least she could do was shed a few tears when he sailed away from her made him feel ungrateful. But swallowing his pride would be a small price to pay to straighten matters between them.

What she'd said about wanting a baby right away

made him feel soft inside every time he thought about it. He'd yearned for them to start a family long before now, but Carol had always wanted to wait. Now she appeared eager. He didn't question her motivation. He was too damned grateful.

A knock on his door jerked his attention across the room. "Yes?"

Seaman Layle stepped forward. "The Captain would like to see you, sir."

Steve nodded and said, "I'll be right there."

Carol sat at the end of the examination table, holding a thin piece of tissue over her lap. The doctor would be in any minute to give her the news she'd been waiting to hear for the past month. Okay, so her period was two weeks late. There could be any number of reasons. For one thing, she'd been under a good deal of stress lately. For another...

Her thoughts came to a grinding halt as Dr. Stewart stepped into the room. His glasses were perched on the end of his nose and his brow compressed as he read over her chart.

"Well?" she asked, unable to disguise the trembling eagerness in her voice.

"Congratulations, Carol," he said, looking up with a grandfatherly smile. "You're going to be a mother."

Chapter 7

Carol was almost afraid to believe what Dr. Stewart was telling her; her hand flew to her heart. "You mean, I'm pregnant?"

The doctor looked up at her over the edge of his bifocals. "This is a surprise?"

"Oh, no...I knew—or at least I thought I knew." The joy that bubbled through her was unlike anything she had ever known. Ready tears blurred her vision and she bit her lower lip to hold back the tide that threatened to overwhelm her.

The doctor took her hand and gently patted it. "You're not sure how you feel—is that it?"

"Of course I do," she said, in a voice half an

octave higher than usual. "I'm so happy I could just..."

"Cry?" he inserted.

"Dance," she amended. "This is the most wonderful thing that's ever happened to me since..."

"Your high-school prom?"

"Since I got married. I'm divorced now, but...Steve, he's my ex-husband, will marry me again...at least, I think he will. I'm not going to tell him about this right away. I don't want him to marry me again just because of the baby. I won't say a word about this. Or maybe I should? I don't know what to do, but thank you, Doctor, thank you so much."

A fresh smile began to form at the edges of his mouth. "You do whatever you think is best. Now, before we discuss anything else I want to go over some key points with you."

"Oh, of course, I'll do anything you say. I'll quit smoking and give up junk food, and take vitamins. If you really think it's necessary, I'll try to eat liver once a week."

His gaze reviewed her chart. "It says here you don't smoke."

"No, I don't, but I'd start just so I could quit if it would help the baby."

He chuckled. "I don't think that will be necessary, young lady."

Carol reached for his hand and pumped it several

times. "I can't tell you how happy you've made me."

Still chuckling, the white-haired doctor said, "Tell me the same thing when you're in labor and I'll believe you."

Carol watched as Lindy entered the restaurant and paused to look around. Feeling a little self-conscious, she raised her hand. Lindy waved back and headed across the floor, weaving her way through the crowded tables.

"Hi. Sorry, I'm late."

"No problem." The extra time had given Carol a chance to study the menu. Her stomach had been so finicky lately that she had to be careful what she ate. This being pregnant was serious business and already the baby had made it clear "she" wasn't keen on particular foods—especially anything with tomatoes.

"Everything has been so hectic lately," Lindy said, picking up the menu, glancing at it and setting it aside almost immediately.

"That was quick," Carol commented, nodding her head toward the menu.

"I'm a woman who knows my own mind."

"Good for you," Carol said, swallowing a laugh. "What are you having?"

"I don't know. What are you ordering?"

"Soup and a sandwich," Carol answered, not

fooled. Lindy wasn't interested in eating, she wanted answers. Steve's sister had been bursting with questions from the moment they'd met in the Boeing parking lot.

"Soup and a sandwich sounds good to me," Lindy said, obviously not wanting to waste time with idle chitchat.

Shaking her head, Carol studied Lindy. "Okay, go ahead and ask. I know you're dying to fire away."

Lindy unfolded the napkin and took pains spreading it over her lap. "Steve didn't come home Christmas Eve.... Well, he did, but it was early in the morning, and ever since that night he's been whistling 'Dixie'". She paused and grinned. "Yet every time I said your name, he barked at me to mind my own business."

"We've seen each other since Christmas, too."

"You have?" Lindy pinched her lips together and sadly shook her head. "That brother of mine is so tight-lipped, I can't believe the two of us are related!"

Carol laughed. Unwittingly Lindy had pinpointed the crux of Carol and Steve's marital problems. They were each private people who preferred to keep problems inside rather than talking things out the way they should.

"So you've seen Steve since Christmas," Lindy

prompted. "He must have contacted you after Rush and I moved."

"Actually I was the one who went to him."

"You did? Great."

"Yes," Carol nodded, blushing a little at the memory of how they'd spent that weekend. "It *was* great."

"Well, don't keep me in suspense here. Are you two going to get back together or what?"

"I think it's the 'or what.'"

"Oh." Lindy's gaze dropped abruptly and she frowned. "I don't mind telling you, I'm disappointed to hear that. I'd hoped you two would be able to work things out."

"We're heading in that direction, so don't despair. Steve and I are going to talk about a reconciliation when he returns."

"Oh, Carol, that's wonderful!"

"I think so, too."

"You two always seemed so right together. The first time I saw Steve after you were divorced, I could hardly recognize him. He was so cynical and unhappy. He'd sit around the apartment and watch television for hours, or stare out the window."

"Steve did?" Carol couldn't imagine that. Steve always had so many things going—he'd never taken the time to relax when they were living together. Another problem had been that they didn't share enough of the same interests. Carol blamed herself for that, but she was willing to compromise now that her marriage was about to have new life breathed into it.

"I wasn't joking when I told you he's been miserable. I don't know what prompted you to contact him at Christmastime, but I thank God you did."

Carol smoothed her hand across her abdomen and smiled almost shyly. "I'm glad I did, too."

Steve's letter to Carol was nearly fifty pages in length now. The days, as they often did aboard a submarine, blended together. It felt as if they were six months into this cruise instead of two, but his eagerness to return to Carol explained a good deal of this interminable feeling.

Carol. His heart felt as though it would melt inside his chest every time he thought about her mentioning a baby. The first thing he was going to do after they'd talked was throw out her birth control pills. And then he was going to take her to bed and make slow, easy love to her.

Once he had her back, he wasn't going to risk losing her again.

In the past two months, Steve had made another decision. They needed to clear the air about Todd Larson. He'd promised her that he wouldn't mention the other man's name again, but he had to, just once, and then it would be finished. Laid to rest forever.

Finding Todd in their shower hadn't been the only thing that had led Steve to believe Carol and her employer were having an affair. There had been plenty of other clues. Steve just hadn't recognized them in the beginning.

For one, she'd been working a lot of overtime, and didn't seem to be getting paid for it. At first Steve hadn't given it much credence, although he'd been angry that often she couldn't see him off to sea properly. At the time, however, she'd seemed as sorry about it as he was.

His return home after a ten-week absence had been the real turning point. Until that tour, Carol had always been eager to make love after so many weeks apart. Normally they weren't in the house ten minutes before they found themselves in the bedroom. But not that time. Carol had greeted him with open arms, but she'd seemed reluctant to hurry to bed. He had gotten what he wanted, but fifteen minutes later she'd made some silly excuse about needing groceries and had left the house.

None of these events had made much sense at the time. Steve had suspected something might be wrong, but he hadn't known how to ask her, how to approach her without sounding like an insecure schoolboy. Soon afterward he'd flown east for a two-week communication class. It was when he'd arrived home unexpectedly early that he'd found Carol and Todd together.

The acid building up in his stomach seemed to explode with pain and Steve took in several deep breaths until the familiar ache passed. All these months he'd allowed Carol to believe he'd condemned her solely because he'd discovered another man in their home. It was more than that, much more, and it was time he freed his soul.

"Carol? Are you here?"

Carol remained sitting on the edge of the bathtub and pressed her hand over her forehead. "I'm in here." Her voice sounded weak and sick—which was exactly how she felt. The doctor had given her a prescription to help ease these dreadful bouts of morning sickness, but it didn't seem to be doing much good.

"Carol?" Once more Lindy's voice vibrated down the hallway and Carol heard the sound of approaching footsteps. "Carol, what's wrong? Should I call a doctor?"

"No...no, I'll be fine in a minute. My stomach has been a little queasy lately, is all."

"You look awful."

"I can't look any worse than I feel." Her feeble attempt at humor apparently didn't impress Lindy.

"I take it the sale at the Tacoma Mall doesn't interest you?"

"I tried to call," Carol explained, "but you'd already left. You go ahead without me."

"I'll do no such thing," Lindy answered vehemently. "You need someone to take care of you. When was the last time you had a decent meal?"

Carol pressed her hand over her stomach. "Please, don't even mention food."

"Sorry."

Lindy helped her back into a standing position and led her down the hallway to her bedroom. Carol was ashamed to have Steve's sister see the house when it looked as if a cyclone had gone through it, but she'd had so little energy lately. Getting to work and home again drained her. She went to bed almost immediately after dinner and woke up exhausted the next morning.

No one had told her being pregnant could be so demanding on her health. She'd never felt more sickly in her life. Her appointment with Dr. Stewart wasn't for another two weeks, but something had to be done. She couldn't go on like this much longer.

The April sun seemed to smile down on Steve as he stepped off the *Atlantis*. He paused and breathed in the glorious warmth of afternoon in the Pacific

Northwest. Carol wouldn't be waiting for him, he knew. She had no way of knowing when he docked.

But she needn't come to him. He was going to her. The minute he got home, showered and shaved, he was driving over to her house. He was so ready for this.

They were going to talk, make love and get married. Maybe not quite that simply, but close.

He picked up his mail and let himself into the apartment. Standing beside the phone, he listened to the messages on his answering machine. Three were from Lindy, who insisted he call first thing when he returned home.

He reached for the phone while he flipped through his assorted mail.

"You rang?" he asked cheerfully, when his sister answered.

"Steve? I'm so glad you called."

"What's wrong? Has Rush decided he's made a terrible mistake and decided to give you back to your dear, older brother to straighten out?" His sister didn't have an immediate comeback or a scathing reply, which surprised him.

"Steve, it's Carol."

His blood ran cold with fear. "What happened?"

"I don't know, but I wanted to talk to you before you went to see her," she said and hesitated. "You were planning on going there right away, weren't you?''

"Yes. Now tell me what's the matter with Carol."

"She's been sick."

"How sick?" His heart was thundering against his chest with worry.

"I... don't think it's anything...serious, but I thought I should warn you before you surprise her with a visit. She's lost weight and looks terrible, and she'll never forgive you if you show up without warning her you're in town."

"Has she seen a doctor?"

"I...don't know," Lindy confessed. "She won't talk about it."

"What the hell could be wrong?"

The line seemed to vibrate with electricity. "If you want the truth, I suspect she's pregnant."

Chapter 8

"Pregnant?" Steve repeated and the word boomeranged against the walls of his mind with such force that the mail he'd been sorting slipped from his fingers and fell to the floor. He said it again. "Pregnant. But...but..."

"I probably shouldn't have said anything." Lindy's soft voice relayed her confusion. "But honestly, Steve, I've been so worried about her. She looks green around the gills and she's much too thin to be losing so much weight. I told her she should see a doctor, but she just smiles and says there's nothing to worry about."

The wheels in Steve's mind were spinning fast.

"The best thing I can do is talk to her, and find out what's happening."

"Do that, but for heaven's sake be gentle with her. She's too fragile for you to come at her like Hulk Hogan."

"I wouldn't do that."

"Steve, I'm your sister. I know you!"

"Okay, okay I'll talk to you later." He hung up the phone but kept his hand on the receiver while he mulled over his sister's news. Carol had said she wanted to have a baby, and she knew how he felt about the subject. He'd longed for a family since the first year they were together.

However, they weren't married now. No problem. Getting remarried was a minor detail. All he had to do was talk to the chaplain and make the arrangements. And if what Lindy said was true, the sooner he saw the chaplain, the better.

Without forethought he jerked the receiver off the hook and jabbed out Carol's number with his index finger. After two rings, he decided this kind of discussion was better done in person.

He showered, changed clothes and was halfway out the door when he remembered what Lindy had said about letting Carol know he was coming. Good idea.

He marched back over to the phone and dialed her number one more time.

No answer.

"Damn." He started pacing the floor, feeling restless, excited and nervous. He couldn't stay in the apartment; the walls felt as if they were closing in on him. He'd spent the last three months buried in the belly of a nuclear submarine and hadn't experienced a twinge of claustrophobia. Twenty minutes inside his apartment, knowing what he now did, and he was going ape.

He had to get out there even if it meant parking outside Carol's house and waiting for her to return.

He rushed out to his car and was grateful when it started right away after sitting for three months.

He was going to be a father! His heart swelled with joy and he experienced such a sense of elation that he wanted to throw back his head and shout loud enough to bring down brick walls.

A baby. His and Carol's baby. His throat thickened with emotion, and he had to swallow several times to keep from breaking down and weeping right there on the freeway. A new life. They were going to bring a tiny little being into this world and be accountable for every aspect of the infant's life. The responsibility seemed awesome. His hands gripped the steering wheel and he sucked in a huge breath as he battled down his excitement and fears.

He was going to be a good father. Always loving and patient. Everything would be right for his son…or daughter. Male chauvinist that he was, he yearned for a son. They could have a daughter the second time, but the thought of Carol giving him a boy felt right in his mind.

But he had so much to learn, so much to take care of. First things first. Steve tried to marshal his disjointed thoughts. He had to see to Carol's health. If this pregnancy was as hard on her as Lindy implied, then he wanted Carol to quit her job. He made good money; she should stay home and build up her strength.

The drive to Carol's house took less than fifteen minutes, and when Steve pulled up and parked he noticed her car in the driveway with the passenger door opened. His heart felt like it was doing jumping jacks, he was so eager to see her.

The front door opened and Carol stepped outside and to her car, grabbing a bag of groceries.

"Carol." She hadn't seen him.

She turned abruptly at the sound of her name. "Steve," she cried out brokenly and dropped the brown shopping bag. Without the least bit of hesitation, she came flying across the lawn.

He met her halfway, and wrapping his arms around her waist, he closed his eyes to the welcome feel of her body against his. His happiness couldn't be contained and he swung her around. Her lips were all over his face, kissing him, loving him, welcoming him.

Steve drank in her love and it humbled him. He held her gently, fearing he would hurt her, and kissed her with an aching tenderness, his mouth playing over the dewy softness of hers.

His hands captured her face and her deep blue eyes filled with tears as she smiled tremulously at him. "I've missed you so much. These have been the longest three months of my life."

"Mine, too." His voice nearly choked, and he kissed her again in an effort to hide the tide of emotion he was experiencing.

Steve picked up the scattered groceries for her and they walked into the house together.

"Go ahead and put those in the kitchen. Are you hungry?"

She seemed nervous and flittered from one side of the room to the other.

"I could fix you something if you'd like," she suggested, her back braced against the kitchen counter.

Steve's eyes held hers, and the emotion that had rocked him earlier built with intensity every minute he was in her presence. "You know what I want," he whispered, hardly able to speak.

Carol relaxed, and blushed a little. "I want to make love with you so much."

He held his hands out to her and she walked toward him, locking her arms around his neck. She pressed her weight against him and Steve realized how slender she was, how fragile. Regret slammed into his chest with all the force of a wrecking ball against a concrete wall. She was nurturing his child within her womb, for God's sake, and all he could think about was getting her into bed. He hadn't even asked her how she was feeling. All he cared about was satisfying his own selfish lusts.

"Carol..." His breath was slow and labored. Gently he tried to break free, because he couldn't think straight when she was touching him.

"Hmm?" Her hands were already working at his belt buckle, and her mouth was equally busy.

He felt himself weakening. "Are you sure? I mean, if you'd rather not..."

She released his zipper and when her hands closed around his naked hardness, he thought he would faint. His eyes rolled toward the ceiling. "Don't...don't you think we should talk?" he managed to say.

"No."

"But—"

She broke away and looked up at him, her eyes hungry with demand. "Steven Kyle, what is your problem? Do you or do you not want to make love?"

"I think...we should probably talk first. Don't

you?'' He didn't know if she would take him seriously with his voice shaking the way it was.

She grinned, and when her gaze dropped to below his waistline, they rounded. ''No. Because neither one of us is going to be able to say anything worth listening to until we take care of other things....''

It wasn't possible to love a woman any more than he did Carol at that moment, Steve thought. She reached for his hand and led him out of the kitchen and into the bedroom.

Like a lost sheep, he followed.

The newborn moon cast silvery shadows on the wall opposite the bed, and Steve sighed, feeling sated and utterly content. Carol slept at his side, her arm draped around his middle and her face nestled against his shoulder. Her tousled hair fell over his chest and he ran his fingers through it, letting the short, silky length slip through his hands.

Gently he brushed a blond curl off her cheek and twisted his head so that he could kiss her temple. She stirred and sighed in her sleep. He grinned. If he searched for a hundred years he would never find a woman who could satisfy him the way Carol did.

They hadn't talked, hadn't done anything but make love until they were both so exhausted that sleep dominated their minds. They may not have voiced the words, but the love between them was so secure it would take more than a bulldozer to rock it this time. Steve may not have had a chance to say the words, but his heart had been speaking them from the minute Carol had led him to bed.

Bringing the blanket more securely over her shoulders, he wrapped his arm around her and studied her profile in the fading moonlight. What Lindy told him was true. Carol had lost weight; she was as slender as a bamboo shoot, and much too pale. She needed someone to take care of her and, he vowed in his heart, he would be the one.

He almost wished she would roll over so that he could place his hand on her abdomen and feel for himself the life that was blossoming there. He felt weak with happiness every time he thought about their baby. He closed his eyes at the sudden longing that seared through his blood.

Carol hadn't yet told him that she was pregnant but he was sure she would in the morning. Until then, he would be content.

He closed his eyes and decided to sleep.

Steve woke first. Carol didn't so much as stir when he climbed out of bed and reached for his clothes. Silently he tiptoed out of the room and gently closed the door. She needed her sleep.

He made himself a pot of coffee and piddled around the kitchen, putting away the groceries that had been sitting on the counter all night. He pulled open the vegetable bin and carelessly tossed a head of lettuce in there. The drawer refused to close and he discovered the problem to be a huge shriveled up sweet potato. He took it out and, with an over the head loop shot Michael Jordan would have envied, tossed it into the garbage.

Carol and sweet potatoes. Honestly. The last time he'd looked inside her refrigerator, it had been filled with the stuff in every imaginable form.

He supposed he should get used to that kind of thing. It was a well-known fact that women often experienced weird food cravings when they were pregnant. Sweet potatoes were only one step above pickles and ice cream.

Just a minute! That had been last Christmas...before Christmas.

Steve's heart seemed to stop and slowly he straightened. Chewing on the inside of his lip, he closed the refrigerator door. Carol had been stuffing down the sweet potatoes long before he'd accepted her dinner invitation. Weeks before, from the look of it.

His thoughts in chaos, he stumbled into the living room and slumped into the chair. An icy chill settled over him. No. He refused to believe it, refused to condemn her on anything so flimsy. Then his gaze fell on a pair of knitting needles. He reached for her pattern book and noted the many designs for infant wear.

His heart froze. The last time he'd been by the house, Carol had been knitting a baby blanket. When he'd asked her about it, she'd told him it was for a friend. His snort of laughter was mirthless. Sure, Carol! More lies, more deceit.

And come to think of it, on Christmas Eve she'd pushed her knitting aside so that he couldn't see it. She'd been knitting the *same* blanket for the *same* friend then, too.

He was still stewing when Carol appeared. She smiled at him so sweetly as she slipped her arms into her robe.

"Morning," she said with a yawn.

"Morning."

His gruffness must have stopped her. "Is something wrong?"

Such innocent eyes... She'd always been able to fool him with that look. No more.

"Steve?"

"You're pregnant, aren't you?"

She released her breath in a long, slow sigh. "I wondered if you'd guess. I suppose I should have told you right away, but...we got sidetracked, didn't we?"

He could hardly stand to look at her.

"You're not angry, are you?" she asked, her eyes suddenly reflecting uncertainty.

Again such innocence, such skill. "No, I suppose not."

"Oh, good," she said with a feeble smile, "you had me worried there for a minute."

"One question?"

"Sure."

"Just whose baby is it?"

Chapter 9

"Whose baby is it?" Carol repeated, stunned. She couldn't believe Steve would dare to ask such a question when the answer was so obvious.

"That's what I want to know."

His face was drawn extremely tight—almost menacing. She moved into the room and sat across from him, her heart ready to explode with dread. She met his look squarely, asking no quarter, giving none. The prolonged moment magnified the silence.

"I'm three months pregnant. This child is yours," she said, struggling to keep her voice even.

"Don't lie to me, Carol. I'm not completely dense." The anger that seeped into his expression was fierce enough to frighten her. Steve vaulted to his feet and started pacing in military fashion, each step precise and clipped, as if the drill would put order to his thoughts and ultimately to his life.

Carol's fingernails dug into the fabric on the sides of the overstuffed chair and her pulse went crazy. Her expression, however, revealed none of the inner turmoil she was experiencing. When her throat felt as if it would cooperate with her tongue, she spoke. "How can you even think such a thing?"

Steve splayed his fingers and jerked them through his hair in an action that seemed savage enough to yank it out by the roots. "I should have known something was wrong when you first contacted me at Christmastime."

Carol felt some color flush into her cheeks; to her regret it probably convinced Steve she was as guilty as he believed.

"That excuse about not wanting to spend Christmas alone was damn convenient. And if that wasn't obvious enough, your little seduction scene should have been. God knows, I fell for it." He whirled around to face her. "You did plan that, didn't you?"

"I...I..."

"Didn't you?" he repeated, in harsh tones that demanded the truth.

Miserable and confused, Carol nodded. She had

no choice but to admit to her scheme of seducing him.

One corner of his mouth curved up in a half smile, but there was no humor or amusement in the action. The love that had so recently shone from his eyes had been replaced by condemnation.

"If only you would let me explain." She tried again, shocked by this abrupt turn of events. Only a few hours before, they'd lain in each other's arms and spoken of a reconciliation. The promise that had sprung to life between them was wilting and she was powerless to stop it.

"What could you possibly say that would change the facts?" he demanded. "I was always a fool when it came to you. Even after a year apart I hadn't completely come to terms with the divorce and you, no doubt, knew that and used it to your advantage."

"Steve, I—"

"It's little wonder," he continued, not allowing her to finish speaking, "that you considered me that perfect patsy for this intrigue. You used my love for you against me."

"Okay, so I planned our lovemaking Christmas Eve. You're right about that. I suppose I was pretty obvious about the whole thing when you think about it. But I had a reason. A damn good one."

"Yes, I know."

Carol hadn't realized a man's eyes could be so cold.

"What do you know?" she asked.

"That cake you're baking in your oven isn't mine."

"Oh, honestly, Steve. Your paranoia is beginning to wear a little thin. I'm doing my damnedest to keep my cool here, but you're crazy if you think anyone else could be the father."

He raised his index finger. "You're good. You know that? You're really very good. That fervent look about you, as though I'm going off the deep end to even suspect you of such a hideous deed. Just the right amount of indignation while keeping your anger in check. Good, very good."

"Stop that," she shouted. "You're being ridiculous. When you get in this mood, nothing appeases you. Everything I say becomes suspect."

His hand wiped his face free of expression. "If I didn't know better, I could almost believe you."

She hated it when Steve was like this. He was so convinced he was right that no amount of arguing would ever persuade him otherwise. "I'm going to tell you one last time, and then I won't say it again. Not ever. We—as in you and I, Steve—are going to have a baby."

Steve stared at her for so long that she wasn't sure what he was thinking. He longed to believe her—she could recognize that yearning in his eyes—and yet something held him back. His Adam's apple moved up and down, and he clenched his jaw so tightly that the sides of his face went white. Still the inner struggle continued while he glared at her, as if commanding the truth—as if to say he could deal with anything as long as it was true.

Carol met that look, holding her gaze as steady and sure as was humanly possible. He wanted the truth, and she'd already given it to him. Nothing she could say would alter the facts: he was her baby's father.

Steve then turned his back on her. "The problem is, I desperately want to believe you. I'd give everything I've managed to accumulate in this life to know that baby was mine."

Everything about Steve, the way he stood with his shoulders hunched, his feet braced as if he expected a blow, told Carol he didn't believe her. Her integrity was suspect.

"I...my birthday—I was thirty," she said, faltering as she scrambled to make him recognize the truth. "It hit me then that my childbearing years were numbered. Since the divorce I've been so lonely, so unhappy, and I thought a baby would help fill the void in my life."

He turned to look at her as she spoke, then closed his eyes and nodded.

Just looking at the anguish in his face was almost more than Carol could bear. "I know you never believed me about Todd, but there's only been one lover in my life, and that's you. I figured that you owed me a baby. I thought if I invited you to spend Christmas with me and you accepted, that I could probably steer us into the bedroom. None of the problems we had in our marriage had extended there."

"Carol, don't—this isn't necessary. I already know you were—"

"Yes, it is. Please, Steve, you've got to listen to me. You've got to understand."

He turned away from her again, but Carol continued talking because it was the only thing left for her to do. If she didn't tell him now, there might never be another chance.

"I didn't count on anything more happening between us. I'd convinced myself I was emotionally separated from you by that time and all I needed was the baby…"

"You must have been worried when I didn't fall into your scheme immediately."

"What do you mean?" Carol felt frantic and helpless.

"I didn't immediately suggest we get back together—that must have had you worried. After Christmas Eve we decided to leave things as they were.'' He walked away from her, but not before she saw the tilt of righteous indignation in his profile. ''That visit to my apartment...what was your excuse? Ah yes, a button you'd found and thought might be mine. Come on, Carol, you should have been more original than that. As excuses go, that's about as flimsy as they get.''

''All right, if you want me to admit I planned that seduction scene, too, then I will. I didn't get pregnant the way I planned in December...I had to try again. You had to know swallowing my pride and coming to you wasn't easy.''

He nodded. ''No, I don't suppose it was.''

''Then you believe me?''

''No.''

Carol hung her head in frustration.

''Naturally only one night of lovemaking wasn't enough,'' he said with a soft denunciation. ''It made sense to plan more than one evening together in case I started questioning matters later. I'm pleased that you did credit me with some intelligence. Turning up pregnant after one time together would have seemed much too convenient. But twice... Well, that sounds far more likely.''

Carol was speechless. Once more Steve had tried and found her guilty, choosing to believe the worst possible scenario.

''Fool that I am, I should have known something

was up by how docile and loving you were. So willing to forget the past, forgive and go on with the
future. Then there was all that talk about us starting
a family. That sucked me right in, didn't it? You
know, you've always known how much I want children.''

"There's nothing I can say, is there?"

"No," he admitted bleakly. "I wonder what you
would have told me next summer when you gave
birth—although months premature, astonishingly the
baby would weigh six or seven pounds and obviously
be full term. Don't you think I would have ques-
tioned you then?"

She kept her mouth shut, refusing to be drawn into
this kind of degrading verbal battle. From experience
she knew nothing she could say would vindicate her.

"If you don't want to claim this child, Steve, that's
fine, the loss is yours. My original intent was to raise
her alone anyway. I'd thought…I'd hoped we could
build a new life together, but it's obvious I was
wrong.''

"Dead wrong. I won't let you make a fool of me
a second time."

A strained moment passed before Carol spoke, and
when she did her voice was incredibly weak. "I think
it would be best if you left now."

He answered her with an abrupt nod, turned away

and went to her bedroom to retrieve his shirt and shoes.

Carol didn't follow him. She sat, feeling numb and growing more ill with each minute. The nausea swelled up inside her until she knew she was going to empty her stomach. Standing, she rushed into the bathroom and leaned over the toilet in a ritual that had become all too familiar.

When she'd finished, she discovered Steve waiting in the doorway, watching her. She didn't know how long he'd been there.

"Are you all right?"

She nodded, not looking at him, wanting him to leave so that she could curl into a tight ball and lick her wounds. No one could hurt her the way Steve did. No other man possessed the power.

He didn't seem to believe she was going to be fine, and slowly he came into the bathroom. He wet a washcloth and handed it to her, waiting while she wiped her face. Then, gently, he led her back into the bedroom and to the bed. Carol discovered that lying down did seem to ease the dizzy, sick feeling.

Steve took his own sweet time buttoning his shirt, apparently stalling so that he could stick by her in case she was sick a second time, although she knew he would never have admitted he cared. If she'd had the energy, Carol would have suggested he go, because for every minute he lingered it was more dif-

ficult for her to bear seeing him. She didn't want him
to care about her—how could he when he believed
the things he did? And yet, every now and again she
would find him watching her guardedly, his eyes
filled with worry.

"When do you see the doctor next?" He walked
around the foot of the bed and resumed an alleged
search for his socks.

"Two weeks." Her voice was faint and barely audible.

"Don't you think you should give him a call
sooner?"

"No." She refused to look at him.

Steve apparently found what he wanted. He sat on
the edge of the mattress and slowly, methodically put
on his shoes. "How often does this sort of thing happen?" he asked next.

"It doesn't matter." Some of her energy returned,
and she tested her strength by sitting up. "Listen,
Steve, I appreciate your concern, but it just isn't necessary. My baby and I are going to be just fine."

He didn't look convinced. His brooding gaze revealed his thoughts, and when he looked at her, his
expression softened perceptibly. It took a moment for
his eyes to drop to her hand, which rested on her
abdomen.

The change that came over him was a shock. His
face tightened and his mouth thinned. A surge of

anger shot through her. "You don't want to claim our daughter, then it's your loss."

"The baby isn't mine."

The anguish in his voice was nearly Carol's undoing. She bit her lower lip and shook her head with mounting despair. "I can't believe you're actually saying that. But you'll never know, will you, Steve? All your life you're going to be left wondering. If she has dark eyes like yours and dark hair, that will only complicate your doubts. No doubt the Kyle nose will make you all the more suspicious. Someday you're going to have to face the fact that you've rejected your own child. If you can live with that, then so be it."

He twisted around and his fists were knotted into tight fists. "You were pregnant at Christmas and you're trying to pawn this pregnancy off on me."

"That is the most insulting thing you've ever said to me."

He didn't answer her for a long time. "You've insulted my intelligence. I may have loved you, but I'm not a blind fool."

"They don't come any blinder."

"Explain the milk?"

"What?" Carol hadn't a clue to what he was talking about.

"At Christmas, after we'd made love, we had a snack. Remember?"

Carol did.

"You poured yourself a glass of milk and I commented because you used to dislike it. We were married five years and the only time I can remember you having milk was with cold cereal. You could live your whole life without the stuff. All of a sudden you're drinking it by the glassful."

With deliberate calm Carol rolled her gaze toward the ceiling. "Talk about flimsy excuses. You honestly mean to say you're rejecting your own child because I drank a glass of milk an entire month before I was pregnant?"

"That isn't everything. I saw your knitting Christmas Eve, although you tried to hide it from me. Later, I asked you about it and you claimed it was a baby blanket. It was the same piece you were working on at Christmas, wasn't it?"

"Yes, but…"

"That blanket's for your baby isn't it, Carol? There never was any friend."

Frustration mounting in volcanic proportions, she yelled, "All right, it wasn't for any friend—that's what you want to hear."

"And then there were the sweet potatoes. Good God, you had six containers full of yams that night…pregnant women are said to experience silly cravings. And that's what it was, wasn't it—a craving?"

Standing, Carol felt the weight of defeat settle on her shoulders. No amount of arguing would change anything now. Steve had reasoned everything out in his own mind and found her answers lacking. There was no argument she could give him that would change what he'd already decided.

"Well?" he demanded. "Explain those things away, if you can."

She felt as if she were going to burst into helpless tears at any second. For six years she'd loved this man and given him the power to shatter her heart. "You're the only man I know who can put two and two together and come up with five, Steve," she said wearily.

"For God's sake, quit lying. Quit trying to make me doubt what's right before my eyes. You wanted to trick me into believing that baby is mine, and by God, it almost worked."

If he didn't leave soon, Carol was going to throw him out. "I think you should leave."

"Admit it!" he shouted.

Nothing less would satisfy him. She slapped her hands against her thighs and feigned a sorrowful sigh. "I guess you're just too smart for me. I should have known better than to try to fool you."

Steve turned and marched to the front door, but stopped, his hand gripping the knob. "What's he going to do about it?"

"Who?"

"Todd."

It took every dictate of Carol's control not to scream that her former employer had nothing to do with her being pregnant. "I don't have anything more to say to you."

"Is he going to divorce Joyce and marry you?"

With one hand cradled around her middle, Carol pointed to the door with the other.

"I have a right to know," Steve argued. "If he isn't going to help you, something should be done."

"I don't need anything—especially from you."

"As much as I'd like to walk away from you, I can't. If you find yourself in trouble, call me. I'll always be there for you."

"If you want to help me, then get out of my life. This baby is mine and mine alone." There was no anger in her words; her voice was low and controlled...and sad, unbelievably sad.

Steve hesitated and his lingering seemed to imply that something would change. Carol knew otherwise.

"Goodbye, Steve."

He paused, then whispered, "Goodbye."

The pain in his voice would haunt her all her days, she thought, as Steve turned and walked out of her life.

The loud pounding noise disrupted Steve's restless slumber and he sat up and glared at the front door of his apartment.

GET 2

HOW TO GET YOUR 2 FREE BOOKS AND FREE GIFT!

1. Peel off the MIRA® sticker on the front cover. Place it in the space provided at right. This automatically entitles you to receive two free books and an exciting surprise gift.

2. Send back this card and you'll get 2 "The Best of the Best™" books. These books have a combined cover price of $11.98 or more in the U.S. and $13.98 or more in Canada, but they are yours to keep absolutely FREE!

3. There's <u>no</u> catch. You're under <u>no</u> obligation to buy anything. We charge nothing – ZERO – for your first shipment. And you don't have to make any minimum number of purchases – not even one!

4. We call this line "The Best of the Best" because each month you'll receive the best books by some of today's most popular authors. These authors show up time and time again on all the major bestseller lists and their books sell out as soon as they hit the stores. You'll like the convenience of getting them delivered to your home at our special discount prices . . . and you'll love your *Heart to Heart* subscriber newsletter featuring author news, horoscopes, recipes, book reviews and much more!

5. We hope that after receiving your free books you'll want to remain a subscriber. But the choice is yours – to continue or cancel, anytime at all! So why not take us up on our invitation, with no risk of any kind. You'll be glad you did!

6. And remember...we'll send you a surprise gift ABSOLUTELY FREE just for giving THE BEST OF THE BEST a try.

SPECIAL FREE GIFT!
We'll send you a fabulous surprise gift, absolutely FREE, simply for accepting our no-risk offer!

Visit us online at
www.mirabooks.com

® and TM are registered trademar of Harlequin Enterprises Limited.

BOOKS FREE!

THE BEST OF THE BEST™ — Here's How it Works:

Accepting your 2 free books and gift places you under no obligation to buy anything. You may keep the books and gift and return the shipping statement marked "cancel." If you do not cancel, about a month later we will send you 4 additional books and bill you just $4.74 each in the U.S., or $5.24 each in Canada, plus 25¢ shipping & handling per book and applicable taxes if any.* That's the complete price and — compared to cover prices starting from $5.99 each in the U.S. and $6.99 each in Canada — it's quite a bargain! You may cancel at any time, but if you choose to continue, every month we'll send you 4 more books, which you may either purchase at the discount price or return to us and cancel your subscription.

*Terms and prices subject to change without notice. Sales tax applicable in N.Y. Canadian residents will be charged applicable provincial taxes and GST. Credit or Debit balances in a customer's account(s) may be offset by any other outstanding balance owed by or to the customer.

"Who is it?" he shouted, and the sound of his own voice sent shooting pains through his temple. He moaned, tried to sit up and in the process nearly fell off the sofa.

"Steve, I know you're in there. Open up."

Lindy. Damn, he should have known it would be his meddling sister. He wished to hell she would just leave him alone. He'd managed to put her off for the past week, avoiding talking to her, inventing excuses not to see her. Obviously that hadn't been good enough because here she was!

"Go away," he said, his voice less loud this time. "I'm sick." That at least was the truth. His head felt like someone had used it for batting practice.

"I have my own key and I'll use it unless you open this door right now."

Muttering under his breath, Steve weaved across the floor until he reached the door. The carpet seemed to pitch and roll like a ship tossed about in a storm. He unbolted the lock and stepped aside so Lindy could let herself in. He knew she was about to parade into his apartment like an angel of mercy prepared to save him from hell and damnation.

He was right.

Lindy came into the room with the flourish of a suffragette marching for equality of the sexes. She stopped in the middle of the room, hands placed righteously on her hips, and studied him as though viewing the lowest form of human life. Then slowly she began to shake her head with obvious disdain.

"You look like hell," she announced.

Steve almost expected bugles to follow her decree. "Thank you, Mother Theresa."

"Sit down before you fall down."

Steve did as she ordered simply because he didn't have the energy to argue. "Would you mind not talking so loud?"

With one hand remaining on her hip, Lindy marched over to the window and pulled open the drapes.

Steve squinted under the force of the sunlight and shaded his eyes. "Was that really necessary?"

"Yes." She walked over to the coffee table and picked up an empty whiskey bottle, as though by touching it she was exposing herself to an incurable virus. With her nose pointed toward the ceiling, she walked into the kitchen and tossed it in the garbage. The bottle made a clanking sound as it hit against other bottles.

"How long do you intend to keep yourself holed up like this?" she demanded.

He shrugged. "As long as it takes."

"Steve, for heaven's sake be reasonable."

"Why?"

She couldn't seem to find an answer and that

pleased him because he wasn't up to arguing with her. He knew there was a reason to get up, get dressed and eat, but he hadn't figured out what it was yet. He'd taken a week of leave in order to spend time with Carol. Now he would give anything to have to report to duty—anything to take his mind off his ex-wife.

His mouth felt like a sand dune had shifted there while he slept. He needed something cold and wet. With Lindy following him, he walked into the kitchen and got himself a beer.

To his utter amazement, his sister jerked it out of his hand and returned it to the refrigerator. "From the look of things, I'd say you've had enough to drink."

He was so stunned, he didn't know what to say.

She pointed her index finger toward a kitchen chair, silently ordering him to sit. From the determined look she wore, Steve decided not to test her.

Before he could object, she had a pot of coffee brewing and was rummaging through the refrigerator looking for God knew what. Eggs, he realized when she brought out a carton.

She insisted he eat, which he did, but he didn't like it. While he sat at the table like an obedient child, Lindy methodically started emptying his sink, which was piled faucet-high with dirty dishes.

"You don't need to do that," he objected.

"Yes, I know."

"Then don't...I can get by without any favors from you." Now that he had something in his stomach, he wasn't about to be led around like a bull with a ring through his nose.

"You need something," she countered. "I'm just not sure what. I suspect it's a swift kick in the seat of the pants."

"You and what army, little sister."

Lindy declined to answer. She poured herself a cup of coffee, replenished his and claimed the chair across the table from him. "Okay," she said, her shoulders rising with an elongated sigh. "What happened with Carol?"

At the mention of his former wife's name, Steve's stomach clenched in a painful knot. Just thinking about her carrying another man's child produced such an inner agony that the oxygen constricted his lungs and he couldn't breathe.

"Steve?"

"Nothing happened between us. Absolutely nothing."

"Don't give me that. The last time we talked, you were as excited as a puppy about her being pregnant. You could hardly wait to see her. What's happened since then?"

"I already told you—nothing!"

Lindy slumped forward and braced her hand against her forehead. "You've buried yourself in this apartment for an entire week and you honestly expect me to believe that?"

"I don't care what you believe."

"I'm to blame, aren't I?"

"What?"

"I shouldn't have said a word about Carol and the baby, but she'd been so sick and I've been so concerned about her." Lindy paused and lightly shook her head. "I still am."

Steve hated the way his heart reacted to the news that Carol was still sickly. He didn't want to care about her, didn't want to feel this instant surge of protectiveness when it came to his ex-wife. For the past week, he'd tried to erase every memory of her from his tortured mind. Obviously it hadn't worked, and the only thing he'd managed to develop was one hell of a hangover.

"I shouldn't have told you," Lindy repeated.

"It wouldn't have made one bit of difference; I would have found out sooner or later."

Lindy's hands cupped the coffee mug. "What are you going to do about it?"

Steve shrugged. "Nothing."

"Nothing? But Steve, that's your baby."

He let that pass, preferring not to correct his sister.

"What's between Carol and me isn't any of your business. Leave it at that."

She seemed to weigh his words carefully. "I wish I could."

"What do you mean by that?"

"Carol looks awful. I really think she needs to see her doctor. Something's wrong, Steve. She shouldn't be this sick."

He shrugged with feigned indifference. "That's her problem."

Lindy's jaw sagged open. "I can't believe you. Carol is carrying your child and you're acting like she got pregnant all by herself."

Steve diverted his gaze to the blue sky outside his living-room window and shrugged. "Maybe she did," he whispered.

Chapter 10

Carol sat at her desk and tried to concentrate on her work. This past seven days had been impossible. Steve honestly believed she was carrying another man's child, and nothing she could ever say would convince him otherwise. It was like history repeating itself and all the agony of her divorce had come back to haunt her.

Only this time Carol was smarter.

If Steve chose to believe such nonsense, that was his problem. She wanted this baby and from the first had been prepared to raise her daughter alone. Now if only she could get over these bouts of nausea and the sickly feeling that was with her almost every day and night. Most of it she attributed to the emotional upheaval in her life. Within a couple of weeks it would pass and she would feel a thousand times better—at least, that was what she kept telling herself.

"Hi."

A familiar, friendly voice invaded Carol's thoughts. "Lindy!" she said, directing her attention to Steve's sister. "What are you doing here?"

"Risking my job and my neck. Can we meet later? I've got to talk to you; it's important."

As fond as Carol was of her former sister-in-law, she knew there was only one subject Lindy would want to discuss, and that was Steve. Her former husband was a topic Carol preferred to avoid. Nor was she willing to justify herself to his sister, if Lindy started questioning her about the baby's father. It would be better for everyone involved if she refused to meet her, but the desperate worry in Lindy's steady gaze frightened her.

"I suppose you want to ask me about Steve," Carol said slowly, thoughtfully. "I don't know that any amount of talking is going to change things. It'd be best just to leave things as they are."

"Not you, too."

"Too?"

"Steve's so closed mouthed you'd think your name was listed as classified information."

Carol picked up the clipboard and flipped over a

page, in an effort to pretend she was exceptionally busy. "Maybe it's better this way," she murmured, but was unable to disguise the pain her words revealed.

"Listen, I've got to get back before someone important—like my supervisor—notices I'm missing," Lindy said, scribbling something on a pad and ripping off the sheet. "Here's the address to my apartment. Rush is on sea trials, so we'll be alone."

"Lindy…"

"If you care anything about my brother you'll come." Once more those piercing eyes spelled out his sister's concern.

Carol took the address, and frowned. "Let me tell you right now that if you're trying to orchestrate a reconciliation, neither one of us will appreciate it."

"I…"

"Is Steve going to mysteriously arrive around the same time as I do?"

"No. I promise he won't. Good grief, Carol, he won't even talk to me anymore. He isn't talking to anyone. I'm not kidding when I say I'm worried about him."

Carol soaked in that information and frowned, growing concerned herself.

"You'll come?"

Against her better judgment, she nodded. Like her ex-husband, she didn't want to talk to anyone, and especially not to someone related to Steve. The pain of his accusations was still too raw to share with someone else.

Yet she knew she would be there to talk about whatever it was Lindy found so important, although she also knew that nothing Lindy could say would alter her relationship with Steve.

At five-thirty, Carol parked her car outside Lindy's apartment building. She regretted agreeing to the meeting, but couldn't see any way of escaping without going back on her word.

Lindy opened the door and greeted her with a weak smile. "Come in and sit down. Would you like something cold to drink? I just finished making a pitcher of iced tea."

"That sounds fine." Carol still wasn't feeling well and would be glad when she saw her doctor for her regular appointment. She took a seat in the living room while Lindy disappeared into the kitchen.

Lindy returned a couple of minutes later with tall glasses filled with iced tea.

"I wish I could say you're looking better," Lindy said, handing Carol a glass and a colorful napkin.

"I wish I could say I was, too."

Lindy sat across from her and automatically crossed her long legs. "I take it the medication the doctor gave you for the nausea didn't help?"

"It helped some."

"But generally you're feeling all right?"

Carol shrugged. She'd never been pregnant before and had nothing to compare this experience to. "I suppose."

Lindy's fingers wiped away the condensation on the outside of her glass. She hedged, and her gaze drifted around the room. "I think the best way to start is to apologize."

"But what could you have possibly done to offend me?"

Lindy's gaze moved to Carol's, and she released a slow breath. "I told Steve I suspected you were pregnant."

"It's true," Carol answered with a gentle smile. She would be a single mother, and although she would have preferred to be married, she was pleased and proud to be carrying this child.

"I know…but it would have been far better coming from you. I left a message for Steve to call me once he returned from his deployment. I was afraid he was going to come at you with his usual caveman tactics and you've been so ill lately… It's a weak excuse, I know."

"Lindy, for goodness' sake, don't worry about it. This baby isn't a deep, dark secret." Remembering the life she was nurturing in her womb was what had gotten her through the bleakest hours of this past week. Steve might choose to reject his daughter, but he could never take away this precious gift he had unknowingly given her.

"I don't know what's going on with my brother," Lindy muttered, dropping her gaze to her tea. "I wish Rush were here. If anyone could talk some sense into him, it's my husband."

"Get used to him being away when you need him most. It's the lot of a Navy wife. The Navy blues doesn't always refer only to their dress uniform, you know."

Lindy nodded. "I'm learning that; I'm also learning I'm much stronger than I thought I was. Rush was involved in an accident last year in the Persian Gulf—you probably read about it in the papers— well, really that doesn't have anything to do with Steve, but he was with me the whole time when we didn't know if Rush was dead or alive. I can't even begin to tell you how good he was, how supportive. In a crisis, my brother can be a real trooper."

"Yes, I know." Carol paused and took a sip of her tea. On more than one occasion in their married life, she had come to admire Steve's levelheadedness in dealing with both major and minor emergencies. It was in other matters, like trust and confidence in her love, that he fell sadly short.

"I don't understand him anymore," Lindy admitted. "He was ecstatic when I mentioned my suspicions about you being pregnant...I thought he was going to go right through the ceiling he was so excited. He was bubbling over like a little kid. I know he drove over to your place right after that and then we didn't hear from him again. I phoned, but he just barked at me to leave him alone, and when I went to see him...well, that's another story entirely.''

Carol stiffened. It was better to deal with Lindy honestly since it was apparent Steve hadn't told her. ''He doesn't believe the baby is his.''

Lindy's brow folded into a dark, brooding frown. ''But that's ridiculous.''

Carol found it somewhat amazing that her former sister-in-law would believe her without question and her ex-husband wouldn't.

''I...can't believe this.'' Lindy pressed her palm over her forehead, lifting her bangs, and her mouth sagged open. ''But, sadly, it explains a good deal.'' As if she couldn't remain sitting any longer, Lindy got up and started walking around the room, moving from one side to the other without direction. ''What is that man's problem? Good grief, someone should get him to face a few fundamental facts here.''

Carol smiled. It felt good to have someone trust and believe her.

''What are you going to do? I mean, I assumed Steve was going to remarry you, but...''

''Obviously that's out of the question.''

''But...''

"Single women give birth every day. It's rather commonplace now for a woman to choose to raise a child on her own. That was my original intention."

"But, Steve…"

"Steve is out of my life." Her hand moved to her stomach and a soft smile courted the edges of her mouth. "He gave me what I wanted. Someday he'll be smart enough to calculate dates, but when he does it'll be too late."

"Oh, Carol, don't say that. Steve loves you so much."

"He's hurt me for the last time. He can't love me and accuse me of the things he has. It's over for us, and there's no going back."

"But he does love you." Lindy walked around a bit more and then plopped down across from Carol. "When he wouldn't talk to me on the phone, I went over to the apartment. I've never seen him like this. He frightened me."

"What's wrong?" Carol was angry with herself for caring, but she did.

"He'd been drinking heavily."

"That's not like Steve."

"I know," Lindy said heatedly. "I didn't know when he'd eaten last, so I fixed him something, which was a mistake because once he had something in his stomach he got feisty again and wanted me to leave."

"Did you?"

"No." Lindy started nibbling on the corner of her mouth. "I kept asking him questions about you, which only made him more angry. I soon learned you were a subject best avoided."

"I can imagine."

"After a while, he fell asleep on the sofa and I stayed around and cleaned up the apartment. It was a mess. Then...I heard Steve. I thought at first he was in the middle of a bad dream and I went to wake him, but when I came into the living room, I found him sitting on the end of the davenport with his hands over his face. He was weeping, Carol. As I've never seen a man weep before—heart-wrenching sobs that came from the deepest part of his soul. I can't even describe it to you."

Carol lowered her gaze to her hands, which had begun to tremble.

"This is the first time I've seen my brother cry, and his sobs tore straight through my heart. I couldn't stand by and do nothing. I wanted to comfort him and find out what had hurt him so badly. I'm his sister, for heaven's sake—he should be able to talk to me. But he didn't want me anywhere near him and ordered me out of the apartment. I left, but I haven't been able to stop thinking about it since."

A tear spilled out of the corner of Carol's eye and left a moist trail down the side of her face.

"By the time I got home I was crying, too. I don't know what to do anymore."

Carol's throat thickened. "There's nothing you can do. This is something Steve has to work out himself."

"Can't you talk to him?" Lindy pleaded. "He loves you so much and it's eating him alive."

"It won't do any good." Carol spoke from bitter experience.

"How can two people who obviously love each other let this happen?"

"I wish I knew." Carol's voice dropped to a whispered sob.

"What about Steve and the baby?"

"He doesn't want to have anything to do with this pregnancy. That's his decision, Lindy."

"But it's the wrong one! Surely you can get him to realize that."

She shook her head sadly. "Once Steve decides on something, his mind is set. He's too stubborn to listen to reason."

"But you love him."

"I wish I could deny that, but I do care about him, with all my heart. Unfortunately that doesn't change a thing."

"How can you walk away from him like this?"

Carol's heart constricted with pain. "I've never left Steve. Not once. He's always been the one to walk away."

Chapter 11

"I'd do anything I could to make things right be
tween me and Steve," Carol told Lindy, "but it isn't
possible anymore."

"Why not?" Lindy pleaded. Carol knew it was
hard for Lindy to understand when her own recent
marriage was thriving. "You're both crazy in love
with each other."

The truth in that statement was undeniable. Although Steve believed her capable of breaking her
wedding vows and the worst kind of deceit, he continued to love her. For her part, Carol had little pride
when it came to her ex-husband. She should have cut
her losses the minute he'd accused her of having an

affair, walked away from her and filed for the divorce. Instead she'd spent the next year of her life in limbo, licking her wounds, pretending the emotional scars had healed. It had taken Christmas Eve to show her how far she still had to go to get over loving Steve Kyle.

"You can't just walk away from him," Lindy pleaded. "What about the baby?"

"Steve doesn't want anything to do with my daughter."

"Give him time, Carol. You know Steve probably better than anyone. He can be such a stubborn fool sometimes. It just takes awhile for him to come to his senses. He'll wake up one morning and recognize the truth about the baby."

"I have to forget him for my own sanity." Carol stood, delivered her empty iced-tea glass to the kitchen and prepared to leave. There wasn't anything Lindy could say that would change the facts. Yes, she did love Steve and probably always would, but that didn't alter what he believed.

Lindy followed her to the front door. "If you need something, anything at all, please call me."

Carol nodded. "I will."

"Promise?"

"Promise." Carol knew that Lindy realized how difficult it was for her to ask for help. Impulsively she hugged Steve's sister. From now on, Lindy would be her only link to Steve and Carol was grateful for the friendship they shared.

Steve had to get out of the apartment before he went crazy. He'd spent the past few days drowning his misery in a bottle and the only thing it had brought him was more pain.

He showered, shaved and dressed. Walking would help clear his mind.

With no real destination in mind, he headed toward the waterfront. He got as far as Pike Place Market and aimlessly wandered among the thick crowds there. The colorful sights of the vegetable and meat displays and the sounds of cheerful vendors helped lift his spirits.

He bought a crisp, red Delicious apple and ate it as he ambled toward the booths that sold various craft items designed to attract the tourist trade. He paused and examined a sculpture made of volcanic ash from Mount Saint Helens. Another booth sold scenic photos of the Pacific Northwest, and another, thick, hand-knit Indian sweaters.

"Could I interest you in something?" a friendly older woman asked. Her long silver hair framed her face, and she offered him a wide smile.

"No thanks, I'm just looking." Steve paused and glanced over the items on her table. Sterling silver jewelry dotted a black velvet cloth—necklaces, earrings and rings of all sizes and shapes.

"You can't buy silver anywhere for my prices," the woman said.

"It's very nice."

"If jewelry doesn't interest you, perhaps these will." She stood and pulled a box of silver objects from beneath the table, lifting it up for him to inspect.

The first thing Steve noticed was a sterling-silver piggy bank. He smiled recalling how he and Carol had dumped their spare change in a piggy bank for months in an effort to save enough for a vacation to Hawaii. They'd spent it instead for the closing costs on the house.

"This is a popular item," the woman told him, bringing out a baby rattle. "Lots of jewelry stores sell these, but no one can beat my prices."

"How much?" Steve couldn't believe he'd asked. What the hell would he do with a baby rattle—especially one made of sterling silver.

The woman stated a reasonable price. "I'll take it," he said, astonished to hear the words come out of his mouth.

"Would you like one with blue ribbon or pink?"

Already Steve regretted the impulse. What was he planning to do? Give it to Carol? He'd decided the best thing for him to do as far as his ex-wife was concerned was to never see her again.

"Sir? Blue or pink?"

"Blue," he answered in a hoarse whisper. For the son he would probably never father. Blue for the color of Carol's eyes when she smiled at him.

By the time Steve walked back to the apartment, the sack containing the silver baby rattle felt like it weighed thirty pounds. By rights, he thought, he should toss the silly thing in the garbage. But he didn't.

He set it on the kitchen counter and opened the refrigerator, looking for something to eat, but nothing interested him. When he turned, the rattle seemed to draw his gaze. He stared at it for a long moment, yearning strongly to press it into the hand of his own child.

Blood thundered in his ears and his heart pounded so hard and fast that his chest ached. He would save the toy for Lindy and Rush whenever they had children, he decided.

Feeling only slightly better, he moved into the living room and turned on the television. He reached for the *TV Guide*, flipped through the pages, sighed and turned off the set. A second later, he rushed to his feet.

He didn't know who the hell he was trying to kid. That silver rattle with the pretty blue ribbon was for

Carol and her baby, and it was going to torment him until he got rid of it.

He could mail her the toy and be done with the plaything. Or have Lindy give it to her without letting Carol know it had come from him. Or...or he could just set it on the porch and let her find it.

The last idea appealed to him. He would casually drive by her neighborhood, park his car around the block and wait until it was dark enough to sneak up and leave the rattle on the front step. He was the last person she would ever suspect would do something like that.

With his plan formulated, Steve drove to Carol's house. He was half a block away from her place when he noticed her car. She was leaving. This would work out even better. He could follow her and when she got where she was going, he could place the rattle inside her car. That way she would assume someone had mistaken her car for their own and inadvertently set the rattle inside. There wasn't anything she could do but take it home with her.

Carol headed north on Interstate 5, and her destination was a matter of simple deduction. She was going to the Northgate Mall. Lord, that woman loved to shop. The minute she steered onto the freeway on-ramp, Steve knew exactly where she was headed. They'd been married for five years, and their year apart hadn't changed her. The smug knowledge produced a smile.

But Carol exited before the mall.

Steve's heart started to pound. He was three cars behind her, but if she wasn't going shopping, he didn't know what she was planning. Maybe she was rendezvousing with Todd. Maybe all those times she'd told him she was shopping Carol had actually been meeting with her employer. The muscles in his stomach clenched into a knot so tight and painful that it stole his breath.

If there'd been any way to turn the car around, Steve would have done it, but he was trapped in the center lane of traffic and forced to follow the heavy flow.

It wasn't until they'd gone several blocks that Steve noticed the back side of the mall. Perhaps she'd found a shortcut and had never bothered to tell him about it.

Carol turned onto a busy side street, and against his better judgment, he followed her. A few minutes later, when Carol turned into the large parking lot at Northgate Mall, Steve felt almost giddy with relief.

She parked close to the J.C. Penney store, and Steve eased his vehicle into a slot four spaces over. On a whim, he decided to follow her inside. He'd always wondered what women found so intriguing about shopping.

He was far enough behind her on the escalator to almost lose her. Standing at the top, he searched until he found her standing in women's fashions, sorting through a rack of dresses. It took him a minute to realize they were maternity dresses. Although she'd lost several pounds, she must be having difficulty finding things that fit her, he realized. According to his calculations, she was five months pregnant—probably closer to six.

He lounged around while she took a handful of bright spring dresses and moved into the changing room. Fifteen minutes passed before she returned, and to Steve it felt like a lifetime.

When she returned, she went back to the rack and replaced all but one of the dresses. She held up a pretty blue one with a wide sailor's collar and red tie and studied it carefully. Apparently she changed her mind because she hung it back up with the others. Still she lingered an extra minute, continuing to examine the outfit. She ran her fingers down the sleeve to catch the price tag, read it, shook her head and reluctantly walked away.

The minute she was out of sight, Steve was at the clothing rack. Obviously she wanted the dress, yet she hadn't bought it. He checked the price tag and frowned. It was moderately priced, certainly not exorbitant. If she wanted it, which she apparently did, then she should have it.

For the second time in the same day, Steve found himself making a purchase that was difficult to rationalize. It wasn't as if he had any use for a maternity dress. But why not? he asked himself. If he left the rattle in her car it shouldn't make any difference if he added a dress. It wasn't likely that she would tie him to either purchase. Let her think her fairy godmother was gifting her.

From his position at the cash register, Steve saw Carol walk through the infant's department. She ran her hand over the top rail of a white Jenny Lind crib and examined it with a look of such sweet anticipation that Steve felt guilty for invading her privacy.

"Would you like this dress on the hanger or in a sack?" the salesclerk asked him.

It took Steve a moment to realize she was talking to him. "A sack, please." He couldn't very well walk through the mall carrying a maternity dress.

Carol bought something, too, but Steve couldn't see what it was. Infant T-shirts or something like that, he guessed. His vantage point in the furniture department wasn't the best. Carol started to walk toward him, and he turned abruptly and pretended to be testing out a recliner.

Apparently she didn't see him, and he settled into the seat and expelled a sigh of relief.

"Can I help you?" a salesclerk asked.

"Ah, no, thanks," he said, getting to his feet.

Carol headed down the escalator, and Steve scooted around a couple of women pushing baby strollers in an effort not to lose sight of her.

Carol's steps were filled with purpose as she moved down the wide aisle to women's shoes. She picked up a red low-heeled dress shoe that was on display, but when the clerk approached, she smiled and shook her head. Within a couple of minutes she was on her way.

Feeling more like a fool with every minute, Steve followed her out of the store and into the heart of the mall. The place was packed, as it generally was on Saturday afternoon. Usually Steve avoided the mall on weekends, preferring to do his shopping during the day or at night.

He saw Carol stop at a flower stand and buy herself a red rosebud. She'd always been fond of flowers, and he was pleased that she treated herself to something special.

She'd gone only a few steps when he noticed that her steps had slowed.

Something was wrong. He could tell from the way she walked. He cut across to the other side, where the flow of shoppers was heading in the opposite direction. Feeling like a secret government agent, he pressed himself against the storefront in an effort to watch her more closely. She had pressed her hand to her abdomen and her face had gone deathly pale. She was in serious pain, he determined as a sense of alarm filled him. Steve could feel it as strongly as if he were the one suffering.

Although he was certain she had full view of him, Carol didn't notice. She cut across the streams of shoppers to the benches that lined the middle of the concourse and sat. Her shoulders moved up and down as though she were taking in deep breaths in an effort to control her reaction to whatever was happening. She closed her eyes and bit her lower lip.

The alarm turned to panic. He didn't know what to do. He couldn't rush up to her and demand to know what was wrong. Nor could he casually stroll by and pretend he just happened to be shopping and had stumbled upon her. But something needed to be done—someone had to help her.

Steve had never felt more helpless in his life. Not knowing what else he could do, he walked up and plopped himself down next to her.

"Hi," he said in a falsely cheerful voice.

"Steve." She looked at him, her eyes brimming with tears. She reached for his hand, gripping it so hard her nails cut into his flesh.

All pretense was gone, wiped away by the stampeding fear he sensed in her.

"What's wrong?"

She shook her head. "I...I don't know."

Her eyes widened and he was struck by how yellow her skin was. He took her hand in both of his. "You're in pain?"

She nodded. Her fear palatable. "I'm so afraid."

"What do you want me to do?" He debated on whether he should could call for an ambulance or contact her doctor and have him meet them at the hospital.

"I...don't know what's wrong. I've had this pain twice, but it's always gone away after a couple of minutes." She closed her eyes. "Oh, Steve, I'm so afraid I'm going to lose my baby."

Chapter 12

Restless, Steve paced the corridor of the maternity ward in Overlake Hospital, his hands stuffed inside his pants pockets. He felt as though he were carrying the world on his shoulders. Each passing minute tightened the knot in his stomach until he was consumed with worry and dread.

He wanted to see Carol—he longed to talk to her—but there wasn't anything more for him to say. He'd done what he could for her, and by rights he should leave. But he couldn't walk away from her. Not now. Not when she needed him.

Not knowing what else to do, he found a pay phone and contacted his sister.

"Lindy, it's Steve."

"Steve, how are you? I'm so glad you phoned; I haven't stopped thinking about you."

She sounded so pleased to hear from him, and he swallowed down his guilt for the way he'd treated her. He'd been rude and unreasonable when she'd only been showing concern for him.

"I'm fine," he said hurriedly, "Listen, I'm at Overlake Hospital…"

"You're at the hospital? You're fine, but you're at Overlake? Good God, what happened? I knew it, I just knew something like this was going to happen. I felt it…"

"Lindy, shut up for a minute, would you?"

"No, I won't shut up—I'm family, Steve Kyle. Family. If you can't come to me when you're hurting, just who can you go to? You seem to think I'm too young to know anything about emotional pain, but you're wrong. When Paul dumped me it wasn't any Sunday-school picnic."

"I'm not the one in need of medical attention— it's Carol."

"Carol!" His blurted announcement seemed to sweep away all his sister's pent-up frustration. "What's wrong?" she asked quietly.

"I don't exactly know; the doctor's still with her. I think she might be losing the baby. She needs a woman—I'm the last person who should be here. I didn't know who else to call. Can you come?''

"Of course. I'll be there as fast as I can."

It seemed as though no more than a couple of minutes had passed before Lindy came rushing down the hall. He stood at the sight of her, immensely grateful. Relief washed over him and he wrapped his arms around her.

"The doctor hasn't come out yet," he explained before she could ask. He released her and checked his watch. "It's been over an hour now."

"What happened?"

"I'm not sure. Carol started having some kind of abdominal pains. I phoned her gynecologist, and after I explained what was happening, he suggested we meet him here."

"You said you thought Carol might be having a miscarriage?"

"Good Lord, I don't know anything about this woman stuff. All I can tell you is that she was in agony. I did the only thing I could—I got her here." The ten minutes it took to get Carol to the emergency room had been emotionally draining. She was terrified of losing the baby and had wept almost uncontrollably. Through her sobs she'd told him how much she wanted her baby and how this pregnancy would be her only opportunity. Little of what she'd said had made sense to Steve. He'd tried to find the words to assure her, but he hadn't really known what to say.

Just then Steve noticed Carol's physician, Dr. Stewart, push open the swinging door and walk toward the waiting area. He met him halfway.

"How is she?" he asked, his heart in his throat.

The gynecologist rubbed his hand down the side of his jaw and shook his head. His frown crowded his brows together. "She's as good as can be expected."

"The baby?"

"The pregnancy is progressing nicely...thus far."

Although the child wasn't his and Carol had tried to trick him into believing otherwise, Steve still felt greatly relieved knowing that her baby wasn't in any immediate danger.

"I'm sorry to keep you waiting so long, but quite frankly Carol's symptoms had me stumped. It's unusual for someone her age to suffer from this sort of problem."

"What problem?" Lindy blurted out.

"Gall bladder."

"Gall bladder," Steve repeated frowning. He didn't know what he'd expected, but it certainly hadn't been that.

"She tells me she's been suffering from flulike symptoms, which she accepted as morning sickness. There wasn't any reason for either of us to assume otherwise. Some of her other discomforts can be easily misinterpreted as well.

"The most serious threat at the moment is that she's dangerously close to being dehydrated. Predictably that has prompted other health risks."

"What do you mean?" Lindy asked.

"Her sodium and potassium levels have dropped and her heart rate is erratic. I've started an IV and that problem should take care of itself within a matter of hours."

"What's going to happen?"

Once more, Dr. Stewart ran a hand down the side of his face and shook his head. His kind eyes revealed his concern. "I've called in a surgeon friend of mine, and we're going to do a few more preliminary tests. But from what I'm seeing at this point, I don't think we can put off operating. Her gall bladder appears to be acutely swollen and is causing an obstruction."

"If you do the surgery, what will happen to the baby?" For Carol's sake, Steve prayed for the tiny life she was carrying.

Dr. Stewart's sober expression turned grim. "There's always a risk to the pregnancy when anesthesia is involved. I'd like to delay this, but I doubt that we can. Under normal conditions gall-bladder surgery can be scheduled at a patient's convenience, but not in Carol's case, I fear. But I want you to know, we'll do everything I can to save the child.''

"Please try." Carol had looked at him with such terror and helplessness that he couldn't help being affected. He would do everything humanly possible to see that she carried this child to full term.

"Please do what you can," Lindy added her own plea. "This child means a great deal to her."

Dr. Stewart nodded. "Carol's sleeping now, but you can see her for a couple of minutes, if you'd like. One at a time."

Steve looked to Lindy, who gestured for him to go in first. He smiled his appreciation and followed the grandfatherly doctor into Carol's room.

As Dr. Stewart had explained, she was sleeping soundly. She looked incredibly fragile with tubes stretching down from an IV pole to connect with the veins in her arm.

Steve stood beside her for several minutes, loving her completely. Emotion clogged his throat and he turned away. He loved her; he always would. No matter what had happened in the past, he couldn't imagine a future without Carol.

"How is she?" Lindy asked when he came out of the room.

He found he couldn't answer her with anything more than a short nod.

Lindy disappeared and returned five minutes later.

By then Steve had had a chance to form a plan of action, and he felt better for it.

As Lindy stepped toward him, he held her gaze with newfound determination. He and Carol were both fools if they thought they could stay apart. It wasn't going to work. Without Carol he was only half-alive. And she'd admitted how miserable she'd been during their year's separation.

"I'm going to marry her," Steve informed his sister brusquely.

"What?" Lindy looked at him as though she'd misheard him.

"I'm going to get the chaplain to come to the hospital, and I'm going to marry Carol."

Lindy studied him for several moments. "Don't you think she should have some say in this?"

"Yes...no."

"But I thought...Carol told me you didn't believe the baby is yours."

"It isn't."

Lindy rolled her eyes, then shook her head, her features tight with impatience. "That is the most ridiculous thing you've ever said. Honestly, Steve, where do you come up with these crazy ideas?"

"What idea? That the baby isn't mine, or remarrying Carol?"

"Both!"

"Whether or not I'm the father doesn't make one

bit of difference. I've decided it doesn't matter. From here on out, I'm claiming her child as mine.''

''But...''

''I don't care. I love Carol and I'll learn to love her baby. That's the end of it.'' Once the decision had been made, it felt right. The two of them had played a fool's game for over a year, but no more—he wouldn't stand for it. ''I'm not going to put up with any arguments from you or from Carol. I want her as my wife—we were wrong ever to have gone through with the divorce. All I'm doing now is correcting a mistake that should never have happened,'' he told his sister in a voice that men jumped to obey.

Lindy took a moment to digest his words. ''Don't you think you should discuss this in a rational matter with Carol? Don't you think she should have some input into her own life?''

''I suppose. But she needs me—although she isn't likely to admit it.''

''You've had just as difficult a time recognizing that fact yourself.''

''Not anymore.''

''When do you plan to tell her?''

Steve didn't know. He'd only reached this conclusion in the last five minutes, but already he felt in control of his life again.

''Well?'' his sister pressed.

"I haven't figured out when.... Before the surgery, I think, if it can be arranged."

"Steve, you're not thinking clearly. Carol isn't going to want to be married sitting in a hospital bed, looking all sickly and pale."

"The sooner we get this settled the better."

"For whom?" Lindy prompted.

"For both of us."

Lindy threw up her hands. "Sometimes the things you say utterly shock me."

"They do?" Steve didn't care—he felt as if he could float out of the hospital, he was so relieved. Carol would probably come through the surgery with flying colors and everything would fall into place the way it should have long ago. This had certainly been a crazy day. He'd bought a sterling silver rattle, followed Carol around a shopping mall like an FBI agent, driven her to the hospital, then made a decision that would go a long way toward assuring their happy future. Steve sighed deeply, feeling suddenly weary.

"Is there any other bombshell you'd care to hit me with?" Lindy asked teasingly.

Steve paused and then surprised her by nodding. Some of the happiness he'd experienced earlier vanished. There was one other decision he'd made—one not as pleasant but equally necessary.

"Should I sit down for this one?" Lindy asked,

still grinning. She slipped her arm around his waist and looked up at him.

"I don't think so."

"Well, don't keep me in suspense, big brother."

Steve regarded her soberly. "I'm leaving the Navy."

Chapter 13

Carol opened her eyes slowly. The room was dim, the blinds over the window closed. She frowned when her gaze fell on the IV stand, and she tried to raise herself.

"You're in the hospital." Steve's voice was warm and caressing.

She lowered her head back to the pillow and turned toward the sound. Steve stood at her bedside. From the ragged, tired look about him, she guessed he'd been standing there all night.

"How long have you been here?" she asked hoarsely, testing her tongue.

"Not very long."

She closed her eyes and grinned. "You never could tell a decent lie."

He brushed the hair from her cheek and his fingers lingered on her face as though he needed to touch her. She knew she should ask him to leave, but his presence comforted her. She needed him. She didn't know how he'd happened to be at Northgate Mall, but she would always be grateful he'd found her when he did.

Her hand moved to her stomach, and she flattened it there. "The baby's all right?"

Steve didn't answer her for a moment, and a sickening sense of dread filled her. Her eyes flew open. The doctor had repeatedly assured her that the baby was safe, but something might have happened while she had slept. She'd been out for hours and much of what had taken place after they arrived at the hospital remained foggy in her mind.

"Everything's fine with the pregnancy."

"Thank God," she whispered fervently.

"Dr. Stewart said you were near exhaustion." He reached for her hand and laced his fingers with hers. His thumb worked back and forth on the inside of her wrist.

"I think I could sleep for a week," Carol said, her voice starting to sound more sure. It seemed as though it had been years since she'd had a decent rest. Even before her pregnancy had been confirmed she'd felt physically and emotionally drained, as if she were running on a treadmill, working as fast as her legs would carry her and getting nowhere.

"How do you feel now?"

Carol had to think about it. "Different. I don't know how to describe it. I'm not exactly sick and I'm not in any pain, but something's not right, either."

"You should have recognized that weeks ago. According to Dr. Stewart, you've probably been feeling ill for months."

"They know what's causing the problem?" Her heart started to work doubly hard. Not until the severe attack of pain in the shopping mall had she been willing to admit something could be wrong with her.

"Dr. Stewart thinks it could be your gall bladder."

"My what?"

"Gall bladder," he repeated softly. "I'm sure he can explain it far better than I can, but from what I understand it's a pear-shaped pouch close to the liver."

Carol arched her brows at his attempt at humor and offered him a weak smile. "That explains it."

Steve grinned back at her, and for a moment everything went still. His eyes held such tenderness that she dared to hope again—dared to believe he'd discovered the truth about her and their baby. Dared to let the love that was stored in her heart shine through her eyes.

"I never thought I'd see you again," she said, and her voice quivered with emotion.

Steve lowered his gaze briefly. "I couldn't stay away. I love you too much."

"Oh, Steve, how could we do this to each other? You think such terrible things of me and I can't bear it anymore. I keep telling myself the baby and I would be better off without you, and then I feel only half alive. When we're separated, nothing feels right in my life—nothing is good."

"When I'm not with you, I'm only a shell." He raised her hand to his lips and kissed her knuckles.

Carol felt the tears gather in her eyes and she turned her head away, unwilling to have Steve witness her emotion. No man would ever be more right for her, and no man could ever be so wrong.

She heard the sound of a chair being pushed to the side of the bed. "I want us to remarry," he said firmly. "I've thought it over. In fact, I haven't thought of anything else in the past fifteen hours— and I'm convinced this is the right thing for us to do."

Carol knew it was right, too. "But what about the baby?" she whispered. "You think—"

"From this moment on, the child is mine in my

heart and in my soul. He's a part of you and that's the only important thing.''

"She," Carol corrected absently. "I'm having a girl."

"Okay…whatever you want as long as we're together.''

Carol's mind flooded with arguments, but she hadn't the strength to fight him. The intervening months would convince Steve that this child was his far better than any eloquent speeches she could give him now. By the time the baby was born, his doubts would have vanished completely. In the meantime they would find a way to settle matters—that was essential because they were both so miserable apart.

"Will you marry me, Carol, a second time?''

"I want to say yes. Everything within me is telling me it's the right thing to do…for me and for the baby. But I'm frightened, too."

"I'm going to be a good husband and father, I promise you that."

"I know you will."

"I made another decision yesterday—one that will greatly affect both our lives." His hand pressed against the side of her face and gently brushed the hair from her temple. "I'm leaving the Navy."

Carol couldn't believe her ears. The military was Steve's life; it had been his goal from the time he was a teenager. His dream. He'd never wanted to be or do anything else.

"But you love your work."

"I love you more," he countered.

"It's not an either-or situation, Steve. I've lived all these years as a Navy wife, I've adjusted."

A hint of a smile touched his face. "I won't be separated from you again."

For Steve's sake, Carol had always put on a happy face and seen him off with a cheerful wave, but she'd hated the life, dreading their months apart. Always had and always would. The promise of a more conventional marriage seemed too good to be true. Her head was swimming at the thought of him working a nine-to-five job. She wanted this—she wanted it badly.

"You're the most important person in my life. I'm getting out of the Navy so I can be the kind of husband and father I should be."

"Oh, Steve." The joy that cascaded through her at that moment brought tears to her eyes.

"I can't think of any other way to show you how serious I am."

Neither could Carol. Nevertheless his announcement worried her. Navy life was in Steve's blood, and she didn't know if he could find happiness outside the only career he'd ever known.

"Let's not make such a major decision now," she

suggested reluctantly. "There'll be plenty of time to talk about this later."

Steve's eyes filled with tenderness. "Whatever you say."

Humming softly, a nurse wandered into the room and greeted them. "Good morning."

"Morning," Carol answered.

The room was bathed in the soft light of day as the middle-aged woman opened the blinds.

"I'm sorry, but there won't be any breakfast for you this morning. Dr. Stewart will be in later, and I'm sure he'll schedule something for you to eat this afternoon."

Carol didn't feel the least bit hungry. Her appetite had been almost nonexistent for months.

"I'll check on you in an hour," the woman said on her way out the door.

Carol nodded. "Thank you." She was filled with nagging questions about what was going to happen. Naturally she hoped Dr. Stewart could give her a prescription and send her home, but she had the feeling she was being overly optimistic.

Steve must have read the doubt in her eyes because he said, "From what Dr. Stewart told me, he's going to have you complete a series of tests this morning. Following those, we'll be able to make a decision."

"What kind of tests? What kind of decision?"

"Honey, I don't know, but don't worry. I'm not leaving you—not for a minute."

Carol hated to be such a weakling, but she was frightened. "Whatever happens, whatever they have to do, I can take it," she said a little shakily.

"I know you can, love. I know you can."

As promised, for the next few hours Carol underwent several tests. She was pinched, poked and prodded and wheeled to several corners of the hospital. As Steve promised, he was with her each time they took her into another and waiting when she returned.

"Quit looking so worried," she told him, when she'd been wheeled back to her room once more. "I'm going to be fine."

"I know."

She slept after that and woke late in the afternoon. Once more Steve was at her bedside, leaning forward, his face in his hands.

"Bad news?" she asked.

He smiled and Carol could tell by the stiff way his mouth moved that the action was forced.

"What's wrong?" she demanded.

He stood and came to stand beside her. She gave him her hand, her eyes wide with fear.

"Dr. Stewart assured me that under normal conditions, gall bladder surgery is optional. But not in your case. Your gall bladder is acutely swollen and is causing several complications to vital organs. It has to be removed, and the sooner the better.''

Carol expelled her breath and nodded. She'd feared something like this, but she was young and healthy and strong; everything would be fine.

''He's called in a surgeon and they've scheduled the operating room for you first thing tomorrow morning.''

Carol swallowed her worry. ''I can handle that.''

''This isn't minor surgery, Carol. I don't think you'd appreciate me minimizing the risks.''

''No...no, I wouldn't.''

''Dr. Stewart and his associate will be back later today to explain the details of what they'll be doing. It's major surgery, but you have several things in your favor.''

She nodded, appreciating the fact that she would know precisely what the medical team would be doing to her body.

''What about the baby?''

Steve's expression tightened and he lifted his eyes from hers. ''The pregnancy poses a problem.''

''What kind of problem?''

''If the surgery could be delayed, Dr. Stewart would prefer to do that, but it can't be. Your life is at risk.''

''What about the pregnancy?'' Carol demanded.

"I'm not agreeing to anything until I hear what will happen to my baby."

Steve's eyes revealed myriad emotions. Worry and fear dominated, but there was something else—something that took her an extended moment to analyze. Something that clouded his features and ravaged his face. Regret, she decided, then quickly changed her mind. It was more than that—a deep inner sorrow, even remorse.

When Steve spoke, it was as if each word had to be tugged from his mouth. "I'm not going to coat the truth. There's a chance the anesthesia will terminate the pregnancy."

"I won't do it," she cried automatically. "The whole thing's off. I'm not doing anything that will hurt my baby."

"Carol, listen to reason…"

"No." She twisted her head so that she wouldn't have to look at him. As long as she drew a single breath there was no way she would agree to do anything that would harm her daughter.

"Honey," he whispered. "We don't have any choice. If we delay the surgery, you could die."

"Then so be it."

"No." He almost shouted the word. "There's a risk to the baby, but one we're both going to have to take. There's no other choice."

She closed her eyes, unwilling to argue with him further. Her mind was made up.

"Carol, I don't like this any better than you do."

She refused to look at him and pinched her lips together, determined not to murmur a single word. Nothing he could say would change her mind.

The silence in the room was magnified to deafening proportions.

"I love you, Carol, and I can't allow you to chance your life for a baby. If the worst happens and the pregnancy is terminated, then we'll have to accept it. There'll be other children—lots more—and the next time there won't be any question about who the father is."

If Steve had driven a stake into her heart, he couldn't have hurt her more. No words had ever been more cruel. No wonder he was so willing to tell her he'd decided to accept this child as his own. She would likely lose the baby, and believing what he did, Steve no doubt felt that was for the best.

Carol jerked her head around so fast she nearly dislocated her neck. "The next time there won't be any questions?" she repeated in a small, still voice.

"I know this is painful for you, but—"

"I want *this* baby."

"Carol, please..."

"How long have you known about this danger?" Steve looked stunned by her anger. "Dr. Stewart told me about the possibility after I brought you to the hospital yesterday.''

Exactly what she'd expected. Everything Steve had done, everything he'd said from that point on was suddenly suspect. He wanted them to remarry and he was going to leave the Navy. His reasoning became as clear as water to her: he didn't really long for a change in their life-style, nor had his offer to leave the Navy been a decision based on his desire to build a strong marital relationship. He didn't dread their separations as she always had—he'd thrived on them. But if he wasn't in the military, then he could spend his days watching her. There would be no opportunity for her to have an affair. And when she became pregnant a second time, he would have the assurance that the baby was indeed his. His offer hadn't been made from love but from fear rooted in a lack of trust.

It amazed her, now that she thought about it, that he would be willing to give up such a promising career for her. He really did love her, in his own way, but not enough. Ultimately he would regret his decision, and so would she. But by then it would be too late.

''I'm probably doing a bad job of this,'' he said, and rammed his fingers through his hair. ''I should have let Dr. Stewart explain everything to you.''

''No,'' she said dispassionately. ''What you've

told me explains a good deal. You've been completely up-front with me and I appreciate what it cost you to tell me this. I...I think it's my turn to be honest with you now.''

A dark frown contorted his features. ''Carol...''

''No, it's time you finally learned the truth. I hesitated when you asked me to marry you and there's a reason. You don't need to worry about me, Steve. You never had to. My baby's father has promised to take care of me. When my plan to trick you didn't work, I contacted him and told him I was pregnant. He thought about it for a couple of days and has decided to marry me himself. I appreciate your offer, but it isn't necessary.''

Steve looked as if she'd slipped a knife into his stomach.

''You're lying.''

''No, for once I'm telling you the truth. Go back to your life and I'll go on with mine. We'll both be far happier this way.''

He didn't move for several minutes. His hands curved around the raised railing at the side of the bed and she swore his grip was strong enough to permanently mark the bars. His eyes hardened to chips of glacial ice.

''Who is the father?'' he demanded.

Carol closed her eyes, determined not to answer.

''Who is he?''

She looked away, but his fingers closed around her chin and forced her face back toward him.

"Todd?"

She was sick of hearing that name. "No."

"Who?"

"No one you know," she shouted.

"Is he married?"

"No."

A pounding, vibrating silence followed.

"Is this what you really want?"

"Yes," she told him. "Yes...."

A year seemed to pass before she heard him leave the room. When he did, each step he took away from her sounded like nails being pounded into a coffin.

It was finished. There was no going back now. Steve Kyle was out of her life and she'd made certain he would never come back.

Carol felt as if she were walking through a thick bog, every step was hindered, her progress painstakingly slow. A mist rose from the marsh, blocking her view, and she struggled to look into the distance, seeking the light, but she was met instead by more fog.

A soft cry—like that of a small animal—reverberated around her, and it took her a minute to realize she was the one who had made the sound.

She wasn't in any pain. Not physically anyway.

The agony she suffered came from deep inside—a weight of grief so heavy no human should ever be expected to carry it. Carol couldn't understand what had happened or why she felt this crippling sense of loss.

Then it came to her.

Her baby...they couldn't delay the surgery. The fog parted and a piece of her memory slipped into place. Steve had walked away from her, and soon after he'd gone she'd suffered another attack that had doubled her over with excruciating pain. The hospital staff had called for Dr. Stewart and surgery had been arranged immediately. The option of waiting for even one day had been taken out of her hands.

Now Steve was out of her life and she'd lost her baby, too.

Moisture ran down the side of her face, but when she tried to lift her hand, she found she hadn't the strength.

A sob came, wrenched from her soul. There would be no more children for her. She was destined to live alone for the rest of her life.

"Nurse, do something. She's in pain."

The words drifted from a great distance, and she tossed her head to and fro in an effort to discover the source. She saw no one in the fog. No one.

Once more the debilitating sense of loneliness overtook her and she was alone. Whoever had been there had left her to find her own way through the darkness.

More sobs came—her own, she realized—erupting in deafening sound all around her.

Then she felt something—a hand she thought—warm and gentle, press over her abdomen. The weight of it was a comfort she couldn't describe.

"Your baby's alive," the voice told her. "Can you feel him? He's going to live and so are you!"

It was a voice of authority, a voice of a man who spoke with confidence; a voice few would question.

A familiar voice.

The dark fog started to close in again and Carol wanted to shout for it to stop. She stumbled toward the light, but it was shut off from her, and she found herself trapped in a black void, defenseless and lost. She didn't know if she would ever have the strength to escape it.

A persistent squeak interrupted Carol's sleep. A wheel far off in the distance was badly in need of oil. The irritating ruckus grew louder until Carol decided it would be useless to try to ignore it any longer.

She opened her eyes to discover Steve's sister standing over her.

"Lindy?"

"Carol, oh, Carol, you're awake."

"Shouldn't I be?" she asked. Her former sister-in-law looked as if she were about to burst into tears.

"I can't believe it. We've been so worried.... No one thought you were going to make it." Lindy cupped her hands over her mouth and nose. "We nearly lost you, Carol Kyle!"

"You did?" This was news to her. She had little memory. The dreadful pain had returned—she remembered that. And then she'd been trapped in that marsh, lost and confused, but it hadn't felt so bad. She had been hot—so terribly hot—she recalled, but there were pleasant memories there, too. Someone had called out to her from there, assured her. She couldn't place what the voice had said, but she remembered how she'd struggled to walk toward the sound of it. The voice hadn't always been comforting. Carol recalled how one time it had shouted at her, harsh and demanding. She hadn't wanted to obey it then and had tried to escape, but the voice had followed her relentlessly, refusing to leave her alone.

"How do you feel?"

"Like I've been asleep for a week."

"Make that two."

"Two?" Carol echoed, shocked. "That long?"

"All right, *almost* two weeks. It's actually been ten days. You had emergency surgery and then everything that could go wrong did. Oh, Carol, you nearly died."

"My baby's okay, isn't she?" From somewhere deep inside her heart came the reassurance that whatever else had happened, the child had survived. Carol vividly remembered the voice telling her so.

"Your baby is one hell of a little fighter."

Carol smiled. "Good."

Lindy moved a chair closer to the bed and sat down. "The doctor said he felt you'd come out of it today. You made a turn for the better around midnight."

"What time is it now?"

Lindy checked her watch. "About 9:00 a.m."

Already her eyes felt incredibly heavy. "I think I could sleep some more."

"As well you should."

Carol tried to smile. "So my daughter is a fighter.... Maybe I'll name her Sugar Ray Kyle."

"Go ahead and get some rest. I'll be here when you wake up."

Already Carol felt herself drifting off, but it was a pleasant sensation. The warm black folds closed their arms around her in a welcoming embrace.

When she stirred a second time, she discovered Lindy was at her bedside reading.

"Is this a vigil or something?" she asked, grinning. "Every time I wake up, you're here."

"I wanted to be sure you were really coming out of it," Lindy told her.

"I feel much better."

"You *look* much better."

The inside of her mouth felt like a sewer. "Do you have any idea how long it'll be before I can go home?"

"You won't. You're coming to live with Rush and me for a couple of weeks until you regain your strength. And we won't take no for an answer."

"But—"

"No arguing!" Lindy's smile softened her brook-no-nonsense tone.

"I don't deserve a friend as good as you," Carol murmured, awed by Lindy's generosity.

"We should be sisters, and you know it."

Carol chose not to answer that. She preferred to push any thoughts of her ex-husband from her mind.

"This probably isn't the time to talk about Steve."

It wasn't, but Carol didn't stop her.

"I don't know what you said to him, but he doesn't seem to think you want to see him again. Carol, he's been worried sick over you. Won't you at least talk to him?"

A lump the size of a goose egg formed in her throat. "No," she whispered. "I don't want to have anything to do with Steve. We're better off divorced."

Chapter 14

"I'm not an invalid," Carol insisted, frowning at her ex-sister-in-law as she carried her own breakfast dishes to the sink.

"But you've only been out of the hospital a week," Lindy argued, flittering around her like a mother hen protecting her smallest chick.

"For heaven's sake, sit down," Carol cried, "before you drive me crazy!"

"All right, all right."

Carol shared a knowing smile with Rush Callaghan, Lindy's husband. He was a different man than the Rush Carol had known before his marriage to Lindy. He smiled openly now. Laughed. Carol had been fond of Rush, but he'd always been so very serious—all Navy. The military wouldn't find a man more loyal than Rush, but loving Lindy had changed him—and for the better. Lindy had brought sunshine and laughter into his life and brightened his world in a wide spectrum of rainbow colors.

"Come on, Lindy," Rush said, "you can walk me to the door and kiss me goodbye."

With an eagerness that made Carol smile, her good friend escorted Rush to the front door and lingered there several minutes.

When she returned, Lindy walked blindly into the kitchen, wearing a dazed, contented grin. She plopped herself down in a chair, reached for her empty coffee cup and sighed. "He'll be gone for a couple of days."

"Are you going to suffer those Navy blues?"

"I suppose," Lindy said. She lifted her mug and rested her elbows on the table. "I'm a little giddy this morning because Rush and I reached a major decision last night." She smiled and the sun seemed to shine through her eyes. "We're going to start a family. Our first wedding anniversary is coming up soon, and we thought this would be a good way to celebrate."

"Sweet potatoes," Carol said, grinning from ear to ear. "They worked for me."

Lindy gave her a look that insinuated that perhaps

Navy Blues

Carol should return to the hospital for much-needed psychiatric treatment. "What was that?"

"Sweet potatoes. You know—yams. I heard a medical report over the news last year that reported the results of a study done on a tribe in Africa whose diet staple was sweet potatoes. The results revealed a higher estrogen level in the women and they attributed that fact to the yams."

"I see."

Lindy continued to study her closely. Carol giggled. "I'm not joking! They really work. I wanted to get pregnant and I couldn't count on anything more from Steve than Christmas Eve, so I ate enough sweet potatoes for my body to float in the hormone."

"One night did it?" Lindy's interest was piqued, although she struggled not to show it.

"Two actually—but who knows how long it would have taken otherwise. I ate that vegetable in every imaginable form—including some I wouldn't recommend. If you want, I'll loan you my collection of recipes."

A slow smile spread over Lindy's face, catching in her lovely brown eyes. "I want!"

Carol rinsed her plate and stuck it inside the dishwasher.

"Let me do that!" Lindy insisted, jumping to her feet. "Honest to goodness, Carol. You're so stubborn."

"No, please, I want to help. It makes me feel like I'm being useful." She never had been one to sit and do nothing. This period of convalescence had been troubling enough without Lindy babying her.

"You're recovering from major surgery for heaven's sake!" Steve's sister insisted.

"I'm fine."

"Now, maybe, but a week ago...."

Even now Carol had a difficult time realizing how close she'd come to losing her life. It was the voice that had pulled her back, refusing to let her slip into the darkness, the voice that had urged her to live. Something deep within her subconscious had demanded she cling to life when it would have been so easy to surrender.

"Lindy, I need to ask you something." Unexpectedly Carol's mind was buzzing with doubts about the future.

"Sure, what is it?"

"If anything were to happen to me after the baby's born—"

"Nothing's going to happen to you," Lindy argued.

"Probably not." Carol pulled out the kitchen chair and sat down. She didn't want to sound as though she had a death wish, but with the baby came a responsibility she hadn't thought of before her illness. "I don't have much in the way of family. My mother died several years ago—soon after Steve…soon after I was married. She and my father were divorced years before, and I hardly know him. He has another family and I rarely hear from him.''

Lindy nodded. ''Dr. Elgin, the surgeon, asked us to contact any close family members and Steve phoned your father. He…he couldn't come.''

''He's a busy man,'' Carol said, willingly offering an excuse for her father, the way she had for most of her life. ''But if I were to die,'' she persisted, ''there'd be no one to raise my baby.''

''Steve…''

Carol shook her head. ''No. He'll probably marry again and have his own family someday. And if he doesn't, he'll be so involved in the Navy he won't be much good for raising a child.'' It was so much to ask of anyone, even a friend as near and dear as Lindy. ''Would you and Rush consider being her guardians?''

''Of course, Carol,'' Lindy assured her warmly. ''But nothing's going to happen to you.''

Carol smiled. ''I certainly plan on living a long, productive life, but something like this surgery hits close to home.''

''I'll talk it over with Rush, but I'm sure he'll be more than willing for us to be your baby's guardians.''

"Thank you," Carol said, and impulsively hugged Lindy. Steve's family had always been good to her.

"Okay, now that that's settled, how about a hot game of gin rummy? I feel lucky."

"Sure…" Carol paused and her eyes rounded. Her hand moved to the slight curve of her stomach as her heart filled with happiness.

"Are you all right?"

"I'm fine. The baby just moved—she does that quite a bit now—but never this strong."

"Does it hurt?"

Carol shook her head. "Not in the least. I don't know how to describe it, but every time she decides to explore her little world, I get excited. In four short months I'll be holding my daughter. Oh, Lindy, I can hardly believe it…I can hardly wait."

"Have you ever considered the possibility that *she* might be a *he*?"

"Nope. Not once. The moment I decided to get pregnant, I put my order in for a girl. The least Steve could do was get that right." His name slipped out unnoticed, but as soon as it left her lips, Carol stiffened. She was doing her utmost to disentangle him from her life, peeling away the threads that were so securely wrapped around her soul. There was no going back now, she realized. She'd confirmed every insulting thing he'd ever accused her of.

The mention of Steve seemed to subdue them both.

"Have you chosen a name for the baby?" Lindy asked a little too brightly in an all too apparent effort to change the subject.

Carol dropped her gaze. She'd originally intended to name the baby Stephanie, after Steve, but she'd since decided against that. There would be enough reminders that Steve was her baby's father without using his name. "Not yet," she answered.

"And you're feeling better?"

"Much." Although she was enjoying staying with Lindy and Rush, Carol longed to go back to her own home. Now that Steve was completely out of her life, living with his sister was flirting with misery. Twice Lindy had tried to casually bring Steve into their conversation. Carol had swiftly stopped her both times, but she didn't know who it was harder on—Lindy or herself. She didn't want to hear about Steve, didn't want to think about him.

Not anymore. Not again.

"So how are you feeling, young lady?" Dr. Stewart asked as he walked into the examination room. "I'll have you know you gave us all quite a scare."

"That's what I hear." This was her first appointment to see Dr. Stewart since she'd left the hospital. She'd been through a series of visits with the surgeon, Dr. Elgin, and everything was progressing as it should with the post-surgery healing.

"And how's that little fighter been treating you lately?" he asked with an affectionate chuckle, eyeing Carol's tummy. "Is the baby moving regularly now?"

She nodded eagerly. "All the time."

"Excellent."

"She seems determined to make herself felt."

"This is only the beginning," Dr. Stewart said chuckling. "Wait a few months and then tell me what you think."

The nurse came into the room and Carol lay back on the examination table while the doctor listened for the baby's heartbeat. He grinned and Carol smiled back. Her world might be crumbling around the edges, but the baby filled her with purpose and hope for a brighter future.

"You've returned to work?"

She nodded. "Part-time for the next couple of weeks, then full-time depending on how tired I get. Despite everything, I actually feel terrific."

He helped her into an upright position. "It's little wonder after what you went through—anything is bound to be an improvement." As he spoke he made several notations in her file. "You were one sick young lady. I don't mind telling you," Dr. Stewart added, looking up from her chart, "I was greatly impressed with that young man of yours."

Carol's smile was forced and her heart lurched at the reference to Steve. "Thank you."

"He wouldn't leave your side—not for a moment. Dr. Elgin commented on the fact just the other day. We both believe it was his love that got you through those darkest hours. He was determined that you live." He paused and chuckled softly. "I don't think God Himself would have dared to claim you."

Carol dropped her gaze, not knowing how to comment.

"He's a fine young man. Navy?"

"Yes."

"Give him my regards, will you?"

Carol nodded, her eyes avoiding his.

"Continue with the vitamins and make an appointment to see me in a couple of weeks." He gently patted Carol's hand and moved out of the room.

From the doctor's office, Carol returned to work. But when she pulled into the Boeing parking lot, she sat in her car for several moments, mulling over what Dr. Stewart had told her.

It was Steve's voice that called to her in the dark fog. Steve had been the one who'd comforted her. And when she'd felt the pull of the night, it was he who had demanded she return to the light. According to Dr. Stewart, he'd refused to leave her side.

Carol hadn't known.

She was stunned. She'd purposely lied to him, wanting to hurt him for being so insensitive about the possibility of the surgery claiming their baby's life. She'd been confused and angry because so much of what he wanted for her revealed his lack of faith in her integrity.

She'd sent him away and yet he'd refused to leave her to suffer through the ordeal alone.

Before she returned to her own job section, Carol stopped off to see Lindy.

"Hi," Lindy greeted, looking up from her desk. "What did the doctor have to say?"

"Take your vitamins and see me in two weeks."

"That sounds profound."

Carol scooted a chair toward Lindy's desk and clasped her purse tightly between her hands. The action produced a wide-eyed stare from her former sister-in-law.

"Something Dr. Stewart did say was profound," Carol stated in even tones, although the information Dr. Stewart had given her had shaken her soul.

"Oh? What?"

"He told me Steve was with me every minute after the surgery. He claimed it was Steve who got me through it alive."

"He was there, all right," Lindy confirmed readily. "No one could get him to leave you. You know how stubborn he is. I think he was afraid that if he walked away, you'd die.''

''You didn't tell me that.''

''Of course I didn't! If you'll recall, I've been forbidden to even mention his name. You practically have a seizure if I so much as hint that there could be someone named Steve distantly related to either of us.''

''But I'd told him the baby wasn't his.... I sent him away.''

''You told him what?'' Lindy demanded, her eyes as round as dinner plates. ''Why? Carol, how could you? Oh, good grief—it isn't any wonder you two have problems. It's like watching a boxing match. You seem to take turns throwing punches at each other.''

''He...didn't say anything?''

''No. Steve never tells me what's going on in his life. No matter what's happened between you two, he won't say a word. I still don't know the reason you divorced in the first place. Even Rush isn't sure what happened. Steve's like that—he keeps everything to himself.''

''And he stayed with me, even after I said I wouldn't remarry him,'' Carol murmured, feeling worse by the moment.

''There will never be anyone else for him but you, Carol,'' Lindy murmured. Some of the indignation had left her, but she still carried an affronted look, as if she wanted to stand up and defend her brother.

Carol didn't need Lindy's outrage in order to feel guilty. Lying had never set well with her, but Steve had hurt her so badly. She would like to think that she'd been delirious with pain at the time and not herself, but that wasn't the case. When she'd told Steve that she was going to accept another man's marriage proposal, she'd known exactly what she was doing.

"I owe him so much," Carol murmured absentmindedly.

"According to the surgeon and Dr. Stewart, you owe Steve your life."

Carol's gaze held Lindy's. "Why didn't you say something earlier?"

Lindy tossed her hands into the air. "You wouldn't let me. Remember?"

"I know…I'm sorry." Carol felt like weeping. Lindy was right, so very right. Her relationship with Steve was like a championship boxing match. Although they loved each other, they continued to strike out in a battle of words and deeds.

It wasn't until after she got home and had time to think matters through that Carol decided what she needed to do—what she had to do.

It wouldn't be easy.

* * *

Steve read the directions on the back of the frozen dinner entrée and turned the dial on the oven to the appropriate setting. He never had been much of a cook, choosing to eat most of his meals out. Lately, however, even that was more of an effort than he wanted to make. He'd been reduced to frozen TV dinners.

While they were married, Carol had—

Steve ground his thoughts to a screeching halt as he forced the name of his ex-wife from his mind. It astonished him how easily she slipped in where he desperately didn't want her. Yet he was doing everything he could to try to forget the portion of his life that they'd shared.

But that was more easily said than done.

He hadn't asked Lindy about Carol since she'd been released from the hospital. He wanted to know if Todd Larson was giving her the time she needed from work to heal properly. The amount of control it demanded to avoid the subject of Carol with his sister depleted his energy. He was like a man lost in the middle of a desert, dying of thirst. And water was well within sight, but he dared not drink.

Carol had her own life, and now that she and the baby were safe, she was free to seek her own happiness. As he could—only there would be little contentment in his life without her.

The sound of the doorbell caught him by surprise.

He tossed the frozen dinner into the oven and headed to the front door, determined to get rid of whoever was there. He wasn't in any mood for company.

"Hello, Steve."

Carol stood on the other side of the threshold, and he was so shocked to see her that someone could have blown him over with the toot of a toy whistle.

"Carol...how are you?" he asked, his voice stiff, his body tense as though mentally preparing for pain.

"I'm doing much better."

She answered him with a gentle smile that spoke of reluctance and regret. Just looking at her tore through his middle.

"Would you like to come in?" he asked. Refusing her entry would be rude, and they'd done more than their share of hurting each other.

"Please."

He stepped aside, pressing himself against the door. She looked well, her coloring once more pink and healthy. Her eyes were soft and appealing when he dared to meet her gaze, which took effort to avoid.

Carol stood in the center of his living room, staring out the window at the panorama of the city. Steve had the impression, though, that she wasn't really looking at the view.

"Would you like something to drink?" he asked when she didn't speak immediately.

"No thanks...this will only take a moment."

Now that he'd found his bearings, Steve forced himself to relax.

"I was in to see Dr. Stewart this afternoon," she said, and her voice pitched a little as if she were struggling to get everything out. "He...he told me how you were with me after the surgery."

"Listen, Carol, if you've come to thank me, it isn't necessary. If you'd told me who the baby's father is, I would have gone for him. He could have stayed with you, but—"

"I lied," Carol interrupted, squaring her shoulders.

He let her words soak into his mind before he responded. "About what?"

"Marrying the baby's father. I told you that because I was so hurt by what you'd said."

"What I'd said?" He couldn't recall doing or saying anything to anger her. The fact was, he'd done everything possible to show her how much he loved and cared about her.

"You suggested it would be better if I did lose this child," she murmured, and her voice trembled even more, "because next time you could be certain you were the father."

She seemed to want him to respond to that.

"I remember saying something along those lines."

Carol closed her eyes as if her patience was depleted and she was seeking another share. "I couldn't take any more of your insults, Steve."

Everything he said and did was wrong when it came to Carol. He wanted to explain, but doubted that it would do any good. "My concern was for you. Any husband would have felt the same way, pregnancy or no pregnancy."

"You aren't my husband."

"I wanted to be."

"That was another insult!" she cried, and a sheen of tears brightened her eyes.

"My marriage proposal was an insult?" he shouted, hurt and stunned.

"Yes...no. The offer to leave the Navy was what bothered me most."

"Then far be it from me to offend you again." There was no understanding this woman. He was willing to give up everything that had ever been important to him for her sake, and she threw the offer back in his face with some ridiculous claim. To hear her tell it, he'd scorned her by asking her to share his life.

The silence stretched interminably. They stood only a few feet apart, but the expanse of the Grand Canyon could have stretched between them for all the communicating they were doing.

The problem, Steve recognized, was that they were both so battle scarred that it was almost impossible for them to talk to each other. Every word they muttered became suspect. No subject was safe. They weren't capable of discussing the weather without finding something to fight about.

"I didn't come here to argue with you," Carol said in weary, reluctant tones. "I wanted to thank you for everything you did. I apologize for lying to you—it was a rotten thing to do."

It was on the tip of his tongue to suggest that he'd gotten accustomed to her lies, but he swallowed the cruel barb. He'd said and done enough to cause her pain in the last couple of years—there was no reason to hurt her more. He would only regret it later. She would look at him with those big blue eyes of hers and he would see all the way to her soul and know the agony he viewed there was of his making. Her look would haunt him for days afterward.

She turned and started to walk away, and Steve knew that if he let her go there would be no turning back. His heart and mind were racing. His heart with dread, his mind with an excuse to keep her. Any excuse.

"Carol—"

Already she was at the front door. "Yes?"

"I...have you eaten?"

Her brow creased, as if food was the last thing on her mind. Her gaze was weary as though she couldn't trust him. "Not yet."

"Would you like to go out with me? For dinner?"
She hesitated.

"The last time you were at the apartment, you said something about a restaurant you wanted to try close to here," he said, reminding her. She'd come to his place with a silly button in her hand and lovemaking on her mind. Things had been bad between them then, and had gone steadily downhill ever since.

She nodded. "The Mexican Lindo."

"Shall we?"

Still she didn't look convinced. "Are you sure this is what you want?"

Now it was his turn to nod. He wanted it so much he could have wept. "Yes, I want this," he admitted.

Some of the tiredness left her eyes and a gentle smile touched her lovely face. "I want it, too."

Steve felt like leaping in the air and clicking his heels. "I'll be just a minute," he said hurriedly. He walked into his kitchen and with a quick twist of his wrist, he turned off the oven. He would toss the aluminum meal later.

For now, he had a dinner date with the most beautiful woman in the world.

Chapter 15

Elaborately decorated Mexican hats adorned the white stucco walls of the restaurant. A spicy, tangy scent wafted through the dining area as Carol and Steve read the plastic-coated menu.

Steve made his decision first.

"Cheese enchiladas," Carol guessed, her eyes linking with his.

"Right. What are you going to have?"

She set aside the menu. "The same thing—enchiladas sound good."

The air between them remained strained and awkward, but Carol could sense how desperately they were each trying to ignore it.

"How are you feeling?" Steve asked after a cumbersome moment of silence. His eyes were warm and tender and seemed to caress her every time he looked in her direction.

"A thousand times better."

He nodded. "I'm glad." He lifted the fork and absently ran his fingers down the tines.

"Dr. Stewart asked me to give you his regards," Carol said in an effort to make conversation. There were so few safe topics for them.

"I like him. He's got a lot of common sense."

"The feeling's mutual—Dr. Stewart couldn't say enough good things about you."

Steve chuckled. "You sound surprised."

"No. I know the kind of man you are." Loving, loyal, determined, proud. Stubborn. She hadn't spent five years of her life married to a stranger.

The waitress came to take their order, and returned a couple of minutes later with a glass of milk for Carol and iced tea for Steve.

"I'm pleased we have this opportunity to talk before I'm deployed," he said, and his hand closed around the tall glass.

"When will you be leaving?"

"In a couple of weeks."

Carol nodded. She was nearly six months pregnant now and if Steve was at sea for the usual three, he might not be home when the baby was born. It all depended on when he sailed.

"I used to hate it when you went to sea." The words slipped from her lips without thought. She hadn't meant to make a comment one way or the other about his tour. It was a part of his life and one she had accepted when she agreed to marry him.

"You hated my leaving?" He repeated her words as though he was certain he'd heard her incorrectly. His gaze narrowed. "You used to see me off with the biggest smile this side of the Mississippi. I always thought you were happy to get me out of your hair."

"That was what I wanted you to think," she confessed with some reluctance. "I might have been smiling on the outside, but on the inside I was dreading every minute of the separation."

"You were?"

"Three months may not seem like a long time to you, but my life felt so empty when you were on the *Atlantis*." The first few years of their marriage, Carol had likened Steve's duty to his sub to a deep affection for another woman who whimsically demanded his attention whenever she wanted him. It wasn't until later that she realized how silly it was to be jealous of a nuclear submarine. She'd done everything possible to keep occupied when he was at sea.

"But you took all those community classes," he

argued, breaking into her thoughts. "I swear you had something scheduled every night of the week."

"I had to do something to fill the time so I wouldn't go stir crazy."

"You honestly missed me?"

"Oh, Steve, how could you have doubted it?"

He flattened his hands on the table and slowly shook his head. "But I thought...I honestly believed you enjoyed it when I was away. You used to tell me it was the only time you could get anything accomplished." His voice remained low and incredulous. "My being underfoot seemed to be a detriment to all your plans."

"You had to know how I felt, or you wouldn't have suggested leaving the Navy."

Steve lowered his gaze and shrugged. "That offer was for me as much as you."

"So you could keep an eye on me—I figured that out on my own. If you held a regular nine-to-five job, then you could keep track of my every move and make sure there wasn't any opportunity for me to meet someone else."

"I imagine you found that insulting."

She nodded. "I don't know any woman who wouldn't."

A heavy silence followed, broken only by the waitress delivering their meals and reminding them that the plates were hot.

Steve studied the steaming food. "I suppose that was what you meant when you said my marriage proposal was an insult?"

Carol nodded, regretting those fiery words now. It wasn't the proposal, but what had followed that she'd taken offense to. "I could have put it a little more tactfully, but generally, yes."

Steve expelled his breath forcefully and reached for his fork. "I can't say I blame you. I guess I wasn't thinking straight. All I knew was that I loved…love you," he corrected. "And I wanted us to get married. Leaving the Navy seemed an obvious solution."

Carol let that knowledge soak into her thoughts as she ate. They were both quiet, contemplative, but the silence, for once, wasn't oppressive.

"I dreaded your coming home, too," Carol confessed partway through her meal.

Steve's narrowed gaze locked with hers, and his jaw clenched until she was sure he would damage his teeth, but he made no comment. It took her a moment to identify his anger. He'd misconstrued her comments and assumed the worst—the way he always did with her. He thought she was referring to the guilt she must have experienced upon his return. Hot frustration pooled in the pit of her stomach, but she forced herself to remain calm and explain.

"I could never tell what you were thinking when

you returned from a deployment," she whispered, her voice choked and weak. "You never seemed overly pleased to be back."

"You're crazy. I couldn't wait to see you."

"It's true you couldn't get me in bed fast enough, but I meant in other ways."

"What ways?"

She shrugged. "For the first few days and sometimes even longer, it was like you were a different man. You would always be so quiet...so detached. There was so little emotion in your voice—or your actions."

"Honey, I'd just spent a good portion of that tour four hundred feet below sea level. We're trained to speak in subdued, monotone voices. If my voice inflections bothered you, why didn't you say something?"

She dropped her gaze and shrugged. "I was so pleased to have you back that I didn't want to say or do anything to cause an argument. It was such a small thing, and I would have felt like a fool for mentioning it."

Steve took a deep breath. "I know what you mean—I couldn't very well comment on how glad you were to see me leave without sounding like an insecure jerk—which I was. But that's neither here nor there."

"I wish I'd said something now, but I was trying

so hard to be the kind of wife you wanted. Please know that I was always desperately lonely without you.''

Steve took a couple more bites, but his interest in the food had obviously waned. ''I can understand why you felt the need for...companionship.''

Carol froze and a thread of righteous anger weaved it's way down her spine. ''I'm going to forget you said that,'' she murmured, having difficulty controlling her trembling voice.

Steve looked genuinely surprised. ''Said what?''

Carol simply shook her head. They would only argue if she pressed the subject, and she didn't have the strength for it. ''Never mind.''

Her appetite gone, she pushed her plate aside. ''You used to sit and stare at the wall.''

''I beg your pardon?'' Steve was finished with his meal, too, and scooted his plate aside.

''When you came home from a tour,'' she explained. ''For days afterward, you hardly did a thing. You were so detached.''

''I was?'' Steve mulled over that bit of insight. ''Yes, I guess you're right. It always takes me a few days to separate myself from the my duties aboard the *Atlantis*. It's different aboard the sub, Carol. I'm different. When I'm home, especially after being at sea several weeks, it takes time to make the adjustment.''

"You're so unfeeling...I don't know how to explain it. Nothing I'd say or do would get much reaction from you. If I proudly showed off some project I'd completed in your absence, you'd smile and nod your head or say something like 'That's nice, dear.'"

Steve grinned, but the action revealed little amusement. "Reaction is something stringently avoided aboard the sub, too. I'm an officer. If I panic, everyone panics. We're trained from the time we're cadets to perform our duties no matter what else is happening. There's no room for emotion."

Carol chewed on the corner of her lower lip.

"Can you understand that?"

She nodded. "I wish I'd asked you about all this years ago."

"I didn't realize I behaved any differently. It was always so good to get home to you that I didn't stop to analyze my behavior."

The waitress came and took away their plates.

"We should have been honest with each other instead of trying to be what we thought the other person wanted," Carol commented, feeling chagrined that they'd been married five years and had never really understood each other.

"Yes, we should have," he agreed. "I'm hoping it isn't too late for us to learn. We could start over right now, determined to be open and honest with each other.''

"I think we should," Carol agreed, and smiled.

Steve's hand reached across the table for hers. "I'd like us to start over in other ways, too—get to know each other. We could start dating again the way we did in the beginning.''

"I think that's a good idea.''

"How about walking down to the waterfront for an ice-cream cone?" he suggested after he'd paid the tab.

Carol was stuffed from their dinner, but did not want their evening to end. Their love had been given a second chance, and she was grabbing hold of it with both hands. They were wiser this time, more mature and prepared to proceed cautiously.

"Are you insinuating that I need fattening up?" she teased, lacing her fingers with his.

"Yes," he admitted honestly.

"How can you say that?" she asked with a soft laugh. She may have lost weight with the surgery, but the baby was filling out her tummy nicely, and it was obvious that she was pregnant. "I eat all the time now. I didn't realize how sick I'd been and now everything tastes so good.''

"Cherry vanilla?''

"Ooo, that sounds wonderful. Double-decker?''

"Triple," Steve answered and squeezed her hand.

Lacing their fingers like high-school sweethearts, they strolled down to the steep hill toward the waterfront like young lovers eager to explore the world.

As he promised, Steve bought them each huge ice-cream cones. They sat on one of the benches that lined the pier and watched the gulls circle overhead.

Carol took a long, slow lick of the cool dessert and smiled when she noted Steve watching her. "I told you I've really come to appreciate my food lately."

His gaze fell to the rounded swell of her stomach. "What did Dr. Stewart have to say about the baby?"

Carol flattened her hand over her abdomen and glowed with an inner happiness that came to her whenever she thought about her child. "This kid is going to be just fine."

He darted his gaze away as though he was uncomfortable even discussing the pregnancy. "I'm pleased for you both. You'll be a good mother, Carol."

Once more frustration settled on her shoulders like a dark shroud. Steve still didn't believe the baby was his. She wasn't going to argue with him. He was smart enough to figure it out.

"Do you need anything?" he surprised her by asking next. "I'd be happy to do what I can to help. I'm sure the medical expenses wreaked havoc with your budget, and you're probably counting on that income to buy things for the baby. I'd like to pitch in, if you'd let me."

His offer touched her heart and she took a minute to swallow the tears that burned the back of her eyes at his generosity.

"Thank you, Steve, that means a lot to me, but I'm all right financially. It'll be tight for a couple of months, but nothing I can't handle. I've managed to save quite a bit over the past year."

He stood, buried his hands in his pockets and walked along the edge of the pier. Carol joined him, licking the last of the ice cream off her fingertips.

Steve looked down and smiled into her eyes. "Here," he said and used his index finger to wipe away a smudge near the corner of her mouth.

He paused and his gaze seemed to consume her face. His eyes, so dark and compelling, studied her as if she were some angelic being and he was forbidden to do anything more than gaze upon her. His brow compressed and his eyes shifted to her mouth. As if against his will, he ran his thumb along the seam of her lower lip and gasped softly when her tongue traced his handiwork. He tested the slickness with the tip of his finger, slowly sliding it back and forth, creating a delicate kind of friction.

Carol was filled with breathless anticipation. Everything around them, the sights, the sounds, the smells of the waterfront, seemed to dissolve with the feeling. He wanted to kiss her, she could feel it with every beat of her heart. But he held back.

Then, in a voice that was so low, so quiet, it could hardly be counted as sound, he said. "Can I?"

In response, Carol turned and slipped her arm around his neck. His eyes watched her, and a fire seemed to leap from them, a feral glow that excited her all the more.

She could feel the tension in him, his whole body seemed to vibrate with it.

His mouth came down on hers, open and eager. Carol groaned and instinctively swayed closer to him. His tongue plunged quickly and deeply into her mouth and she met it greedily. He tasted and teased and withdrew, then repeated the game until the savage hunger in them both had been pitched to a fevered level. Still his lips played over hers, and once the urgent need had been appeased, the kiss took on a new quality. His mouth played a slow, seductive rhythm over hers—a tune with which they were both achingly familiar.

He couldn't seem to get enough of her and even after the kiss had ended, he continued to take short, sweet samples of her lips, reluctant to part for even a minute. Finally he buried his head in the curve of her neck and took in short raspy breaths.

Carol surfaced in slow, reluctant degrees, her head

buzzing. She clung to him as tightly as he held on to her.

"We have an audience," Steve whispered with no element of alarm apparent in his tone or action.

Carol opened her eyes to find a little girl about five years old staring up at them.

"My mom and dad do that sometimes," she said, her face wrinkled with displeasure, "but not where lots of people can see them."

"I think you have a smart mom and dad," Steve answered, his voice filled with chagrin. Gently he pulled away from Carol and wrapped his arm around her waist, keeping her close to his side. "'Bye," he told the preschooler.

"'Bye," she said with a friendly wave, and then ran back to a boy who appeared to be an older brother who was shouting to gain her attention.

The sun was setting, casting a rose-red hue over the green water.

They walked back to where Steve had parked his car and he opened her door for her. "Can I see you again?" he asked, with an endearing shyness.

"Yes."

He looked almost surprised. "How about tomorrow night? We could go to a movie."

"I'd like that. Are you going to buy me popcorn?"

He smiled, and from the look in his eyes he would be willing to buy her the whole theater if he could.

Chapter 16

Steve found himself whistling as he strolled up the walkway to Carol's house. He felt as carefree as a college senior about to graduate. Grand adventures awaited him. He had every detail of their evening planned. He would escort Carol to the movies, as they'd agreed, then afterward he would take her out for something to eat. She needed to gain a few pounds and it made him feel good to spend money on her.

When they arrived back at the house, she would invite him in for coffee and naturally he would agree. Once inside it would take him ten...fifteen minutes at the most to steer her into the bedroom. He was starved for her love, famished by his need for her.

The kiss they'd shared the night before had convinced him this was necessary. He was so crazy in love with this woman that he couldn't wait another night to take her to bed. She was right about them starting over—he was willing to do that. It was the going-nice-and-slow part he objected to. He understood exactly what she intended when she decided they could start over. It was waiting for the lovemaking that confused him. Good Lord, they'd been married five years. It wasn't as if they were virgins anticipating their wedding night.

"Hi," Carol said and smiled, opening the door for him.

"Hi." Steve couldn't take his eyes off her. She was wearing the blue maternity dress he'd bought for her the day he'd followed her around like the KGB. "You look beautiful," he said in what had to be the understatement of the year. He'd heard about women having a special glow about them when they were pregnant—Carol had never been more lovely than she was at that moment.

"Do you like it?" she asked and slowly whirled around showing off the dress to full advantage. "Lindy bought it for me. She said she found it on sale and couldn't resist. It was the craziest thing because I'd tried on this very dress and loved it, but decided I really couldn't afford to be spending money on myself. She gave me a silver baby rattle, too. I have a feeling Aunt Lindy is going to spoil this baby.''

''You look…marvelous.''

''I'm getting so fat,'' she said, and chuckled. To prove her point, she scooped her hands under the soft swell of her abdomen and turned sideways to show him. She smiled, and her eyes sparkled as she jerked her head toward him and announced, ''The baby just kicked.''

''Can I feel?'' Steve had done everything he could to convince himiself this child was his. Unfortunately he knew otherwise. But he loved Carol, and he'd love her baby. He would learn to—already he truly cared about her child. Without this pregnancy there was no way of knowing if they would ever have gotten back together.

''Here.'' She reached for his hand and placed it over the top of her stomach. ''Feel anything?''

He shook his head. ''Nothing.''

''Naturally she's going to play a game of cat and mouse now.''

Steve removed his hand and flexed his fingers. Some of the happiness he'd experienced earlier seeped out of him, replaced with a low-grade despondency. He wanted her baby to be his with a desperation that threatened to destroy him. But he couldn't change the facts.

"I checked the paper and the movie starts at seven," Carol said, interrupting his thoughts.

He glanced at his watch. "We'd better not waste any time then." While Carol opened the entryway closet and removed a light sweater and her purse, Steve noted the two gallons of paint sitting on the floor.

"What are you painting?" he asked.

"The baby's room. I thought I'd tackle that project this weekend. I suddenly realized how much I have to do yet to get ready."

"Do you want any help?" He made a halfhearted offer, and wished almost immediately that he hadn't. It wasn't the painting that dissuaded him. Every time Carol so much as mentioned anything that had to do with the baby, her eyes lit up like the Fourth of July. His reaction was just as automatic, too. He was jealous, and that was the last thing he wanted Carol to know.

She closed the closet door and studied him, searching his eyes. He boldly met her look, although it was difficult, and wasn't disappointed when she shook her head. "No thanks, I've got everything under control."

"You're sure?"

"Very."

There was no fooling Carol. She might as well

have read his thoughts, because she knew and her look told him as much.

"I'm trying," he said, striving for honesty. "I really am trying."

"I know," she murmured softly.

They barely spoke on the way to the theater and Carol hardly noticed what was happening with the movie. She'd witnessed that look on Steve's face before when she started talking about the baby. So many subjects were open to them except that one. She didn't know any man more blind than Steve Kyle. If she were to stand up in the middle of the show and shout out that she was having his child, he wouldn't hear her. He'd buried his head so deep in the sand when it came to her pregnancy that his brain was plugged.

Time would teach him, if only she could hold on to her patience until then.

Steve didn't seem to be enjoying the movie any more than she was. He shifted in his seat a couple of times, crossed and uncrossed his legs and munched on his popcorn as if he were chewing bullets.

Carol shifted, too. She was almost six months pregnant and felt eight. The theater seat was uncomfortable and the baby had decided to play baseball, using Carol's ribs for batting practice.

She braced her hands against her rib cage and leaned to one side and then scooted to the other.

"Are you all right?" Steve whispered halfway through the feature film.

Carol nodded. She wanted to explain that the baby was having a field day, exploring and kicking and struggling in the tight confines of her compact world, but she avoided any mention of the pregnancy.

"Do you want some more popcorn?"

Carol shook her head. "No thanks."

Ten minutes passed in which Carol did her utmost to pay attention to the show. She'd missed so much of the plot already that it was difficult to understand what was happening.

Feeling Steve's stare, Carol diverted her attention to him. He was glaring at her abdomen, his eyes wide and curious. "I saw him move," he whispered, his voice filled with awe. "I couldn't believe it. He's so strong."

"She," Carol corrected automatically, smiling. She took his hand and pressed it where she'd last felt the baby kick. He didn't pull away but there was some reluctance in his look.

The baby moved again, and Carol nearly laughed aloud at the astonishment that played over Steve's handsome features.

"My goodness," he whispered. "I had no idea."

"Trust me," she answered, and grinned. "I didn't, either."

Irritated by the way they were disrupting the movie, the woman in the row in front of them turned around to press her finger over her lips. But when she saw Steve's hand on Carol's stomach, she grinned indulgently and whispered, "Never mind."

Steve didn't take his hand away. When the baby punched her fist on the other side of Carol's belly, she slid his hand over there. She loved the slow, lazy grin that curved up the edges of his mouth. The action caused her to smile too. She tucked her hand over his and soon they both went back to watching the action on the screen. But Steve kept his fingers where they were for the rest of the movie, gently caressing the rounded circle of her tummy.

By the time the film was over, Carol's head was resting on Steve's shoulder. Although the surgery had been weeks before, it continued to surprise her how quickly she tired. She'd worked that day and was exhausted. It irritated her that she could be so weak. Steve had mentioned getting something to eat after the movie, but she was having difficulty hiding her yawns from him.

"I think I'd better take you home," he commented once they were outside the theater.

"I'm sorry," she murmured, holding her hand to her mouth in a futile effort to hold in her tiredness.

"I'm not used to being out so late two nights running."

Steve slipped his arm around her shoulders. "Me, either."

He steered her toward his car and opened the passenger door for her. Once she was inside, he gently placed a kiss on her cheek.

She nearly fell asleep on the short ride home.

"Do you want to come in for some coffee?" she offered when he pulled up to the curb in front of her house.

"You're sure you're up to this?" he asked, looking doubtful.

"I'm sure."

Carol thought she detected a bounce to his step as he came around to help her out of the car, but she couldn't be sure. Steve Kyle said and did the most unpredictable things at times.

Once inside he took her sweater, and while he was hanging it up for her, she went into the kitchen and got down the coffee from the cupboard. Steve moved behind her and slipped his arms around her waist.

"I don't really want coffee," he whispered and gently caught her earlobe between his teeth.

"You don't?"

"No," he murmured.

His hands explored her stomach in a loving caress

and Carol felt herself go weak. "I...I wish you'd said something earlier."

"It was a pretense." His mouth blazed a moist trail down the side of her neck.

"Pretense," she repeated in a daze.

As if he were a puppet master directing her actions, Carol turned in his arms and raised her face to his, anticipating his kiss. Her whole body felt as if it were rocking with the force of her heartbeat, anticipating the touch of his mouth over hers.

Steve didn't keep her waiting long. His hands cradled her neck and his lips found hers, exploring them as though he wished to memorize their shape. She parted her mouth in welcome, and his tongue touched hers, then delicately probed deeper in a sweet, unhurried exploration that did incredible things to her. Desire created a churning, boiling pool deep in the center of her body.

His fingers slipped from her nape to tangle with her hair. Again and again, he ran his mouth back and forth over hers, pausing now and again to tease her with a fleck of his tongue against the seam of her lips. "I thought about doing this all day," he confessed.

"Oh, Steve."

His hands searched her back, grasping at the material of her dress as he claimed her mouth in a kiss that threatened to burst them both into searing flames. With a frustrated groan, he drew his arms around her front, searching. His breath came in ragged, thwarted gasps.

Carol could feel the heavy pounding of his heart and she pressed her open mouth to the hollow at the base of his throat, loving the way she could feel his pulse hammer there.

"Damn," he muttered, exasperated. "Where's the opening to this dress?"

It took Carol a moment to understand his question. "There is none."

"What?"

"I slip it on over my head…there aren't any buttons."

"No zipper?"

"None."

He muffled a groan against her neck and Carol felt the soft puffs of warm air as he chuckled. "This serves me right," he protested.

"What does?"

He didn't answer her. Instead, he cradled her breasts in his palms, bunching the material of her dress in the process. Slowly he rotated his thumb over her swollen, sensitive nipples until she gasped, first with shock and surprise, then with the sweet sigh of pleasure.

"Is it good, honey?" he asked, then kissed her,

teasing her with his tongue until she was ready to collapse in his arms.

"It's very good," she told him when she could manage to speak, although her voice was incredibly low.

"I want you." He took her hand and pressed it down over his zipper so that she could feel for herself his bulging hardness.

"Oh, Steve." She ran her long fingernails over him.

Exquisitely aroused, he made small hungry sounds and whispered in a voice that shook with desire. "Come on, honey, I want to make love in a bed."

She made a weak sound of protest. "No." It demanded every ounce of fortitude she possessed to murmur the small word.

"No?" he repeated stunned.

"No." There was more conviction in her voice this time. "So many of our discussions end up in the bedroom."

"Carol, dear God, talking was the last thing I had in mind."

"I know what you want," she whispered. "I think we should wait…it's too soon."

"Wait," he murmured, dragging in a deep breath. "Wait," he said again. "All right, if that's what you honestly want—then fine, anything you say." Reluctantly he released her. "I'm going to have to get out of here while I still can, though. Walk me to the door, will you?''

Carol escorted him to her front door and his hungry kiss revealed all his pent-up frustration.

''You're sure?'' he asked one last time, giving her a round-eyed look that would put a puppy to shame.

''No...I'm not the least bit sure,'' she admitted, and when his eyes widened even more, she laughed aloud at the excitement that flared to life so readily. ''I don't like this any better than you do,'' she told him, ''but I honestly think it's necessary. When the time's right we'll know it.''

He shut his eyes and nodded. ''I was afraid of that.''

Chapter 17

Carol woke before seven Saturday morning, determined to get an early start on painting the baby's bedroom. She dressed in a old pair of summer shorts with a wide elastic band and a Seahawk T-shirt that had once been Steve's. A western bandana knotted at the base of her skull covered her blond hair. She looked like something out of the movie *Aliens*, she decided, smiling.

Oh, well, she wouldn't be seeing Steve. She regretted turning down his offer of help now, but it was too late for second thoughts. She hadn't seen him since the night they'd gone to the movies, nor had he phoned. That concerned her a little, but she tried not to let it bother her.

He was probably angry about her not letting him spend the night. Well, for his information, she'd been just as frustrated as he was. She'd honestly wanted him to stay—in fact, she'd tossed and turned in bed for a good hour after he'd left her, mulling over her decision. It may have been the right one, but it didn't take away this ache of loneliness, or ease her own sexual frustration.

For six years the only real communication between them had been on a mattress. It was long past time they started building a solid foundation of love and trust. Those qualities were basic to a lifetime relationship, and they'd both suffered for not cultivating them.

By nine, Carol had the bedroom floor carpeted with a layer of newspapers. The windows were taped and she was prepared to do the cutting in around the corners and ceiling.

She carried the stepladder to the far side of the room and, humming softly, started brushing on the pale pink paint.

"What are you doing on that ladder?"

The voice startled her so much that she nearly toppled from her precarious perch. "Steve Kyle," she cried, violently expelling her breath. "You scared me half out of my mind."

"Sorry," he mumbled, frowning.

"What are you doing here?"

"I...I thought you could use some help." He held up a white sack. "Knowing you, you probably forgot to eat breakfast. I brought you something."

Now that she thought about it, Carol realized she hadn't had anything to eat.

"Thanks," she said grinning, grateful to see him. "I'm starved."

Climbing down the stepladder, she set aside the paint and brush and reached for the sack. "Milk," she said taking out a small carton, "and a muffin with egg and cheese." She smiled up at him and brushed her mouth over his cheek. "Thanks."

"Sit," he ordered, turning over a cardboard box as a mock table for her.

"What about you?"

"I had orange juice and coffee on the way over here." Hands on his hips, he surveyed her efforts. "Good grief, woman, you must have been at this for hours."

"Since seven," she said between bites. "It's going to be a scorcher today, and I wanted to get an early start."

He nodded absently, then turned the cap he was wearing around so that the brim pointed toward his back. Next, he picked up the paintbrush and coffee can she'd been using to hold paint. "I don't want you on that ladder, understand?"

"Aye, aye, Captain."

He responded to her light sarcasm with a soft chuckle. "Have you missed me?" he asked, turning momentarily to face her.

Carol dropped her gaze and nodded. "I thought you might be angry about the other night when you wanted to stay and—"

"Carol, no," he objected immediately. "I understood and you were right. I couldn't call—I've had twenty-four-hour duty."

Almost immediately Carol's spirits lifted and she placed the wrapper from her breakfast inside the paper sack. "Did you miss *me*?" she asked, loving the way his eyes brightened at her question.

"Come here and I'll show you how much."

Laughing, she shook her head. "No way, fellow. I'd like my baby's bedroom painted before she makes her debut." Carol noted the way Steve's face still tightened at the mention of her pregnancy and some of the happiness she'd experienced by his unexpected visit evaporated. He'd told her he was trying to accept her child and she believed him, but her patience was wearing perilously thin. After all, this child was his, too, and it was time he acknowledged the fact.

Pride drove her chin so high that the back of her neck ached. She reached for another paintbrush, her shoulders stiff with frustration. "I can do this myself, you know."

"I know," he returned.

"It isn't like I'm helpless."

"I know that, too."

Her voice trembled a little. "It isn't like you really want this baby."

An electric silence vibrated between them, arcing and spitting tension. Steve reacted to it first by lowering his brush.

"Carol, I'm sorry. I didn't mean to say or do anything to upset you. My offer to help is sincere—I'd like to do what I can, if you'll let me."

She bit into her lower lip and nodded. "I...I was being oversensitive, I guess."

"No," he hurried to correct her, "the problem is mine, but I'm dealing with it the best way I know how. I need time, that's all."

His gaze dropped to her protruding stomach and Carol saw a look of anguish flitter through his eyes, one so fleeting, so transient that for a second she was sure she was mistaken.

"Well," she said, drawing in a deep breath. "Are we going to paint or are we going to sit here and grumble at each other all day?"

"Paint," Steve answered, swiping the air with his brush, as if he were warding off pirates.

Carol smiled, then placed the back of her hand over her forehead and sighed. "My hero," she said teasingly.

By noon the last of the walls were covered and the white trim complete around the window and door.

Carol stepped back to survey their work. "Oh, Steve," she said with an elongated sigh. She slipped her arm around his waist. "It's lovely."

"I sincerely hope you get the girl you want so much, because a boy could take offense at all this pink."

"I am having a girl."

"You're sure?" He cocked his eyebrows with the question, his expression dubious.

"No-o-o, but my odds are fifty-fifty, and I'm choosing to think positive."

His arm tightened around her waist. "You've got paint in your hair," he said, looking down at her.

Wrinkling her nose, she riffled her fingers through her bangs. Steve's hand stopped her. His eyes lovingly stroked her face as if he meant to study each feature and commit it to memory. His gaze filled with such longing, such adoration that Carol felt as if she were some heavenly creature he'd been forbidden to touch. He raised his hand to her mouth and she stopped breathing for a moment.

His touch was unbelievably delicate as he rubbed the back of his knuckles over her moist lips. He released her and backed away, his breath audible.

Carol lifted her hand to the side of his face and

he closed his eyes when the tips of her fingers grazed his cheek.

"Thank you for being here," she whispered. "Thank you for helping."

"I always want to be with you." He placed his hand over hers, intertwining their fingers. Tenderly, almost against his will, he lowered his knuckles to her breast, dragging them across the rigid, sensitive tip. Slowly. Gently. Back and forth. Again and again.

Carol sucked in her breath at the wild sensation that galloped through her blood. Her control was slipping. Fast. She felt weak, as though she would drop to the floor, and yet she didn't let go of his hand, pinning it against her throbbing nipple.

"How does that feel?" he asked, and he rotated his thumb around and around, intensifying the pleasure.

"...so good," she told him, her voice husky and barely audible.

"It's good for me, too."

His eyes were closed. As Carol watched his face harden with desire she knew her features were equally sharp.

He kissed her then, and the taste of him was so sweet, so incredibly good. His lips teased hers, his tongue probing her mouth, tracing first her upper and then her lower lip in a leisurely exercise. The kiss grew sweeter yet, and deeper.

Steve broke away and pressed his forehead against hers while taking in huge, ragged puffs of air. "There's something you should know."

"What?" She wrapped her hands around his middle, craving the feel of his body against her own.

"The orders for the *Atlantis* came in. I have to leave tomorrow."

Carol went stock-still. "Tomorrow?"

"I'm sorry, honey. I'd do anything I could to get out of this, but I can't."

"I…know."

"I got some Family-grams so you can let me know when the baby's born."

Carol remembered completing the short telegram-like messages while they were married. She was allowed to send a handful during the course of a tour, but under strict conditions. She wasn't allowed to use any codes, and she was prohibited from relaying any unpleasant news. She had forty-six words to tell him everything that was happening in her life. Forty-six words to tell him when his daughter was born, forty-six words to convince him this baby was his.

His hand slipped inside the waistband of her summer shorts and flattened over the baby. "I'll be waiting to hear."

Carol didn't know what to tell him. The baby could very well be born while he was away. It all depended on his schedule.

"I'd like to be here for you."

"I'll be fine.... Both of us will." Carol felt as if she was going to dissolve into tears, her anguish was so keen. Her hand reached for his face and she traced his eyebrows, the arch of his cheek, his nose and his mouth with fingers that trembled with the strength of her love.

His hands slid behind her and cupped her buttocks, lifting her so that the junction between her thighs was nestled against the strong evidence of his desire.

"I want to make love," she whispered into his mouth, and then kissed him.

He shut his eyes. "Carol, no—you were right, we should wait. We've done this too often before...we..."

She hooked her left leg around his thigh and felt a surge of triumph at the shudder that went through him.

"Carol..."

Before he could think or move, she jerked the T-shirt off her head and quickly disposed of her bra. Her mouth worked frantically over his, darting her tongue in and out of his mouth, kissing him with a hunger that had been building within her for months. Her fingers worked feverishly at the buttons of his shirt. Once it was unfastened, she pulled his shirttails free of his waistband and bared his chest. Having achieved her objective, she leaned toward him just enough so that her bare breasts grazed his chest.

The low rumbling sound in Steve's throat made her smile. Slowly then, with unhurried ease, she swayed her torso, taking her pleasure by rubbing her distended nipples over the tense muscles of his upper body.

Steve's breathing came in short, rasping gasps as he spoke. "Maybe I was a bit hasty..."

Carol locked her hands behind his head. "How long will you be gone?" she asked, knowing full well the answer.

"Three months."

"You were too hasty."

"Does this mean...you're willing?"

"I was willing the other night."

"Oh, dear God, Carol, I want you so much."

She rubbed her thigh over his engorged manhood and he groaned. "I know what you want." She kissed him with all the pent-up longings of her heart. "I want you, too. Do you have any idea how much?"

He darted his tongue over one rigid nipple, feasting and sucking at her until she gave a small cry.

He lifted his head and chuckled. "Good, then the feeling's mutual."

With that, he swung her into his arms and carried her into the bedroom. Very gently he laid her atop the mattress and leaned over her, his upper body pinning her to the bed.

He stared down at her and his eyes darkened, but not with passion. It was something more, an emotion she couldn't readily identify.

"Will I...is there any chance I'll hurt the baby?" He whispered the question, his gaze narrowed and filled with concern.

"None."

He sighed his relief. "Oh, Carol, I love you so much."

She closed her eyes and directed his mouth to hers. She loved him, too, and she was about to prove how much.

Carol woke an hour before the alarm was set to ring. Steve slept soundly at her side, cuddling her spoon-fashion, his hand cupping the warm underside of her breast.

They'd spent the lazy afternoon making slow, leisurely love. Then they'd showered, eaten and made love again, with the desperation that comes of knowing it would be three months before they saw each other again.

It was morning. Soon he would be leaving her again. A lump of pain began to unflower inside her. It was always this way when Steve left. For years she'd hid her sorrow behind a cheerful smile, but she couldn't do that anymore. She couldn't disguise how weak and vulnerable she was without him.

Not again.

When it became impossible to hold back the tears, she silently slipped from the bed, donned her robe and moved into the kitchen. Once there, she put on a pot of coffee just so she'd be doing something.

Steve found her sitting at the table with a large pile of tissues stacked next to her coffee cup. She looked up at him, and sobbed once, and reached for another Kleenex.

"G-g-good m-morning," she blubbered. "D-did you sleep well?"

Obviously bewildered, Steve nodded. "You didn't?"

"I s-slept okay."

Watching her closely, he walked over to the table. "You're crying."

"I know that," she managed between sobs.

"But why?"

If he wasn't smart enough to figure that out then he didn't deserve to know.

"Carol, are you upset because I'm leaving?"

She nodded vigorously. "Bingo—give the man a Kewpie doll."

He knelt down beside her, took her free hand and kissed the back of it. He rubbed his thumb over her knuckles and waited until she swallowed and found her voice.

"I hate it when you have to leave me," she confessed when she could talk. "Every time I think we're getting somewhere you sail off into the sunset."

"I'm coming back."

"Not for three months." She jerked the tissue down both sides of her face. "I always c-cry when you go. You just never see me. This t-time I can't...h-hold it in a minute longer."

Steve knelt in front of her and wrapped his arms around her middle. With his head pressed over her breast, one hand rested on top of her rounded stomach.

"I'll be back, Carol."

"I...know."

"But this time when I return, it'll be special."

She nodded because speaking had become impossible.

"We'll have a family."

She sucked in her breath and nodded.

"Dammit, Carol, don't you know that I hate leaving you, too?"

She shrugged.

"And worse, every time I go, I regret that we aren't married. Don't you think we should take care of that next time?"

She hiccuped. "Maybe we should."

Chapter 18

"This works out great," Lindy said, standing in line for coffee aboard the ferry *Yakima* as it eased away from the Seattle wharf, heading toward Bremerton. "You can drop me off at Susan's and I can ride home with Rush. I couldn't have planned this any better myself."

"Glad to help," Steve answered, but his thoughts weren't on his sister. Carol continued to dominate his mind. He'd left her only a couple of hours earlier and it felt as if years had passed—years or simply minutes, he couldn't decide which.

She'd stood on the front porch as he walked across the lawn to his car. The morning sunlight had silhouetted her figure against the house. Tears had brightened her eyes and a shaky smile wobbled over her mouth. When he'd opened the car door and looked back, she'd raised a hand in silent farewell and done her best to send him off with a proud smile.

Steve had stood there paralyzed, not wanting to leave her, loving her more than he thought it was possible to care about anyone. His gaze centered on her abdomen and the child she carried and his heart lurched with such pain that he nearly dropped to his knees. There stood Carol, the woman he loved and would always love, and she carried another man's child. The anguish built up inside him like steam ready to explode out of a teakettle. But as quickly as the emotion came, it left him. The baby was Carol's, a part of her, an innocent. This child deserved his love. It shouldn't matter who the father was. If Steve was going to marry Carol—which he fully intended to do—she came as part of a package deal. Carol and the baby. He sucked in his breath, determined to do his best for them both.

Now, hours later, the picture of her standing there on the porch continued to scorch his mind.

"Lindy," he said, as they reached a table, "I need you to do something for me."

"Sure. Anything."

Steve pulled out his checkbook and set it on the

table. "I want you to go to the J.C. Penney store and buy a crib, and a few other things."

"Steve, listen…"

"The crib's called the Jenny Lind—at least I think it was." The picture of Carol running her hand over the railing that day he'd followed her came to his mind. "It's white, I remember that much. I don't think you'll have any trouble knowing which one I mean once you see their selection."

"I take it you want the crib for Carol?"

"Of course. And while you're there, pick out a high chair and stroller and whatever else you can find that you think she could use."

"Steve, no."

"No!" He couldn't believe his sister. "Why the hell not?"

"When I agreed to do you a favor, I thought you wanted me to pick up your cleaning or check on the apartment—that sort of thing. If you want to buy things for Carol, I'm refusing you point-blank. I won't have anything to do with it."

"Why?" Lindy and Carol were the best of friends. His sister couldn't have shocked him more if she'd suggested he leap off the ferry.

"Remember the dress?" Lindy asked, and her chest heaved with undisguised resentment. "I felt like a real heel giving her that, and worse, lying about it." Her face bunched into a tight frown.

"Carol was as excited as a kid at Christmas over that maternity dress, and I had to tell her I'd seen it on sale and thought of her and how I hoped against hope that it would fit." She paused and glared at him accusingly. "You know I'm not the least bit good at lying. It's a wonder Carol didn't figure it out. And if I didn't feel bad enough about the dress, the rattle really did it."

Steve frowned, too. He'd asked Lindy to make up some story about the dress and the toy so that Carol wouldn't know he'd been following her that afternoon. Those had been dark days for him—and for Carol.

"Did you know," Lindy demanded, cutting into his thoughts and waving her finger under his nose, "Carol got all misty over that silver rattle?" The look she gave Steve accused him of being a coward. "*I* nearly started crying by the time she finished."

Steve's hand cupped the Styrofoam container of coffee. "I'm glad she liked it."

"It was the first thing anyone had given her for the baby, and she was so pleased that she could barely talk." Lindy paused and slowly shook her head. "I felt like the biggest idiot alive to take credit for that."

"If you'll recall, sister dearest, Carol didn't want to have anything to do with me at the time."

Lindy's eyes rounded with outrage. "And little wonder. You are so dense sometimes, Steve Kyle."

Steve ignored his sister's sarcasm and wrote out a check, doubling the amount he'd originally intended. "Buy her a bunch of baby clothes while you're at it...and send her a huge bouquet of roses when she's in the hospital, too."

"Steve...I don't know."

He refused to argue with her. Instead, he tore off the check, and slipped it across the table.

Lindy took it and studied the amount. She arched her eyebrows and released a soft, low whistle. "I'm not hiding this. I'm going to tell Carol all these gifts are from you. I refuse to lie this time."

"Fine...do what you think is best."

Steve watched as she folded the check in half and stuck it inside a huge bag she called her purse.

"Actually you may be sorry you trusted me with this task later," Lindy announced, looking inordinately pleased about something.

She said this with a soft smile, and her eyes sparkled with mischief.

"Why's that?"

Lindy rested her elbows on the tabletop and sighed. "Rush and I are planning to start our family."

The thought of his little sister pregnant did funny things to Steve. She was ten years younger than he was and he'd always thought of her as a baby herself. An equally strange image flittered into this mind— one of his friend Rush holding an infant in his arms. The thought brought a warm smile with it. When it came to the Navy, Rush knew everything there was to know. Every rule, every regulation—he loved military life. Rush was destined to command ships and men. But when it came to babies—why, Rush Callaghan wouldn't know one end from the other. One thing Steve did know about his friend, though—he knew Rush would love his children with the same intensity that he loved Lindy. Any brother and uncle-to-be couldn't ask for anything more.

"Rush will be a good father," Steve murmured, still smiling.

"So will you," Lindy countered.

Blood drained from his heart and brain at his sister's comment. "Yes," Steve admitted, and the word felt as if it had been ripped from his soul. He was going to love Carol's child; he accepted the baby then as surely as he knew the moon circled the earth. When the little one was born, he was going to be as proud and as pleased as if she were his own seed.

"Yes," he repeated, stronger this time, his heart throbbing with a newly discovered joy. "I plan on taking this parenting business seriously."

"Good," Lindy said, and opened her purse once

more. She drew out a plastic dish and spoon. "I take it you and Carol are talking to each other now."

Smiling, Steve took a sip of his coffee and nodded, thinking about how well they'd "communicated" the day before. "You could say that," he answered, leaning back in his chair, content in the knowledge that once he returned they would remarry.

"There were times when I was ready to give up on you both," Lindy said, shaking her head. "I don't know anyone more stubborn than you. And Carol's so damn proud; there's no reasoning with her, either."

They'd both learned lessons in those areas. Painful ones.

"Take care of her for me, Lindy," he said, his eyes appealing to his sister. "I'm worried about her. She's so fragile now, delicate in body and spirit."

"I don't think she'll be working much longer, but I'll make a point of stopping in and seeing her as often as I can without being obvious about it."

Her job had been an area they'd both avoided discussing, because ultimately it involved Todd. As much as possible, Steve avoided all thoughts of the sporting good store where Carol was employed.

"I'd appreciate that," he murmured.

"If you think it's necessary, I could suggest picking her up and driving her to work with me."

"That's miles out of your way."

"No, it isn't," she returned, giving him an odd look. "Rush's and my apartment is less than a mile from Carol's place. In fact, I drive right past her street on my way to work anyway. It wouldn't be any trouble to swing by and pick her up."

"True, but Larson's is the opposite direction from the Boeing plant."

"Larson's? What's Larson's?"

"Larson's Sporting Goods where Carol works." Even saying it brought an unreasonable surge of anger. It had always bothered him to think of Carol having anything to do with the store.

"Carol doesn't work at a sporting goods store. She works for Boeing," Lindy informed him crisply, looking at him as though he'd recently landed from Mars. "She's been there over a year now."

"Boeing?" Steve repeated. "She works for Boeing? I...I didn't know that."

"Is Larson's the place she used to work?"

Steve nodded, wondering how much his sister knew about Carol's relationship with the owner.

"I think she mentioned it once. As I recall, they were having lots of financial troubles. She was putting in all kinds of extra hours and not getting paid. Not that it mattered, she told me. The couple who owned the place were friends and she was doing what she could to help out. I understand they're still in business. Carol never told me why she decided to change jobs.''

Steve chewed on that information. Apparently for all their talk about honest communication they'd done a poor job of it. Again.

Lindy removed the lid from the Tupperware dish and started stirring some orange concoction that faintly resembled mashed carrots.

''Good Lord, that looks awful.''

''This?'' She pointed the spoon at the container. ''Trust me, it's dreadful stuff.''

''What is it?''

Lindy's gaze linked with his. ''You mean you don't know?''

''If I did, do you think I'd be asking?''

''It's sweet potatoes.''

''Sweet potatoes?'' he echoed, wrinkling his nose. ''What are you doing eating them at this time of year? I thought they were a holiday food.''

''I just told you.''

''No, you didn't.'' He didn't know what kind of guessing game Lindy was playing now, but apparently he'd missed some important clues.

''Rush and I are trying to get me pregnant.''

''Congratulations, you already told me that.''

''That's why I'm eating the sweet potatoes,'' Lindy went on to explain in a voice that was slow and clear, as though she were explaining this to a preschooler.

Steve scratched the area behind his left ear. "Obviously I'm missing something here."

"Obviously!"

"Well, don't keep me in suspense. You want to have a baby so you're eating sweet potatoes."

Lindy nodded. "Three times a day. At least, that was what Carol recommended."

"Why would she do that?"

Lindy offered him another one of those looks usually reserved for errant children or unusually dense adults. "Because she told me how well eating this little vegetable worked for her."

Steve's brow folded into a wary frown.

"Apparently she heard this report on the radio about yams raising a woman's estrogen level and she ate them by the bowlful getting ready for Christmas Eve with you." Lindy reached inside her purse and pulled out several index cards. "She was generous enough to copy down some recipes for me. How does sweet potato and ham casserole sound?" she asked, and rolled her eyes. "I don't think I'll be sampling that."

"Sweet potatoes," he repeated.

Lindy's gaze narrowed to thin slits. "That's what I just got done saying."

If she'd slammed a hammer over his head, the ef-

fect would have been less dramatic. Steve's heart felt
as if it was about to explode. His mind whirled at
the speed of a thousand exploding stars. A super-
nova—his own. Everything made sense then. All the
pieces to the bizarre and intricate puzzle slipped
neatly into place.

Slowly he rose to his feet, while bracing his hands
against the edge of the table. His gaze stretched toward Seattle and the outline of the city as it faded
from view.

"Steve?" Lindy asked, concern coating her voice.
"Is something wrong?"

He shook his head. "Lindy," he said reaching for
her hand and pumping it several times. "Lindy. Oh,
Lindy," he cried, his voice trembling with emotion.
"I'm about to become a father."

Chapter 19

An overwhelming sense of frustration swamped Steve as the *Atlantis* sailed out of Hood Canal. As he sat at his station, prepared to serve his country for another tour, two key facts were prominent in his mind. The first was that he was soon to become a father and the second, that it would be three interminable months before he could talk to Carol.

He'd been a blind fool. He'd taken a series of circumstantial evidence about Carol's pregnancy and based his assumption solely on a series of events he'd misinterpreted. He remembered so clearly the morning he'd made his less-than-brilliant discovery. He'd gone into Carol's living room and sat there, his heart and mind rebelling at what he'd discovered...what he thought he'd learned.

Carol had come to him warm from bed, her eyes filled with love and laughter. He'd barely been able to tolerate the sight of her. He recalled the stunned look she'd given him when he first spoke to her. The shock of his anger had made her head reel back as though he'd slapped her. Then she'd stood before him, her body braced, her shoulders rigid, the proud tilt of her chin unyielding while he'd blasted his accusations at her like fiery balls from a hot cannon.

He'd been so confident. The sweet potatoes were only the beginning. There was the knitting and the milk and a hundred little things she'd said and done that pointed to one thing.

His heart ached at the memory of how she'd swallowed her self-respect and tried to reason with him. Her hand had reached out to him, implored him to listen. The memory of the look in her eyes was like the merciless sting of a whip as he relived that horrible scene.

Dear God, the horrible things he'd said to her.

He hadn't been able to stop taunting her until she'd told him what he wanted to hear. Repeatedly he'd shouted at her to confirm what he believed until she'd finally admitted he was too smart for her.

Steve closed his eyes to the agony that scene produced in his mind. She'd silently stood there until her voice had come in desperate, throat-burning rasps that sounded like sobs. That scene had been shockingly similar to another in which he'd set his mind based on a set of circumstances and refused to believe her.

Steve rubbed a hand wearily across his face. Carol had never had an affair with Todd. She'd tried to tell him, begged him to believe her, and he'd refused.

"Oh, God," he whispered aloud, tormented by the memory. He buried his face in his hands. Carol had endured all that from him and more.

So much more.

Carol was miserable. She had six weeks of this pregnancy left to endure and each day that passed seemed like a year. Next time she decided to have a baby, she was going to plan the event so that she wouldn't spend the hottest days of the summer with her belly under her nose.

She no longer walked—she waddled. Getting in and out of a chair was a major production. Rolling over in bed was like trying to flip hotcakes with a toothpick. By the time she made it from one position to another, she was panting and exhausted.

It was a good thing Steve wasn't around. She was tired and irritable and ugly. So ugly. If he saw her like this he would take one look and be glad they were divorced.

The doorbell chimed and Carol expelled her breath, determined to find a way to come to a standing position from the sofa in a ladylike manner.

"Don't bother to get up," Lindy said, letting herself in the front door. "It's only me."

"Hi," Carol said, doing her best to smile, and failing.

"How do you feel?"

She planted her hands on her beach-ball-size stomach. "Let me put it this way—I have a much greater appreciation of what my mother went through. I can also understand why I'm an only child!"

Lindy giggled and plopped down on the chair. "I can't believe this heat," she said, waving her hand in front of her face.

"*You* can't! I can't see my feet anymore, but I swear my ankles look like tree trunks." She held one out for Lindy's inspection.

"Yup—oak trees!"

"Thanks," Carol groaned. "I needed that."

"I have something that may brighten your day. A preordered surprise."

With an energy Carol envied, Steve's sister leaped out of the chair and held open the front door.

"Okay, boys," she cried. "Follow me."

Two men marched through the house carrying a huge box.

"What's that?" Carol asked, struggling to get out

of her chair, forgetting her earlier determination to be a lady about it.

"This is the first part of your surprise," Lindy called from the hallway.

Carol found the trio in the baby's bedroom. The oblong shaped box was propped against the wall. "A Jenny Lind crib," she murmured, reading the writing on the outside of the package. For months, every time she was in the J.C. Penney store she'd looked at the Jenny Lind crib. It was priced far beyond anything she could afford, but she hadn't seen any harm in dreaming.

"Excuse me," the delivery man said, scooting past Carol.

She hadn't been able to afford a new crib and had borrowed one from a friend, who'd promised to deliver it the following weekend.

"Lindy, I can't allow you to do this," Carol protested, although her voice vibrated with excitement.

"I didn't." She looked past Carol and pointed to the other side of the bedroom. "Go ahead and put the dresser there."

"Dresser!" Carol whirled around to find the same two men carrying in another huge box. "This is way too much."

"This, my dear, is only the beginning," Lindy told her, and her smile was that of a Cheshire cat.

"The beginning?"

One delivery man was back, this time with a mattress and several sacks.

Rush followed on the man's heels, carrying a toolbox in his hand. "Have screwdriver, will travel," he explained, grinning.

"The stroller, high chair and car seat can go over in that corner," Lindy instructed with all the authority of a company foreman.

Carol stood in the middle of the bedroom with her hand pressed over her heart. She was so overcome she couldn't speak.

"Are you surprised?" Lindy asked, once the delivery men had completed their task.

Carol nodded. "This isn't from you?"

"Nope. My darling brother gave me specific instructions on what he wanted me to buy for you—right down to the model and color. Before the *Atlantis* sailed he wrote out a check and listed the items he wanted me to purchase. Rush and I had a heyday in that store."

"Steve had you do this?" Carol pressed her lips tightly together and exhaled slowly through her nose in an effort to hold in the emotion. She missed him so much; each day was worse than the one before. The morning he'd left, she'd cried until her eyes burned. He probably wouldn't be back in time for the baby's birth. But even if he was, it really wouldn't matter because Steve Kyle was such an id-iot, he still hadn't figured out this child was his own.

"And while we're on the subject of my dim-witted brother," Lindy said, turning serious, "I think you should know he was the one who bought you the maternity dress and the rattle, too."

"Steve did?"

Lindy nodded. "You two were going through a rough period and he didn't think you'd accept them if you knew he was the one who bought them."

"We're always going through a rough period," Carol reported sadly.

"I wouldn't say that Steve is so dim-witted," Rush broke in, holding up the instructions for assem-bling the crib. "Otherwise, he'd be the one trying to make sense out of this instead of me."

"Consider this practice, Rush Callaghan, since you'll be assembling another one in a few months."

The screwdriver hit the floor with a loud clink. "Lindy," Rush breathed in a burst of excitement. "Does this mean what I think it does?"

Steve wrote a journal addressed to Carol every day. It was the only thing that kept him sane. He poured out his heart and begged her forgiveness for being so stupid and so blind. It was his insecurities and doubts that had kept him from realizing the truth. Now that he'd accepted what had always been right before his eyes, he was astonished. No man had ever been so obtuse.

Every time Steve thought about Carol and the baby, which was continually, he would go all soft inside and get weak in the knees. Steve didn't know what his men thought. He wasn't himself. His mood swung from high highs to lower lows and back again. All the training he'd received paid off because he did his job without pause, but his mind was several thousand miles away in Seattle, with Carol and his baby.

His baby.

He repeated that phrase several times each night, letting the sound of it roll around in his mind, comforting him so he could sleep.

Somehow, someway, Steve was going to make this up to Carol. One thing he did know—the minute he was back home, he was grabbing a wedding license and a chaplain. They were getting married.

The last day that Carol was scheduled to work, the girls in the office held a baby shower in her honor. She was astonished by their generosity and humbled by what good friends she had.

Because she couldn't afford anything more than a three-month leave of absence, she was scheduled to return. A temporary had been hired to fill her position and Carol had spent the week training her.

"The shower surprised you, didn't it?" Lindy commented on the way out to the parking lot.

"I don't think I realized I had so many friends."

"This baby is special."

Carol flattened her hands over her abdomen. "Two weeks, Lindy. Can you believe in just two short weeks, I'll be holding my own baby?"

"Steve's due home around that time."

Carol didn't dare to hope that Steve could be with her when her time came. Her feelings on the subject were equally divided. She wanted him, needed him, but she would rather endure labor alone than have Steve with her, believing she was delivering another man's child.

"He'll be here," Lindy said with an unshakable confidence.

Carol bit into her lower lip and shook her head. "No, he won't. Steve Kyle's got the worst timing of any man I've ever known."

Carol let herself into the house and set her purse down. She ambled across the living room and caught a glimpse of herself in the hallway mirror as she walked toward the baby's bedroom. She stopped, astonished at the image that flashed back at her.

She looked as wide as a battleship. Everyone had been so concerned about the weight she lost when she'd been so sick. Well, she'd gained all that back and more. She'd become a walking, breathing Goodyear blimp.

Her hair needed washing and hung in limp blond strands, and her maternity top was spotted with dressing from the salad she'd eaten at lunch. She looked and felt like a slob. And she felt weird. She didn't know how to explain it. Her back ached and her feet throbbed.

Tired, hungry and depressed, she tried to lift her spirits by strolling around the baby's room, gliding her hand over the crib railing and restacking the neatly folded diapers.

According to Lindy and Rush, the *Atlantis* was due into port any day. Carol was so anxious to see Steve. She needed him so much. For the past two years, she'd been trying to convince herself she could live a good life without him. It took days like this one—when the sky had been dark with thunderclouds all afternoon, she'd gained two pounds that she didn't deserve and she felt so...so pregnant—to remind her how much she did need her ex-husband.

The doorbell chimed once, but before Carol could make it halfway across the living room, the front door flew open.

"Carol." Steve burst into the room and slowly dropped his sea bag to the floor when he saw her. His eyes rounded with shock.

Carol knew she looked dreadful.

"Honey," he said, taking one step toward her. "I'm home."

"Steve Kyle, how could you do this to me?" she cried and unceremoniously burst into tears.

Chapter 20

Steve was so bewildered by Carol's tears that he stood where he was, not moving, barely thinking, unsure how to proceed. Handling a pregnant woman was not something listed in the Navy operational manual.

"Go away," she bellowed.

"You want me to leave?" he asked, his voice tight and strained with disbelief. This couldn't be happening—he was prepared to fall at her knees, and she was tossing him out on his ear!

With hands held protectively over her face, Carol nodded vigorously.

For three months he'd fantasized about this moment, dreamed of holding her in his arms and kissing her. He'd envisioned placing his hands over her extended belly and begging her and the baby's forgiveness. The last thing he'd ever imagined was that she wouldn't even listen to him. He couldn't let her do it.

Cautiously, as though approaching a lost and frightened kitten, Steve advanced a couple of steps.

Carol must have noticed because she whirled around, refusing to face him.

"I...I know the baby's mine," he said softly, hoping to entice her with what he'd learned before sailing.

In response, she gave a strangled cry of rage. "Just go. Get out of my house."

"Carol, please, I love you...I love the baby."

That didn't appease her, either. She turned sideways and jerked her index finger toward the door.

"All right, all right." Angry now, he stormed out of the house and slammed the door, but he didn't feel any better for having vented his irritation. Fine. If she wanted to treat him this way, she could do without the man who loved her. Their baby could do without a father!

He made it all the way to his car, which was parked in the driveway. He opened the door on the driver's side and paused, his gaze centered on the house. The frustration nearly drowned him.

Hell, he didn't know what he'd done that was so terrible. Well, he did…but he was willing to make it up to her. In fact, he was dying to do just that.

He slammed the car door and headed back to the house, getting as far as the front steps. He stood there a couple of minutes, jerked his hand through his hair hard enough to bruise his scalp, then returned to his car. It was obvious his presence wasn't sought or appreciated.

Not knowing where else to go, Steve drove to Lindy's.

Rush opened the door and Steve burst past him without a word of greeting. If anyone understood Carol it was his sister, and Steve needed to know what he'd done that was so wrong, before he went crazy.

"What the hell's the matter with Carol?" he demanded of Lindy, who was in the kitchen. "I was just there and she kicked me out."

Lindy's gaze sought her husband's, then her eyes widened with a righteousness that was barely contained. "All right, Steve, what did you say to her this time?"

"Terrible things like I loved her and the baby. She wouldn't even look at me. All she could do was cover her face and weep." He started pacing in a kitchen that was much too small to hold three people, one of whom refused to stand still.

"You're sure you didn't say anything to insult her?"

"I'm sure, dammit." He splayed his fingers through his hair, nearly uprooting a handful.

Once more Lindy looked to Rush. "I think I better go over and talk to her."

Rush nodded. "Whatever you think."

Lindy reached for her purse and left the apartment.

"Women," Steve muttered. "I can't understand them."

"Carol's pregnant," Rush responded, as though that explained everything.

"She's been pregnant for nine months, for God's sake. What's so different now?"

Rush shrugged. "Don't ask me." He walked across the kitchen, opened the fridge and took out a beer, silently offering it to Steve.

Steve shook his head. He wasn't interested in drinking anything. All he wanted was for this situation to be squared away with Carol.

Rush helped himself to a beer and moved into the living room, claiming the recliner. A slow smile spread across his face. "In case you haven't heard, Lindy's pregnant."

Steve stopped pacing long enough to share a grin with his friend. "Congratulations."

"Thanks. I'm surprised you didn't notice."

"Good grief, man, she could only be a few months along."

"Not her," Rush teased. "Me. The guys on the *Mitchell* claim I've got that certain glow about me."

Despite his own troubles, Steve chuckled. He paused, standing in the middle of the room, and checked his watch. "What could be taking Lindy so long? She should have phoned long before now."

Rush studied his own timepiece. "She's only been gone a few minutes. Relax, will you?"

Steve honestly tried. He sat on the edge of the sofa and draped his hands over his bent knees. "I suppose I'm only getting what I deserve." His fingers went through his hair once more. If this continued he would be bald before morning.

The national news came on and Rush commented on a recent senate vote. Hell, Steve didn't even know what his friend was talking about. Didn't care, either.

The phone rang and Steve bounced off the sofa as if the telephone had an electronic device that sent a shot of electricity straight through him.

"Answer that," Rush said, chuckling. "It might be a phone call."

Steve didn't take time to say something sarcastic. "Lindy?" he demanded.

"Oh, hi, Steve. Yes, it's Lindy."

"What's wrong with Carol?"

"Well, for one thing she's having a baby."

"Everyone keeps telling me that. It isn't any deep, dark secret, you know. Of course she's having a baby. My baby!"

"I mean she's having the baby *now*."

"Now?" Steve suddenly felt so weak, he sat back down. "Well, for God's sake she should be at the hospital. Have you phoned the doctor? How far apart are the contractions? What does she plan to do about this?"

"Which question do you want me to answer first?"

"Hell, I don't know." His voice sounded like a rusty door hinge. His knees were shaking, his hands were trembling and he'd never felt so unsure about anything in his life.

"I did phone Dr. Stewart," Lindy went on to say, "if that makes you feel any better."

It did. "What did he say?"

"Not much, but he said Carol could leave for the hospital anytime."

"Okay...okay," Steve said, pushing down the panic that threatened to consume him. "But I want to be the one to drive her there. This is my baby—I should have the right."

"Oh, that won't be any problem, but take your time getting here. Carol wants to wash her hair first."

"What?" Steve shouted, bolting to his feet.

"There's no need to scream in my ear, Steven Kyle," Lindy informed him primly.

Steve's breath came in short, uneven rasps. "I'm on my way...don't leave without me."

"Don't worry. Now, before you hang up on me, put Rush on the line."

Whatever Lindy said flew out his other ear. Carol was in labor—their baby was going to be born anytime, and she was styling her hair! Steve dropped the phone to the carpet and headed toward the front door.

"What's happening?" Rush asked, standing.

Steve paused. "Lindy's with Carol. Carol's hair is in labor and the baby's getting washed."

"That explains everything," Rush said, and picked up the phone.

By the time Steve arrived at the house, his heart was pounding so violently, his rib cage was in danger of being damaged. He leaped out of the car, left the door open and sprinted toward the house.

"Where is she?" he demanded of Lindy. He'd nearly taken the front door off its hinges, he'd come into the house so fast.

His sister pointed in the direction of the bedroom.

"Carol," he called. He'd repeated her name four more times before he walked into the bedroom. She was sitting on the edge of the mattress, her hands resting on her abdomen, taking in slow, even breaths.

Steve fell to his knees in front of her. "Are you all right?"

She gave him a weak smile. "I'm fine. How about you?"

He placed his hands over hers, closed his eyes and expelled his breath. "I think I'm going to be all right now."

Carol brushed a hand over his face, gently caressing his jawline. "I'm sorry about earlier...I felt so ugly and I didn't want you to see me until I'd had a chance to clean up."

The frenzy and panic left him and he reached up a hand and hooked it around her neck. Gently he lowered her mouth to his and kissed her in a leisurely exploration. "I love you, Carol Kyle." He released her and lifted her maternity top enough to kiss her swollen stomach. "And I love you, Baby Kyle."

Carol's eyes filled with tears.

"Come on," he said, helping her into an upright position. "We've got a new life to bring into the world and we're going to do it together."

Sometime around noon the following day, Carol woke in the hospital to discover Steve sleeping across the room from her, sprawled in the most uncomfortable position imaginable. His head was tossed back, his mouth open. His leg was hooked over the side of the chair and his arms dangled like cooked noodles at his side, the knuckles of his left hand brushing the floor.

"Steve," she whispered, hating to wake him. But if he stayed in that position much longer, he wouldn't be able to move his neck for a week.

Steve jerked himself awake. His leg dropped to the floor with a loud thud. He looked around him as though he couldn't remember where he was or even who he was.

"Hi," Carol said, feeling marvelous.

"Hi." He wiped a hand over his face, then apparently remembered what he was doing in her hospital room. A slow, satisfied smile crept over his features. "Are you feeling all right?"

"I feel fantastic."

He moved to her side and claimed her hand with both of his. "We have a daughter," he said, and his voice was raw with remembered emotion. "I've never seen a more beautiful little girl in my life."

"Stephanie Anne Kyle," she told him. "Stephanie for her father and Anne for my mother."

"Stephanie," Steve repeated slowly, then nodded. "She's incredible. You're incredible."

"You cried," Carol whispered, remembering the tears that had run down the side of Steve's face when Dr. Stewart handed him their daughter.

"I never felt any emotion more powerful in my life," he answered. "I can't even begin to explain it.'' He raised her hand to his lips and briefly closed his eyes. ''You'd worked so hard and so long and then Stephanie was born and squalling like crazy. I'd been so concerned about you that I'd hardly noticed her and then Dr. Stewart wrapped her in a blanket and gave her to me. Carol, the minute I touched her something happened in my heart. I felt so humble, so awed, that I'd been entrusted with this tiny life.'' He placed his hand over his heart as if it were marked by their daughter's birth and she would notice the change in him. ''Stephanie is such a beautiful baby. We'd been up most of the night and you were exhausted. But I felt like I could fly, I was so excited. Poor Rush and Lindy, I think I talked their heads off.''

''I was surprised you slept here.''

He ran the tips of his fingers over her cheek. ''I had to be with you. I kept thinking about everything I'd put you through. I was so wrong, so very wrong about everything, and yet you loved me through it all. I should have known from the first that you were innocent of everything bad I've ever believed. I was such a fool...such an idiot. I nearly ruined both our lives.''

''It's in the past and forgotten.''

''We're getting married.'' He said it as if he expected an argument.

"I think we should," Carol agreed, "seeing that we have a daughter."

"I never felt unmarried," Steve admitted. "There's only one woman in my life, and that's the way it'll always be."

"We may have divorce papers, but I never stopped being your wife."

The nurse walked into the room, tenderly cradling a soft pink bundle. "Are you ready for your daughter, Mrs. Kyle?"

"Oh, yes." Carol reached for the button that would raise the hospital bed to an upright position. As soon as she was settled, the nurse placed Stephanie Anne Kyle in her mother's arms.

Following the nurse's instructions, Carol bared her breast and gasped softly as Stephanie accepted her mother's nipple and sucked greedily.

"She's more beautiful every time I see her," Steve said, his voice filled with wonder. The rugged lines of his face softened as he gazed down on his daughter. Gently he drew one finger over her velvet-smooth cheek. "But she'll never be as beautiful as her mother is to me right this minute."

Love and joy flooded Carol's soul and she gently kissed the top of her daughter's head.

"We're going to be all right," Steve whispered.

"Yes, we are," Carol agreed. "We're going to be just fine—all three of us."

*   *   *   *   *

Don't forget to look for Debbie Macomber's
next emotional navy story—

NAVY BRAT,

featuring Erin McNamara and Brandon Davis.

Coming in early 2004 from Silhouette Books.

But first, there's

311 PELICAN COURT

coming from MIRA Books
in September 2003.

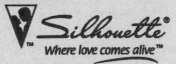

He was the handsomest man in the bar, and he couldn't keep his eyes off her.

It was all Erin MacNamera could do to keep her own coffee-brown eyes trained away from him. He sat on the bar stool, his elbows braced against the polished mahogany counter, and he nonchalantly held a bottle of imported beer in his hand.

Against her will, Erin's gaze meandered back to him. He seemed to be waiting for attention, and smiled, his mouth lifting sensuously at the edges. Erin quickly looked away and tried to concentrate on what her friend was saying.

"...Steve and me."

Erin hadn't a clue as to what she'd missed. Aimee talked nonstop, especially when she was upset. The reason Erin and her co-worker were meeting was that Aimee wanted to discuss the problems she was having in her marriage.

Marriage was something Erin fully intended to avoid, at least for a good long while. She was focusing her energies on her career as an employment counselor and on teaching a class called Women in Transition two evenings a week at South Seattle Community College. Helping others through a time of painful transition was what Erin had been born to do.

"Erin," Aimee whispered, "the man at the bar is staring at us."

"Oh?"

Aimee stirred the swizzle stick in her daiquiri, then licked the end as she stared across the room, her eyes studying the good-looking man. "It's you who interests him."

"How can you be so sure?"

"Because I'm married."

"He doesn't know that," Erin argued.

"Sure he does." Aimee leaned across the table. "Married women give off vibes and single men pick them up like sonar. I tried to send him a signal, but it didn't work. He knew immediately. You on the other hand, are giving off single vibes and he's zeroing in on that like a bee does pollen. My guess is that the minute I'm out of here he's going to make a beeline for you." She stood hurriedly, smiled at her own wit, then added, "The pun was an accident— clever but unintentional. We'll talk some other time." She winked suggestively. "Good luck."

"Ah…" Erin was at a loss as to what to do. For the majority of her adult life she'd avoided romantic relationships. Not by design. It had just worked out that way. Her social life had been sadly neglected since Howie Riverside had asked her to the Valentine's Day dance and her tender young heart had been all aflutter.

Then it happened. The way it always had. Her father, a career navy man, had been transferred, and they had moved three days before the dance. Somehow, Erin had never quite regained her stride. After three more moves before college, Erin had felt like a social pygmy when it came to dealing with men….

"Hello."

And he was standing next to her.

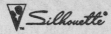